THE MOON POOL &
THE CONQUEST OF THE MOON POOL

With regards of

A. Merritt

Virgil Finlay

Alias the Night Wind

BY VARICK VANARDY

The Blue Fire Pearl: The Complete Adventures
of Singapore Sammy, Volume 1

BY GEORGE F. WORTS

Clovelly

BY MAX BRAND

Drink We Deep

BY ARTHUR LEO ZAGAT

The Gun-Brand

BY JAMES B. HENDRYX

Jan of the Jungle

BY OTIS ADELBERT KLINE

Minions of the Moon

BY WILLIAM GREY BEYER

Tarzan and the Jewels of Opar

BY EDGAR RICE BURROUGHS

War Lord of Many Swordsmen:
The Adventures of Norcross, Volume 1

BY W. WIRT

THE MOON POOL
&
THE CONQUEST OF
THE MOON POOL

ABRAHAM MERRITT

PRIMARY ILLUSTRATOR

VIRGIL FINLAY

INTRODUCTION BY

WILL MURRAY

ALTUS PRESS
2017

© 2017 Steeger Properties, LLC, under license to Altus Press • First Edition—2017

EDITED AND DESIGNED BY
Matthew Moring

ASSOCIATE EDITOR
Ray Riethmeier

PUBLISHING HISTORY
"Introduction" appears here for the first time. Copyright © 2017 Will Murray. All
    rights reserved.
"The Moon Pool" originally appeared in the June 22, 1918 issue of *All-Story Weekly*
    magazine (Vol. 85, No. 3). Copyright © 1918 by The Frank A. Munsey
    Company.
"The Conquest of the Moon Pool" originally appeared in the February 15 & 22, and
    March 1, 8, 15 & 22, 1919 issues of *All-Story Weekly* magazine (Vol. 94, No.
    4–Vol. 95, No. 2). Copyright © 1919 by The Frank A. Munsey Company.
Images copyright © 1939, 1940, and 1948 by The Frank A. Munsey Company and
    Popular Publications, Inc., and assigned to Steeger Properties, LLC. All rights
    reserved.
"A. Merritt (1884–1943)" appears here for the first time. Copyright © 2017 Will
    Murray. All rights reserved.
"About the Author" originally appeared in the October 25, 1930 issue of *Argosy*
    magazine (Vol. 216, No. 2). Copyright © 1930 by The Frank A. Munsey
    Company. Copyright renewed © 1957 and assigned to Steeger Properties, LLC.
    All rights reserved.

THANKS TO
Will Murray

ISBN
978-1-61827-306-2

Visit *altuspress.com* for more books like this.
Printed in the United States of America.

TABLE OF CONTENTS

INTRODUCTION

A CENTURY HAS now passed since the debut of Abraham Grace Merritt in the pages of Munsey's *All-Story Weekly*. His 1917 short fantasy, "Through the Dragon Glass," was well received, but not especially noteworthy. Merritt started a sequel, but abandoned it, later claiming that he did not care for sequels.

Yet a year later "The Moon Pool" appeared in the June 22, 1918 issue. The haunting novelette of an unearthly encounter with an indescribable entity dwelling in a pool concealed in a Polynesian ruin caused a sensation among readers of that magazine during the days when science fiction had yet to earn a magazine of its own.

Weird Tales and *Amazing Stories* still lay a few years ahead in the post-war future. Outré works such as those that Merritt would come to specialize in were colloquially described by magazine editors as "impossible" or "different" stories. Science fiction was a genre yet to be named and codified. And the common term fantasy suggested *Grimm's Fairy Tales*, not heroic fiction.

The overwhelming clamor for another such "different" work motivated Merritt to overcome his instinctual distaste for sequels and rush out *The Conquest of the Moon Pool*, an enormous sequel dwarfing the seminal novelette in length. Where "The Moon Pool" comprised about 19,000 words, its followup ran as a sequel in six parts, sprawling over 118,000 words of exciting prose and running through February 15 to March 22, 1918 issues of *All-Story*.

The sequel was a natural. Indeed, it was hinted at in the promised expedition mentioned in the first story's headnote and climax. Readers demanded to read about the further explorations of the mysterious Moon Pool and the spiritual horrors it harbored.

However, they received something very different from their ethereal, if not supernatural, expectations. Here was a full-blown "lost world" saga in the high-adventure vein of H. Rider Haggard and Edgar Rice Burroughs. Nor did it disappoint. Least of all did it disappoint *All-Story* editor Robert H. Davis, who raved that *The Conquest of the Moon Pool* was "… a story so weird, so soul-stirring, and of such tense and terrible interest to every human being that even the title 'different' but weakly describes its uncanny fascination."

While *The Conquest of the Moon Pool* was radically different in tone and atmosphere than its predecessor, veering completely into the yet-unnamed realm of science fiction, few appreciators of the original story failed to be captivated by this expansion. Thus did A. Merritt detonate as a supernova star in the early era before the science fiction and fantasy genres came into their own, a formative era when they were essentially the same thing.

Nor was his fame limited to a pulp magazines. A hardcover edition of *The Moon Pool* was published by the respectable G.P. Putnam's Sons in 1919, shortly followed by yet another version in which the primary antagonist was renamed for political reasons. Dr. Von Herzdorf had been the original villain, but Merritt transformed the German into a Russian named Marakinoff as World War I passions gave way to fears of the spreads of Communism. Merritt himself later regretted allowing this variant version. Unfortunately, that repudiated Boni & Liveright edition provided the text that was most often reprinted in subsequent decades.

By fusing both magazines stories, the author created a unified whole that instantly became a classic of the genre, then sometimes styled the "scientific romance." Yet many critics—among them H.P. Lovecraft—thought that the eerie power of the original novelette was lost in Merritt's methodical revision. Readers with long memories as well as the new inter-war generation of science fiction fans periodically begged Munsey editors to reprint it in the pages of *Argosy*, the only surviving successor to *All-Story Weekly*.

Eventually, they caved in. The original "Moon Pool" novelette was selected to lead the premier issue of *Famous Fantastic Mysteries* in 1939. *The Conquest of the Moon Pool* did not see print again in its unrevised form until 1948. While the germinal "Moon Pool" has from time to time been anthologized, *The Conquest of the Moon Pool* has remained out of print for nearly 70 years, its last official republication in *Fantastic Novels* magazine, September, 1948.

In this Altus Press edition we reprint for the first time in one volume both seminal stories as they were originally published 100 years ago, along with Virgil Finlay's stunning illustrations that accompanied their acclaimed magazine reprinting.

Merritt went on to write a semi-sequel to *The Conquest of the Moon Pool* called *The Metal Master*, as well as penning several other novels and short stories which he produced at irregular intervals, quickly establishing himself as one of the great fantasy writers of the first half of the 20th century. A 1930s poll asked *Argosy* readers to name their favorite story ever to run in the magazine. By an overwhelming margin, Merritt's *The Ship of Ishtar* was selected—and duly reprinted. The author was almost uniformly lauded, often emulated, but never surpassed in his lifetime, and was considered only second in popularity and lasting influence to an earlier *All-Story* discovery, Edgar Rice Burroughs of Tarzan and John Carter of Mars fame.

Such was his renown that a pulp magazine was named after him posthumously: *A. Merritt's Fantasy Magazine*. Nor did the wartime decline of the pulps and the passing of the influential author in 1943 diminish Merritt's popularity. His novels began appearing in the new medium of the paperback novel during, and so when the fantasy field boomed in the 1960s and '70s Merritt was firmly in the forefront of the new wave that included writers as varied as J.R.R. Tolkien and Robert E. Howard.

Later generations of readers, writers and critics have attempted to unseat the emperor of fantasy fiction from his opulent throne, and to some degree they have succeeded—but only because the passage of time has caused the florid style of fiction that Merritt practiced to fall out of common currency.

The world was a larger, more mysterious place in Merritt's time. And the lure of the unexplored corners of the planet was strong in the imaginations of actual explorers and armchair enthusiasts alike. Nothing can turn back the clock, whether it is marking the advancement of time, knowledge or literature. But a century after his first appearance in print, the works of A. Merritt are still being reprinted and read—and appreciated by generation he could scarcely imagine.

Abraham Merritt had a formative influence on the writers who were his contemporaries, as well as those who followed. They ranged from H.P. Lovecraft to contemporaries as Jack Williamson, Arthur Leo Zagat, Edmond Hamilton and Henry Kuttner. Although many of Merritt's concepts and characters went on to become tropes and ultimately cliches, they were exceedingly fresh when he wrote them. Well into the 21st Century, they continue to be recycled—the popular TV series *Lost* among the prominent examples.

No one today writes purple prose like A. Merritt. Nor should they. But that does not make the author or his works a relic of a long-gone era. Rather, Merritt and his handful of memorable novels represent the vanguard of an emerging literature, and one that resonates even more strongly today than it did when the writer was exploring his craft through the vehicle of his unsurpassed imagination.

Now, prepare to encounter the indescribable Dweller in the Moon Pool... exactly as an enthralled generation of fantasy readers first did one hundred years ago....

THE MOON POOL

TO THE EDITOR OF ALL-STORY MAGAZINE:

The International Association of Science has directed me to place before you the following narrative with the view, if you are agreeable, of publication as soon as possible. Because of your extraordinarily large circulation and its diffusion not only throughout the United States, but throughout the reading world, it was felt that yours was the ideal medium to bring the facts before the greatest audience and so enable the association to right a wrong which, but for Dr. Goodwin's very understandable and perhaps entirely human hesitation, would never have gained headway.

The association in selecting you as the subject of this request, took into consideration the fact that the space limitations of newspapers are such that the complete narrative of Dr. Goodwin could not be published therein, whereas with you this handicap does not exist. It was also convinced that so important and unusual a document could not communicate its unique impression of truth and sincerity unless read in its entirety exactly as it was before the International Association of Science, April 18, 1918.

I have been authorized to announce that we have discovered that Dr. Goodwin is now actually on his way to the Caroline Islands, and that the association is preparing an expedition to follow him speedily; to save him if it can arrive in time; at the least to investigate and to destroy if possible, and if necessary, the cause of his journey.

The maps which Dr. Goodwin received from Dr. Throckmartin accompany this manuscript. It is our desire that they be published with it for the guidance of other scientists or courageous men who may be impelled on reading it to follow us with another expedition. For it is not at all certain that the human expedients planned by the association can cope with phenomena so clearly beyond the range of present human knowledge as that which Dr. Throckmartin describes as emanating from what he calls "the moon pool," and that which Dr. Goodwin saw onboard the *Southern Queen*. Again it may be that this unearthly dweller in the prehistoric island ruins of the South Seas is only one of many. Further, there is the hint conveyed by the underground chanting heard by Dr. Throckmartin; raising the question of the existence of considerable other forces or creatures possessing powers or knowledge of which we are densely ignorant, and in the exercise of which the world must be deeply concerned.

It is unnecessary to say to you that Dr. Walter T. Goodwin, Ph.D., F.R.G.S., *et cetera*, though in his early thirties, is known as the foremost of American botanists, and that Dr. David Throckmartin's scientific reputation is so great that even the cloud that has gathered about his memory could not blacken his achievements.

For those who would follow us, full information as to the methods of the expedition can be secured at the office of the president of the association.

Our foremost purpose in asking publication is, however, as I have said, to remove the shadow from the name of Dr. Throckmartin, of his young wife, and of his brilliant young associate, Dr. Charles Stanton, who accompanied him on his ill-fated journey.

The association has entrusted this explanation and the narrative of Dr. Goodwin to Mr. A. Merritt, who has courteously volunteered to set it before you together with other facts which we have asked him to communicate to you verbally.

Respectfully yours,
THE INTERNATIONAL ASSOCIATION OF SCIENCE,
Per J.B.K., President.

CHAPTER I

THE THROCKMARTIN MYSTERY

I BREAK A silence of three years to clear the name of Dr. David Throckmartin and to lift the shadow of scandal from that of his wife and of Dr. Charles Stanton, his assistant. That I have not found the courage to do so before, all men who are jealous of their scientific reputations will understand when they have heard what I have written. How strongly I attest to my belief in the truth of what I am about to lay before you will be equally clear as you listen and realize, as I do, the storm of ridicule and disbelief it is sure to bring upon me. Yet I hope that you will also believe before this narrative is finished.

Let me recapitulate what, until now, has actually been known of the Throckmartin expedition to the island of Ponape in the Carolines—the Throckmartin Mystery, as it is called.

Dr. Throckmartin set forth early in 1915 to make detailed observations of Nan-Matal, that extraordinary group of island ruins, remains of a high and prehistoric civilization, that are clustered along the east shore of Ponape. With him went his wife to whom he had been wedded less than half a year. The daughter of Professor Frazier-Smith, she was as deeply interested and almost as well informed as he, upon these relics of a vanished race that titanically strew certain islands of the Pacific and form the basis for the theory of a submerged Pacific continent.

Mrs. Throckmartin, it will be recalled, was much younger, fifteen years at least, than her husband. Dr. Charles Stanton, who accompanied them as Dr. Throckmartin's assistant, was about her age. These three and a Swedish woman, Thora Helversen, who had been Edith Throckmartin's nurse in babyhood and who was entirely devoted to her, made up the expedition.

Dr. Throckmartin planned to spend a year among the ruins, not only of Ponape, but of Lele—the twin centers of that colos-

sal riddle of humanity whose answer has its roots in immeasurable antiquity; a weird flower of man-made civilization that
blossomed ages before the seeds of Egypt were sown; of whose
arts we know little and of whose science and secret knowledge
of nature nothing.

He carried with him complete equipment for his work and
gathered at Ponape a dozen or so natives for laborers. They went
straight to Metalanim harbor and set up their camp on the
island called Uschen-Tau in the group known as the Nan-
Matal. You will remember that these islands are entirely unin-
habited and are shunned by the people on the main island.

Three months later Dr. Throckmartin appeared at Port
Moresby, Papua. He came on a schooner manned by Solomon
Islanders and commanded by a Chinese half-breed captain. He
reported that he was on his way to Melbourne for additional
scientific equipment and whites to help him in his excavations,
saying that the superstition of the natives made their aid negligible. He went immediately on board the steamer *Southern
Queen* which was sailing that same morning. Three nights later
he disappeared from the *Southern Queen* and it was officially
reported that he had met death either by being swept overboard
or by casting himself into the sea.

A relief-boat sent with the news to Ponape found the
Throckmartin camp on the island Uschen-Tau and a smaller
camp on the island called Nan-Tauach. All the equipment,
clothing, supplies were intact. But of Mrs. Throckmartin, of Dr.
Stanton, or of Thora Helversen they could find not a single
trace!

The natives who had been employed by the archeologist were
questioned. They said that the ruins were the abode of great
spirits—*ani*—who were particularly powerful when the moon
was at the full. On these nights all the islanders were doubly
careful to give the ruins wide berth. Upon being employed, they
had demanded leave from the day before full moon until it was
on the wane and this had been granted them by Dr. Throckmartin. Thrice they had left the expedition alone on these nights.

On their third return they had found the four white people gone and they "knew that the *ani* had eaten them." They were afraid and had fled.

That was all.

The Chinese half caste was found and reluctantly testified at last that he had picked Dr. Throckmartin up from a small boat about fifty miles off Ponape. The scientist had seemed half mad but he had given the seaman a large sum of money to bring him to Port Moresby and to say, if questioned, that he had boarded the boat at Ponape harbor.

That, gentlemen, is all that has been known of the fate of the Throckmartin expedition.

Why, you will ask, do I break silence now; and how came I in possession of the facts I am about to set forth?

To the first I answer: I was at the Geographical Club last evening and overheard two members talking. They mentioned the name of Throckmartin and I became, frankly, eavesdropper. One said:

"Of course what probably happened was that Throckmartin killed them all. It's a dangerous thing for a man to marry a woman so much younger than himself and then throw her into the necessarily close company of exploration with a man as young and as agreeable as Stanton was. The inevitable happened, no doubt. Throckmartin discovered; avenged himself. Then followed remorse and suicide."

"Throckmartin didn't seem to be that kind," said the other thoughtfully.

"No, he didn't," agreed the first.

"Isn't there another story?" went on the second speaker. "Something about Mrs. Throckmartin running away with Stanton and taking the woman, Thora, with her? Somebody told me they had been recognized in Singapore recently."

"You can take your pick of the two stories," replied his vis-à-vis. "It's one or the other I suppose."

It was neither one nor the other, gentlemen. I know—and I answer now the second question—because I was with Throckmartin when he—vanished. I know what he told me and I know what my own eyes saw. Incredible, abnormal, against all the known facts of our science as it was, I testify to it. And it is my intention, after sending you this, to sail to Ponape, to go to the Nan-Matal and to the islet beneath whose frowning walls dwells the mystery that Throckmartin sought and found—and at the last sought and found Throckmartin!

I attach herewith a copy of the map of the islands that he gave me. I attach also his sketch of the great courtyard of Nan-Tauach, the location of the moon door, his recollection of the probable location of the moon pool and the passage to it and his approximation of the position of the shining globes. If I do not return and there are any with enough belief, scientific curiosity, and courage to follow, I leave them in these a plain trail.

I will now proceed straightforwardly with my narrative.

For six months I had been on the d'Entrecasteaux Islands gathering data for the concluding chapters of my book upon "Flora of the Volcanic Islands of the South Pacific." The day before, I had reached Port Moresby and had seen my specimens safely stored on board the *Southern Queen*. As I sat on the upper deck that morning I thought, with homesick mind, of the long leagues between me and Melbourne and the longer ones between Melbourne and New York.

It was one of Papua's yellow mornings, when she shows herself in her most somber, most baleful mood. The sky was a smoldering ocher. Over the island brooded a spirit sullen, implacable and alien; filled with the threat of latent, malefic forces waiting to be unleashed. It seemed an emanation from the untamed, sinister heart of Papua herself—sinister even when she smiles. And now and then, on the wind, came a breath from unexplored jungles, filled with unfamiliar odors, mysterious, and menacing.

It is on such mornings that Papua speaks to you of her immemorial ancientness and of her power. I am not unduly imaginative but it is a mood that makes me shrink—I mention it because it bears directly upon Dr. Throckmartin's fate. Nor is the mood Papua's alone. I have felt it in New Guinea, in Australia, in the Solomons and in the Carolines. But it is in Papua that it seems most articulate. It is as though she said: "I am the ancient of days; I have seen the earth in the throes of its shaping; I am the primeval; I have seen races born and die and, lo, in my breast are secrets that would blast you by the telling, you pale babes of a puling age. You and I ought not be in the same world; yet I am and I shall be! Never will you fathom me and you I hate though I tolerate! I tolerate—but how long?"

And then I seem to see a giant paw that reaches from Papua toward the outer world, stretching and sheathing monstrous claws.

All feel this mood of hers. Her own people have it woven in them, part of their web and woof; flashing into light unexpectedly like a soul from another universe; masking itself as swiftly.

I fought against Papua as every white man must on one of her yellow mornings. And as I fought I saw a tall figure come striding down the pier. Behind him came a Kapa-Kapa boy swinging a new valise. There was something familiar about the tall man. As he reached the gangplank he looked up straight into my eyes, stared at me for a moment and waved his hand. It was Dr. Throckmartin!

Coincident with my recognition of him there came a shock of surprise that was definitely—unpleasant. It was Throckmartin—but there was something disturbingly different about him and the man I had known so well and had bidden farewell less than a year before. He was then, as you know, just turned forty, lithe, erect, muscular; the face of a student and of a seeker. His controlling expression was one of enthusiasm, of intellectual keenness, of—what shall I say—expectant search. His ever eagerly questioning brain had stamped itself upon his face.

I sought in my mind for an explanation of that which I had felt on the flash of his greeting. Hurrying down to the lower deck I found him with the purser. As I spoke he turned and held out to me an eager hand—and then I saw what the change was that had come over him!

He knew, of course, by my face the uncontrollable shock that my closer look had given me. His eyes filled and he turned bruskly to the purser; then hurried off to his stateroom, leaving me standing, half dazed.

At the stair he half turned.

"Oh, Goodwin," he said. "I'd like to see you later. Just now—there's something I must write before we start—"

He went up swiftly.

"'E looks rather queer—eh?" said the purser. "Know 'im well, sir? Seems to 've given you quite a start, sir."

I made some reply and went slowly to my chair. I tried to analyze what it was that had disturbed me so; what profound change in Throckmartin that had so shaken me. Now it came to me. It was as though the man had suffered some terrific soul searing shock of rapture and horror combined; some soul cataclysm that in its climax had remolded his face deep from within, setting on it the seal of wedded joy and fear. As though indeed ecstasy supernal and terror infernal had once come to him hand in hand, taken possession of him, looked out of his eyes and, departing, left behind upon him ineradicably their shadow.

Gone was Throckmartin's old eager look, utterly gone, and in its place was this—something—I had never seen before on any face. I caught myself wondering what his face must have been when the seal was stamped freshly upon it. And what in the name of all knowledge was the agency that had done this thing! For it came to me suddenly that the true reason for the distress, the deep perturbation and amaze that he stirred in me was that the two expressions were mingled, inextricably, lay side by side, not contending but in some frightful fashion—harmonious! That was what shocked. For how could hate and love, ecstasy and horror, heaven and hell mix, join hands—kiss? Yet these were what, close embraced, lay on Throckmartin's face!

If I seem to dwell on this, have patience; it is necessary indeed.

Alternately I looked out over the port and paced about the deck, striving to read the riddle; to banish it from my mind. And all the time still over Papua brooded its baleful spirit of ancient evil, unfathomable, not to be understood; nor had it lifted when the *Southern Queen* lifted anchor and steamed out into the gulf.

CHAPTER II

DOWN THE MOON PATH

I WATCHED WITH relief the shores sink down behind us; welcomed the touch of the free sea wind. We seemed to be drawing away from something malefic; something that lurked within the island spell I have described, and the thought crept into my mind, spoke—whispered rather—from Throckmartin's face.

I had hoped—and within the hope was an inexplicable shrinking, an unexpressed dread—that I would meet Throckmartin at lunch. He did not come down and I was sensible of a distinct relief within my disappointment. All that afternoon I lounged about uneasily but still he kept to his cabin. Nor did he appear at dinner.

Dusk and night fell swiftly. I was warm and went back to my deck-chair. The *Southern Queen* was rolling to a disquieting

swell and I had the place to myself. I had looked my fellow passengers over while we were at table. They were a scant dozen. A couple of English officials and their wives, engrossed in "shop" and bulwarked by the English unapproachableness of the first night out; a clerk or two; a shoe salesman from Brisbane; a scattering of others—none of them worth breaking my solitude for, I decided.

Over the heavens was a canopy of cloud, glowing faintly and testifying to the moon riding behind it. There was much phosphorescence. Now and then, before the ship and at the sides, arose those strange little swirls of mist that steam up from the Southern Ocean like the breath of sea monsters, whirl for a moment and disappear. I lighted a cigarette and tried once more to banish from my mind Throckmartin's face—and unsuccessfully as ever.

Suddenly the deck door opened and through it came Throckmartin himself. He paused uncertainly, looked up at the sky

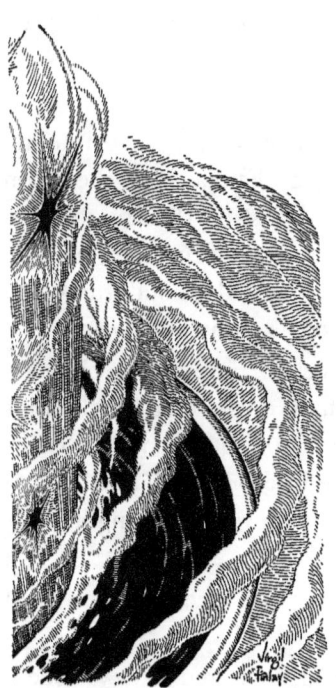

She threw herself squarely within its diabolical splendor....

with a curiously eager, intent gaze, hesitated, then closed the door behind him.

"Throckmartin," I called. "Come sit with me. It's Goodwin."

Immediately he made his way to me. Sitting beside me with a gasp of relief that I noted curiously. His hand touched mine and gripped it with a tenseness that hurt. His hand was ice-like. I puffed up my cigarette and by its glow scanned him closely. He was

watching a large swirl of the mist that was passing before the
ship. The phosphorescence beneath it illumined it with a fitful
opalescence. I saw fear in his eyes. The swirl passed; he sighed;
his grip relaxed and he sank back.

"Throckmartin," I said, wasting no time in preliminaries.
"What's wrong? Can I help you?"

He was silent.

"Is your wife all right and what are you doing here when I
heard you had gone to the Carolines for a year?" I went on.

I felt his body grow tense again. He did not speak for a
moment and then:

"I'm going to Melbourne, Goodwin," he said. "I need a few
things—need them urgently. And more men—white men."

His voice was low; preoccupied. It was as though the brain
that dictated the words did so perfunctorily, half impatiently;
aloof, watching, strained to catch the first hint of approach of
something dreaded.

"You are making progress then?" I asked. It was a banal question, put forth in a blind effort to claim his attention.

"Progress?" he repeated. "Progress—"

He stopped abruptly; rose from his chair, gazed intently
toward the north. I followed his gaze. Far, far away the moon
had broken through the clouds. Almost on the horizon, you
could see the faint luminescence of it upon the quiet sea. The
distant patch of light quivered and shook. The clouds thickened
again and it was gone. The ship raced southward, swiftly.

Throckmartin dropped into his chair. He lighted a cigarette
with a hand that trembled. The flash of the match fell on his
face and I noted with a queer thrill of apprehension that its
unfamiliar expression had deepened; become curiously intensified as though a faint acid had passed over it, etching its lines
faintly deeper.

"It's the full moon tonight, isn't it?" he asked, palpably with
studied inconsequence.

"The first night of full moon," I answered. He was silent

again. I sat silent too, waiting for him to make up his mind to speak. He turned to me as though he had made a sudden resolution.

"Goodwin," he said. "I do need help. If ever man needed it, I do. Goodwin—can you imagine yourself in another world, alien, unfamiliar, a world of terror, whose unknown joy is its greatest terror of all; you all alone there; a stranger! As such a man would need help, so I need—"

He paused abruptly and arose to his feet stiffly; the cigarette dropped from his fingers. I saw that the moon had again broken through the clouds, and this time much nearer. Not a mile away was the patch of light that it threw upon the waves. Back of it, to the rim of the sea was a lane of moonlight; it was a gleaming gigantic serpent racing over the rim of the world straight and surely toward the ship.

Throckmartin gazed at it as though turned to stone. He stiffened to it as a pointer does to a hidden covey. To me from him pulsed a thrill of terror—but terror tinged with an unfamiliar, an infernal joy. It came to me and passed away—leaving me trembling with its shock of bitter sweet.

He bent forward, all his soul in his eyes. The moon path swept closer, closer still. It was now less than half a mile away. From it the ship fled; almost it came to me, as though pursued. Down upon it, swift and straight, a radiant torrent cleaving the waves, raced the moon stream. And then— "Good God!" breathed Throckmartin, and if ever the words were a prayer and an invocation they were.

And then, for the first time—I saw—*it!*

The moon path, as I have said, stretched to the horizon and was bordered by darkness. It was as though the clouds above had been parted to form a lane—drawn aside like curtains or as the waters of the Red Sea were held back to let the hosts of Israel through. On each side of the stream was the black shadow cast by the folds of the high canopies. And straight as a road between the opaque walls gleamed, shimmered and danced the shining, racing, rapids of the moonlight.

Far, it seemed immeasurably far, along this stream of silver fire I sensed, rather than saw, something coming. It drew into sight as a deeper glow within the light. On and on it sped toward us—an opalescent mistiness that swept on with the suggestion of some winged creature in darting flight. Dimly there crept into my mind memory of the Dyak legend of the winged messenger of Buddha—the Akla bird whose feathers are woven of the moon rays, whose heart is a living opal, whose wings in flight echo the crystal clear music of the white stars—but whose beak is of frozen flame and shreds the souls of unbelievers. Still it sped on, and now there came to me sweet, insistent tinklings—like a pizzicati on violins of glass, crystalline, as purest, clearest glass transformed to sound. And again the myth of the Akla bird came to me.

BUT NOW it was close to the end of the white path; close up to the barrier of darkness still between the ship and the sparkling head of the moon stream. And now it beat up against that barrier as a bird against the bars of its cage. And I knew that this was no mist born of sea and air. It whirled with shimmering plumes, with swirls of lacy light, with spirals of living vapor. It held within it odd, unfamiliar gleams as of shifting mother-of-pearl. Coruscations and glittering atoms drifted through it as though it drew them from the rays that bathed it.

Nearer and nearer it came, borne on the sparkling waves, and less and less grew the protecting wall of shadow between it and us. The crystalline sounds were louder—rhythmic as music from another planet.

Now I saw that within the mistiness was a core, a nucleus of intenser light—veined, opaline, effulgent, intensely alive. And above it, tangled in the plumes and spirals that throbbed and whirled were seven glowing lights.

Through—all the incessant but strangely ordered movement of the—*thing*—these lights held firm and steady. They were seven—like seven little moons. One was of a pearly pink, one of delicate nacreous blue, one of lambent saffron, one of the emerald you see in the shallow waters of tropic isles; a deathly white; a ghostly amethyst; and one of the silver that is seen only when the flying fish leap beneath the moon. There they shone—these seven little varicolored orbs within the opaline mistiness of whatever it was that, poised and expectant, waited to be drawn to us on the light filled waves.

The tinkling music was louder still. It pierced the ears with a shower of tiny lances; it made the heart beat jubilantly—and checked it dolorously. It closed your throat with a throb of rapture and gripped it tight like the hand of infinite sorrow!

Came to me now a murmuring cry, stilling the crystal clear notes, it was articulate—but as though from something utterly foreign to this world. The ear took the cry and translated with conscious labor into the sounds of earth. And even as it compassed, the brain shrank from it irresistibly and simultaneously it seemed, reached toward it with irresistible eagerness.

"Av-o-lo-ha! Av-o-lo-ha!" So the cry seemed to throb.

The grip of Throckmartin's hand relaxed. He walked stiffly toward the front of the deck, straight toward the vision, now but a few yards away from the bow. I ran toward him and gripped him—and fell back. For now his face had lost all human semblance. Utter agony and utter ecstasy—there they were side by side, not resisting each other; unholy inhuman companions blending into a look that none of God's creatures should wear—and deep, deep as his soul! A devil and a God dwelling harmoniously side by side! So must Satan, newly fallen, still divine, seeing heaven and contemplating hell, have looked.

And then—swiftly the moon path faded! The clouds swept over the sky as though a hand had drawn them together. Up from the south came a roaring squall. As the moon vanished what I had seen vanished with it—blotted out as an image on a magic lantern; the tinkling ceased abruptly—leaving a silence like that which follows an abrupt and stupendous thunder clap. There was nothing about us but silence and blackness!

Through me there passed a great trembling as one who had stood on the very verge of the gulf wherein the men of the Louisades say lurks the fisher of the souls of men, and has been plucked back by sheerest chance.

Throckmartin passed an arm around me.

"It is as I thought," he said. In his voice was a new note; of the calm certainty that has swept aside a waiting tenor of the unknown. "Now I know! Come with me to my cabin, old friend. For now that you too have seen I can tell you"—he hesitated— "what it was you saw," he ended.

As we passed through the door we came face to face with the ship's first officer. Throckmartin turned quickly, but not soon enough for the mate to see and to stare at him with amazement. His eyes went questioningly to me.

With a strong effort of will Throckmartin composed his face into at least a semblance of normality.

"Are we going to have much of a storm?" he asked.

"Yes," said the mate. Then the seaman, getting the better of his curiosity, added, profanely: "We'll probably have it all the way to Melbourne."

Throckmartin straightened as though with a new thought. He gripped the officer's sleeve eagerly.

"You mean at least cloudy weather for"—he hesitated—"for the next three nights, say?"

"And for three more," replied the mate.

"Thank God!" cried Throckmartin, and I think I never heard such relief and hope as was in his voice.

The sailor stood amazed. "Thank God," he repeated. "Thank— what d'ye mean?"

But Throckmartin was moving onward to his cabin. I started to follow. The first officer stopped me.

"Your friend," he said, "is he ill?"

"The sea!" I answered hurriedly. "He's not used to it. I am going to look after him."

I saw doubt and disbelief in the seaman's eyes but I hurried on. For I knew now that Throckmartin was ill indeed—but that it was a sickness the ship's doctor nor any other could heal.

CHAPTER III

"DEAD! ALL DEAD!"

THROCKMARTIN WAS SITTING on the side of his berth as I entered. He had taken off his coat. He was leaning over, face in hands.

"Lock the door," he said quietly, not raising his head. "Close the portholes and draw the curtains—and—have you an electric flash in your pocket—a good, strong one?"

He glanced at the small pocket flash I handed him and clocked it on. "Not big enough I'm afraid," he said. "And after all"—he hesitated—"it's only a theory."

"What's only a theory?" I asked in astonishment.

"Thinking of it as a weapon against—what you saw." he said, with a wry smile.

"Throckmartin," I cried. "What was it? Did I really see—that thing—there in the moon path? Did I really hear—"

"This, for instance," he interrupted.

Softly he whispered: "Av-o-lo-ha!" With the murmur I seemed to hear again the crystalline unearthly music; an echo of it, faint, sinister, mocking, jubilant.

"Throckmartin," I said. "What was it? What are you flying from, man? Where is your wife—and Stanton?"

"Dead!" he said monotonously. "Dead! All dead!" Then as I recoiled in horror—"All dead. Edith, Stanton, Thora—dead—or worse. And Edith in the moon pool—with them—drawn by what you saw on the moon path—and that wants me—and that has put its brand upon me—and pursues me."

With a vicious movement he ripped open his shirt.

"Look at this," he said. I gazed. Around his chest, an inch above his heart, the skin was white as pearl. This whiteness was sharply defined against the healthy tint of the body. He turned and I saw it ran around his back. It circled him. The band made a perfect cincture about two inches wide.

"Burn it!" he said, and offered me his cigarette. I drew back. He gestured—peremptorily. I pressed the glowing end of the cigarette into the ribbon of white flesh. He did not flinch nor was there odor of burning nor, as I drew the little cylinder away, any mark upon the whiteness.

"Feel it!" he commanded again. I placed my fingers upon the band. It was cold—like frozen marble.

He handed me a small penknife.

"Cut!" he ordered. This time, my scientific interest fully aroused, I did so without reluctance. The blade cut into flesh. I waited for the blood to come. None appeared. I drew out the knife and thrust it in again, fully a quarter of an inch deep. I might have been cutting paper so far as any evidence followed that what I was piercing was human skin and muscle.

Another thought came to me and I drew back, revolted.

"Throckmartin," I whispered. "Not leprosy!"

"Nothing so easy," he said. "Look again and find the places you cut."

I looked, as he bade me, and in the white ring there was not a single mark. Where I had pressed the blade there was no trace. It was as though the skin had parted to make way for the blade and then had quietly closed again.

Throckmartin arose and drew his shirt about him.

"Two things you have seen," he said. "*It*—and its mark—the seal it placed on me that gives it, I think, the power to follow me. Seeing, you must believe my story. Goodwin, I tell you again that my wife is dead—or worse—I do not know; the prey of—what you saw; so, too, is Stanton; so Thora. How—" He stopped for a moment, then continued:

"And I am going to Melbourne for the things to empty its den and its shrine; for dynamite to destroy it and its lair—if anything made on earth will destroy it; and for white men with courage to use them. Perhaps—perhaps after you have heard, you will be one of these men?" He looked at me a bit wistfully. "And now—do not interrupt me, I beg of you, till I am through—for"—he smiled wanly—"the mate may be wrong.

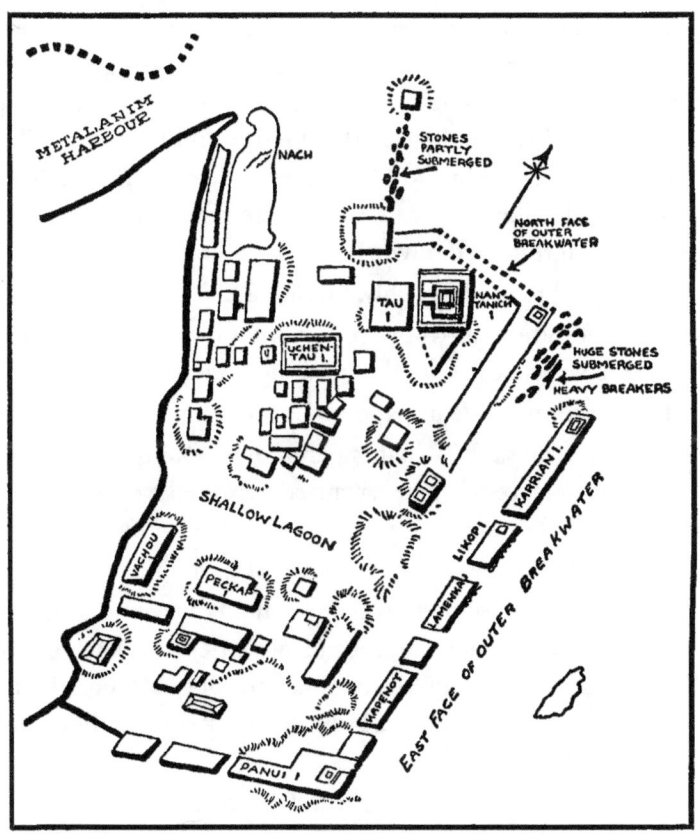

A copy of the map of the islets of the Nan-Matal, which
Dr. Throckmartin gave Dr. Goodwin. It in its turn is a
copy of the official sketch plan by F.W. Christian, the first
explorer to map the Caroline Islands' mysterious maze.

And if he is"—he arose and paced twice about the room—"if he is I may not have time to tell you."

"Throckmartin," I answered, "I have no closed mind. Tell me—and if I can I will help."

He took my hand and pressed it.

"Goodwin," he began, "if I have seemed to take the death of my wife lightly—or rather"—his face contorted—"or rather—if I have seemed to pass it by as something not of first importance to me—believe me it is not so. If the rope is long enough—if what the mate says is so—if there is cloudy weather until the moon begins to wane—I can conquer—that I know. But if it does not—if the dweller in the moon pool gets me—then must you or some one avenge my wife—and me—and Stanton. Yet I cannot believe that God would let a thing like that conquer! But why did He then let it take my Edith? And why does He allow it to exist? Are there things stronger than God, do you think, Goodwin?"

He turned to me feverishly. I hesitated.

"I do not know just how you define God," I said. "If you mean the will to know, working through science—"

He waved me aside impatiently.

"Science," he said. "What is our science against—that? Or against the science of whatever cursed, vanished race that made it—or made the way for it to enter this world of ours?"

With an effort he regained control of himself.

"Goodwin," he said, "do you know at all of the ruins on the Carolines; the Cyclopean, megalithic cities and harbors of Ponape and Lele, of Kusaie, of Ruk and Hogolu, and a score of other islets there? Particularly, do you know of the Nan-Matal and Metalanim?"

"Of the Metalanim I have heard and seen photographs," I said. "They call it, don't they, the Lost Venice of the Pacific?"

"Look at this map," said Throckmartin. He handed me the map. "That," he went on, "is Christian's map of Metalanim harbor and the Nan-Matal. Do you see the rectangles marked Nan-Tauach?"

"Yes," I said.

"There," he said, "under those walls is the moon pool and the seven gleaming lights that raise the dweller in the pool and the altar and shrine of the dweller. And there in the moon pool with it lies Edith and Stanton and Thora."

"The dweller in the moon pool?" I repeated half-incredulously.

"The thing you saw," said Throckmartin solemnly. A solid sheet of rain swept the ports, and the *Southern Queen* began to roll on the rising swells. Throckmartin drew another deep breath as of relief, and drawing aside a curtain peered out into the night. Its blackness seemed to reassure him. At any rate, when he sat again he was calm.

"There are no more wonderful ruins in the world than those of the island Venice of Metalanim on the east shore of Ponape," he said almost casually. "They take in some fifty islets and cover with their intersecting canals and lagoons about twelve square miles. Who built them? None knows. When were they built? Ages before the memory of present man, that is sure. Ten thousand, twenty thousand, a hundred thousand years ago—the last more likely.

"All these islets, Goodwin, are squared, and their shores are frowning sea-walls of gigantic basalt blocks hewn and put in place by the hands of ancient man. Each inner water-front is faced with a terrace of those basalt blocks which stand out six feet above the shallow canals that meander between them. On the islets behind these walls are Cyclopean and time-shattered fortresses, palaces, terraces, pyramids; immense courtyards strewn with ruins—and all so old that they seem to wither the eyes of those who look on them.

"There has been a great subsidence. You can stand out of Metalanim harbor for three miles and look down upon the tops of similar monolithic structures and walls twenty feet below you in the water.

"And all about, strung on their canals, are the bulwarked islets with their enigmatic giant walls peering through the dense growths of mangroves—dead, deserted for incalculable ages; shunned by those who live near.

"You as a botanist are familiar with the evidence that a vast shadowy continent existed in the Pacific—a continent that was not rent asunder by volcanic forces as was that legendary one of Atlantis in the Eastern Ocean. My work in Java, in Papua, and in the Lactones had set my mind upon this Pacific lost land. Just as the Azores are believed to be the last high peaks of Atlantis, so evidence came to me steadily that Ponape and Lele and their basalt bulwarked islets were the last points of the slowly sunken western land clinging still to the sunlight, and had been the last refuge and sacred places of the rulers of that race which had lost their immemorial home under the rising waters of the Pacific.

"I believed that under these ruins I might find the evidence of what I sought. Time and again I had encountered legends of subterranean networks beneath the Nan-Matal, of passages running back into the main island itself; basalt corridors that followed the lines of the shallow canals and ran under them to islet after islet, linking them in mysterious chains.

"My—my wife and I had talked before we were married of making this our great work. After the honeymoon we prepared for the expedition. It was to be my monument. Stanton was as enthusiastic as ourselves. We sailed, as you know, last May in fulfillment of our dreams.

"At Ponape we selected, not without difficulty, workmen to help us—diggers. I had to make extraordinary inducements before I could get together my force. Their beliefs are gloomy, these Ponapeans. They people their swamps, their forests, their mountains and shores with malignant spirits—*ani* they call them. And they are afraid—bitterly afraid of the isles of ruins and what they think the ruins hide. I do not wonder—now! For their fear has come down to them through the ages, from the people 'before their fathers,' as they call them, who, they say, made these mighty spirits their slaves and messengers.

"When they were told where they were to go, and how long we expected to stay, they murmured. Those who, at last, were tempted made what I thought then merely a superstitious proviso that they were to be allowed to go away on the three nights of the full moon. Would to God I had heeded them and gone too!"

He stopped and again over his face the lines etched deep.

"We passed," he went on, "into Metalanim harbor. Off to our left—a mile away arose a massive quadrangle. Its walls were all of forty feet high and hundreds offset on each side. As we passed it our natives grew very silent; watched it furtively, fearfully. I knew it for the ruins that are called Nan-Tauach, the 'place of frowning walls.' And at the silence of my men I recalled what Christian had written of this place; of how he had come upon its 'ancient platforms and tetragonal enclosures of stonework; its wonder of tortuous alleyways and labyrinth of shallow canals; grim masses of stonework peering out from behind verdant screens; Cyclopean barricades,' and of how, when he had turned into its ghostly shadows, straightway the merriment of our guides was hushed and conversation died down to whispers. For we were close to Nan-Tauach—the place of lofty walls, the most remarkable of all the Metalanim ruins." He arose and stood over me.

"Nan-Tauach, Goodwin," he said solemnly—"a place where merriment is hushed indeed and words are stifled; Nan-Tauach—where the moon pool lies hidden—lies hidden behind the moon rock, but sends its diabolic soul out—even through the prisoning stone." He raised clenched hands. "Oh, God," he breathed, "grant me that I may blast it from earth!"

He was silent for a little time.

"Of course I wanted to pitch our camp there," he began again quietly, "but I soon gave up that idea. The natives were panic-stricken—threatened to turn back. 'No,' they said, 'too great *ani* there. We go to any other place—but not there.' Although, even then, I felt that the secret of the place was in Nan-Tauach, I found it necessary to give in. The laborers were essential to the success of the expedition, and I told myself that after a little time had passed and I had persuaded them that there was nothing anywhere that could molest them, we would move our tents to it. We finally picked for our base the islet called Uschen-Tau—you see it here—" He pointed to the map. "It was close to the isle of desire, but far enough away from it to satisfy our men. There was an excellent camping-place there and a spring of fresh water. It offered, besides, an excellent field for preliminary work before attacking the larger ruins. We pitched our tents, and in a couple of days the work was in full swing."

CHAPTER IV

THE MOON ROCK

"**I DO NOT** intend to tell you now," Throckmartin continued, "the results of the next two weeks, Goodwin, nor of what we found. Later—if I am allowed. I will lay all that before you. It is sufficient to say that at the end of those two weeks I had found confirmation for many of my theories, and we were well under way to solve a mystery of humanity's youth—so we thought. But enough. I must hurry on to the first stirrings of the inexplicable thing that was in store for us.

"The place, for all its decay and desolation, had not infected us with any touch of morbidity—that is not Edith, Stanton or myself. My wife was happy—never had she been happier. Stanton and she, while engrossed in the work as much as I, were of the same age, and they frankly enjoyed the companion-ship that only youth can give youth. I was glad—never jealous.

"But Thora was very unhappy. She was a Swede, as you know,

and in her blood ran the beliefs and superstitions of the North-land—some of them so strangely akin to those of this far south-ern land; beliefs of spirits of mountain and forest and water—werewolves and beings malign. From the first she showed a curious sensitivity to what, I suppose, may be called the 'influ-ences' of the place. She said it 'smelled' of ghosts and warlocks.

"I laughed at her then—but now I believe that this sensitiv-ity of what we call primitive people is perhaps only a clearer perception of the unknown which we, who deny the unknown, had lost. It is a *rapprochement* toward an acknowledgment of other forces which, no doubt, betrays them to the very forces they sense and fear. It was what made Thora first to feel—what was to happen. A prey to these fears, she followed my wife about like a shadow; carried with her always a little sharp hand-ax, and although we twitted her about the futility of chopping fantoms with such a weapon she would not relinquish it.

"Two weeks slipped by, and at their end the spokesman for our natives came to us. The next night was the full of the moon, he said. He reminded me of my promise. They would go back to their village next morning; they would return after the third night, as at that time the power of the *ani* would begin to wane with the moon. They left us sundry charms for our 'protection' and solemnly cautioned us to keep as far away as possible from Nan-Tauach during their absence—although their leader po-litely informed us that, no doubt, we were stronger than the spirits. Half-exasperated, half-amused I watched them go.

"No work could be done without them, of course, so we decided to spend the days of their absence junketing about the southern islets of the group. Under the moon the ruins were inexpressibly weird and beautiful. We marked down several spots for subsequent exploration, and on the morning of the third day set forth along the east face of the breakwater for our camp on Uschen-Tau, planning to have everything in readiness for the return of our men the next day.

"We landed just before dusk, tired and ready for our cots. It was only a little after ten o'clock that Edith awakened me.

" 'Listen!' she said. 'Lean over with your ear close to the ground!' I did so, and seemed to hear, far, far below, as though coming up from great distances, a faint chanting. It gathered strength, died down, ended; began, gathered volume, faded away into silence.

" 'It's the waves rolling on rocks somewhere,' I said. 'We're probably over some ledge of rock that carries the sound.'

" 'It's the first time I've heard it,' replied my wife doubtfully. We listened again. Then through the dim rhythms, deep beneath us, another sound came. It drifted across the lagoon that lay between us and Nan-Tauach in little tinkling waves. It was music—of a sort; I won't describe the strange effect it had upon me. You've felt it—"

"You mean on the deck?" I asked. Throckmartin nodded.

"I went to the flap of the tent." he continued, "and peered out. As I did so Stanton lifted his flap and walked out into the moonlight, looking over to the other islet and listening. I called to him.

" 'That's the queerest sound!' he said. He listened again. 'Crystalline! Like little notes of translucent glass. Like the bells of crystal on the sistrums of Isis at Dendarah Temple,' he added half-dreamily. We gazed intently at the island. Suddenly, on the gigantic sea-wall, moving slowly, rhythmically, we saw a little group of lights. Stanton laughed.

" 'The beggars!' he exclaimed. 'That's why they wanted to get away, is it? Don't you see, Dave, it's some sort of a festival—rites of some kind that they hold during the full moon! That's why they were so eager to have us *keep* away, too.'

"I felt a curious sense of relief, although I had not been sensible of any oppression. The explanation seemed good. It explained the tinkling music and also the chanting—worshipers, no doubt, in the ruins—their voices carried along passages I now knew honeycombed the whole Nan-Matal.

" 'Let's slip over,' suggested Stanton—but I would not.

" 'They're a difficult lot as it is.' I said. 'If we break into one of their religious ceremonies they'll probably never forgive us. Let's keep out of any family party where we haven't been invited.'

" 'That's so,' agreed Stanton.

In her blood ran the beliefs and superstitions of the Northland... beliefs of spirits of mountain and forest and water... werewolves and spirits malign.

"The strange tinkling music, if music it can be called, rose and fell, rose and fell—now laden with sorrow, now filled with joy.

" 'There's something—something very unsettling about it,' said Edith at last soberly. 'I wonder what they make those sounds with. They frighten me half to death, and, at the same time, they make me feel as though some enormous rapture was just around the corner.'

"I had noted this effect, too, although I had said nothing of it. And at the same time there came to me a clear perception that the chanting which had preceded it had seemed to come from a vast multitude—thousands more than the place we were contemplating could possibly have held. Of course, I thought, this might be due to some acoustic property of the basalt; an amplification of sound by some gigantic sounding-board of rock; still—" 'It's devilish uncanny!' broke in Stanton, answering my thought.

"And as he spoke the flap of Thora's tent was raised and out into the moonlight strode the old Swede. She was the great Norse type—tall, deep-breasted, molded on the old Viking lines. Her sixty years had slipped from her. She looked like some ancient priestess of Odin." He hesitated. "She knew," he said slowly, "something more far-seeing than my science had given her sight. She warned me—she warned me! Fools and mad that we are to pass such things by without heed!" He brushed a hand over his eyes.

"She stood there," he went on. "Her eyes were wide, brilliant, staring. She thrust her head forward toward Nan-Tauach, regarding the moving lights; she listened. Suddenly she raised her arms and made a curious gesture to the moon. It was—an archaic—movement; she seemed to drag it from remote antiquity—yet in it was a strange suggestion of power. Twice she repeated this gesture and—the tinklings died away! She waited a moment longer and then turned to us.

" 'Go!' she said, and her voice seemed to come from far distances. 'Go from here—and quickly! Go while you may. They have called—' She pointed to the islet. "They know you are here. They wait.' Her eyes widened further. 'It is there,' she wailed. 'It beckons—the—the—'

"She fell at Edith's feet, and as she fell over the lagoon came again the tinklings, now with a quicker note of jubilance—almost of triumph.

"We ran to Thora, Stanton and I, and picked her up. Her head rolled and her face, eyes closed, turned as though drawn full into the moonlight. I felt in my heart a throb of unfamiliar fear—for her face had changed again. Stamped upon it was a look of mingled transport and horror—alien, terrifying, strangely revolting. It was"—he thrust his face close to my eyes—"what you see in mine!"

For a dozen heart-beats I stared at him, fascinated; then he sank back again into the half-shadow of the berth.

"I managed to hide her face from Edith," he went on. "I thought she had suffered some sort of a nervous seizure. We carried her into her tent. Once within the unholy mask dropped from her, and she was again only the kindly, rugged old woman. I watched her throughout the night. The sounds from Nan-Tauach continued until about an hour before moon-set. In the morning Thora awoke, none the worse, apparently. She had had bad dreams, she said. She could not remember what they were—except that they had warned her of danger. She was oddly sullen, and I noted that throughout the morning her gaze returned again half-fascinatedly, half-wonderingly to the neighboring isles.

"That afternoon the natives returned. They were so exuberant in their apparent relief to find us well and intact that Stanton's suspicions of them were confirmed. He slyly told their leader that 'from the noise they had made on Nan-Tauach the night before they must have thoroughly enjoyed themselves.'

"I think I never saw such stark terror as the Ponapean manifested at the remark! Stanton himself was so plainly startled that he tried to pass it over as a jest. He met poor success! The men seemed panic-stricken, and for a time I thought they were about to abandon us—but they did not. They pitched their camp at the western side of the island—out of sight of Nan-Tauach. I noticed that they built large fires, and whenever I awoke that night I heard their voices in slow, minor chant—one of their song 'charms,' I thought drowsily, against evil *ani*. I heard nothing else; the place of frowning walls was wrapped in silence—no lights showed. The next morning the men were quiet, a little depressed, but as the hours wore on they regained their spirits, and soon life at the camp was going on just as it had before.

"You will understand, Goodwin, how the occurrences I have related would excite the scientific curiosity. We rejected immediately, of course, any explanation admitting the supernatural. Why not? Except the curiously disquieting effects of the tinkling music and Thora's behavior there was nothing to warrant any such fantastic theories—even if our minds had been the kind to harbor them.

"Our—symptoms let me call them—could all very easily be accounted for. It is unquestionable that the vibrations created by certain musical instruments have definite and sometimes extraordinary effect upon the nervous system. We accepted this as the explanation of the reactions we had experienced in hearing the unfamiliar sounds. Thora's nervousness, her superstitious apprehensions, had wrought her up to a condition of semi-somnambulistic hysteria. Science could readily explain her part in the night's scene.

"We came to the conclusion that there must be a passageway between Ponape and Nan-Tauach, known to the natives—and used by them during their rites. Ceremonies were probably held in great vaults or caverns beneath the ruins—for certainly a race which could have cut and set into place the enormous basalt blocks that formed them would have had little difficulty in hollowing out caverns, even had none existed before. Evidence of such subterranean passages we had already discovered.

We decided at last that on the next departure of our laborers we would set forth immediately to Nan-Tauach. We would investigate during the day, and at evening my wife and Thora would go back to camp, leaving Stanton and me to spend the night on the island, observing from some safe hiding-place what might occur.

"The moon waned; appeared crescent in the west; waxed slowly toward the full. Before the men left us they literally prayed us to accompany them. Their importunities only made us more eager to see what it was that, we were now convinced, they wanted to conceal from us. At least that was true of Stanton and myself. It was not true of Edith. She was thoughtful, abstracted—reluctant. Thora, on the other hand, showed an unusual restlessness, almost an eagerness to go. Goodwin"—he paused—"Goodwin, I know now that the poison was working in Thora—and that women have perceptions that we men lack—forebodings, sensings. Would to God I had known it then—Edith!" he cried suddenly. "Edith—come back to me! Forgive me!"

I stretched the decanter out to him. He drank deeply. Soon he had regained control of himself.

"When the men were out of sight around the turn of the harbor," he went on, "we took our boat and made straight for Nan-Tauach. Soon its mighty sea-wall towered above us. We passed through the water-gate with its gigantic hewn prisms of basalt and landed beside a half-submerged pier. In front of us stretched a series of giant steps leading into a vast court strewn with fragments of fallen pillars. In the center of the court, beyond the shattered pillars, rose another terrace of basalt blocks, concealing, I knew, still another enclosure.

"And now, Goodwin, for the better understanding of what follows and to guide you, should I—not be able—to accompany you when you go there, listen carefully to my description of this place: Nan-Tauach is literally three rectangles. The first rectangle is the sea-wall, built up of monoliths—hewn and squared, twenty feet wide at the top. To get to the gateway in the sea-wall you pass along the canal marked on the map between Nan-Tauach and the islet named Tau. The entrance to the canal is hidden by dense thickets of mangroves; once through these the way is clear. The gigantic steps lead up from the landing of the sea-gate through the entrance to the court-yard.

"This courtyard is surrounded by another basalt wall, rect-angular, following with mathematical exactness the march of the outer barricades. The sea-wall is from thirty to forty feet high—originally it must have been much higher, but there has been subsidence in parts. The wall of the first enclosure is fifteen feet across the top and its height varies from twenty to fifty feet—here, too, the gradual sinking of the land has caused portions of it to fall.

"Between the terrace of this enclosure and the sea-wall is, on each side, a considerable space. It is covered with little thick-ets of fern, of eucalyptus, shrubs; hibiscus vines run riot, cover-ing the fragments with their flowers.

"Within this courtyard is the second enclosure. Its terrace, of the same basalt as the outer walls, is about twenty feet high. Entrance is gained to it by many breaches which time has made in its stonework. This is the inner court, the heart of Nan-Tauach! There lies the great central vault with which is associ-ated the one name of living being that has come to us out of the mists of the past. The natives say it was the treasure-house of Chau-te-leur, a mighty king who reigned long 'before their fathers.' As Chau is the ancient Ponapean word both for sun and king, the name means, without doubt, 'place of the sun king.' It is a memory of a dynastic name of the race that ruled the Pacific continent, now vanished—just as the rulers of ancient Crete took the name of Minos and the rulers of Egypt the name of Pharaoh.

"And opposite this place of the sun king is the moon rock that hides the moon pool.

"It was Stanton who first found what I call the moon rock.

We had been inspecting the inner courtyard; Edith and Thora were getting together our lunch. I forgot to say that we had previously gone all over the islet and had found not a trace of living thing. I came out of the vault of Chau-te-leur to find Stanton before a part of the terrace studying it wonderingly.

" 'What do you make of this?' he asked me as I came up. He pointed to the wall. I followed his finger and saw a slab of stone about fifteen feet high and ten wide. At first all I noticed was the exquisite nicety with which its edges joined the blocks about it. Then I realized that its color was subtly different—tinged with gray and of a smooth, peculiar—deadness.

" 'Looks more like calcite than basalt,' I said. I touched it and withdrew my hand quickly, for at the contact every nerve in my arm tingled as though a shock of frozen electricity had passed through it. It was not cold as we know cold that I felt. It was a chill force—the phrase I have used—frozen electricity—describes it better than anything else. Stanton looked at me oddly.

" 'So you felt it too,' he said. 'I was wondering whether I was developing hallucinations like Thora. Notice, by the way, that the blocks beside it are quite warm beneath the sun.'

"I felt them and touched the grayish stone again. The same faint shock ran through my hand—a tingling chill that had in it a suggestion of substance, of force. We examined the slab more closely. Its edges were cut as though by an engraver of jewels. They fitted against the neighboring blocks in almost a hair-line. Its base, we saw, was slightly curved, and fitted as closely as top and sides upon the huge stones on which it rested. And then we noted that these stones had been hollowed to follow the line of the gray stone's foot. There was a semicircular depression running from one side of the slab to the other. It was as though the gray rock stood in the center of a shallow cup—revealing half, covering half. Something about this hollow attracted me. I reached down and felt it. Goodwin, although the balance of the stones that formed it, like all the stones of the courtyard, were rough and age-worn—this was as smooth, as even surfaced as though it had just left the hands of the polisher.

" 'It's a door!' exclaimed Stanton. 'It swings around in that little cup. That's what makes the hollow so smooth.'

" 'Maybe you're right,' I replied. 'But how the devil can we open it?'

"We went over the slab again—pressing upon its edges, thrusting against its sides. During one of those efforts I happened to look up—and cried out. For a foot above and on each side of the corner of the gray rock's lintel I had seen a slight convexity, visible only from the angle at which my gaze struck it. These bosses on the basalt were circular, eighteen inches in diameter, as we learned later, and at the center extended two inches only beyond the face of the terrace. Unless one looked directly up at them while leaning against the moon rock—for this slab, Goodwin, *is* the moon rock—they were invisible. And none would dare stand there!

"We carried with us a small scaling-ladder, and up this I went. The bosses were apparently nothing more than chiseled curvatures in the stone. I laid my hand on the one I was examining, and drew it back so sharply I almost threw myself from the ladder. In my palm, at the base of my thumb, I had felt the same shock that I had in touching the slab below. I put my hand back. The impression came from a spot not more than an inch wide. I went carefully over the entire convexity, and six times more the chill ran through my arm. There were, Goodwin, seven circles an inch wide in the curved place, each of which communicated the precise sensation I have described. The convexity on the opposite side of the slab gave precisely the same results. But no amount of touching or of pressing these spots singly or in any combination gave the slightest promise of motion to the slab itself.

" 'And yet—they're what open it,' said Stanton positively.

" 'Why do you say that?' I asked.

" 'I—don't know,' he answered hesitatingly. 'But something

tells me so, Throck,' he went on half earnestly, half laughingly, 'the purely scientific part of me is fighting the purely human part of me. The scientific part is urging me to find some way to get that slab either down or open. The human part is just as strongly urging me to do nothing of the sort and get away while I can!'

"He laughed again—shamefacedly.

" 'Which will it be?' he asked—and I thought that in his tone the human side of him was ascendant.

" 'It will probably stay as it is—unless we blow it to bits,' I said.

" 'I thought of that,' he answered, 'and—I wouldn't dare,' he added soberly enough. And even as I had spoken there came to me the same feeling that he had expressed. It was as though something passed out of the gray rock that struck my heart as a hand strikes an impious lip. We turned away—uneasily, and faced Thora coming through a breach in the terrace.

" 'Miss Edith wants you quick,' she began—and stopped. I saw her eyes go past me and widen. She was looking at the gray rock. Her body grew suddenly rigid; she took a few stiff steps forward and then ran straight to it. We saw her cast herself upon its breast, hands and face pressed against it; heard her scream as though her very soul were being drawn from her—and watched her fall at its foot. As we picked her up I saw steal from her face the look I had observed when first we heard the crystal music of Nan-Tauach—that un-human mingling of opposites!"

CHAPTER V

AV-O-LO-HA

"**WE CARRIED THORA** back, down to where Edith was waiting. We told her what had happened and what we had

found. She listened gravely, and as we finished Thora sighed
and opened her eyes.

" 'I would like to see the stone,' she said. 'Charles, you stay
here with Thora.' We passed through the outer court silently—
and stood before the rock. She touched it, drew back her hand
as I had; thrust it forward again resolutely and held it there.
She seemed to be listening. Then she turned to me.

" 'David,' said my wife, and the wistfulness in her voice hurt
me—'David, would you be very, very disappointed if we went
from here—without trying to find out any more about it—
would you?'

"Goodwin, I never wanted anything so much in my life as I
wanted to learn what that rock concealed. You will understand—the cumulative curiosity that all the happenings had
caused; the certainty that before me was an entrance to a place
that, while known to the natives—for I still clung to that
theory—was utterly unknown to any man of my race; that
within, ready for my finding, was the answer to the stupendous
riddle of these islands and a lost chapter of the history of humanity. There before me—and was I asked to turn away, leaving
it unread!

"Nevertheless, I tried to master my desire, and I answered—
'Edith, not a bit if you want us to do it.'

"She read my struggle in my eyes. She looked at me searchingly for a moment and then turned back toward the gray rock.
I saw a shiver pass through her. I felt a tinge of remorse and
pity!

" 'Edith,' I exclaimed, 'we'll go!'

"She looked at me again. 'Science is a jealous mistress,' she
quoted. 'No, after all it may be just fancy. At any rate, you can't
run away. No! But, Dave, I'm going to stay too!'

" 'You are not!' I exclaimed. 'You're going back to the camp
with Thora. Stanton and I will be all right.'

" 'I'm going to stay,' she repeated. And there was no changing her decision. As we neared the others she laid a hand on my arm.

" 'Dave,' she said, 'if there should be something—well—inexplicable tonight—something that seems—too dangerous—will you promise to go back to our own islet tomorrow, or, while we can, and wait until the natives return?'

"I promised eagerly—for the desire to stay and see what came with the night was like a fire within me.

"And would to God that I had not waited another moment. Goodwin; would to God that I had gathered them all together then and sailed back on the instant through the mangroves to Uschen-Tau!

"We found Thora on her feet again and singularly composed. She claimed to have no more recollection of what had happened after she had spoken to Stanton and to me in front of the gray rock than she had after the seizure on Uschen-Tau. She grew sullen under our questioning, precisely as she had before. But to my astonishment, when she heard of our arrangements for the night, she betrayed a febrile excitement that had in it something of exultance.

"We had picked a place about five hundred feet away from the steps leading into the outer court. I would have preferred going into the inner enclosure, but I feared for Edith. Besides, it was better to go slowly until we knew what was opposed to us. And there was no place in the heart of the ruins where we could hide—except in the vault, and none of us liked to think of that. The spot we had selected was well hidden. We could not be seen, and yet we had a clear view of the stairs and the gateway. We settled down just before dusk to wait for whatever might come. I was nearest the giant steps; next me Edith; then Thora, and last Stanton. Each of us had with us automatic pistols, and all, except Thora, had rifles.

"Night fell. After a time the eastern sky began to lighten, and we knew that the moon was rising; grew lighter still, and the orb peeped over the sea; swam suddenly into full sight.

Edith gripped my hand, for, as though the full emergence into the heavens had been a signal, we heard begin beneath us the deep chanting. It came from illimitable depths.

"The moon poured her rays down upon us, and I saw Stanton start. On the instant I caught the sound that had roused him. It came from the inner enclosure. It was like a long, soft sighing. It was not human; seemed in some way—mechanical. I glanced at Edith and then at Thora. My wife was intently listening. Thora sat, as she had since we had placed ourselves, elbows on knees, her hands covering her face.

"And then suddenly from the moonlight flooding us there came to me a great drowsiness. Sleep seemed to drip from the rays and fall upon my eyes, closing them—closing them inexorably. I felt Edith's hand relax in mine, and under my own heavy lids saw her nodding. I saw Stanton's head fall upon his breast and his body sway drunkenly. I tried to rise—to fight against the profound desire for slumber that pressed in on me.

"And as I fought I saw Thora raise her head as though listening; saw her rise and turn her face toward the gateway. For a moment she gazed, and my drugged eyes seemed to perceive within it a deeper, stronger radiance. Thora looked at us. There was infinite despair in her face—and expectancy. I tried again to rise—and a surge of sleep rushed over me. Dimly, as I sank within it, I heard a crystalline chiming; raised my lids once more with a supreme effort, saw Thora, bathed in light, standing at the top of the stairs, and then—sleep took me for its very own—swept me into the very heart of oblivion!

"Dawn was breaking when I wakened. Recollection rushed back on me and I thrust a panic-stricken hand out toward Edith; touched her and felt my heart give a great leap of thankfulness. She stirred, sat up, rubbing dazed eyes. I glanced toward Stanton. He lay on his side, back toward us, head in arms.

"Edith looked at me laughingly. 'Heavens! What sleep!' she said. Memory came to her. Her face paled. 'What happened?' she whispered. 'What made us sleep like that?' She looked over to Stanton, sprang to her feet, ran to him, shook him. He turned over with a mighty yawn, and I saw relief lighten her face as it had lightened my heart.

"Stanton raised himself stiffly. He looked at us. 'What's the matter?' he exclaimed. 'You look as though you've seen ghosts!'

"Edith caught my hands. 'Where's Thora?' she cried. Before I could answer she ran out into the open calling: 'Thora! Thora!'

"Stanton stared at me. 'Taken!' was all I could say. Together we went to my wife, now standing beside the great stone steps, looking up fearfully at the gateway into the terraces. There I told them what I had seen before sleep had drowned me. And together then we ran up the stairs, through the court and up to the gray rock.

"The gray rock was closed as it had been the day before, nor was there trace of its having opened. No trace! Even as I thought this Edith dropped to her knees before it and reached toward something lying at its foot. It was a little piece of gay silk. I knew it for part of the kerchief Thora wore about her hair. She lifted the fragment; hesitated. I saw then that it had been cut from the kerchief as though by a razor-edge; I saw, too, that a few threads ran from it—down toward the base of the slab; ran to the base of the gray rock and—under it! The gray rock was a door! And it had opened and Thora had passed through it!

"I think, Goodwin, that for the next few minutes we all were a little insane. We beat upon that diabolic entrance with our hands, with stones and clubs. At last reason came back to us. Stanton set forth for the camp to bring back blasting powder and tools. While he was gone Edith and I searched the whole islet for any other clue. We found not a trace of Thora nor any indication of any living being save ourselves. We went back to the gateway to find Stanton returned.

"Goodwin, during the next two hours we tried every way in our power to force entrance through the slab. The rock within effective blasting radius of the cursed door resisted our drills. We tried explosions at the base of the slab with charges covered by rock. They made not the slightest impression on the surface beneath, expending their force, of course, upon the slighter resistance of their coverings.

"Afternoon found us hopeless, so far as breaking through the rock was concerned. Night was coming on and before it came we would have to decide our course of action. I wanted to go to Ponape for help. But Edith objected that this would take hours and after we had reached there it would be impossible to persuade our men to return with us that night, if at all. What then was left? Clearly only one of two choices: to go back to our camp and wait for our men to return and on their return try to persuade them to go with us to Nan-Tauach. But this would mean the abandonment of Thora for at least two days. We could not do it; it would have been too cowardly.

"The other choice was to wait where we were for night to come; to wait for the rock to open as it had the night before, and to make a sortie through it for Thora before it could close again. With the sun had come confidence; at least a shattering of the mephitic mists of superstition with which the strangeness of the things that had befallen us had clouded for a time our minds. In that brilliant light there seemed no place for fantoms.

"The evidence that the slab had opened was unmistakable, but might not Thora simply have *found* it open through some mechanism still working after ages, and dependent for its action upon laws of physics unknown to us upon the full light of the moon? The assertion of the natives that the *ani* had greatest power at this time might be a far-flung reflection of knowledge which had found ways to use forces contained in moonlight, as we have found ways to utilize the forces in the sun's rays. If so, Thora was probably behind the slab, sending out prayers to us for help.

"But how explain the sleep that had descended upon us? Might it not have been some emanation from plants or gaseous emanations from the island itself? Such things were far from uncommon, we agreed. In some way the period of their greatest activity might coincide with the period of the moon, but if this were so why had not Thora also slept?

"There, indeed, we faced an impasse. It might be, of course, that Thora had been resistant to such emanations, as certain of us are resistant and immune from various bacteria. It was possible. And it might still be that our first theory was correct and that Nan-Tauach was a sacred place: a gathering point for priests possessing fragments of the ancient secrets, vanished knowledge, and the resented intruders. We knew the command certain primitive folk have of sleep sounds and vapors. It might be that here was the true explanation.

"But whatever the truth, our path lay clear before us. We had to spend that night on Nan-Tauach!

"As dusk fell we looked over our weapons. Edith was an excellent shot with both rifle and pistol. With the idea that the

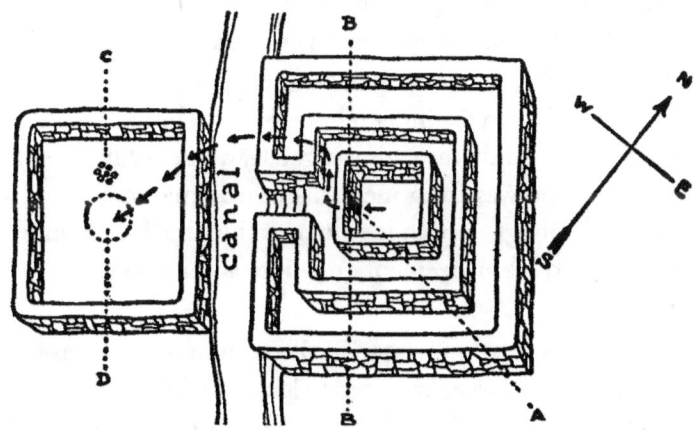

Dr. Throckmartin's sketch of the location of the moon door.
The passageways, the probable location of the moon pool deep
under Tau Islet, and the conjectured location of the seven
lights. A is the moon rock on Nan-Tauach; B B is the bosses
above it which control its opening; the arrows indicate Dr.
Throckmartin's probable course beneath the walls and under
the canal. C are the moon lights, and D the cavern of the
moon pool on Tau Islet. Proper measurements are not observed
in the sketch; the idea being solely to determine position.

impulse toward sleep was the result either of emanations such
as I have described or man-made, we constructed, rough-and-
ready but effective, neutralizes, which we placed over our
mouths and nostrils. We had decided that my wife was to
remain in the hiding-place. Stanton would take up a station on
the far side of the stairway and I would place myself opposite
him on the side near Edith. The place I picked out was less than
five hundred feet from her, and I could reassure myself now
and as to her safety as it looked down upon the hollow wherein
she crouched. As the phenomena had previously synchronized
with the rising of the moon, we had no reason to think they
would occur any earlier this night. From our respective stations
Stanton and I could command the gateway entrance. His position gave him also a glimpse of the outer courtyard.

"A faint glow in the sky heralded the moon. I kissed Edith,
and Stanton and I took our places. The moon dawn increased
rapidly; the disk swam up, and in a moment it seemed was
shining in full radiance upon ruins and sea.

"As it rose there came as on the night before the curious little
sighing sound from the inner terrace. I saw Stanton straighten
up and stare intently through the gateway, rifle ready. Even at
the distance he was from me, I discerned amazement in his
eyes. The moonlight within the gateway thickened, grew stronger. I watched his amazement grow into sheer wonder.

"I arose.

"'Stanton, what do you see?' I called cautiously. He waved a
silencing hand. I turned my head to look at Edith. A shock ran
through me. She lay upon her side. Her face was turned full
toward the moon. She was in deepest sleep!

"As I turned again to call to Stanton, my eyes swept the head
of the steps and stopped, fascinated. For the moonlight had
thickened more. It seemed to be—curdled—there; and through
it ran little gleams and veins of shimmering white fire. A languor
passed through me. It was not the ineffable drowsiness of the
preceding night. It was a sapping of all will to move. I tore my

eyes away and forced them upon Stanton. I tried to call out to him. I had not the will to make my lips move! I had struggled against this paralysis and as I did so I felt through me a sharp shock. It was like a blow. And with it came utter inability to make a single motion. Goodwin, I could not even move my eyes!

"I saw Stanton leap upon the steps and move toward the gateway. As he did so the light in the courtyard grew dazzlingly brilliant. Through it rained tiny tinklings that set the heart to racing with pure joy and stilled it with terror.

"And now for the first time I heard that cry, *'Av-o-lo-ha! Av-o-lo-ha!,'* the cry you heard on deck. It murmured with the strange effect of a sound only partly in our own space—as though it were part of a fuller phrase passing through from another dimension and losing much as it came; infinitely caressing, infinitely cruel!

"On Stanton's face I saw come the look I dreaded—and yet knew would appear; that mingled expression of delight and fear. The two lay side by side as they had on Thora, but were intensified. He walked on up the stairs; disappeared beyond the range of my fixed gaze. Again I heard the murmur—*'Av-o-lo-ha!'* There was triumph in it now and triumph in the storm of tinklings that swept over it.

"For another heart-beat there was silence. Then a louder burst of sound and ringing through it Stanton's voice from the courtyard—a great cry—a scream—filled with ecstasy insupportable and horror unimaginable! And again there was silence. I strove to burst the invisible bonds that held me. I could not. Even my eyelids were fixed. Within them my eyes, dry and aching, burned.

"Then Goodwin—I first saw the inexplicable! The crystalline music swelled. Where I sat I could take in the gateway and its basalt portals, rough and broken, rising to the top of the wall forty feet above, shattered, ruined portals—unclimbable. From this gateway an intenser light began to flow. It grew, it gushed, and into it, into my sight, walked Stanton.

"Stanton! But—God! What a vision!"

He ceased. I waited—waited.

CHAPTER VI

INTO THE MOON POOL

"GOODWIN," THROCKMARTIN SAID at last, "I can describe him only as a thing of living light. He radiated light; was filled with light; overflowed with it. Around him was a shining cloud that whirled through and around him in radiant swirls, shimmering tentacles, luminescent, coruscating spirals.

"I saw his face. It shone with a rapture too great to be borne by living men, and was shadowed with insuperable misery. It was as though his face had been remolded, by the hand of God and the hand of Satan, working together and in harmony. You have seen it on my face. But you have never seen it in the degree that Stanton bore it. The eyes were wide open and fixed, as though upon some inward vision of hell and heaven! He walked like the corpse of a man damned who carried within him an angel of light!

"The music swelled again. I heard again the murmuring—'Av-o-lo-ha!' Stanton turned, facing the ragged side of the portal. And then I saw that the light that filled and surrounded him had a nucleus, a core—something shiftingly human shaped—that dissolved and changed, gathered itself, whirled through and beyond him and back again. And as this shining nucleus passed through him Stanton's whole body pulsed with light. As the luminescence moved, there moved with it, still and serene always, seven tiny globes of light like seven little moons.

"So much I saw and then swiftly Stanton seemed to be lifted—levitated—up the unscalable wall and to its top. The glow faded from the moonlight, the tingling music grew fainter.

I tried again to move. The spell still held me fast. The tears were running down now from my rigid lids and they brought relief to my tortured eyes.

"I have said my gaze was fixed. It was. But from the side, peripherally, they took in a part of the far wall of the outer enclosure. Ages seemed to pass and I saw a radiance stealing along it. Soon there came into sight the figure that was Stanton. Far away he was—on the gigantic wall. But still I could see the shining spirals whirling jubilantly around and through him; felt rather than saw his tranced face beneath the seven lights. A swirl of crystal notes, and he had passed. And all the time, as though from some opened well of light, the courtyard gleamed and sent out silver fires that dimmed the moon-rays, yet seemed strangely to be a part of them.

"Ten times he passed before me so. The luminescence came with the music; swam for a while along the man-made cliff of basalt and passed away. Between times eternities rolled and still I crouched there, a helpless thing of stone with eyes that would not close!

"At last the moon neared the horizon. There came a louder burst of sound; the second, and last, cry of Stanton, like an echo of his first! Again the soft sigh from the inner terrace. Then— utter silence. The light faded; the moon was setting and with a rush life and power to move returned to me. I made a leap for the steps, rushed up them, through the gateway and straight to the gray rock. It was closed—as I knew it would be. But did I dream it—or did I hear, echoing through it as though from vast distances a triumphant shouting—*'Av-o-lo-ha! Av-o-lo-ha!'*

"I remembered Edith. I ran back to her. At my touch she wakened; looked at me wanderingly; raised herself on a hand.

" 'Dave!' she said, 'I slept—after all.' She saw the despair on my face and leaped to her feet. 'Dave!' she cried. 'What is it? Where's Charles?'

"I lighted a fire before I spoke. Then I told her. And for the balance of that night we sat before the flames, arms around each other—like two frightened children."

Suddenly Throckmartin held his hands out to me appealingly.

"Goodwin, old friend!" he cried. "Don't look at me as though I were mad. It's truth, absolute truth. Wait—" I comforted him as well as I could. After a little time he took up his story.

"Never," he said, "did man welcome the sun as we did that morning. As soon as it was light we went back to the courtyard. The basalt walls whereon I had seen Stanton were black and silent. The terraces were as they had been. The gray slab was in its place. In the shallow hollow at its base was—nothing. Nothing—nothing was there anywhere on the islet of Stanton— not a trace, not a sign on Nan-Tauach to show that he had ever lived.

"What were we to do? Precisely the same arguments that had kept us there the night before held good now—and doubly good. We could not abandon these two; could not go as long as there was the faintest hope of finding them—and yet for love of each other how could we remain? I loved my wife, Goodwin—how much I never knew until that day; and she loved me as deeply.

" 'It takes only one each night,' she said. 'Beloved, let it take me.'

"I wept, Goodwin. We both wept.

" 'We will meet it together,' she said. And it was thus at last that we arranged it."

"That took great courage indeed, Throckmartin," I interrupted. He looked at me eagerly.

"You do believe then?" he exclaimed.

"I believe," I said. He pressed my hand with a grip that nearly crushed it.

"Now," he told me, "I do not fear. If I—fail, you will prepare and carry on the work."

I promised. And—God forgive me—that was three years ago.

"It did take courage," he went on, again quietly. "More than courage. For we knew it was renunciation. Each of us in our hearts felt that one of us would not be there to see the sun rise. And each of us prayed that the death, if death it was, would not come first to the other.

"We talked it all over carefully, bringing to bear all our power of analysis and habit of calm, scientific thought. We considered minutely the time element in the phenomena. Although the deep chanting began at the very moment of moonrise, fully five minutes had passed between its full lifting and the strange sighing sound from the inner terrace. I went back in memory over the happenings of the night before. At least fifteen minutes had intervened between the first heralding sigh and the intensification of the moonlight in the courtyard. And this glow grew for at least ten minutes more before the first burst of the crystal notes. Indeed, more than half an hour must have elapsed, I calculated, between the moment the moon showed above the horizon and the first delicate onslaught of the tinklings.

"The sighing sound—of what had it reminded me? Of course—of a door revolving and swishing softly along its base.

" 'Edith!' I cried. 'I think I have it! The gray rock opens five minutes after upon the moonrise. But whoever or whatever it is that comes through it must wait until the moon has risen higher, or else it must come from a distance. The thing to do is not to wait for it, but to surprise it before it passes out the door. We will go into the inner court early. You will take your rifle and pistol and hide yourself where you can command the opening—if the slab does open. The instant it moves I will enter. It's our best chance, Edith. I think it's our only one.'

"My wife demurred strongly. She wanted to go with me. But I convinced her that it was better for her to stand guard without, prepared to help me if I were forced from what lay behind the rock again into the open.

"The day passed too swiftly. In the face of what we feared our love seemed stronger than ever. Was it the flare of the spark before extinguishment? I wondered. We prepared and ate a good dinner. We tried to keep our minds from anything but the scientific aspect of the phenomena. We agreed that whatever it was its cause must be human, and that we must keep that fact in mind every second. But what kind of men could create such prodigies? We thrilled at the thought of finding perhaps the remnants of a vanished race, living perhaps in cities over whose rocky skies the Pacific rolled; exercising there the lost wisdom of the half-gods of earth's youth.

"At the half-hour before moonrise we two went into the inner courtyard. I took my place at the side of the gray rock. Edith crouched behind a broken pillar twenty feet away, slipped her rifle-barrel over it so that it would cover the opening.

"The minutes crept by. The courtyard was very quiet. The darkness lessened and through the breaches of the terrace I watched the far sky softly lighten. With the first pale flush the stillness became intensified. It deepened—became unbearably—expectant. The moon rose, showed the quarter, the half, then swam up into full sight like a great bubble.

"Its rays fell upon the wall before me and suddenly upon the convexities I have described seven little circles of light sprang out. They gleamed, glimmered, grew brighter—shone. The gigantic slab before me turned as though on a pivot, sighing softly as it moved.

"For a moment I gasped in amazement. It was like a conjurer's trick. And the moving slab I noticed was also glowing, becoming opalescent like the little shining circles above.

"Only for a second I gazed and then with a word to Edith flung myself through the opening which the slab had uncovered. Before me was a platform and from the platform steps led downward into a smooth corridor. This passage was not dark; it glowed with the same faint silvery radiance as the door. Down it I raced. As I ran, plainer than ever before, I heard the chant-

ing. The passage turned abruptly, passed parallel to the walls of
the outer courtyard and then once more led abruptly downward.
Still I ran, and as I ran I looked at the watch on my wrist. Less
than three minutes had elapsed.

"The passage ended. Before me was a high vaulted arch. For
a moment I paused. It seemed to open into space; a space filled
with lambent, coruscating, many-colored mist whose brightness
grew even as I watched. I passed through the arch and stopped
in sheer awe!

"In front of me was a pool. It was circular, perhaps twenty
feet wide. Around it ran a low, softly curved lip of glimmering
silvery stone. Its water was palest blue. The pool with its silvery
rim was like a great blue eye staring upward.

"Upon it streamed seven shafts of radiance. They poured
down upon the blue eye like cylindrical torrents; they were like
shining pillars of light rising from a sapphire floor.

"One was the tender pink of the pearl; one of the aurora's
green; a third a deathly white; the fourth the blue in mother-
of-pearl; a shimmering column of pale amber; a beam of amethyst; a shaft of molten silver. Such are the colors of the seven
lights that stream upon the moon pool. I drew closer, awestrick-
en. The shafts did not illumine the depths. They played upon
the surface and seemed there to diffuse, to melt into it. The pool
drank them!

"Through the water tiny gleams of phosphorescence began
to dart, sparkles and coruscations of pale incandescence. And
far, far below I sensed a movement, a shifting glow as of something slowly rising.

"I looked upward, following the radiant pillars, to their
source. Far above were seven shining globes, and it was from
these that the rays poured. Even as I watched their brightness
grew. They were like seven moons set high in some caverned
heaven. Slowly their splendor increased, and with it the splendor of the seven beams streaming from them. It came to me
that they were crystals of some unknown kind set in the roof

of the moon pool's vault and that their light was drawn from the moon shining high above them. They were wonderful, those lights—and what must have been the knowledge of those who set them there!

"Brighter and brighter they grew as the moon climbed higher, sending its full radiance down through them. I tore my gaze away and stared at the pool. It had grown milky, opalescent. The rays gushing into it seemed to be filling it; it was alive with sparklings, scintillations, glimmerings. And the luminescence I had seen rising from its depths was larger, nearer!

"A swirl of mist floated up from its surface. It drifted within the embrace of the rosy beam and hung there for a moment. The beam seemed to embrace it, sending through it little shining corpuscles, tiny rosy spiralings. The mist absorbed the rays, was strengthened by it, gained substance. Another swirl sprang into the amber shaft, clung and fed there, moved swiftly toward the first and mingled with it. And now other swirls arose, here and there, too fast to be counted, hung poised in the embrace of the light steams; flashed and pulsed into each other.

"Thicker and thicker still they arose until the surface of the pool was a pulsating pillar of opalescent mist; steadily growing stronger; drawing within it life from the seven beams falling upon it; drawing to it from below the darting, red atoms of the pool. Into its center was passing the luminescence I had sensed rising from the far depths. And the center glowed, throbbed— began to send out questing swirls and tendrils—

"There forming before me was *that* which had walked with Stanton, which had taken Thora—the thing I had come to find!

"With the shock of realization my brain sprang into action. My hand fell to my pistol and I fired shot after shot into its radiance. The place rang with the explosions and there came to me a sense of unforgivable profanation. Devilish as I knew it to be, that Chamber of the Moon Pool seemed also—in some way—holy. As though a god and a demon dwelt there, inextricably commingled.

"As I shot the pillar wavered; the water grew more disturbed. The mist swayed and shook; gathered itself again. I slipped a second clip into the automatic and another idea coming to me took careful aim at one of the globes in the roof. From thence I knew came the force that shaped the dweller in the pool. From the pouring rays came its strength. If I could destroy them I could check its forming. I fired again and again. If I hit the globes I did no damage. The little motes in their beams danced with the motes in the mist, troubled. That was all.

"Up from the pool like little bells, like bubbles of crystal notes rose the tinklings. Their notes were higher, had lost their sweetness, were angry, as it were, with themselves.

"And then out from the inexplicable, hovering over the pool, swept a shining swirl. It caught me above the heart; wrapped itself around me. I felt an icy coldness and then there rushed over me a mingled ecstasy and horror. Every atom of me quivered with delight and at the same time shrank with despair. There was nothing loathsome in it. But it was as though the icy soul of evil and the fiery soul of good had stepped together within me. The pistol dropped from my hand.

"So I stood while the pool gleamed and sparkled; the streams of light grew more intense and the mist glowed and strengthened. I saw that its shining core had shape—but a shape that my eyes and brain could not define. It was as though a being of another sphere should assume what it might of human semblance, but was not able to conceal that what human eyes saw was but a part of it. It was neither man nor woman; it was unearthly and androgynous. Even as I found its human semblance it changed. And still the mingled rapture and terror held me. Only in a little corner of my brain dwelt something untouched; something that held itself apart and watched. Was it the soul? I have never believed—and yet—

"Over the head of the misty body there sprang suddenly out seven little lights. Each was the color of the beam beneath which it rested. I knew now that the dweller was—complete!

"And then—behind me I heard a scream. It was Edith's voice. It came to me that she had heard the shots and followed me. I felt every faculty concentrate into a mighty effort. I wrenched myself free from the gripping tentacle and it swept back. I turned to catch Edith, and as I did so slipped—fell. As I dropped I saw the radiant shape above the pool leap swiftly for me!

"There was the rush past me and as the dweller paused, straight into it raced Edith, arms outstretched to shield me from it! God!"

He trembled.

"She threw herself squarely within its diabolic splendor," he whispered. "She stopped and reeled as though she had encountered solidity. And as she faltered it wrapped its shining self around her. The crystal tinklings burst forth jubilantly. The light filled her, ran through and around her as it had with Stanton, and I saw drop upon her face—the look. From the pillar came the murmur—*'Av-o-lo-ha!'* The vault echoed it.

" 'Edith!' I cried. 'Edith!' I was in agony. She must have heard me, even through the—thing. I saw her try to free herself. Her rush had taken her to the very verge of the moon pool. She tottered; and in an instant—she fell—with the radiance still holding her, still swirling and winding around and through her—into the moon pool! She sank, Goodwin, and with her went—the dweller!

"I dragged myself to the brink. Far down I saw a shining, many-colored nebulous cloud descending; caught a glimpse of Edith's face, disappearing; her eyes stared up to me filled with supernal ecstasy and horror. And—vanished!

"I looked about me stupidly. The seven globes still poured their radiance upon the pool. It was pale-blue again. Its sparklings and coruscations were gone. From far below there came a muffled outburst of triumphant chanting!

" 'Edith!' I cried again. 'Edith, come back to me!' And then a darkness fell upon me. I remember running back through the shimmering corridors and out into the courtyard. Reason had left me. When it returned I was far out at sea in our boat wholly estranged from civilization. A day later I was picked up by the schooner in which I came to Port Moresby.

"I have formed a plan; you must hear it, Goodwin—" He fell upon his berth. I bent over him. Exhaustion and the relief of telling his story had been too much for him. He slept like the dead.

CHAPTER VII

THE DWELLER COMES

ALL THAT NIGHT I watched over him. When dawn broke I went to my room to get a little sleep myself. But my slumber was haunted.

The next day the storm was unabated. Throckmartin came to me at lunch. He looked better. His strange expression had waned. He had regained much of its old alertness.

"Come to my cabin," he said. There, he stripped his shirt from him. "Something is happening," he said. "The mark is smaller." It was as he said.

"I'm escaping," he whispered jubilantly. "Just let me get to Melbourne safely, and then we'll see who'll win! For, Goodwin, I'm not at all sure that Edith is dead—as we know deaths—nor that the others are. There was something outside experience there—some great mystery."

And all that day he talked to me of his plans.

"There's a natural explanation, of course," he said. "My theory is that the moon rock is of some composition sensitive to the action of moon rays; somewhat as the metal selenium is to sun rays. There is a powerful quality in moonlight, as both science and legends can attest. We know of its effect upon the mentality, the nervous system, even upon certain diseases.

"The moon slab is of some material that reacts to moonlight. The little circles over the top are, without doubt, its operating agency. When the light strikes them they release the mechanism that opens the slab, just as you can open doors with sunlight by an ingenious arrangement of selenium-cells. Apparently it takes the strength of the full moon to do this. We will first try a concentration of the rays of the nearly full moon upon these circles to see whether that will open the rock. If it does we will be able to investigate the pool without interruption from—from—what emanates.

"Look, here on the chart are their locations. I have made this in duplicate for you in the event of something happening to me."

He worked upon the chart a little more. "Here," he said, "is where I believe the seven great globes to be. They are probably hidden somewhere in the ruins of the islet called Tau, where they can catch the first moon rays. I have calculated that when I entered I went so far this way—here is the turn; so far this way, took this other turn and ran down this long, curving corridor to the hall of the moon pool. That ought to make lights, at least approximately, here." He pointed.

"They are certainly cleverly concealed, but they must be open to the air to get the light. They should not be too hard to find. They must be found." He hesitated again. "I suppose it would be safer to destroy them, for it is clearly through them that the phenomena of the pool is manifested; and yet, to destroy so wonderful a thing! Perhaps the better way would be to have some men up by them, and if it were necessary, to protect those below, to destroy them on signal. Or they might simply be covered. That would neutralize them. To destroy them—" He hesitated again. "No, the phenomena is too important to be destroyed without fullest investigation." His face clouded again. "But it is not human; it can't be," he muttered. He turned to me and laughed. "The old conflict between science and too frail human credulity!" he said.

Again—"We need half a dozen diving-suits. The pool must be entered and searched to its depths. That will indeed take courage, yet in the time of the new moon it should be safe, or perhaps better after the dweller is destroyed or made safe."

We went over plans, accepted them, rejected them, and still the storm raged—and all that day and all that night.

I hurry to the end. That afternoon there came a steady light-

Stanton's whole body pulsed with light... seemed to be lifted... levitated up the unscalable wall....

ening of the clouds which Throckmartin watched with deep uneasiness. Toward dusk they broke away suddenly and soon the sky was clear. The stars came twinkling out.

"It will be tonight," Throckmartin said to me. "Goodwin, friend, stand by me. Tonight it will come, and I must fight."

I could say nothing. About an hour before moonrise we went to his cabin. We fastened the portholes tightly and turned on the electrics. Throckmartin had some queer theory that the electric rays would be a bar to his pursuer. I don't know why. A little later he complained of increasing sleepiness.

"But it's just weariness," he said. "Not at all like that other drowsiness. It's an hour till moonrise still," he yawned at last. "Wake me up a good fifteen minutes before."

He lay upon the berth. I sat thinking. I came to myself with a start. What time was it? I looked at my watch and jumped to the porthole. It was full moonlight; the orb had been up for fully half an hour. I strode over to Throckmartin and shook him by the shoulder.

"Up, quick, man!" I cried. He rose sleepily. His shirt fell open at the neck and I looked, in amazement, at the white band around his chest. Even under the electric light it shone softly, as though little flecks of light were in it.

Throckmartin seemed only half-awake. He looked down at his breast, saw the glowing cincture, and smiled.

"Oh, yes," he said drowsily, "it's coming—to take me back to Edith! Well, I'm glad."

"Throckmartin!" I cried. "Wake up! Fight."

"Fight!" he said. "No use; keep the maps; come after us."

He went to the port and drowsily drew aside the curtain. The moon traced a broad path of light straight to the ship. Under its rays the band around his chest gleamed brighter and brighter; shot forth little rays; seemed to move.

He peered out intently and, suddenly, before I could stop him, threw open the port. I saw a glimmering presence moving swiftly along the moon path toward us, skimming over the waters.

And with it raced little crystal tinklings and far off I heard a long-drawn murmuring cry.

On the instant the lights went out in the cabin, evidently throughout the ship, for I heard shoutings above. I sprang back into a corner and crouched there. At the porthole was a radiance; swirls and spirals of living white cold fire. It poured into the cabin and it was filled with dancing motes of light, and over the radiant core of it shone seven little lights like tiny moons. It gathered Throckmartin to it. Light pulsed through and from him. I saw his skin turn to a translucent, shimmering whiteness like illumined porcelain. His face became unrecognizable, inhuman with the monstrous twin expressions. So he stood for a moment. The pillar of light seemed to hesitate and the seven lights to contemplate me. I shrank further down into the corner. I saw Throckmartin drawn to the port. The room filled with murmuring. I fainted.

When I awakened the lights were burning again.

But of Throckmartin there was no trace!

Gentlemen, there are some things we are doomed to regret all our life. Born in me then was a great fear. I suppose I was unbalanced by what I had seen. I could not think clearly. But there came to me the sheer impossibility of telling the ship's officers what I had seen; what Throckmartin had told me. They would accuse me, I felt, of his murder. At neither appearance of the phenomena had any save our two selves witnessed it. I was certain of this because they would surely have discussed it. Why none had seen it I do not know.

The next morning when Throckmartin's absence was noted, I merely said that I had left him early in the evening. It occurred to no one to doubt me, or to question me further. His strangeness had caused much comment; all had thought him half-mad. And so it was officially reported that he had fallen or jumped from the ship during the failure of the lights, the cause of which was another mystery of that night.

Afterward, the same inhibition held me back from making his and my story known to my fellow scientists.

But this inhibition is suddenly dead, and I am not sure that its death is not a summons from Throckmartin.

I go to Nan-Tauach, gentlemen, to make amends for my cowardice by seeking out the dweller.

And, gentlemen, I stake all my reputation, all my faith, all that I hold sacred and dear that what I have written here is absolute truth.

THE CONQUEST OF
THE MOON POOL

TO THE EDITOR OF ALL-STORY WEEKLY:

December 5, 1918.

The International Association of Science takes the greatest pleasure in notifying you that, after long discussion and hesitation by the executive council, the decision has been made to pass to you for presentation in your publication the further narrative of Dr. Walter T. Goodwin, Ph.D., F.R.G.S., *et cetera*, relating his experiences in quest of the solution and possible destruction of the extraordinary phenomena emanating from that group of prehistoric ruins in the Caroline Islands known as the Nan-Matal.

The delay of the International Association in making definite reply to the many and compelling appeals of yourself and your readers for additional information upon Dr. Goodwin's surprising adventure was due, frankly, sir, to a very real doubt not as to the expediency of revealing at this time certain features of these later observations, but as to the actual danger to humanity such revelation might involve.

Still, in view of your courtesy and courage in printing, on June 22, 1918, under the title of "The Moon Pool," so extraordinary and (as the association was well aware) so apparently incredible a recital; in view, too, of the fact that no other agency of publicity could have presented to so great and widely spread an audience the evidence clearing the names of Dr. David Throckmartin, his devoted wife, and his equally devoted young associate, Dr. Charles Stanton, of the cloud of scandal that had gathered over them, the International Association realizes that it owes you a very real debt of gratitude indeed.

Furthermore, the response of your readers touched us profoundly. Enough money to equip a score of expeditions and enough offers of personal service to have manned many score were tendered; and besides them many valuable suggestions for coping with the powerful, inexplicable and clearly unhuman manifestations of unknown, mysterious energy described by Dr. Goodwin in his first narrative. But before these could be received the association's own expedition of relief was on its way.

The tragic fate of that heroic party, lost with all others on board the steamer Adelaide, when destroyed by the German raider Von Moltke in the Papuan Gulf, has been recorded by the public prints; and while the association was considering the formation of a second expedition we were confronted by a development that changed radically the whole situation.

This development was the return of Dr. Goodwin himself, bearing news that made a second expedition, for the present at least, not only inadvisable, but apparently useless. And it is the astonishing, the disquieting import of his news, the menacing potentialities within it, that is the cause of our long delay in answering you.

Nevertheless, a way seems to have been found both to accede to your appeal and to neutralize the danger in doing so. Dr. Goodwin is now preparing his narrative, but it will, of necessity, be a month or more before you can receive it; this not only because the history cannot adequately be presented within less than one hundred thousand words, but also because when finished it must be submitted to the executive council for possible censorship and approval. And here I wish to warn you, sir, that because of subtle dangers involved in its presentation there are bound to be elisions, or at least glossings over, of certain facts, circumstances and conclusions. When we tell you that we believe our duty to the world's welfare demands this, you will, I know, sir, be the first to acquiesce to these deletions.

But notwithstanding these precautions it will be through you that the world will learn of calamity narrowly escaped; catastrophe beside which the war, terrible as it was, is but a pleasant dream; cataclysm, indeed, which threatened to destroy all civilization as we know it, to deliver to a monstrous slavery all of our race dwelling on the face of our planet and, at last, to annihilate it.

Let me say further that the narrative of Dr. Goodwin, amazing in the best sense of that word as it may be, is fully supported by proofs brought forward by him and accepted by this association. His evidence will be dealt with in purely scientific expositions of all phases of his investigations after (may we say the more popular) aspects of his experiences have been revealed by you.

That the whole viewpoint of science upon the history of humanity, of its evolution and of the character and potentialities of certain forms of universal energy, and particularly that form of etheric and magnetic vibration we call light, must be revised from their foundations is certain. Disconcerting as this may be to science, out of the new humility created and the new research and experimentation demanded by Dr. Goodwin's discoveries, there is bound to come a broader and a better and an invincible knowledge.

The association will, as before, avail itself of the courteous services of Mr. A. Merritt to convey to you Dr. Goodwin's manuscript when it is ready, and, orally, a full and personal explanation of the causes of our hesitation, now only to be hinted in this communication.

Respectfully yours,
THE INTERNATIONAL ASSOCIATION OF SCIENCE,
Per J.B.K., President.

P.S.—Let me recall to your memory the fact that in 1899 the Caroline Islands were bought by Germany from Spain for twenty-five million pesetas, that since that time German domination of them has been complete, and, further, that they have been the field of a number of German scientific expeditions.

Allow me also to inform you that the German chapter of the association, although outlawed from the parent body early in the war, preserves its entity as an independent unit and numbers among its members some of the most acute, daring and far-seeing scientists that atavistic and war-crazed nation has ever produced.

J.B.K.

CHAPTER I

THE DWELLER IN
THE MOON POOL

IN BEGINNING THIS narrative I find it necessary to refer, briefly, to my original recital printed in the *All-Story Weekly* of June 22, 1918, under the title of "The Moon Pool," of the causes that led me into the adventure of which it is to be the history. For in so much as that recital was confession, so the adventure was expiation of a promise broken and an intellectual coward-ice that held me silent when by speaking I could have checked a great wrong before it had taken root.

At last I did speak, knowing full well that in doing so I was putting in jeopardy my scientific reputation—as dear to me as honor to any woman; and after speaking, acted—knowing equally well that by my action I threw down my life as stake in an unknown game with death. More than life and reputation no man can offer in repayment of error.

But was it error? In the light of what followed it may be the very inhibition which my long training as a scientist had imposed upon me—that rigid reluctance to testify to the exis-tence of a thing seemingly outside of science, that almost un-conquerable sensitiveness to the possible disbelief and ridicule of my colleagues—was but the hand of a higher power placed over my mouth, stilling me until the appointed time: holding me back until that exact moment when my going would forge the last links in the chain to bind the Dweller.

For certainly had I spoken that dread night on the *Southern Queen,* when the monstrous, shining Thing of living light and mingled rapture and horror embraced Throckmartin and drew him from his cabin down the moon path to its lair beneath the Moon Pool, I would have been written lunatic or worse. And so, perhaps, would I have been written by my brothers in science if three years of biting remorse had not etched my words with the acid of conviction invincible.

Had I set forth for that group of Southern Pacific islets called the Nan-Matal, where the Moon Pool lay hidden, a day before or after, I would not have found Olaf Huldricksson, hands lashed to the wheel of his ravished *Brunhilda,* steering it even in his sleep down the track of the Dweller, and of the wife and babe the Dweller had snatched from him. Nor would I have picked up Larry O'Keefe from the wreck of his flying boat fast sinking under the long swells of the Pacific. And without O'Keefe and Huldricksson that weird and almost unthinkably fantastic drama enacted beyond the Moon Pool's gates must have had a very different curtain.

The remorse of a botanist, the burning, bitter hatred of a Norse seaman, the breaking of a wire in a flying-boat's wing—all these meeting at one fleeting moment formed the slender tripod upon which rested the fate of humanity! Could that universal irony which seems to mold our fortunes go further?

And yet always I think, it is upon such fragile chances that the wheel we call life rolls, and always are they the determinators of its course. What is chance but the working out of a lofty mathematics in which every thought, every action, every happening since the world began to spin around the sun is a factor? And what is life, moment by moment, but the constant totaling of these vast equations?

A hundred thousand years ago a stinging gnat escaped the sweep of a trapped mammoth's trunk—and in the glory of Egypt the horse of a Pharaoh on which one of its progeny lighted threw, under its sting, the Pharaoh, destroying a dynasty. Had the mammoth crushed its tormentor the gnat which killed the Pharaoh would not have been—nor can we say any other would at that precise moment have been at that precise place to work Pharaoh's bane. Time, place, and effect were all determined one hundred thousand years before.

Fifty thousand years ago a bullock fled from a tiger, and two thousand years ago the augurs of Nero, reading in a beast of that same bullock's blood evil omens, held back Nero's armies and a nation won respite from slavery.

And those chances of a hundred thousand years ago were determined by chances a hundred thousand years before them; and so back to the first quickening of life in the primeval slime.

A woman kisses and an empire falls; a horse stumbles and a race bows its neck to the yoke; a child asks a question and gods die.

To Fate the Spinner come countless myriads of threads, each stretching back to the dim beginnings. Fate weaves them—but she does not make them. And the pattern of her web, I think, is not determined by her but by the threads as they come. So it was that there crept toward her that strange, supernally beautiful, supernally dreadful thread I have called the Dweller; an alien thread that once woven in her web would have changed forever the pattern that is humanity. But even as she reached for it, there came to her hand other threads that in her swift fingers bound and covered and thrust back at last the radiant menace. Had they not been there—

But there they were—O'Keefe and Huldricksson and I; Larry O'Keefe and Olaf Huldricksson and I, and Lakla of the flower face and wide, golden eyes, Lakla the Handmaiden of the Silent Ones, and the Three who had fashioned the Dweller from earth's secret heart—each thread in its place.

And so humanity lives!

And now let me recall to those who read my first narrative, and to make plain to those who did not, what it was that took me on my quest; that enigmatic prelude in which the Dweller first tried its growing power.

Early in 1915, Dr. David Throckmartin, one of America's leaders in archeological and ethnological research, set out for the Caroline Islands, accompanied by his young wife, Edith, his equally youthful associate, Dr. Charles Stanton, and Mrs. Throckmartin's nurse from babyhood, Thora Helverson. Their destination was that extraordinary cluster of artificially squared, basalt-walled islets off the eastern coast of Ponape, the largest Caroline Island, known as the Nan-Matal. It was Throckmartin's belief that in those prehistoric ruins lay the clue to the lost and highly civilized race which had peopled that ancient continent, which, sinking beneath the waters of the Pacific, had left in the myriads of islands we call Polynesia only its highest flung peaks.*

The Funafuti borings of 1897, definitely proving the existence of this continent, had also shown that its subsidence had taken place at a comparatively recent date—not more than from fifty thousand to one hundred thousand years ago.

Dr. Throckmartin planned to spend a year on the Nan-Matal, hoping that within its shattered temples and terraces, its vaults and Cyclopean walls, or in the maze of secret tunnels that running under the sea threaded together the islets, he would recover not only a lost page of the history of our race, but also, perhaps, a knowledge that had vanished with it. For that this dead people had commanded powers, had wielded energies unknown to us, is not only proved by the astonishing character of their crumbling remains, but, as it has been written by one world-famous student of them, by "echoes of sublime theogenies and philosophies still heard in the oral traditions and folk lore of many Polynesian groups."

The subsequent fate of this expedition formed what became known, until my confession in April before the International Association of Science, as the Throckmartin mystery. Three months after the little party had landed at Ponape, and had been accompanied to the ruins by a score of reluctant native workmen—reluctant because all the islanders shun the Nan-Matal as a haunted place—Dr. Throckmartin appeared alone at Port Moresby, Papua.

---

* For more detailed observations on these points refer to G. Volkens, *"Uber die Karolinen Insel Yap,"* in Verhandlungen Gesellschaft Erdkunde Berlin, xxvii (1901); J.S. Kubary. *"Ethnographische Beiträge zur Kentniss des Karolinen Archipels"* (Leiden, 1889-1892); De Abrade *"Historia del Conflicto de las Carolinas, etc."* (Madrid, 1886).

There he said that he was going to Melbourne to employ some white workmen to help him in his excavations, the superstitions of the natives making their usefulness negligible. He took passage on the *Southern Queen,* sailing the same day that he appeared, and three nights later he vanished utterly from that vessel.

It was officially reported that he had either fallen from the ship or had thrown himself overboard. A relief party sent to the Nan-Matal for the others in his party found no trace of his wife, of Stanton, or of Thora Helverson. The native workmen, questioned, said that, on the nights of the full moon the *ani* or spirits of the ruins had great power; that on these nights no Ponapean would go within sight or sound of them, and that by agreement with Throckmartin they had been allowed to return to their homes on these nights, leaving the expedition "to face the spirits alone, as being white, they were no doubt stronger than the *ani.*"

After the full of the moon on the third month of the expedition's stay, the natives had returned to the Throckmartin camp only to find it deserted. And then, "knowing that the *ani* had been stronger," they had fled.

Enlightened civilization, rejecting such a story as a preposterous figment of the primitive mind, crystallized the mystery

Ever radiant plumes and spirals expanding, the core of the Shining One waxed as it drew into itself the life force of these lost ones....

into a scandal having two versions: one, that Throckmartin, discovering that his wife and Dr. Stanton had betrayed him, had in his rage killed them, together with the old nurse, afterward in remorse committing suicide; the other that Stanton and Mrs. Throckmartin, taking Thora with them, had abandoned Throckmartin and had hidden themselves and their guilty passion in China.

These were the lies that my silence allowed to take root and flourish—for I had been a passenger with Throckmartin on the *Southern Queen:* I had been with him when that wondrous horror which had followed him down the moon path after it had set its unholy seal upon him snatched him from the vessel; and he had told me his story, and I had promised, God forgive me, that if the Dweller took him as it had taken his wife and Stanton and Thora, I would follow.

He had told me his story, and I knew that story was true—for twice I had seen the inexplicable power which Throckmartin, discovering, had loosed upon himself and those who loved him; that unearthly Thing that left on the faces of its prey soul-deep lines of mingled agony and rapture, of joy celestial and misery infernal, side by side, as though the hand of God and the hand of Satan working in harmony had etched them!

Nor can I better describe the Dweller than I did to the members of the association—as I first beheld it on that first night out from Papua when it came racing over the horizon to claim Throckmartin.

We two were on the upper deck. He had not yet summoned the courage to tell me of what had befallen him—held back, as I was during the years, by the fear of disbelief. Storm threatened but suddenly far to the north, the clouds parted, and upon the waters far away the moon shone.

Swiftly the break in the high-flung canopies advanced toward us and the silver rapids of the moon stream between them came racing down toward the *Southern Queen* like a gigantic, shining serpent writhing over the rim of the world. And down its shimmering length a pillared radiance sped! It reached the barrier of blackness that still held between the ship and the head of the moon stream and beat against it with a swirling of shimmering misty plumes, throbbing lacy opalescences and vaporous spiralings of living light.

Pulsing through it were glittering atoms and coruscations, drawn, it seemed, from the moon rays pouring on it. And all about it was a storm of sweet, insistent tinklings as of pizzi-cati on violins of glass or little sparkling-white crystals tuned to sound: strangely compelling and as strangely disquieting. At once they played upon the heart like little fiery fingers of desire and tiny cold fingers of death.

Then, as the protecting shadow grew less. I saw that within the pillar was a core, a nucleus of intense light—veined, opal-escent, vital. Above, tangled in the swirls and plumes and spi-ralings, yet ever firm, and steady in all the incessant movement, were seven lights like seven little moons. One was of a pearly rose, one of delicate nacreous blue, one of lambent saffron, one of emerald, a deathly white, a ghostly amethyst, and one of gleaming silver.

Through the gusts of tinklings came a murmuring cry as of a calling from another sphere—making soul and body shrink from it irresistibly and reach toward it with an infinite longing.

"Av-o-lo-ha! Av-o-lo-ha!" it sighed.

Straight toward the radiant vision walked Throckmartin, his face transformed from all human semblance by unholy blend-ing of agony and rapture that had fallen over it like a mask! And then—the clouds closed, the moon path was blotted out, and where the shining Thing had been was—nothing!

What had been there was—the Dweller!

It was after I had beheld that apparition that Throckmartin told me what would have been, save for what my own eyes had seen, his incredible story. How, upon a first night of the full moon, camping on another shore, they had seen lights moving on the outer bulwarks of that islet of the Nan-Matal, called Nan-Tauach, the "place of frowning walls," and faintly to them over the waters had crept the crystalline music, while far beneath, as though from vast distant caverns, a mighty muffled chanting had risen; how, on going to Nan-Tauach next day, they had found set within the inner of its three titanic terraces, and opposite that mysterious vault which Admiral Sir Cyprian Bridge and Christian named "the treasure house of Chau-ta-

"I saw a white fire that shone like stars in a swirl of
mist and I stood helpless while the sparkling devil pulled
my dear ones over the ship's rail into the eerie light.
I saw them a little while whirling away in the moon
track behind the ship—and then they were gone!"

leur, the sun king," a slab of stone, gray and cold and strangely
repellent to the touch; above it and on each side a rounded
breast of basalt in each of which were seven little circles that
gave to the hand that same alien shock, "as of frozen electricity," that contact with the gray slab gave.

And that night, when sleep had seemed to drop down upon
them from the moon, but before the sleep had conquered him,

he had seen the court of the gray rock curdle with light, while into it walked Thora, bathed and filled with a pulsing effulgence beside which all earthly light was shadow!

He told me of their search for Thora at dawn, when the slumber had fallen from their eyes, and of their discovery of her kerchief caught beneath the lintel of the gray slab, betraying that it had opened, and opening, closed upon her; of their efforts to force it, and of the vigil that night when Stanton was taken and walked—"like a corpse in which flamed a god and a devil" in the embrace of the Dweller upon the shattered walls of Tauach, vanishing at last through the moon door, even as had Thora. And the muffled, distant, mighty chanting as of a multitude that hailed his passage.

After that, of the third night, when his wife and he watched despairingly beside the moon door, waiting for it to open, hoping to surprise the shining Thing that came through it, and surprising, conquer it; of their wait until the moon swam up and its full light shone upon the terrace; of the sudden gleaming out of the little circles under its rays and of the sighing murmur of the moon door, swinging open as its hidden mechanism responded to the force of the light falling on the circles; and of his mad rush down the glimmering passage beyond the moon-door portal to the threshold of the wondrous Chamber of the Moon Pool.

Absorbed, silent, marveling, I listened as he described that place of mystery—a vaulted arch that seemed to open into space; a space filled with lambent, coruscating, many-colored mist whose brightness grew even as he watched; before him an awesome pool, circular, perhaps twenty feet wide. Around it a low, softly curving lip of glimmering, silvery stone. The pool's water was palest blue. Within its silvery rim it was like a great, blue eye staring upward.

Upon it streamed seven shafts of radiance. They poured down upon it like torrents; they were like shining pillars of light rising from a sapphire floor. One was the tender pink of the pearl; one of the aurora's green; a third a deathly white; the fourth the blue in mother-of-pearl; a shimmering column of pale amber; a beam of amethyst; a shaft of molten silver. The pool drank them!

And even as Throckmartin gazed, he saw run through the blue water tiny gleams of phosphorescence, sparkles and cor-uscations of pale incandescence, and far, far down in its depths he sensed a movement, a shifting gleam as of some radiant body slowly rising.

Mists then began to float up from the surface, tiny swirls that held and hung in the splendor of the seven shafts, absorb-ing their glory and at last coalescing into the shape I had seen and that he called—the Dweller.

He had raised his pistol and sent bullet after bullet into it. And as he did so, out from it swept a gleaming tentacle. It caught him above the heart; wrapped itself round him. Over him rushed a mingled ecstasy and horror. It was, he said, as though the cold soul of evil and the burning soul of good had stepped together within him.

He saw that the shining nucleus of that which he had watched shape itself from vapors and light had form—but a form that eyes and brain could not define; as though a being of another world should assume what it might of human sem-blance, but could not hide that what human eyes saw was still only a part of it. It was neither man nor woman; it was un-earthly and androgynous and even as he found its human sem-blance, that semblance changed, while all the while every atom of him thrilled with interwoven rapture and terror.

Behind him he had heard the swift feet of his wife, racing to his aid. Love gave him power, and he wrested himself from the Dweller. Even as he did so he fell—and saw her rush straight into the radiant glory! Saw, too, the Dweller swiftly wrap its shining mists around her and drew her over the lip of the pool; dragged himself to the verge and watched her sink in its embrace, down, down through the depths—"a shining, many-colored, nebulous cloud, and in it Edith's face, disappearing, her eyes staring up at me filled with ecstasy supernal and infernal horror—and—vanished!"

Then, far below, again the triumphant chanting!

There had come to Throckmartin madness. He had memory of running wildly through glimmering passages; then blackness and oblivion until he found himself far out at sea in the little boat they had used to cruise around the lagoons of the Nan-Matal. He had bribed the half-caste captain of a ship that picked him up to take him to Port Moresby, from whence he intended to go to Melbourne, hoping to find some who would return with him, force the haunted chamber, and battle with him against the Dweller.

And on that third night I cowered in the corner of his cabin and saw the Dweller take him!

Here then you have the prelude.

For three years I was silent, and then, obeying a sudden, irresistible impulse, I gave my narrative to my brothers of the International Association of Science and started, alone, for the Nan-Matal to make reparation. For Throckmartin had not entirely believed that his wife was dead—nor Stanton nor Thora; rather he thought that they might be held in some unearthly bondage.

And he had, too, a vague belief that the deep, underground chantings that had accompanied the disappearance of the Dweller with its victims, pointing clearly as they did to the existence of other beings or powers in its mysterious den, held a vast threat against humanity. How true was his scientific clairvoyance, and yet how far from the amazing, unthinkable truth you are to learn. It was my own conviction that in both he had been right, that I might break that bondage, and if not release the world from the menace, at least discover its nature and forewarn the world; and it was this conviction which now forced me onward at all speed toward the Carolines.

I delayed my departure from America only long enough to get certain instruments and apparatus that long brooding over the phenomena had suggested might be useful in coping with them.

Nine weeks later, with my paraphernalia, I was northward bound from Port Moresby on the *Suwarna*, a swift little copra sloop with a fifty-horse-power motor auxiliary, and heading for Ponape—for the Nan-Matal and the Chamber of the Moon Pool and all that it held for me of soul-shaking awe, of peril beside which bodily death is nothing, and of new and blinding knowledge.

CHAPTER II

"THE SPARKLING DEVIL TOOK THEM!"

WE SIGHTED THE *Brunhilda* some five hundred miles south of Ponape. Soon after we had left Port Moresby the wind had fallen, but the *Suwarna*, although far from being as fragrant as the Javan flower for which she was named, could do her twelve knots an hour. Da Costa, the captain, was a garrulous Portuguese; his mate was a Canton man who had all the marks of long and able service on some pirate junk; his engineer was a half-breed Chino-Malay who had picked up his knowledge of power plants Heaven alone knows where, and who, I had reason to believe, had transferred all his religious impetus to the mechanism which he so faithfully served. At any rate he seldom came out of the little pit which did as the *Suwarna's* engine-room, and seemed to sleep, as it were, always with one ear awake to hear the smallest complaint from his American-built deity. The crew were six huge, chattering Tonga boys.

The *Suwarna* had cut through Finschafen Huon Gulf to the protection of the Bismarcks. She had threaded the maze of the archipelago tranquilly, and we were then rolling over the thousand-mile stretch of open ocean with New Hanover far behind us and our boat's bow pointed straight toward Nukuor of the

Monte Verdes. After we had rounded Nukuor we should, barring accident, reach Ponape in not more than sixty hours.

It was late afternoon, and on the demure little breeze that marched behind us came far-flung sighs of spice-trees and nutmeg flowers. Beneath us the slow, prodigious swells of the Pacific lifted us in gentle, giant hands and sent us as gently down the long, blue wave slopes to the next broad, upward slope. There was a spell of peace over the ocean that was semi-hypnotic, stilling even the Portuguese captain who stood dreamily at the wheel, slowly swaying to the rhythmic lift and fall of the sloop.

There came a winning hail from the Tonga boy lookout draped lazily over the bow.

"Sail he b'long port side!"

Da Costa straightened and gazed while I raised my glass. The vessel was a scant mile away, and must have been visible long before the sleepy watcher had seen her. She was a sloop about the size of the *Suwarna*, without power. All sails set, even to a spinnaker she carried, she was making the best of the little breeze. I tried to read her name, but the vessel jibed sharply as though the hands of the man at the wheel had suddenly dropped the helm—and then with equal abruptness swung back to her course. The stern came in sight, and on it I read *Brunhilda*.

I shifted my glasses to the figure at the wheel. It came to me that there was something odd about him. He was crouching down over the spokes in a helpless, huddled sort of way, and even as I looked the vessel veered again, abruptly as before. I saw the helmsman straighten up and bring the wheel about with a vicious jerk.

He stood so for a moment, looking straight ahead, entirely oblivious of us, and then seemed again to sink down within himself. It came to me that his was the action of a man striving against a weariness unutterable. I swept the deck with my glasses. There was no other sign of life. I turned to find the

Portuguese staring intently and with puzzled air at the sloop, now separated from us by a scant half mile.

"Something veree wrong I think there, sair," he said in his curious English. "The man on deck I know. He is captain and owner of the Brrwun'ild. His name Olaf Huldricksson, what you say—Norwegian. He is eithair veree sick or veree tired—but I do not undweerstand where is the crew and the starb'd boat is gone—"

As he spoke I clearly saw the arms at the wheel of the *Brunhilda* relax, the wheel spin and the vessel lurch about to swell and wind and saw again the helmsman stiffen like a man awakened violently from deep sleep; saw his arms tighten spasmodically and bring the ship once more to her course.

A gleam lighted the eyes of the Portuguese; a cunning speculative light.

"Veree sick or something veree wrong," he repeated. "I t'ink I better go close and see if he need help, sair?"

I read what was passing through his mind. Here, perhaps, was profit, salvage. Still it was the right thing to do. I nodded acquiescence. He shouted an order to the engineer and as he did so the faint breeze died utterly and the sails of the *Brunhilda* flapped down inert. I saw the helmsman glare about him and thought I heard him curse. But we were now nearly abreast and a scant five hundred yards away. The engine of the *Suwarna* died and the Tonga boys leaped to one of the boats.

"You Olaf Huldricksson!" shouted Da Costa. "What's a matter wit' you?"

THE MAN at the wheel turned toward us. As his body lifted I saw that he was a giant of a man; his shoulders enormous, thick chested, strength in every line of him, he towered like a viking of old at the rudder bar of his shark ship.

I raised the glass again; his face sprang into the lens as though he himself had leaped from his deck and was staring at me; and never have I seen a face that was lined and marked as though by ages of unsleeping misery as was that of Olaf Huldricksson!

The bloodshot eyes peered into mine with a look in their depths that might have been in the eyes of the mummy of that ancient Sultan who cursed Buddha Gautama and whose eyes were doomed to live, the Javans say, as long as that Sultan's withered body could defy time!

The glasses dropped from my shaking hand. The two Tonga boys had the boat alongside and were waiting at the oars. The little captain was dropping into it.

"Wait!" I cried. I ran into my cabin, grasped my emergency medical kit and climbed down the rope ladder. The two Tonga boys bent to the oars. We reached the side and Da Costa and I each seized a lanyard dangling from the stays and swung ourselves swiftly on board. Da Costa approached Huldricksson softly.

"What's the matter, Olaf?" he began and then was silent, looking down at the wheel. My gaze followed his and we shrank together involuntarily. For the hands of Huldricksson were lashed fast to the spokes of the wheel by thongs of thin, strong cord. They had been bound so tightly that they were swollen and black, the thongs had bitten so into the sinewy wrists that they were hidden in the outraged flesh, cutting so deeply that blood fell, slow drop by drop, at his feet. We sprang toward him, reaching out hands to his fetters to loose them. Even as we touched them, Huldricksson grew rigid with anger that had in it something diabolic. He aimed a vicious kick at me and then another at Da Costa which sent the Portuguese tumbling into the scuppers.

"Let be!" croaked Huldricksson; his voice was as thick and lifeless as though forced from a dead throat, and I saw that his lips were cracked and dry and his parched tongue was black. "Let be! Go! Let be!" The words beat upon the ears heavily, painfully—like the sinister sobbing of the devil drums of the Solomons that are beaten with adders' heads and of the skins of women flayed alive. It was the dead alive and speaking!

The Portuguese had picked himself up, whimpering with

rage and knife in hand, but as Huldricksson's voice reached him he stopped. Amazement crept into his eyes and as he thrust the blade back into his belt they softened with pity.

"Something veree wrong wit' Olaf," he murmured to me. "I think he crazee!" And then Olaf Huldricksson began to curse us. He did not speak—he howled from that hideously dry mouth his imprecations and I think I never heard such hate and bitterness issue from any man's lips. He cursed us by everything in heaven and earth and hell—yes, and he cursed earth, hell and heaven as well. And all the time his bloodshot eyes roamed the seas and his hands, clenched and rigid on the wheel, dropped blood.

"I go below," said Da Costa nervously. "His wife, his little Freda, they are always wit' him. You wait." He darted down the companionway and was gone. Huldricksson suddenly was silent, slumping down over the wheel, forgetting us.

Da Costa's head appeared at the top of the companion steps.

"There is nobody, nobody," he paused—then—"nobody—nowhere!" His hands flew out in a gesture of utter hopeless incomprehension. "I do not understan'."

Then Olaf Huldricksson opened his dry lips again and as he spoke a thrill ran through me, stopping my heart.

"The sparkling devil took them!" croaked Olaf Huldricksson, "the sparkling devil took them! Took my Helma and my little Freda! The sparkling devil came down from the moon and took them!"

He swayed and two great tears ran down his cheeks. Da Costa moved toward him again and again Huldricksson watched him, once more alertly, wickedly, from his reddened eyes.

I took a hypodermic syringe from my case and filled it with morphine. I drew Da Costa to me.

"Get to the side of him," I whispered, "talk to him." He saw the little syringe in my hand and nodded. He moved over toward the wheel.

"Where is your Helma and Freda, Olaf?" he said.

Huldricksson turned his head toward him. "The shining devil took them," he repeated. "The moon devil that spark—"

A yell broke from him. I had thrust the needle into his arm just above one swollen wrist and had quickly shot the drug through. He struggled to release himself and then began to rock drunkenly side by side. The morphine, taking him in his weakness, worked quickly. Soon over his face we saw a peace descend. The pupils of the staring eyes contracted. Once, twice, he swayed and then his bleeding, prisoned hands held high and still gripping the wheel, he dropped to the deck.

It was with utmost difficulty that we loosed the thongs, but at last it was done. We rigged a little swing and the Tonga boys slung the great inert body over the side into the dory. Soon we had Huldricksson in my bunk. Da Costa sent half his crew over to the sloop in charge of the Cantonese. They took in all sail, stripping Huldricksson's boat to the masts and then with the *Brunhilda* nosing quietly along after us at the end of a long hawser, one of the Tonga boys at her wheel, we resumed the way so enigmatically interrupted.

I HAD cleansed and bandaged the drugged Norseman's lacerated wrists and was sponging the blackened, parched mouth with warm water and a mild antiseptic when the Portuguese softly entered the cabin. I did not hear him until he spoke, so engrossed was I in my thoughts of this mystery of the *Brunhilda*. At first, when Huldricksson had spoken of a "sparkling devil from the moon" I had felt a shock of apprehension. Could it be that on the very threshold of my quest the Dweller had come out to meet me?

But in the light of Huldricksson's fettering this thought had vanished. There had probably occurred on the *Brunhilda* one of those swift, devilish tragedies of the South Seas that ever and anon flare up like lightning out of hell. A mutiny of the only-half-tamed crew, a treacherous blow from behind that had felled the Norseman to the deck, a mordant humor or obscure

superstition that had left him to awaken fettered to the wheel
of his ravished vessel, a carrying away of mother and child to
death or worse than death in some reeking island jungle.

Such a story is a commonplace in those vast reaches of sea
and sea-hidden lairs of cruel and savage tribes. And yet there
was no mark or blow upon the captain's head. Suddenly I was
aware of Da Costa's presence and turned. His unease was
manifest and held, it seemed to me, a queer, furtive anxiety.

"What you think of Olaf, sair?" he asked. I shrugged my
shoulders. "You think he killed his woman and his babee?" He
went on. "You think he crazee and killed all?"

"Nonsense, Da Costa," I answered. "You saw the boat was
gone. His crew mutinied and tied him up the way you saw."

Da Costa shook his head slowly. "No," he said. "No. The crew
did not. Nobody there on board when Olaf was tied."

"What!" I cried, startled. "What do you mean?"

"I mean," he said slowly, "that Olaf tie himself!

"Wait!" he went on at my incredulous gesture of dissent.
"Wait, I show you." He had been standing with hands behind
his back and now I saw that he held in them the same thongs
that had bound Huldricksson. They were bloodstained and each
ended in a broad leather tip skillfully spliced into the cord.
"Look!" he said, pointing to these leather ends. I looked and
saw in them deep indentations as of teeth. I snatched one of
the thongs and opened the mouth of the unconscious man on
the bunk. Carefully I placed the leather within it and gently
forced the jaws shut on it. It was true. Those marks were where
Olaf Huldricksson's teeth had gripped! Dazed I turned to Da
Costa.

"Wait!" he said again. "I show you." He took the cords and
rested his hands on the supports of a chair back. Rapidly he
twisted one of the thongs around his left hand, drew a loose
knot, shifted the cord up toward his elbow. This left wrist and
hand still free and with them he twisted the other cord around
the right wrist; drew a similar knot. His hands were now in the

exact position that Huldricksson's had been on the *Brunhilda* but with cords and knots hanging loose. Then Da Costa reached down his head, took a leather end in his teeth and with a jerk drew the end of the thong that noosed his left hand tight; similarly he drew tight the second.

And then he stood and strained at his fetters. There before my eyes he had pinioned himself so that without aid he could not release himself. And he was exactly as Huldricksson had been!

"You will have to cut me loose, sair," he said. "I cannot move them. It is an old trick on these seas. Sometimes it is necessairy that a man stand at the wheel many hours, without help, and he does this so that if he sleep the wheel wake him, yes, sair."

I looked from him to the man on the bed.

"But why, sair," said Da Costa slowly, "did Olaf have to tie his hands?"

I had no answer.

"We'll have to wait till he awakens, captain," I said. He nodded acquiescence and was silent for a time. "What did you think, sair, of what he said of sparkling devils?" he asked at last. And as he spoke I knew that this was what had been on his mind all along. Clearly he knew something, had heard something, that gave the words I had dismissed an unquieting significance. I looked at him closely.

"I don't know," I said. "Do you?"

He fidgeted, avoided my eyes, and then rapidly, almost surreptitiously crossed himself.

"No," he replied. "I know nothing. Some things I have heard—but they tell many tales on these seas."

He turned, almost abruptly, and started for the door. Before he reached it he turned again. "But this I do know," he half whispered, "I do know I am damned glad there is no full moon tonight." He passed out, leaving me staring after him in amazement. What did the Portuguese know?

I bent over the sleeper. On his face was no trace of that

unholy mingling of opposites, of mingled joy and fear, that the Dweller stamped upon its victims. But with Da Costa's revelations the security I had felt in my theory of the prisoned wrists crumbled. Huldricksson's words came back to me—"The sparkling devil took them!" Nay, they had been even more explicit—"The sparkling devil that came down from the moon!"

They sank upon my heart like weights, carrying subconscious conviction that resisted all my efforts to dismiss. I lifted the sheet from Huldricksson and went over his body minutely, turning it from side to side. The Norseman was, as I have said, a giant, and his mighty, muscled form was clean and white as a girl's. Nowhere was there a trace of that cold, white stain which was the mark of the touch of the Dweller and that had been, on Throckmartin, a shining cincture girdling the body just below the heart.

Throckmartin had believed, and I had believed with him, that the thing I had gone forth to find had no power outside the islet of the moon door and that it was only by virtue of that mark it had been enabled to follow him. But was this true? Huldricksson had been steering straight for Ponape, not away from it—and there was no trace of the Nan-Matal's dread mystery upon him.

Had the Dweller swept down unheralded and unknown upon the *Brunhilda,* drawing down the moon path Olaf Huldricksson's wife and babe even as it had drawn Throckmartin? But if this were so then I must revise much of what I thought I knew of its action, for the ravishing of the *Brunhilda* could mean only one of two things: we had been wrong in our theory that the Dweller's power was limited by place, or else in the years that had passed its power had overcome that limitation.

As I sat thinking the cabin grew suddenly dark and from above came a shouting and patter of feet. Down upon us swept one of the abrupt, violent squalls that are met with in those latitudes. I lashed Huldricksson fast in the berth and ran up on deck.

The long, peaceful swells had changed into angry, choppy waves from the tops of which the spindrift streamed in long, stinging lashes. Behind us the *Brunhilda* pulled and strained on her hawser and Da Costa stood, hatchet in hand, ready to cut if necessary. I could see the rolling white of the Tonga helmsman's eyes watching on the other deck, like a rabbit a serpent, the Portuguese and his weapon, for well he knew there would be little chance for him if the *Suwarna* cast him adrift.

A half-hour passed, and still Da Costa withheld his hand. And then the squall died as quickly as it had arisen. The sea quieted. Over in the west, from beneath the tattered, flying edge of the storm, dropped the red globe of the setting sun; dropped slowly until it was just above the horizon, and then, just before it touched the sea rim, seemed to be drawn down and up into that curious oval, that ever-startling phenomenon of refraction which the ancient Egyptians christened the "gate of the west."

I watched it—and rubbed my eyes and stared again. For over its flaming portal something huge and black moved, like a gigantic beckoning finger!

Da Costa had seen it, too, and he turned the *Suwarna* straight toward the descending orb and its strange shadow. As we approached we saw it was a little mass of wreckage and that the beckoning finger was a wing of canvas, sticking up and swaying with the motion of the waves. On the highest point of the wreckage sat a tall figure calmly smoking a cigarette.

We brought the *Suwarna* too, dropped a boat, and with myself as coxswain pulled toward what I knew now was a wrecked hydroairplane. Its occupant took a long puff at his cigarette, waved a cheerful hand, and shouted a reassuring greeting. And just as he did so a great wave raised itself up behind him, took the wreckage, tossed it high in a swelter of foam, and passed on. When we had steadied our boat, where wreck and man had been was—nothing.

I scanned the water with anxious eyes. Who had been this debonair castaway, and from whence in these far seas had dropped his plane? There came a tug at the side of our boat, two muscular brown hands gripped it close to my left, and a sleek, black, wet head showed its top between them. Two bright, blue eyes that held deep within them a laughing deviltry looked into mine, and a long, lithe body drew itself gently over the thwart and seated its dripping self at my feet.

"Much obliged," said this man from the sea. "I knew somebody was sure to come along when the O'Keefe banshee didn't show up."

"The what?" I asked in amazement.

"The O'Keefe banshee— Oh, yes, pardon me, I'm Larry O'Keefe. It's a far way from Ireland, but not too far for the O'Keefe banshee to travel if the O'Keefe was going to click in."

I looked again at my astonishing rescue. He seemed perfectly serious, and later I was to know how exasperatingly, naïvely, and entirely serious he was on that subject.

"Have you a cigarette?" said Larry O'Keefe. "Mine went out," he added with a grin, as he reached a moist hand out for the little cylinder, took it, lighted it on the match I struck for him, and then gazed at me frankly and with manifest curiosity. I returned the gaze as frankly.

I SAW a lean, intelligent face whose fighting jaw was softened by the wistfulness of the clean-cut lips and the roguishness that lay side by side with the deviltry in the laughing blue eyes; nose of a thoroughbred with the suspicion of a tilt; long, well-knit, slender figure that I knew must have all the strength of fine steel; the uniform of a lieutenant in the Royal Flying Corps of Britain's navy.

He laughed, stretched out a firm hand, and gripped mine.

"Thank you really ever so much, old man," he said.

I liked Larry O'Keefe from the beginning—but I did not dream as the Tonga boys pulled us back to the *Suwarna* how that liking was to be forged into man's strong love for man by fires which souls such as his and mine—and yours who read this—could never dream.

Larry! Larry O'Keefe, where are you now with your leprechawns and banshee, your heart of a child, your laughing blue eyes, and your fearless soul? Shall I ever see you again, Larry O'Keefe, dear to me as some best-beloved younger brother? Larry!

CHAPTER III

LARRY O'KEEFE

PRESSING BACK THE questions I longed to ask, I introduced myself. Oddly enough, I found that he knew me, or rather my work. He had bought, it appeared, my volume upon the peculiar vegetation whose habitat is disintegrating lava rock and volcanic ash, that I had entitled, somewhat loosely, I could now perceive, "Flora of the Craters." For he explained naïvely that he had picked it up, thinking it an entirely different sort of book, a novel, in fact—something like Meredith's "Diana of the Crossways," which he liked greatly.

Seeing, I suppose, my involuntary start of surprise, for the possible ambiguity of the title had never before occurred to me, he hastened to say that he had admired the book hugely, and once starting it, had read it straight through; a statement which I felt sprang more from his courtesy than fact, as the work, although not lacking perhaps in interesting description, is extremely technical and was written for the initiate rather than the layman.

He had hardly finished this explanation before we touched the side of the *Suwarna*, and I was forced to curb my curiosity until we reached the deck. Da Costa greeted us eagerly, and was plainly gratified by the military salute which O'Keefe bestowed upon him.

"You haven't seen a German raider called the *Wolf* about, have you?" he asked with a grin, after he had elaborately thanked the bowing little Portuguese skipper for his rescue. "That thing you saw me sitting on was all that was left of one of his majesty's best little hydroairplanes after that cyclone threw it off as excess baggage. And by the way, about where are we?"

Da Costa gave him our approximate position from the noon reckoning.

O'Keefe whistled. "A good three hundred miles from where I left the H.M.S. *Dolphin* about four hours ago," he said. "That squall I rode in on was some whizzer!

"The *Dolphin*," he went on, calmly divesting himself of his soaked uniform, "was hunting a Hun boy that got out of somewhere about a month ago and has been sneaking around seeking whom he might devour. The *Wolf* has been doing some devouring, too. We heard at Tangaloa that it had been working along these lanes. I went out on a scouting flight. Before I could get back to the *Dolphin* that blow shot up out of nowhere, picked me up, and insisted that I go with it whether or no.

"About an hour ago I thought I saw a chance to dig up and out of it, I turned, and quick went my upper right wing, and down I dropped. Engine began to work loose, and just as I knew something had to come along quick or the banshee of the O'Keefes was due for a long, swift trip from Ireland, I sighted you.

"And here I am, and again I say I'm much obliged to you," finished Larry O'Keefe. "And I'll take another cigarette, if you don't mind."

"I don't know how we can notify your ship, Lieutenant O'Keefe," I said. "We have no wireless."

"Doctair Goodwin," said Da Costa, "we could change our course, sair—perhaps—"

"Thanks—but not a bit of it," broke in O'Keefe. "Lord alone knows where the *Dolphin* is now. Fancy she'll be nosing around looking for me—unless she sights that raider.* Anyway, the

---

* The *Wolf* had truly a remarkable record. This raider was not only equipped with wireless but had, like the *Dolphin,* a hydroairplane. The *Wolf* would pick up wireless messages and, according to the story of a Scotch-American prisoner, who escaped, its sailors would predict days before whether they would have, at a certain time, new sup-

Dolphin is just as apt to run into you as you into her. Maybe we'll strike something with a wireless, and I'll trouble you to put me aboard." He hesitated. "Where are you bound, by the way?" he asked.

"For Ponape," I answered.

"No wireless there," mused O'Keefe. "Beastly hole. Stopped a week ago for fruit. Natives seemed scared to death at us—or something. What are you going there for?"

I saw Da Costa dart a furtive glance at me. It troubled me. I had, of course, told him nothing of the real reasons for my journey, stating simply, when I had employed him, that I wished to go to Ponape where the scientific work I had planned might keep me many weeks. What did the man know, I wondered, and what was the explanation of his remarks in the cabin and of his manifest unease? O'Keefe's sharp eyes had noted the glance and, misinterpreting it and my consequent hesitation, flushed in embarrassment.

"Oh, I beg your pardon," he said. "Maybe I oughtn't to have asked that?"

"It's no secret, lieutenant," I replied, somewhat testily. "I'm about to undertake some exploration work there—a little digging among the ruins on the Nan-Matal."

I looked at the Portuguese sharply as I named the place. I distinctly saw a pallor creep under his skin and again he made swiftly the sign of the cross, glancing as he did so uneasily to the north. I made up my mind then to question him when opportunity came. He turned from his quick scrutiny of the sea and addressed O'Keefe.

---

plies of beer, or coal, or beef—and their predictions always turned out truly. The *Wolf's* airplane usually traveled fifty to sixty miles on its scouting expeditions, and its pilots asserted that they could "spot" a ship ninety miles away from a height of a thousand feet. On her return to Germany, with a small fleet of captured ships, one of these, the *Ignatz Mendi,* passed within a mile of two heavily armed American transports. The commander of the *Ignatz Mendi,* when off Jutland, mistook in the fog a Danish lighthouse for a German torpedo-boat he was expecting. The *Ignatz Mendi* piled up on the beach, and the prisoners within escaped to tell the story of the raider. The *Wolf* made a safe return. J.B.K.

Once, twice, three times, she pressed upon the flower centers....

"There's nothing on board to fit you, lieutenant," he said, looking over the tall figure before him. "But perhaps we can find something while your clothes dry. Will you come to my cabin?"

"Oh, just give me a sheet to throw around me, captain," said O'Keefe, following him. Darkness had fallen, and as the two disappeared I softly opened the door of my own cabin and listened. I could hear Huldricksson breathing deeply and regularly.

I drew my electric-flash, and shielding its rays from my face, looked at him. His sleep was changing from the heavy stupor of the drug into one that was at least on the borderland of the normal. Gently drawing down his jaw, I noted that the tongue had lost its arid blackness and that the mouth secretions had resumed action. Satisfied as to his condition I returned to deck.

O'Keefe was there, looking like a specter in the cotton sheet he had wrapped about him. A deck table had been cleated down and one of the Tonga boys was setting it for our dinner. Soon the very creditable larder of the *Suwarna* dressed the board, and O'Keefe, Da Costa and I attacked it. The night had grown close and oppressive. Behind us the forward light of the *Brunhilda* glided and the binnacle lamp threw up a faint glow in which her black helmsman's face stood out mistily. O'Keefe had looked curiously a number of times at our tow, but had asked no questions.

"You're not the only passenger we picked up today," I told him. "We found the captain of that sloop, lashed to his wheel, nearly dead with exhaustion, and his boat deserted by every one except himself."

"What was the matter?" asked O'Keefe in astonishment.

"We don't know," I answered. "He fought us, and I had to drug him before we could get him loose from his lashings. He's sleeping down in my berth now. His wife and little girl ought to have been on board, the captain here says, but—they weren't."

"Any signs of a fight?" asked O'Keefe.

I shook my head, and again I saw Da Costa swiftly cross

himself. "We'll have to wait until he wakes up to get the story," I concluded.

"**WIFE AND** child gone!" said O'Keefe. "And you saw nothing?"

"From the condition of his mouth he must have been alone at the wheel and without water at least two days and nights before we found him," I replied. "And as for looking for any one on these waters after such a time—it's hopeless."

"That's true," said O'Keefe. "But his wife and baby! Poor, poor devil!"

He was silent for a moment and then began to tell us stories of the great war and of what he had seen in Flanders of broken hearts and homes, and tragedies of motherhood and childhood. He had served there, it appeared, during the first year. He had been wounded at Ypres and, recovering, had been assigned to the naval service. For the last year he had been cruising along the Australian and New Zealand transport lines.

"And I'm homesick for the lark's land with the boche planes playing tunes on their machine guns and the Hun Archies tickling the soles of my feet," said Larry O'Keefe with a sigh. "If you're in love, love to the limit; and if you hate, why, hate like the devil, and if it's a fight you're in, get where the fighting is hottest and fight like hell," sighed Larry. "If you don't, life's not worth the living!"

I watched him as he talked, feeling my liking for him steadily increasing. If I could but have a man like this beside me on the path of unknown peril upon which I had set my feet—I thought wistfully. We sat and smoked a bit, sipping the strong coffee the Portuguese made so well.

Da Costa at last relieved the Cantonese at the wheel. O'Keefe and I drew chairs up to the rail. The brighter stars shone out dimly through a hazy sky; gleams of phosphorescence tipped the crests of the waves and sparkled with an almost angry brilliance as the bow of the *Suwarna* tossed them aside; far to the east a faint silver glow heralded the rising moon. O'Keefe pulled contentedly at a cigarette. The glowing spark lighted the keen, boyish face and the blue eyes, now black and brooding under the spell of the tropic night.

"Are you American or Irish, O'Keefe?" I asked suddenly.

"Why?" he laughed.

"Because," I answered, "from your name and your service I would suppose you Irish—but your command of pure Americanese makes me doubtful." He grinned amiably.

"I'll tell you how that is," he said. "My mother is an American—a Grace, of Virginia. My father was O'Keefe, of Coleraine. And these two loved each other so well that the heart they gave me is half Irish and half American. My father died when I was sixteen. I used to go to the States with my mother every other year for a month or two. But after my father died we used to go to Ireland every other year. And there you are—I'm as American as I am Irish.

"When I'm in love, or excited, or dreaming, or mad I have the brogue. But for the every-day purposes of life I like the United States talk, and I know Broadway as well as I do Binevenagh Lane, and the Sound as well as St. Patrick's Channel; educated a bit at Eton, a bit at Oxford, a bit at Harvard; always too much O'Keefe *cum* Grace money to have to make any; in love lots of times, and never a heartache after that wasn't a pleasant one, and never a real purpose in life until I took the king's shilling and earned my wings; just thirty—and that's me—Larry O'Keefe."

"But it was the Irish O'Keefe who sat out there waiting for the banshee." I laughed.

"It was that," he said somberly, and I heard the brogue creep over his voice like velvet and his eyes grew brooding again. "There's never an O'Keefe for these thousand years that has passed without his warning. An' twice have I heard the banshee calling—once it was when my younger brother died an' once when my father lay waiting to be carried out on the ebb tide."

He mused a moment, then went on: "An' once I saw an *Annir*

Choille, a girl of the green people, flit like a shadow of green fire through the Carntogher woods, an' once at Dunchraig I slept where the ashes of the Dun of Cormac MacConcobar are mixed with those of Cormac an' Eilidh the Fair, all burned in the nine flames that sprang from the harping of Cravetheen, an' I heard the echo of his dead harpings—"

He paused again and then, softly, with that curiously sweet, high voice that only the Irish seem to have, he sang:

"Woman of the white breasts, Eilidh;
Woman of the gold-brown hair, and lips of the red, red rowan,
Where is the swan that is whiter, with breast more soft,
Or the wave on the sea that moves as thou movest, Eilidh."

CHAPTER IV

OLAF'S STORY

THERE WAS A little silence. I looked upon him with wonder. Clearly he was in deepest earnest. I know the psychology of the Gael is a curious one and that deep in all their hearts their ancient traditions and beliefs have strong and living roots. And I was both amused and touched.

Here was this soldier, facing war and all its ugly realities open-eyed and fearless, picking, indeed, the most dangerous branch of service for his own, a modern if ever there was one, appreciative of most unmystical Broadway and yet soberly and earnestly attesting to his belief in banshee, in shadowy people of the woods and fantom harpers! I wondered what he would think if he could see the Dweller and then, with a pang, that perhaps his superstitions might make him an easy prey.

For how then was I to have known that Larry O'Keefe's childlike faith in the existence of these fantasies of the Gaelic imagination was to prove not his weakness but his strong buckler against creatures that not even the imagination of his race could conceive?

He shook his head half impatiently and ran a hand over his eyes; turned to me and grinned.

"Don't think I'm cracked, professor," he said. "I'm not. But it takes me that way now and then. It's the Irish in me. And, believe it or not, I'm telling you the truth."

I looked eastward where the moon, now nearly a week past the full, was mounting.

"You can't make me see what you've seen, lieutenant." I laughed. "But you can make me hear. I've always wondered what kind of a noise a disembodied spirit could possibly make without any vocal cords or breath or any other earthly sound-producing mechanism. How does the banshee sound?"

O'Keefe did not laugh. Instead, he looked at me seriously.

"All right," he said. "I'll show you." From deep down in his throat came first a low, weird sobbing that mounted steadily into a keening whose mournfulness made my skin creep. And then O'Keefe's hand shot out and gripped my shoulder, and I stiffened like stone in my chair—for from behind us, like an echo, and then taking up the cry, swelled a wail that seemed to hold within it a sublimation of the sorrows of centuries! It gathered itself into one heartbroken, sobbing note and died away! O'Keefe's grip loosened, and he rose swiftly to his feet.

"It's all right, Goodwin," he said. "It's for me. It found me— all this way from Ireland."

There was no trace of fear in face or voice. "Buck up, professor," laughed O'Keefe. "There's nothing for you to be afraid of. And never yet was there an O'Keefe who feared the kind spirit that carries the warnin'."

Again the silence was rent by the cry. But now I had located it. It came from my room, and it could mean only one thing— Huldricksson had wakened.

"Forget your banshee!" I gasped, and made a jump for the cabin.

Out of the corner of my eye I noted a look of half-sheepish relief flit over O'Keefe's face, and then he was beside me. Da Costa shouted an order from the wheel, the Cantonese ran up and took it from his hands and the little Portuguese pattered down toward us. My hand on the door, ready to throw it open, I stopped. What if the Dweller were within—what if the new power I feared it had attained had made it not only independent of place but independent of that full flood of moon ray which Throckmartin had thought essential to draw it from the blue pool!

The Portuguese had paused, too, and looking at him I saw my own cravenness reflected. Now, from within, the sobbing wail began once more to rise. O'Keefe pushed me aside and with one quick motion threw open the door and crouched low within it. I saw an automatic flash dully in his hand; saw it cover the cabin from side to side, following the swift sweep of his eyes around it. Then he straightened and his face, turned toward the berth, was filled with wondering pity.

Da Costa and I had stepped in behind him. Through the window streamed a shaft of the moonlight. It fell upon Huldricksson's staring eyes; in them great tears slowly gathered and rolled down his cheeks; from his opened mouth came the wo-laden wailing. I ran to the port and drew the curtains. Da Costa snapped the lights.

The Norseman's dolorous crying stopped as abruptly as though cut. His gaze rolled toward us. And then his whole body reddened with a shock of rage, and at one bound he broke through the strong leashes I had buckled round him and faced us, a giant, naked figure tense with wrath, his eyes glaring, his yellow hair almost erect with the force of the passion visibly surging through him. Da Costa shrunk behind me. O'Keefe, coolly watchful, took a quick step that brought him in front of me.

"Where do you take me?" said Huldricksson, and his voice was thick as the growl of a beast. "Where is my boat?"

I touched O'Keefe gently and stood in front of the giant. He glared at me, and I saw the muscles of the gigantic arms flex and the hands below the bandaged wrists clench. He was berserk—mad!

"Listen, Olaf Huldricksson," I said. "We take you to where the sparkling devil took your Helma and your Freda. We follow the sparkling devil that came down from the moon. Do you hear me?" I spoke slowly, distinctly, striving to pierce the mists that I knew swirled around the strained brain. And the words did pierce. He stared at me for a moment. I heard O'Keefe murmur: "Good stuff! That's the idea. Humor him." Huldricksson stared at me and thrust out a shaking hand. As I gripped it I saw his madness fade, while his great chest heaved and fell. "You say you follow?" he asked falteringly. "You know where to follow? Where it took my Helma and my little Freda?"

"Just that, Olaf Huldricksson," I answered. "Just that! I pledge you my life that I know."

Da Costa stepped forward. "He speaks true, Olaf," he said. "Dr. Goodwin here he follow as he say. You go faster on the *Suwarna* than on the *Br-rw-un'ilda*, Olaf, yes."

The giant Norseman, still gripping my hand, looked at him. "I know you, Da Costa," he said. "You are all right. *Ja!* You are a fair man. Where is the *Brunhilda?*"

"She follow be'ind on a big rope, Olaf," soothed the Portuguese. "Soon you see her. But now lie down an' tell us, if you can, why you tie yourself to your wheel an' what it is that happen, Olaf."

"If you'll tell us how the sparkling devil came it will help us all when we get to where it is, Huldricksson," I said.

On O'Keefe's face there was an expression of well-nigh ludicrous doubt and amazement. He glanced from one to the other. The giant shifted his own tense look from me to the Irishman. I saw a gleam of approval in his eyes. He loosed me, and gripped O'Keefe's arm. *"Staerk!"* he said. *"Ja*—strong, and with a strong heart. A man—*ja!* He comes, too—we shall need him—*ja?*" He turned toward me. I looked toward O'Keefe and saw his doubt deepen.

"He comes," I said, "if he can."

Once more Huldricksson searched me with his glance; once more turned and absorbed O'Keefe in the icy blue of his eyes.

"A man, *ja*," he repeated. He pointed to me. "And you—a man, *ja!* But not the same as him—and me.

"I tell," he said, and seated himself on the side of the bunk. "It was four nights ago. My Freda"—his voice shook—"Mine *Yndling!* She loved the moonlight. I was at the wheel and my Freda and my Helma they were behind me. The moon was behind us and the *Brunhilda* was like a swan-boat sailing down with the moonlight sending her, *ja.*

"I heard my Freda say: 'I see a *nisse* coming down the track of the moon.' And I hear her mother laugh, low, like a mother does when her *Yndling* dreams. I was happy—that night—with my Helma and my Freda, and the *Brunhilda* sailing like a swan-boat, *ja.* I heard the child say, 'The *nisse* comes fast!' And then I heard a scream from my Helma, a great scream—like a mare when her foal is torn from her. I spun round fast, *ja!* I dropped the wheel and spun fast! I saw—" He covered his eyes with his hands.

The Portuguese had crept close to me, and I heard him panting like a frightened dog. O'Keefe, immobile, watched the Norseman narrowly. His hand fell and hate crept into his eyes; a bitter hate; that winged and white-hot hate that makes even the gods tremble.

"I saw a white fire spring over the rail," whispered Olaf Huldricksson. "It whirled round and round, and it shone like—like stars in a whirlwind mist. There was a noise in my ears. It sounded like bells—little bells, *ja!* Like the music you make when you run your finger round goblets. It made me sick and dizzy—the bells' noise.

"My Helma was—*indeholde*—what you say—in the middle of the white fire. She turned her face to me and she turned it on the child, and my Helma's face burned into my heart. Because it was full of fear, and it was full of happiness—of *glaede*. I tell you that the fear in my Helma's face made me ice here"—he beat his breast with clenched hand—"but the happiness in it burned on me like fire. And I could not move—I could not move.

"I said in here"—he touched his head—"I said, 'It is Loki come out of Helvede. But he cannot take my Helma, for Christ lives and Loki has no power to hurt my Helma or my Freda! Christ lives! Christ lives!' I said. But the sparkling devil did not let my Helma go. It drew her to the rail; half over it. I saw her eyes upon the child and a little she broke away and reached to it. And my Freda jumped into her arms. And the fire wrapped them both and they were gone! A little I saw them whirling on the moon track behind the *Brunhilda*—and they were gone!

"The sparkling devil took them! Loki was loosed, and he had power. I turned the *Brunhilda*, and I followed where my Helma and mine *Yndling* had gone. My boys crept up and asked me to turn again. But I would not. They dropped a boat and left me. I steered straight on the path. I lashed my hands to the wheel that sleep might not loose them. I steered on and on and on—

"Where was the God I prayed when my wife and child were taken?" cried Olaf Huldricksson—and it was as though I heard Throckmartin three years before asking that same bitter question. "I have left Him as He left me, *ja!* I pray now to Thor and to Odin, who can fetter Loki!" He sank back, covering again his eyes.

"Olaf," I said, "what you have called the sparkling devil has taken ones dear to me. I, too, was following it when we found you. You shall go with me to its home, and there we will try to take from it your wife and your child and my friends as well. But now that you may be strong for what is before us, you must sleep again."

Olaf Huldricksson looked upon me and in his eyes was that

something which souls must see in the eyes of Him the old Egyptians called the Searcher of Hearts in the Judgment Hall of Osiris.

"You speak the truth!" he said at last slowly. "I will do what you say!"

He stretched out an arm at my bidding. I gave him a second injection. He lay back and soon he was sleeping. I turned toward Da Costa. His face was livid and sweating, and he was trembling pitifully. O'Keefe stirred.

"You did that mighty well, Dr. Goodwin," he said. "So well that I almost believed you myself."

"What did you think of his story, Mr. O'Keefe?" I asked.

His answer was almost painfully brief and colloquial.

"Nuts!" he said. I was a little shocked, I admit. "I think he's crazy, Dr. Goodwin," he corrected himself, quickly. "What else could I think?"

I turned to the little Portuguese without answering.

"There's no need for any anxiety tonight, captain," I said. "Take my word for it. You need some rest yourself. Shall I give you a sleeping draft?"

"I do wish you would, Dr. Goodwin, sair," he answered gratefully. "Tomorrow, when I feel bettair—I would have a talk with you."

I nodded. He had known something then! I mixed him an opiate of considerable strength. He bowed and went to his own cabin.

I locked the door behind him and then, sitting beside the sleeping Norseman, I told O'Keefe my story from end to end. He asked few questions as I spoke; only watched me with a somewhat disconcerting intensity. In the main his inquiries dealt with the sound phenomena accompanying the apparition of the Dweller. He made a few somewhat startling interruptions dealing with Throckmartin's psychology. And after I had finished he cross-examined me rather minutely upon my recollections of the radiant phases upon each appearance, checking these with Throckmartin's observations of the same activities in the Chamber of the Moon Pool.

"And now what do you think of it all?" I asked.

He sat silent for a while, looking at Huldricksson.

"Not what you seem to think, Dr. Goodwin," he answered at last, gravely. "Let me sleep over it and, like the captain, I'll tell you tomorrow. One thing of course is certain—you and your friend Throckmartin and this man here saw—something. But—" he was silent again and then continued with a kindness that I found vaguely irritating—"but I've noticed that when a scientist gets superstitious it—er—takes very hard!

"Here's a few things I can tell you now though," went on O'Keefe, while I struggled to speak—"I pray in my heart that the old *Dolphin* is so busy she'll forget me for a while and that we won't meet anything with wireless on board her going up. Because, Dr. Goodwin, I'd dearly love to take a crack at your Dweller.

"And another thing," said Larry O'Keefe. "After this—cut out the trimmings, Doc, and call me plain Larry, for whether I think you're crazy or whether I don't you're there with the nerve, professor, and I'm *for* you.

"Good night!" said Larry O'Keefe and took himself out to the deck hammock he had insisted upon having slung for him, refusing the captain's importunities to use his own cabin.

And it was with extremely mixed emotions as to his compliment that I watched him go. Superstitious! I, whose pride was my scientific devotion to fact and fact alone! Superstitious—and this from a man who believed in banshees and ghostly harpers and Irish wood nymphs and no doubt in leprechawns and all their tribe!

Half laughing, half irritated and wholly happy in even the part promise of Larry O'Keefe's comradeship on my venture, I arranged a couple of pillows, stretched myself out on two chairs and took up my vigil beside Olaf Huldricksson.

CHAPTER V

A LOST PAGE OF EARTH

WHEN I AWAKENED the sun was streaming through the cabin porthole. Outside a fresh voice lilted. I lay on my two chairs and listened. The song was one with the wholesome sunshine and the breeze blowing stiffly and whipping the curtains. It was Larry O'Keefe at his matins:

"The little red lark is shaking his wings. Straight from the breast of his love he springs."

Larry's voice soared—

"Listen the lilt of the song he sings, All in the morning early, O!"

I sat up and looked at Huldricksson. He was sound asleep and in his sleep he smiled. The voice came nearer my door—

"His wings and his feathers are sunrise red.
He hails the sun and his golden head:
'Good morning, doc, you are long abed.'"

This last was a most irreverent interpolation, I well knew. I opened my door. O'Keefe stood outside laughing. Behind him the Tonga boys clustered, wide toothed and adoring. Even the Cantonese mate had something on his face that served for a grin and Da Costa was beaming. I closed the door behind me.

The *Suwarna,* her engines silent, was making fine headway under all sail, the *Brunhilda* skipping in her wake cheerfully with half her canvas up.

The sea was crisping and dimpling under the wind. Blue and white was the world as far as the eye could reach. Schools of little silvery green flying fish broke through the water rushing on each side of us; flashed for an instant and were gone. Behind us gulls hovered and dipped. The shadow of mystery had retreated far over the rim of this wide awake and beautiful world and if, subconsciously, I knew that somewhere it was brooding and waiting, for a little while at least I was consciously free of its oppression.

"How's the patient?" asked O'Keefe.

He was answered by Huldricksson himself, who must have risen just as I left the cabin. The great Norseman had slipped on a pair of pajamas and, giant torso naked under the sun, he strode out upon us. We all of us looked at him a trifle anxiously. But Olaf's madness had left him. His face was still drawn and in his eyes was much sorrow, but the berserk rage had vanished. He stretched out a hand to us in turn.

"This is Dr. Goodwin, Olaf," said Da Costa. "An' this is Lieutenant O'Keefe, of the English Navy."

Huldricksson bowed, with a touch of grace that revealed him not all rough seaman—and indeed, as I was later to find, the Norwegian had been given gentle upbringing and a fair education before the wanderlust of his race had swept him into these far seas.

He addressed himself straight to me: "You said last night we follow?"

I nodded.

"It is where?" he asked again.

"We go first to Ponape and from there to Metalanim Harbor—to the Nan-Matal. You know the place?"

Huldricksson bowed—a white gleam as of ice showing in his blue eyes.

"It is there?" he asked.

"It is there that we must first search," I answered.

"Good!" said Olaf Huldricksson. "It is good!"

He looked at Da Costa inquiringly and the little Portuguese, following his thought answered his unspoken question.

"We should be at Ponape tomorrow morning early, Olaf."

"Good!" repeated the Norseman. He looked away, his eyes tear filled.

A restraint fell upon us; the embarrassment all men experience when they feel a great sympathy and a great pity, neither of which they quite know how to give expression. By silent consent we discussed at breakfast only the most casual topics.

When the meal was over Huldricksson expressed a desire to go aboard the *Brunhilda*.

The *Suwarna* hove to and Da Costa and he dropped into the small boat. When they reached the *Brunhilda's* deck I saw Olaf take the wheel and the two fall into earnest talk. I beckoned to O'Keefe and we stretched ourselves out on the bow hatch under cover of the foresail. He lighted a cigarette, took a couple of leisurely puffs, and looked at me expectantly.

"Well," I asked, "and what do you think of it now?"

"Well," said O'Keefe, "suppose you tell me what you think—and then I'll proceed to point out your scientific errors." His eyes twinkled mischievously.

"Larry," I replied, somewhat severely, "you may not know that I have a reputation as an observer which, putting aside all modesty, I may say is an enviable one; also that while I have my share of imagination it is purely scientific and deals only with the interpretation of facts. You used a word last night to which I must interpose serious objection. You more than hinted that I had—superstitions. Let me inform you, Larry O'Keefe, that I am solely a seeker, observer, analyst, and synthesist of scientific fact. Facts pass through my mind in exactly the way threads pass through a loom; and I have no more superstition about them than the loom has. I am not"—and I tried to make my tone as pointed as my words—"I am not a believer in fantoms or spooks, leprechawns, banshees, or ghostly harpers."

O'Keefe leaned back and shouted with laughter.

"You're telling me what you think you are, Doc," he said at last, "but not what you think it is."

"Larry," I began indignantly. He saw that I was really hurt and instantly his levity gave way to almost boyish contrition.

"Forgive me, Goodwin," he said. "That was rotten bad taste I know. But if you could have seen yourself solemnly disclaiming the banshee"—another twinkle showed in his eyes—"and then with all this sunshine and this wide-open world"—he shrugged his shoulders—"it's hard to visualize anything such as you and Huldricksson have described."

"I know how hard it is, Larry," I answered. "And don't think I have any idea that the phenomenon is supernatural in the sense spiritualists and table turners have given that word. I do think it is supernormal; energized by a force unknown to modern science—but that doesn't mean I think it outside the radius of science."

"Tell me your theory, Goodwin," he said. I hesitated—for not yet had I been able to put into form to satisfy myself any explanation of the Dweller.

"I think," I said at last, "it is possible that some members of that race peopling the ancient continent which we know existed here in the Pacific and which was destroyed by a comparatively gradual subsidence, have survived. We know that many of these islands are honeycombed with caverns and vast subterranean spaces too great to be so called; literally underground lands, running in many cases far out beneath the ocean floor. It is possible that for some reason the survivors of this race of which I speak sought refuge in these abysmal spaces, one of whose entrances is on the island where Throckmartin's party met its end.

"As for their persistence in these caverns—we know the lost people possessed a high science. This is indisputable. It may be that they had gone far in their mastery of certain universal forms of energy. They may have discovered the secret of that form of magnetic etheric vibration we call light. If so, they would have had no difficulty in maintaining life down there, and, indeed, shielded by earth's crust from the natural forces

which always have surface man more or less at their mercy, they
may have developed a civilization and extended a science immensely more advanced than ours. And unless they have also
developed a complete indifference to conquest and an inflex-
ible determination never to come forth from their world, they
must always continue to be a potential menace to our world."

I paused. His keen face was now all eager attention.

"Have you ever heard of the Chamats?" I asked him. He
shook his head.

"In Papua," I explained, "there is a widespread and immeasurably old tradition that 'imprisoned under the hills' is a race of
giants who once ruled this region 'when it stretched from sun
to sun' and 'before the moon god drew the waters over it'—I
quote from the legend. Not only in Papua but in Borneo and
Java and in fact throughout Malaysia you find this story. And,
so the tradition runs, these people—the Chamats—will one
day break through the hills and rule the world; 'make over the
world' is the literal translation of the constant phrase in the
tale.* Does this convey anything to you, Larry?"

"Something," he nodded. "Go on."

"It conveys something to me," I said, "especially in the light
of what Throckmartin heard and saw and what Huldricksson
and I witnessed. It was Herbert Spencer who said that there
was a foundation of truth in every myth and legend of man;
that man could create nothing of himself—and that it was the
true mission of science to strip the husks from the fact, the
perhaps tremendous fact that was at the root of myth, and not
to pass it by scoffing."

"I know Spencer's kind," interrupted Larry. "He wouldn't
have stuck up his nose at the O'Keefe banshee. Not a bit of it.
He'd have had all the O'Keefes dying off quick so he'd have

---

*   William Beebe, the famous American naturalist and ornithologist, recently fighting in France with America's air forces, called attention to this remarkable belief in
an article not long ago printed in the *Atlantic Monthly*. Still more significant was it
that he noted a persistent rumor that this breaking out of the buried race was close
at hand.—W.J.B.

more chances to put salt on its tail and bottle it up as a laboratory specimen. I'm damned if I know which is worse—the scientific curiosity or the scientific sup—" He stopped guiltily. I looked at him suspiciously, but his face was grave, and after all there was much in what he said. I resumed:

"Now it is possible that these survivors I have mentioned form Spencer's fact basis of the Malaysian legend. It is possible that they are experimenting with their science, and that what I call 'the Dweller' is one of their results. Or it may be that the phenomenon is something that they created long ago and control of which they may have lost; or again it may be some unknown energy that they found when they entered their subterranean realm and which they have learned to control or which controls them.

"This much is sure—the moon door, which is clearly operated by the action of moonlight upon some unknown element or combination in much the same way that the metal selenium functions under sun rays or the electric light, and the crystals through which the moon rays pour down upon the pool their prismatic columns, are humanly made mechanisms. Set within the ruins they would seem to argue for the ancientness of the work. But who can tell when moon door and moon lights were set in their places? Nevertheless, so long as they are humanly made, and so long as it is this flood of moonlight from which the Dweller draws its power of materialization, the Dweller itself, if not the product of the human mind is at least dependent upon the product of the human mind for its appearance."

My pride in this analysis was short lived.

"Wait a minute, Goodwin," said O'Keefe. "Do you mean to say you think that this thing is made of—well—of moonshine?"

"Moonlight," I replied, "is, of course, reflected sunlight. But the rays which pass back to earth after their impact on the moon's surface are profoundly changed. The spectroscope shows that they lose practically all the slower vibrations we call red and infra-red, while the extremely rapid vibrations we call the violet and ultra-violet are accelerated and altered. Many scientists hold that there is an unknown element in the moon—perhaps that which makes the gigantic luminous trails that radiate in all directions from the lunar crater Tycho—whose energies are absorbed by and carried on the moon rays.

"At any rate, whether by the loss of the vibrations of the red or by the addition of this mysterious force, the light of the moon becomes something entirely different from mere modified sunlight—just as the addition or subtraction of one other chemical in a compound of several makes the product a substance with entirely different energies and potentialities. Carbon, for instance, is a food, a fuel, and useful in a host of ways. Add to one atom of carbon an atom of oxygen—CO—and you have carbon monoxid, one of the deadliest gases both to animals and plants known; add another atom of oxygen—CO_2—and you have not only not nearly so deadly a gas to animals but an actual plant food. Why? Ah, that we cannot tell.

"Now these rays. Larry, are given perhaps still another mysterious activity by the transparent globes through which Throckmartin told me they passed in the Chamber of the Moon Pool and whose colors they take. The result is the necessary factor in the formation of the Dweller. There would be nothing scientifically improbable in such a process, Larry. Kubalski, the great Russian physicist, produced crystalline forms exhibiting every faculty that we call vital by subjecting certain combinations of chemicals to the action of highly concentrated, brilliant rays of various colors. Something in light and in nothing else produced their pseudo-vitality.

"We know the extraordinary effect of the Finsen rays, which are only the concentration of the chemical energies in the green and blue of the spectrum, upon malignant cell growths in the human body; and we know that the X-ray can dissolve the normal barrier of matter for us, making the solid transparent. We do not begin to know how to harness the potentialities of light. This hidden race may have learned; and learning, may have created forms with powers and possibilities undreamed by us."

"Listen, Doc," said Larry earnestly, "I'll take everything you say about this lost continent, the people who used to live on it, and their caverns, for granted. But by the sword of Brian Boru, you'll never get me to fall for the idea that a bunch of moonshine can handle a big woman such as you say Throckmartin's Thora was, nor a two-fisted man such as you say Throckmartin was, nor Huldricksson's wife—and I'll bet she was one of those strapping big northern women too—you'll never get me to believe that any bunch of concentrated moonshine could handle them and take them waltzing off along a moonbeam back to wherever it goes. No Doc, not on your life, *jamais de la vie,* as we say at the front—nix!"

"I've told you that what you call moonshine is an aggregate of vibrations with immense potential power, Larry," I answered, considerably irritated. "What we call matter is nothing but a collection of infinitely small particles of electricity—electrons; and the way the electrons are grouped makes of matter man or wood or metal or stone. Light is a magnetic vibration of the ether and is probably composed of similar particles of electricity but functioning in another way from the particles that make matter. Learn the secret of making light and you come close to learning the secret of matter. Why Larry, if you could take *all* the energy out of the sunshine that in one minute covers one square foot of earth, you could blast *all* of earth to bits. And your wonderful wireless is nothing but vibrations—yet it carries words around the world with almost the speed of light itself."

"Yes," said Larry, and you know the kind of apparatus we have to make to catch those vibrations. Why the knock of a gnat on it is like the kick of an elephant! Why, Doc, you could put me up against all the wireless vibrations in the world at eleven o'clock at night when they're heaviest, and all I'd say would be—'That mosquito humming around me is sure dying of old age and general decrepitude.'"

"But—" I began.

"No," he interrupted. "It's wrong. And about the sun— Say! I've seen a New York copper standing at Forty-Second Street and Fifth Avenue for six hours at a stretch with a 110 degree heat beating around him. And all he said when he was relieved was—'Well, about three good cold pails of suds will just about do me.' Three good cold beers Doc, was all he needed to neutralize six hours of the same old rays that in one minute on one square foot have enough energy to blow up the world! And he was right.

"No, no Doc. It's good in theory, but it don't work out. Like my old professor in chemistry at Eton who was always trying the balmiest experiments that never worked out either. But at the end of every fliv he'd run to us cheerfully and say: 'The experiment has failed, gentlemen, but the principle remains the same.' Same way, theoretically, old Archimedes was right when he said that if a man could get a lever long enough he could move the world. But will man ever get hold of that long a lever—*Jamais—de—la—vie!*"

"All right O'Keefe," I answered, now very much irritated indeed. "What's your theory?" And I could not resist adding: "Fairies?"

"Professor," he grinned, "if that Thing's a fairy, it's Irish. There aren't any fairies anywhere but in Ireland. It takes a country with a history to grow the Little People—and Ireland's got more history than all the else of the world put together. If it's a fairy it's Irish and when it sees me it'll be so glad there'll be nothing to it. 'I was lost, strayed or stolen, Larry *avick,*' it'll say, 'an' I was so homesick for the old sod I was desp'rit,' it'll say, an' 'take me back quick before I do any more har-rm!' It'll tell me—an' that's the truth."

I forgot my chagrin in our laughter.

"But I'll tell you what I think," he said soberly. "Down at the first battle of the Marne there were any number of Englishmen who thought they saw the old archers of Crecy and Agincourt, dead these half dozen centuries, twanging their fantom bows and shooting down the Huns by the hundred. And you can find thousands of Frenchmen who see Joan of Arc and Napoleon regularly. It's what the doctors call collective hallucination. Somebody sees something a little queer; his imagination gets to work hard because his nerves are pretty well strained anyway, he says to the next fellow: 'Don't you see it?' and the next fellow says, 'Sure I see it, too!' And there you are—bowmen of Mons, St. George on his white horse, Joan in armor, and all the rest of it."

"If you think that explains Throckmartin and myself, how do you explain Huldricksson, who never saw Throckmartin and didn't see me before the Thing came to the *Brunhilda?*" I asked with, I admit, some heat.

"Now don't get me wrong," replied Larry. "I believe you all saw something all right. But what I think you saw was some kind of gas. All this region is volcanic and islands and things are constantly poking up from the sea. It's probably gas; a volcanic emanation; something new to us and that drives you crazy—lots of kinds of gas do that. It hit the Throckmartin party on that island and they probably were all more or less delirious all the time; thought they saw things; talked it over and—collective hallucination. When they got it bad they most likely jumped overboard one by one. Huldricksson sails into a place where it is and it hits his wife. She grabs the child and jumps overboard. Maybe the moon rays make it luminous—I've seen gas on the front under the moon that looked like a thousand whirling dervish devils. Yes, and you could see the devil's faces in it. And if you got into your lungs nothing could ever make you think you hadn't seen *real* devils."

"But that doesn't explain the moon door and the phenomena of the lights in the Chamber of the Pool," I said at last.

"*You* haven't seen them, have you?" asked Larry. "And Throckmartin admitted he was pretty nearly crazy when he thought *he* did. Well!"

For a time I was silent.

"Larry," I said at last, "whether you are right or I am right, I must go to the Nan-Matal. Will you go with me, Larry?"

"Goodwin," he replied, "I surely will. I'm as interested as you are. If we don't run across the *Dolphin* I'll go. I'll leave word at Ponape, to tell them where I am if they come along, and I'll make arrangements with Da Costa to stop at various points where the old dear may run in and leave messages. If they report me dead for a while there's nobody to care. So that's all right. Only old man, be reasonable. You've thought over this so long, you're going bug, honestly you are."

And again, the gladness that I might have Larry O'Keefe with me, was so great that I forgot to be angry.

CHAPTER VI

THE MOON DOOR OPENS—AND SHUTS

DA COSTA, WHO had come aboard unnoticed by either of us, now tapped me on the arm.

"Doctair Goodwin," he said, "can I see you in my cabin, sair?"

At last, then, he was going to speak. I followed him.

"Doctair," he said, when we had entered, "this is a veree strange thing that has happened to Olaf. Veree strange. An' the natives of Ponape, they have been very much excite' lately. An' none go near the Nan-Matal now, for they say the spirits have got great power and are angree because of that othair partee which they take.

"Of what they fear I know nothing, nothing!" Again that quick, furtive crossing of himself. "But this I have to tell you. There came to me from Ranaloa last month a man, a German, a doctair, like you. His name it was Von Hetzdoip. I take him to Ponape an' the natives there, they will not take him to the Nan-Matal, where he wish to go—no! So I take him. We leave in a boat, with much instrument carefully tied up. I leave him there wit' the boat an' the food. He tell me to tell no one an' pay me not to. But you are a friend an' Olaf he depend much upon you an' so I tell you, sair."

"You know nothing more than this, Da Costa?" I asked. "You're sure?"

"Nothing! Nothing more!" he answered. But I was not so sure. Later I told O'Keefe.

"A German, eh?" He whistled. "Well, that means trouble. Now I'll pray to all the fairies in Ireland that we don't meet up with the *Dolphin*."

His prayers must have been powerful, for the next morning we raised Ponape, without further incident, and before noon the *Suwarna* and the *Brunhilda* had dropped anchor in the harbor. Upon the excitement and manifest dread of the natives, when we sought among them for carriers and workmen to accompany us, I will not dwell. It is enough to say that no payment we offered would induce a single one of them to go to the Nan-Matal. Nor would they say why.

They were sullen and panicky, and I think the most disconcerting thing of all in their attitude, was the open relief they showed when they learned that the British warship might steam in, seeking O'Keefe. It indicated that their fear was deep-rooted and real, indeed.

Finally it was agreed that the *Brunhilda* should be left at Ponape in charge of a half-breed Chinaman, whom both Da Costa and Huldricksson knew and trusted. We piled her long-boat up with my instruments and food and camping equipment. The *Suwarna* took us around to Metalanim Harbor, and there, with the tops of ancient sea walls deep in the blue water beneath us, and the ruins looming up out of the mangroves, a scant mile from us, left us.

Da Costa's anxiety and uneasiness were almost pitiful and I knew that even if we could persuade him to stay with the party, his superstitions would make him worse than useless. His men, too, who had got inklings of the happenings on the *Brunhilda*, were already half mutinous. But there were tears in the eyes of the little Portuguese when he bade us farewell, invoking all the saints to stand by and protect us; and the sorrow in his face and the fervor of his parting grip were eloquent of his conviction that never again would he behold us.

Then, when he had passed with the *Suwarna* out of view, with Huldricksson manipulating our small sail, and Larry at the rudder, we rounded the titanic wall that swept down into the depths, passed monoliths, standing like gigantic sentinels upon its shattered verge, and turned at last into the canal that Throckmartin, on his map, had marked as the passage which, running between frowning Nan-Tauach and its satellite islet, Tau, led straight to the gate of that place of ancient mysteries, where the moon door is portal of that dread chamber wherein the Dweller made itself manifest.

And as we entered that channel we were enveloped by a silence; a silence so intense, so—weighted, that it seemed to have substance; an alien silence that clung and stifled and still stood aloof from us—the living. It was a stillness, such as might follow the long tramping of millions into the grave; it was—paradoxical as it may be—*filled* with the withdrawal of life.

Standing down in the chambered depths of the Great Pyramid I had known something of such silence—but never such intensity as this. Larry felt it and I saw him look at me askance. If Olaf, sitting in the bow, felt it, too, he gave no sign; his blue eyes, with again the glint of ice within them, watched the channel before us.

As we passed, there arose upon our left sheer walls of black basalt blocks, Cyclopean, towering fifty feet or more, broken here and there by the sinking of their deep foundations—and only where they had so broken, had the hand of time been able to crumble them. From these dark ramparts the silence seemed to ooze, and my skin crept as though from hidden places in them scores of eyes, ages dead, peered out upon us.

In front of us the mangroves widened out and filled the canal. On our right the lesser walls of Tau, somber blocks smoothed and squared and set with a cold, mathematical nicety, that filled me with vague awe, slipped by. Through breaks I caught glimpses of dark ruins and of great fallen stones that seemed to crouch and menace us, as we passed. Somewhere there, hidden, were the seven globes that poured the moon fire down upon the Moon Pool.

Now we were among the mangroves and, sail down, the three of us pushed and pulled the boat through their tangled roots and branches. The noise of our passing split the silence, like a profanation, and from the ancient bastions came murmurs— forbidding, strangely sinister. And now we were through, floating on a little open space of shadow-filled water. Before us lifted the gateway of Nan-Tauach, gigantic, broken, incredibly old; shattered portals through which had passed men and women of earth's dawn, old with a weight of years that pressed leadenly upon the eyes that looked upon it, and yet in some curious, indefinable way—menacingly defiant.

Beyond the gate, back from the portals, stretched a flight of enormous basalt slabs, a giant's stairway indeed; and from each side of it marched the high walls that were the Dweller's pathway. None of us spoke as we grounded the boat and dragged it up upon a half-submerged pier. And when we did speak it was in whispers.

"What next?" asked Larry.

"I think we ought to take a look around." I replied in the same low tones. "We'll climb the wall here and take a flash about. The whole place ought to be plain as day from that height."

Huldricksson, his blue eyes alert, nodded. With the greatest difficulty we clambered up the broken blocks, the giant Norseman at times lifting me like a child, and stood at last upon the broad top. From this vantage-point, not only the whole of Nan-Tauach, but all of the Nan-Matal lay at our feet.

To the east and south of us, set like children's blocks in the midst of the sapphire sea, were dozens of islets, none of them covering more than two square miles of surface: each of them a perfect square or oblong within its protecting walls. Behind these walls were grouped ruins—houses, temples, palaces, all the varying abodes of men. On none was there sign of life, save for a few great birds that hovered here and there and gulls dipping in the blue wave beyond.

We turned our gaze down upon the island on which we stood. It was, I estimated, about three-quarters of a mile square. The sea wall enclosed it like the sides of a gigantic box. It was really an enormous basalt-sided open cube, and within it two other open cubes. The enclosure between the first and second wall was stone paved, with here and there a broken pillar and long stone benches.

The hibiscus, the aloe-tree and a number of small shrubs had found place, but seemed only to intensify its stark loneliness. It came to me that this had been the assembling place of those who, thousands upon thousands of years ago, had gathered within this citadel of mystery. Beyond the wall that was its farther boundary was a second enclosure, littered with broken pillars, fragments of stone and numerous small structures; and the second enclosure's limit was the third wall, a terrace not more than twenty feet high. Within it was what had been without doubt the heart of Nan-Tauach—an open space three hundred feet square; at each of its corners a temple.

Directly before us, black and staring like an eyeless socket, was the entrance to the "treasure-house of Chau-ta-Leur" the sun king. The blocks that had formed its doors lay shattered beside it. And opposite it should be, if Throckmartin's story had not been a dream, the gray slab he had named the moon door.

"Wonder where the boche can be?" asked Larry.

I shook my head. There was no sign of life here. Had Von Hetzdorp gone—or had the Dweller taken him, too? Whatever had happened, there was no trace of him below us or on any of the islets within our range of vision. We scrambled down the side of the gateway. Olaf looked at me wistfully.

"We start the search now, Olaf," I said. "And first, O'Keefe, let us see whether the gray stone is really here. After that we will set up camp, and while I unpack you and Olaf search the island. It won't take long."

Larry gave a look at his service automatic and grinned. "Lead on, *Macduff*," he said. We made our way up the steps, through the outer enclosures and into the central square. I confess to a fire of scientific curiosity and eagerness tinged with a dread that O'Keefe's analysis might be true. Would we find the moving slab and, if so, would it be as Throckmartin had described? If so, then even Larry would have to admit that here was something that theories of gases and luminous emanations would not explain; and the first test of the whole amazing story would be passed. But if not—

And there before us, the faintest tinge of gray setting it apart from its neighboring blocks of basalt, was the moon door!

There was no mistaking it. This was, in very deed, the portal through which, as I have told in my narrative so courteously printed by *The All-Story Weekly* last June, Dr. Throckmartin had seen pass that gloriously dreadful apparition he called the Dweller; through it the Dweller had borne in an embrace of living light first Thora, Mrs. Throckmartin's maid, and then Dr. Stanton, his youthful colleague; and through it at last had gone Throckmartin, down the shining tunnel beyond, whose luminous lure led to that enchanted chamber into which streamed the seven moon torrents that drew the Dweller from the wondrous pool that was its lair.

Across its threshold had raced Edith Throckmartin, my lost friend's young bride, fearlessly flying down that haunted passage to aid her husband in his fruitless fight against the Thing—and out of it he himself had rushed, a merciful darkness shrouding consciousness and sight, after he had watched her sink, slowly sink, down through the blue waters of the moon pool, wrapped in the Dweller's coruscating folds, to—what?

And then there seemed to drift out through the stone to face me that inexplicable being of swirling, spiraling plumes and jets of sparkling opalescence, of crystal sweet chimings, of murmuring sighings that Throckmartin had told me stamped upon the faces of its prey wedded anguish and rapture, terror and ecstasy commingled, joy of heaven and agony of hell, the seal of God and devil monstrously mated—and that my own eyes had seen clasp Throckmartin in our cabin of the *Southern Queen* and draw him swiftly down the moon path—here?

What was that portal—more enigmatic than was ever sphinx? And what lay beyond it? What did that smooth stone, whose wan deadness whispered of ages old corridors of time opening out into alien, uinmaginable vistas, hide? It had cost the world of science Throckmartin's great brain—as it had cost Throckmartin those he loved. It had drawn me to it in search of Throckmartin—and its shadow had fallen upon the soul of Olaf the Norseman; and upon what thousands upon thousands more I wondered, since the brains that had conceived it had vanished with their secret knowledge?

Did the Dweller lurk behind it in wait for us? When we found its open-sesame would we find within truths of our world's youth to which the riches of *Ali Baba's* cave were but dross? Was there that within which would force science to recast its hard won theories of humanity, of its evolution, of its painful progress from brute to what we call man—or would we loose upon the world some nameless, blasting evil, some survival of our planet's nightmare hours, some supernormal, inhuman thing spawned by unthinkable travail in a hidden cavern of mother earth?

A barrier of unknown stone—fifteen feet high and ten feet wide; and yet it might bar the way to a lost paradise or hold back a hell undreamed by even crudest brains!

What lay beyond it?

Swiftly the thoughts raced through my mind as I stood staring at the gray slab—and then through me passed a wave of weakness. And not until then did I realize the intense, sub-conscious anxiety that had possessed me; the mordant fear that I had been prey of inexplicable obsession and had by it misled my colleagues of the International Association and through them the entire scientific world.

I stretched out a shaking hand and touched the surface of the slab. A faint thrill passed through my hand and arm, oddly unfamiliar and as oddly unpleasant; as of electric contact holding the very essence of cold. O'Keefe, watching, imitated my action. As his fingers rested on the stone his face filled with astonishment. In Huldricksson's eyes was mingled hope and despair. I beckoned him; he laid a hand on the slab and swiftly withdrew it. But I saw the despair die from his face, leaving only eagerness.

"It is the door!" he said. I nodded. There was a low whistle of astonishment from O'Keefe and he pointed up toward the top of the gray stone. I followed the gesture and saw, above the moon door and on each side of it, two gently curving bosses of rock, perhaps a foot in diameter.

"The moon door's keys," I said.

"It begins to look so," answered Larry. "If we can find them," he added.

"There's nothing we can do till moonrise," I replied. "And we've none too much time to prepare as it is. Come!"

But stark lonely as was that place, I felt, as we passed out, as though eyes were upon me, watching with an intensity of ma-levolence, a bitter hatred. Olaf must have felt it, too, for I saw him glance sharply around and his face hardened. I said nothing, however, nor did he; and a little later we were beside our boat. We lightered it, set up the tent, and as it was now but a short hour to sundown I bade them leave me and make their search. They went off together, and I busied myself with opening some of the paraphernalia I had brought with me.

First of all I took out two Becquerel ray-condensers that I had bought in New York. Their lenses would collect and intensify to the fullest extent any light directed upon them. I had found them most useful in making spectroscopic analysis of luminous vapors, and I knew that at Yerkes Observatory splendid results had been obtained from them in collecting the diffused radiance of the nebulae for the same purpose.

It was my theory that the mechanism operating the moon door responded only to the force of the full light of the moon shining through the seven little circles which Throckmartin had discovered set within each of the bosses above it; just as the Dweller could materialize only under the same full-moon force shining through the varicolored lights. Obviously the time, then, of the door's opening and the phenomenon's materialization must coincide.

With the moon only a few days past its full, it was practically certain that by setting the Becquerel condensers above the bosses I could concentrate enough light upon the circles to set the opening mechanism in motion. And as the ray stream from the waning moon was insufficient to energize the pool, we could enter the chamber free from any fear of encountering its tenant, make our preliminary observations and go forth before the satellite had dropped so far that the concentration in the condensers would fall below that necessary to keep the slab from closing.

I took out also a small spectroscope, easily carried and a few other small instruments for the analysis of certain light manifestations and the testing of metal and liquid. Finally, I put aside my emergency medical kit.

I had hardly finished examining and adjusting these before O'Keefe and Huldricksson returned. They reported signs of a camp at least ten days old beside the northern wall of the outer court, but beyond that no evidence of others beyond ourselves on Nan-Tauach. Moonrise would not occur until nine thirty, and until then there was no use of attacking the moon door.

We prepared supper, ate and talked a little, but for the most part were silent. Even Larry's high spirits were not in evidence; half a dozen times I saw him take out his automatic and look it over. He was more thoughtful than I had ever seen him. Once he went into the tent, rummaged about a bit and brought out another revolver which, he said, he had got from Da Costa, and a half-dozen clips of cartridges. He passed the gun over to Olaf, who took it with a word of thanks.

At last a glow in the southeast heralded the rising moon. I picked up my instruments and the medical kit; Larry and Olaf shouldered each a short ladder that was part of my equipment, and, with our electric-flashes pointing the way, walked up the great stairs, through the enclosures, and straight to the gray stone.

By this time the moon had risen and its clipped light shone full upon the slab. I saw faint gleams pass over it as of fleeting phosphorescence—but so faint were they that I could not be sure of the truth of my observation. The base of the gray stone bisected a curious cuplike depression whose perfectly rounded sides were as smooth as though they had been polished by a jeweler. This half cup was, at its deepest, two and a half feet, and its lip joined the basalt pavement four feet from the barrier of the great slab.

We set the ladders in place. Olaf I assigned to stand before the door and watch for the first signs of its opening—if open it should—and the big sailor accepted the post eagerly, thinking, I suppose, that it would bring him nearer the loved ones he now was sure were within. The Becquerals were set within three-inch tripods, whose feet I had equipped with vacuum rings to enable them to hold fast to the rock.

I scaled one ladder and fastened a condenser over the boss; descended; sent Larry up to watch it, and, ascending the second ladder, rapidly fixed the other in its place. Then, with O'Keefe watchful on his perch, I on mine and Olaf's eyes fixed upon the moon door, we began our vigil. Suddenly there was an exclamation from Larry.

"Seven little lights are beginning to glow on this stone, Goodwin!" he cried. But I had already seen those beneath my lens begin to gleam out with a silvery luster. Swiftly the rays within the condenser began to thicken and increase, and as they did so the seven small circles waxed like stars growing out of the dusk, and with a queer—curdled is the best word I can find to define it—luster entirely strange to me.

I placed a finger upon one of them and received a shock such as I had felt on touching the moon door, only greatly intensified. Clearly a current of some kind was set up within the substance when the moonlight fell upon it. And now the lights were glowing steadily. Beneath me I heard a faint, sighing murmur and then the voice of Huldricksson:

"It opens—the stone turns—"

I began to climb down the ladder. Again came Olaf's voice:

"The stone—it is open—" And then a shriek that came from the very core of his heart; a wail of blended anguish and pity, of rage and despair—and the sound of swift footsteps racing through the wall beneath me!

I DROPPED to the ground. The moon door was wide open, and through it I caught a glimpse of a corridor filled with a faint, pearly vaporous light like earliest misty dawn. But of Olaf I could see—nothing! And even as I stood, gaping, from behind me came the sharp crack of a rifle; I saw the glass of the condenser at Larry's side flash and fly into fragments; saw him drop swiftly to the ground and the automatic in his hand flash once, twice, into the darkness.

Saw, too, the moon door begin to pivot slowly, slowly back into its place!

I rushed toward the turning stone with the wild idea of holding it open. As I thrust my hands against it there came at my back a snarl and an oath and Larry staggered under the impact of a body that had flung itself straight at his throat. He reeled at the lip of the shallow cup at the base of the slab, slipped upon its polished curve, fell and rolled with that which had attacked him, kicking and writhing, straight through the narrowing portal into the mistily luminous passage!

Forgetting all else, I sprang with a cry to his aid. And as I leaped I felt the closing edge of the moon door graze my side. And then, as Larry raised a fist, brought it down upon the temple of the man who had grappled with him and rose from the twitching body unsteadily to his feet, I heard shuddering past me a mournful whisper; spun about as though some giant's hand had whirled me—and stood so, rigid, appalled!

For the end of the corridor no longer opened out into the moonlit square of ruined Nan-Tauach. It was barred by a solid mass of glimmering stone. The moon door had closed!

And where was Olaf Huldricksson? And who was the man at our feet who had brought this calamity down upon us? And what were we to do, prisoned, and my bewildered brain told me, hopelessly prisoned, without food, in the very lair of the Dweller itself?

CHAPTER VII

THE MOON POOL

"**LARRY!**" **I CRIED,** turning to O'Keefe, "the stone has shut! We're caught!"

O'Keefe took a brisk step toward the barrier behind us. There was no mark of juncture with the shining walls; the slab lifted into the sides as closely as a mosaic. "It's shut all right," said Larry. "But if there's a way in, there's a way out. Anyway, Doc, we're right in the pew we've been heading for—so why worry?" He grinned at me cheerfully, and although I could not accept his light-hearted view of the situation, I felt a twinge of shame for my momentary panic. The man on the floor groaned, and O'Keefe dropped swiftly to his knees beside him.

"Von Hetzdorp!" he said.

At my exclamation he moved aside, turning the face so I

could see it. It was clearly German, and just as clearly its pos-sessor was one of considerable force and intellectuality.

The strong, massive brow with orbital ridge unusually de-veloped, the dominant, high-bridged nose, the straight lips with their more than suggestion of latent cruelty, and the strong lines of the jaw beneath a black, pointed beard all gave evidence that here was a personality beyond the ordinary. The hair was closely cropped on the square head, and the short, stocky body with its deep chest and abnormal length of torso as compared to the legs, indicated extraordinary vitality.

Unscrupulous, I thought, looking down upon him, remorse-less, crafty, and with a brain as unmoral as is science itself, for I hold that what we call science is infinitely beyond all code, and is good or bad or neutral only as it is applied by humanity; that, *par example,* the Nature whose laws bring about that con-dition of unstable equilibrium among atoms which we call a high explosive, cannot be blamed if man uses those laws to destroy the bodies of his fellow man instead of leveling rocky barriers to commerce or tearing up the subsoil of earth for a greater fertility—nor can any responsibility for their use be held against the student who, discovering the laws, gave them to man.

"Couldn't be anybody else," said Larry, breaking in on my thoughts. "He must have been watching us over there from Chau-ta-leur's vault all the time. When he saw that we had the slab open I suppose he figured that now we had picked the chestnuts out of the fire, he'd better collect 'em all for himself. So he took a pot shot at me first, and meant to get you and Olaf next. But his aim was bad—too damned good, rather—and when he saw what he'd done he took a crazy chance. That's Heinie all over—"

The man on the corridor's floor stirred, and swiftly O'Keefe ran practised hands over his body; then stood erect, holding out to me two wicked-looking magazine pistols and a knife. "He got one of my bullets through his right forearm, too," he said. "Just a flesh wound, but it made him drop his rifle. Some arsenal, our little German scientist, what?"

I OPENED my medical kit and knelt beside Von Hetzdorp—if indeed it was he. The wound was a slight one, and Larry stood looking on as I bandaged it.

"Got another one of those condensers the Dutchman here broke?" he asked me suddenly. "And do you suppose Olaf will know enough to use it?"

And then it dawned upon me that O'Keefe could not have heard, as I had, the Norseman race into the moon door's passage before the door had closed! I arose swiftly.

"Larry," I answered, "Olaf's not outside! He's in here somewhere!"

His jaw dropped.

"The hell you say!" he whispered.

"Didn't you hear him shriek when the stone opened?" I asked.

"I heard him yell, yes," he said. "But I didn't know what was the matter. And then this wild cat jumped me—" He paused and his eyes widened. "Which way did he go?" he asked swiftly. I pointed down the faintly glowing passage.

"There's only one way," I said.

"Watch that bird close," hissed O'Keefe, pointing to Von Hetzdorp—and pistol in hand stretched his long legs and raced away. I looked down at the German. His eyes were open, and he reached out a hand to me. I lifted him to his feet.

"I have heard," he said. "We follow, quick. If you will take my arm, please, I am shaken yet, yes—" I gripped his shoulder without a word, and the two of us set off down the corridor after Larry. Von Hetzdorp was gasping, and his weight pressed upon me heavily, but he moved with all the will and strength that was in him.

As we ran I took hasty note of the tunnel. I saw that its sides were smooth and polished, and that the light seemed to come not from their surfaces, but from far within them—giving to

Golden-eyed Lakla stood looking down at the sleeping
Larry, and all about her were other eyes....

the walls an illusive aspect of distance and depth; rendering
them in a peculiarly weird way—spacious. The passage turned,
twisted, ran down, turned again. It came to me that the light
that illumined the tunnel was given out by tiny points deep
within the stone, sprang from the points ripplingly and spread
upon their polished faces. Involuntarily I stopped to look more
closely.

"Hurry," gasped Von Hetzdorp. "Explain that later—etheric
vibration—setup in that composition—stones really etheric
lights—stupendous! Hurry!"

Through his panting speech broke a cry from far ahead. It
was Larry's voice.

"Olaf!"

I gripped Von Hetzdorp's arm closer and we sped on. Now we were coming fast to the end of the passage. Before us was a high arch, and through it I glimpsed a dim, shifting luminosity as of mist filled with rainbows. We reached the portal and I drew myself up short, almost tripping the German. For what I was looking into was a chamber that might have been transported from that enchanted palace of the Jinn King that rises beyond the magic mountains of Kaf.

It was filled with a shimmering, prismatic lambency that thickened in the distances to impenetrable veils of fairy opalescence. It was a shine of sorcery!

Before me stood O'Keefe, and a dozen feet in front of him, Huldricksson, with something clasped tightly in his arms. The Norseman's feet were at the verge of a shining, silvery lip of stone within whose oval lay a blue pool. And down upon this pool staring upward like a gigantic eye, fell seven pillars of fantom light—one of them amethyst, one of rose, another of white, a fourth of blue, and three of emerald, of silver and of amber. They fell each upon the azure surface, and I knew that these were the seven streams of radiance, within which the Dweller took shape—now but pale ghosts of their brilliancy when the full energy of the moon stream raced through them.

Then Huldricksson bent and placed on the shining silver lip of the Pool that which he held—and I saw that it was the body of a child! He set it there so gently, bent over the side and thrust a hand down into the water. And as he did so he stiffened strangely, moaned and lurched against the little body that lay before him. Instantly the form moved—and slipped over the verge into the blue. Rigid with horror, I watched Huldricksson recover himself and throw his body over the stone, hands clutching, arms thrust deep down—and then heard from his lips a long-drawn, heart-shriveling cry of pain and of anguish that held in it nothing human!

Close on its wake came a cry from Von Hetzdorp.

"Gott!" shrieked the German. "Drag him back! Quick!"

He leaped forward, but before he could half clear the distance, O'Keefe had leaped too, had caught the Norseman by the shoulders and toppled him backward, where he lay whimpering and sobbing. And as I rushed behind the German I saw Larry lean over the lip of the Pool and cover his eyes with a shaking hand; saw Von Hetzdorp peer down into it with real pity in his cold eyes; heard him murmur—*"Das armes Kind! Ach! das armes Kleine Mädchen!"*

THEN I stared down myself into the Moon Pool, and there, sinking, sinking, was a little maid whose dead face and fixed, terror-filled eyes looked straight into mine; and ever sinking slowly, slowly—vanished! And I knew that this was Olaf's Freda, his beloved *"yndling"* whose mother had snatched her up from the *Brunhilda's* deck when the Dweller had wrapped its awesome, coruscating folds about her, and had drawn her, the child still in her arms, along the moonbeam path to where we stood!

But where was the mother, and where had Olaf found his babe?

Simultaneously, it seemed, we straightened ourselves, the three of us, and looked into each other's faces; each of us, yes, even Von Hetzdorp, shaken to the heart. The German was first to speak.

"You have nitroglycerin there, yes?" he asked, pointing toward my medical kit that I had gripped unconsciously and carried with me during the mad rush down the passage. I nodded and drew it out.

"Hypodermic," he ordered next, curtly; took the syringe, filled it accurately with its one one-hundredth of a grain dosage, and leaned over Huldricksson, who, with arms held out rigidly, was fighting for breath as though a great weight lay on his chest. He rolled up the sailor's sleeves halfway to the shoulder. The arms were white with that same strange semitranslucence that I had seen on Throckmartin's breast where a tendril of the

Dweller had touched him; and his hands were of the same whiteness—like a baroque pearl. Above the line of white, standing out like marble on the bronzed arms, Von Hetzdorp thrust the needle.

"He will need all his heart can do," he said to me.

Then he reached down into a belt about his waist and drew from it a small, flat flask of what seemed to be lead. He opened it and let a few drops of its contents fall on each arm of the Norwegian. The liquid sparkled and instantly began to spread over the skin much as oil or gasoline dropped on water does—only far more rapidly. And as it spread it seemed to draw a sparkling film over the tainted flesh and little wisps of vapor rose from it. The Norseman's mighty chest heaved with agony, and I could see the overstimulated heart beating in a great pulse in his throat. He strove to rise to his feet—but his weakness was too great. His hands clenched. The German gave a grunt of satisfaction at this, dropped a little more of the liquid, and then, watching closely, grunted again and leaned back. Huldricksson's labored breathing ceased, his head dropped upon Larry's knee, and from his arms and hands the whiteness swiftly withdrew.

Von Hetzdorp arose and contemplated us—almost benevolently.

"He will all right be in five minutes," he said. "I know. I do it to pay for that shot of mine, and also because we will need him. Yes." He turned to Larry. "You have a poonch like a mule kick, my young friend," he said. "Some time you pay me for that, too, eh?" He smiled; and the quality of the grimace was not exactly reassuring. Larry looked him over quizzically.

"You're Von Hetzdorp, of course," he said. The German nodded, betraying no surprise at the recognition.

"And you?" he asked.

"Lieutenant O'Keefe of the Royal Flying Corps," replied Larry, saluting. "And this gentleman is Dr. Walter T. Goodwin."

Von Hetzdorp's face brightened.

"The American botanist?" he queried. I nodded.

"*Ach!*" cried Von Hetzdorp eagerly; "but this is fortunate. Long I have desired to meet you. Your work, for an American, is most excellent; surprising. But you are wrong in your theory of the development of the Angiospermae from *Cycadeoidea dacotensis. Ja*—all wrong—"

I was interrupting him with considerable heat, for my conclusions from the fossil *Cycadeoidea* I knew to be my greatest triumph, when Larry broke in upon me rudely.

"Say," he sputtered, "am I crazy or are you? What in damnation kind of a place and time is this to start an argument like that? What's up to us is to fix Olaf here, get his wife back to him, and find a way to get out ourselves.

"Angiospermae, is it?" exclaimed Larry. "*Hell!*"

Von Hetzdorp again regarded him with that irritating air of benevolence.

"You have not the scientific mind, young friend," he said. "The poonch, yes! But so has the mule. You must learn that only the fact is important—not you, not me, not this"—he pointed to Huldricksson—"or its sorrows. Only the fact, whatever it is, is real, yes. But"—he turned to me—"another time—"

Huldricksson interrupted him. The big seaman had risen stiffly to his feet and stood with Larry's arm supporting him. He stretched out his hands to me.

"I saw her," he whispered. "I saw mine Freda when the stone swung. She lay there—just at my feet. I picked her up and I saw that mine Freda was dead. But I hoped—and I thought maybe mine Helma was somewhere here, too. So I ran with mine *Yndling*—here—" His voice broke. "I thought maybe she was not dead," he went on. "And I saw that"—he pointed to the Moon Pool—"and I thought I would bathe her face and she might live again. And when I dipped my hands within—the life left them, and cold, deadly cold, ran up through them into my heart. And mine Freda—she fell—" he covered his eyes, and dropping his head on O'Keefe's shoulder, stood, racked by sobs that seemed to tear at his very soul.

CHAPTER VIII

THE FLAME-TIPPED SHADOWS

VON HETZDORP NODDED his head solemnly as Olaf finished.

"*Ja!*" he said. "That which comes from here took them both—the woman and the child. *Ja!* They came clasped within it and the stone shut upon them. But why it left the child behind I do not understand."

Larry was watching him, in his eyes incredulous indignation and amazement.

"You, too, try to tell me that *something* carried a woman and a child from a ship hundreds of miles away, through the air over the seas to here?" he cried, an edge of contempt in his voice. "*Something* that Dr. Goodwin has said is made of—moonshine—carried a strong woman and a child. How da you know?"

"Because I saw it," answered Von Hetzdorp simply. "Not only did I see it, but hardly had I time to make escape through the entrance before it passed whirling and murmuring and its bell sounds all joyous. *Ja!* It was what you call the squeak close, that."

"Wait a moment," I said—stilling Larry with a gesture. "Do I understand you to say that you were *within* this place?"

Von Hetzdorp actually beamed upon me.

"*Ja*, Dr. Goodwin," he said, "I went in when that which comes from it went out!"

I gaped at him, stricken dumb; into Larry's bellicose attitude crept a suggestion of grudging respect; Olaf, trembling, watched silently.

"Dr. Goodwin and my impetuous young friend, you," went on Von Hetzdorp after a moment's silence—and I wondered vaguely why he did not include Huldricksson in his address—"it is time that we have an understanding. I have a proposition to make to you, also. It is this; we are what you call a bad boat, and all of us are in it. *Ja!* Also in this troublous water we find ourself we need all hands, is it not so? Let us put together our knowledge and our brains and resources—and even a poonch of a mule is a resource," he looked wickedly at O'Keefe, "and pull our boat into quiet waters again. After that—"

"All very well, Von Hetzdorp," interjected Larry angrily; "but I don't feel very safe in any boat with somebody capable of shooting me through the back."

Von Hetzdorp waved a deprecating hand.

"It was natural," he said, "logical, yes. Here is a very great secret, perhaps many secrets to Germany invaluable. You are an enemy of Germany, although why as an Irishman you should be I do not know—" He watched the flush of anger in Larry's face with interest, shook his head and turned to me. "And here, too, is Dr. Goodwin, a Yankee and an enemy. And besides, am I not a scientist, and do I like to see the fruits of my labors taken from me? *Nein!* Dr. Goodwin understands, do you not?"

"I don't understand how anything could justify you in shooting us down from ambush," I replied hotly.

"No?" he said, almost sadly. "And yet that was nothing, nothing, weighed with the possible results. *Ach,*" he sighed, "the point of view of these outlanders! They cannot understand!" He seemed lost in perplexity at our indignation; then resumed: "But it is not important! Let us forget that now and face our situation. My proposal is this: that we join interests, and what you call, see it through together; find our way through this place and learn those secrets of which I have spoken. And when that is done we will go our ways, each to his own land, to make use of them as we may. On my part I offer my knowledge—and it is very valuable, Dr. Goodwin—and my training. You and Lieutenant O'Keefe do the same, and this man Olaf, what he can of his strength, for I do not think his usefulness lies in his brains, *nein.*"

I considered—but after all, what else was there to do? The

*There trembled before us for a moment a faintly luminous
shadow which held, here and there, tiny sparking atoms!*

German was undoubtedly a man of resource and courage, and,
as he said, possessed of special information regarding the phenomena I had come to seek, for this his remarks concerning
the lighting of the corridor and his treatment of Olaf's arms

had plainly shown. What good would there be in—disposing of him? But how much could he be trusted? Larry echoed my thoughts:

"In effect, Goodwin, the professor's proposition is this," he said: "He wants to know what it is that's going on here, and he knows he can't do it by himself. Also he knows we have the drop on him. We're three to his one, and we have all his hardware and cutlery. We could throw him down the Pool if we wanted to, or tie him up and leave him. I haven't the slightest doubt that if he saw a way to do it and to get away with it, he'd do all of that to us. But in the mean time we can do better *with* him than without him—just as *he* can do better *with* us than without us. It is an even break. If you say so, all right. I'll guarantee to watch the professor here for any little German manifestations such as he showed outside."

There was almost a twinkle in Von Hetzdorp's eyes. As Larry ended he bowed.

"It is not just as I would have put it, perhaps," he said, "but in its skeleton he was right. Nor will I turn my hand against you while we are still in danger here. I pledge you my honor on this!" He drew himself up rigidly.

I glanced at Larry half doubtfully and back at the German. Then I thrust out a hand to him. He gripped it, dropped it, and thrust his to Larry. The Irishman hesitated, then with a laugh, took it.

"But I'll just keep the guns, professor," he said. Von Hetzdorp bowed again.

"Now," he said, "to prove my good faith I will tell you what I know. Something I knew of what was occurring here before I was sent"—he corrected himself hurriedly—"before I came. I found the secret of the door mechanism even as you did, Dr. Goodwin. But by carelessness, my condensers were broken. I was forced to wait while I sent for others—and the waiting might be for months. I took certain precautions, and on the first night of this full moon I hid myself within the vault of

Chau-ta-leur. There is"—he hesitated—"there is a something there also which I do not quite understand that—protects. But I did not know this when I first hid myself, *nein!* All I thought was that I could see from there and perhaps come through."

An involuntary thrill of respect for the man went through me at the manifest heroism of this leap in the dark. I could see it reflected in Larry's face.

"I hid in the vault," continued Von Hetzdorp, "and I saw that which comes from here come out. You are," he turned to me, "familiar with its appearance?" I nodded. "But how you learned—well, of that later. I saw, I say, *it* come out. I waited—long hours. At last, when the moon was low, I saw it return—ecstatically—with a man, a native, in embrace enfolded. It passed through the door, and soon then the moon became low and the door closed. I had found it difficult—and had it not been for—whatever it is of protection there in the vault—" He hesitated again, perplexedly.

"The next night," he went on, "more confidence was mine, yes. And after that which comes had gone, I looked through its open door. I said, 'It will not return for three hours. While it is away, why shall I not into its home go through the door it has left open?' So I went—even to here. I looked at the pillars of light and I tested the liquid of the Pool on which they fell, and what I found led me to believe the shape of light emerged from there." I started. Evidently then, he did not *know* just how the Dweller materialized from the Pool. He saw my movement and interpreted it correctly.

"You know how it comes?" he asked eagerly.

"Yes," I answered, "later I will tell you."

"I analyzed that liquid," he went on, "and then I knew I had been right in one phase at least of my theory. That liquid, Dr. Goodwin, is not water, and it is not any fluid known on earth." He handed me a small vial, its neck held in a long thong.

"Take this," he said, "and see."

Wonderingly, I took the bottle; dipped it down into the Pool.

The liquid was extraordinarily light; seemed, in fact, to give the vial buoyancy. I held it to the light. It was striated, streaked, as though little living, pulsing veins ran through it. And its blueness even in the vial, held an intensity of luminousness.

"Radioactive," said Von Hetzdorp. "Some liquid that is intensely radioactive; but what it is I know not at all. Upon the living skin it acts like radium raised to the nth power and with an element most mysterious added. The solution with which I treated him," he pointed to Huldricksson, "I had prepared before I came here, from information I had of what I might find. It is largely salts of radium, and its base is Loeb's formula for the neutralization of radium and X-ray burns. Taking this man at once, before the degeneration had become really active, I could negative it. But after two hours I could have done nothing." He paused a moment.

"Next I studied the nature of these luminous walls. I concluded that whoever had made them, knew the secret of the Almighty's manufacture of light from the ether itself. Colossal! *Ja!* But the substance of these blocks confines an atomic—how would you say—atomic manipulation, a conscious arrangement of electrons, light-emitting, and perhaps indefinitely so. These blocks are lamps in which oil and wick are—electrons drawing light waves from ether itself! A Prometheus, indeed, this discoverer! *Hein?* Hardly had I concluded these investigations before my watch warned me to go. I went. That which comes forth returned—this time empty-handed.

"And the next night I did the same thing. Engrossed in research, I let the moments go by to the clanger point, and Scarcely was I replaced within the vault when the shining thing raced over the walls, and in its grip the woman and child—

"Then you came—and that is all. And now—what is it you know?"

Very briefly I went over my story. His eyes gleamed now and then, but he did not interrupt me.

"A great secret! A colossal secret!" he said at last. "We cannot leave it hidden."

"The first thing to do is to try the door," said Larry, matter of fact.

"There is no use, my young friend," said Von Hetzdorp mildly.

"Nevertheless we'll try," said Larry. We retraced our way through the winding tunnel to the end, but soon even O'Keefe saw that any idea of moving the slab from within was hopeless. We returned to the Chamber of the Pool. The pillars of light were fainter, and we knew that the moon was sinking. On the world outside before long dawn would be breaking. I began to feel thirst—and the blue semblance of water within the silvery rim seemed to glint mockingly as my eyes rested on it.

"*Ja!*" said Von Hetzdorp, reading my thoughts uncannily. "*Ja!* We will be thirsty. And it will be very bad for him of us who loses control and drinks of that, my friend. *Ja!*"

Larry threw back his shoulders as though shaking a burden from them.

"This place would give an angel of joy the willies," he said. "And you two with your damned scientific superstitions would drive a prohibitionist from a trough of grape juice to a vat of rye! We're four able-bodied men up against a bunch of moonshine and a lot of dead ones. Buck up, for God's sake!"

"Do you suggest that we poonch our way out?" asked Von Hetzdorp mildly.

"Forget it, professor," answered Larry almost testily. "If I can forget that bullet of yours that came within an inch of clicking me, you can forget that smash of mine. I suggest that we look around this place and find something that will take us somewhere. You can bet the people that built it had more ways of getting in than that once-a-month family entrance. Doc, you and Olaf take the left wall; the professor and I will take the right."

He loosened one of his automatics with a suggestive movement.

"After you, professor," he said politely. And I knew that

despite the German's apparent frankness and docility he did not trust him.

Nor did I. And how much did Von Hetzdorp really know, I wondered, as the Norseman and I started off. Clearly more than he had told us; and from whence had come the information that had been detailed enough to enable him to prepare an antidote for the exact effects the touch of the Moon Pool produced? So, wondering, I walked with Olaf—and then soon forgot my perplexity in the contemplation of that greater wonder which I was observing.

The chamber widened out from the portal in what seemed to be the arc of an immense circle. The shining walls held a perceptible curve, and from this curvature I estimated that the roof was fully three hundred feet above us. It occurred to me that perhaps the Chamber of the Pool was shaped like half a hollow sphere—an inverted bowl—and as we silently passed on, I was confirmed in this belief, for clearly we were circling. If I were right, the circumference of the place, reckoning the radius at three hundred feet, must be one thousand eight hundred feet—or a little less than a third of a mile.

The floor was of smooth, mosaic-fitted blocks of a faintly yellow tinge. They were not light-emitting like the blocks that formed the walls. The radiance from these latter, I noted, had the peculiar quality of *thickening* a few yards from its source, and it was this that produced the effect of misty, veiled distances. As we walked, the seven columns of rays streaming down from the crystalline globes high above us waned steadily; the glow within the chamber lost its prismatic shimmer and became an even gray tone somewhat like moonlight in a thin cloud.

Now before us, out from the wall, jutted a low terrace. It was all of a pearly rose-colored stone, and above it, like a balustrade, marched a row of slender, graceful pillars of the same hue. The face of the terrace was about ten feet high, and all over it ran a bas-relief of what looked like short-trailing vines, surmounted by five stalks, on the tip of each of which was a flower. Behind the vines ran a design of semiglobes from which branched delicate tendrils. I did not recognize the carved flowers; they were, I thought, some symbolization in which the true form of the original had been lost.

How then could I have known the incredible thing which these stones pictured!

We passed along the terrace. It turned in an abrupt curve. I heard a hail, and there, fifty feet away, at the curving end of a wall identical with that where we stood, were Larry and Von Hetzdorp. Obviously the left side of the chamber was a duplicate of that we had explored. We joined. In front of us the columned barriers ran back a hundred feet, forming an alcove. The end of this alcove was another wall of the same rose stone, but upon it the design of vines was much heavier.

We took a step forward, and then stopped, every muscle rigid. There was a gasp of terrified awe from the Norseman, a guttural exclamation from Von Hetzdorp. For on, or rather within, the wall before us, a great oval began to glow, waxed almost to a flame, and then shone steadily out as though from behind it a light was streaming through the stone itself!

And within the roseate oval two flame-tipped shadows appeared, stood for a moment, and then seemed to float out upon its surface. The shadows wavered; the tips of flame that nimbused them with flickering points of violet and vermilion pulsed outward, drew back, darted forth again, and once more withdrew themselves—and as they did so the shadows thickened—and suddenly there before us stood two figures!

One was a girl—a girl whose great eyes were golden as the fabled lilies of Kwan-Yung that were born of the kiss of the sun upon the amber goddess the demons of Lao-Tz'e carved for him; whose softly curved lips were red as the royal coral, and whose golden-brown hair reached to her knees!

And the second was a gigantic frog—a woman frog, head helmeted with carapace of shell around which a fillet of brilliant yellow jewels shone; enormous round eyes of blue circled with a broad iris of green; monstrous body of banded orange and white girdled with strand upon strand of the flashing yellow gems; six feet high if an inch, and with one webbed paw of its short, powerfully muscled forelegs resting upon the white shoulder of the golden-eyed girl!

CHAPTER IX

"I'D FOLLOW HER THROUGH HELL!"

MOMENTS MUST HAVE passed as we stood in stark amazement, gazing at that incredible apparition. The two figures, although as real as any of those who stood beside me, unfantomlike as it is possible to be, had a distinct suggestion of—projection.

They were there before us—golden-eyed girl and grotesque frog-woman—complete in every line and curve; and still it was as though their bodies passed back through distances; as though, to try to express the well-nigh inexpressible, the two shapes we were looking upon were the end of an infinite number stretching in fine linked chain far away, of which the eyes saw only the nearest, while in the brain some faculty higher than sight recognized and registered the unseen others.

It crossed my mind that so we three-dimensional beings might appear to those dwellers in the hypothetical two-dimensional space we use to help us conceive the fourth dimension. And yet there was nothing of any metaphysical fourth dimension about them; they were actualities—real, breathing, complete.

The gigantic eyes of the frog-woman took us all in—unwinkingly. I could see little glints of phosphorescence shine out within the metallic green of the outer iris ring. She stood upright, her great legs bowed; the monstrous slit of a mouth slightly open, revealing a row of white teeth sharp and pointed as lancets; the paw resting on the girl's shoulder, half covering its silken surface, and from its five webbed digits long yellow claws of polished horn glistening against the delicate texture of the flesh.

But if the frog-woman regarded us all, not so did the maiden of the rosy wall. Her eyes were fastened upon Larry, drinking him in with extraordinary intentness. She was tall, far over the average of woman, almost as tall, indeed, as O'Keefe himself; not more than twenty years old, if that, I thought. Abruptly she leaned forward, the golden eyes softened and grew tender; the red lips moved as though she were speaking.

Larry took a quick step, and his face was that of one who after countless births comes at last upon the twin soul lost to him for ages. The frog-woman turned her eyes upon the girl; her huge lips moved, and I knew that she was talking! The girl held out a warning hand to O'Keefe, and then raised it, resting each finger upon one of the five flowers of the carved vine close beside her. Once, twice, three times, she pressed upon the flower centers, and I noted that her hand was curiously long and slender, the digits like those wonderful tapering ones the painters we call the primitives gave to their virgins.

Three times she pressed the flowers, and then looked intently at Larry once more. A slow, sweet smile curved the crimson lips. She stretched both hands out toward him again eagerly; and then I distinctly saw a burning blush rise swiftly over white breasts and flowerlike face.

And in that instant, like the clicking out of a cinematograph, the pulsing oval faded and golden-eyed girl and frog-woman were gone!

And thus it was that Lakla, the handmaiden of the Silent Ones, and Larry O'Keefe first looked into each other's hearts!

With their evanishment a spell was lifted from us. Olaf Huldricksson ran a hand over a brow from which tiny beads of sweat had sprung; Von Hetzdorp turned to me with an exclamation; Larry stood rapt, gazing at the stone.

"Eilidh," I heard him whisper, "Eilidh of the lips like the red, red rowan and the golden-brown hair!"

"Clearly of the Ranadae," said Von Hetzdorp, "a development of the fossil Labyrinthodonts; you saw her teeth, *ja?*"

"Ranadae, yes," I answered. "But from the Stegocephalia; of the order Ecaudata—"

"Upon what evidence do you base your theory that she was of the Stego—"

I think I never heard such complete indignation as was in O'Keefe's voice as he interrupted the German.

"What do you mean—fossils and Stego whatever it is?" he asked. "She was a girl, a wonder girl—a real girl, and Irish, or I'm not an O'Keefe!"

"We were talking about the frog-woman, Larry," I said, conciliatingly.

His eyes were wild as he regarded us.

"Say," he said, "if you two had been in the Garden of Eden when Eve took the apple, you wouldn't have had time to give her a look for counting the scales on the snake!"

"But I took especial note of the girl, too, Larry," I pleaded mildly, "and she couldn't have been Irish. Now how could she?"

"Couldn't, eh?" he said. "But she was. Didn't you notice the sweet little tilted nose of her, an' the hair an' the eyes like the sunshine? She's a daughter of the old people, of the Taitha-da-Dainn. I'm thinkin' that's who it was, anyway, that made this place on their way to Erin. Not Irish? A girl like that couldn't be anything else!"

He strode swiftly over to the wall. We followed. He sounded the stone. It did not ring hollowly—nor indeed had I expected it to, for the figures had shadowed themselves *through* the terrace, and had stood upon its surface. Larry paused, stretched his hand up to the flowers on which the tapering fingers of the golden-eyed girl had rested.

"It was here she put up her hand," he murmured. He pressed caressingly the carved calyxes, once, twice, a third time even as she had—and silently and softly the wall began to split; on each side a great stone pivoted slowly, and before us a portal stood,

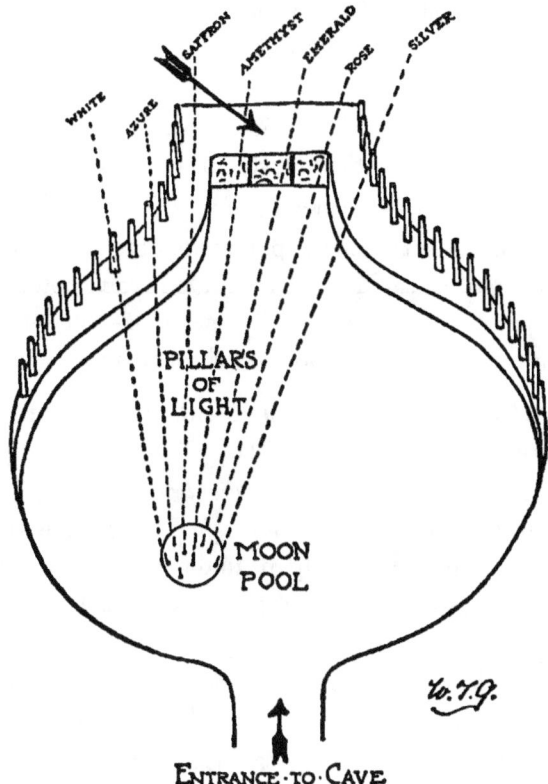

*Dr. Goodwin's diagrammatic sketch of the Moon Pool
Chamber showing the color arrangement and approximate
position of the seven pillars of light. The arrow points
to the wall through which the expedition passed down
into the caverns, and upon which the mysterious forms of
the golden-eyed girl and the frog-woman appeared.*

opening into a narrow corridor glowing with the same rosy
luster that had gleamed around the flame-tipped shadows!

O'Keefe leaped forward. I caught him by the arm. The far
wall of the tunnel that had been revealed was not more than
eight feet from where we were, and it ran, apparently, at right
angles to the entrance. There was little of it to be seen, therefore,
save the space just in front of us—and I will confess that my
nerves were slightly shaken.

"What's the matter?" he asked.

"Wait," I answered. "Don't rush in there. Let us go together and carefully."

"Come, then, quickly," he said, curiously distrait. "I won't wait. I must follow. That's what she meant, you know."

"What she meant?" I echoed stupidly.

"What she meant when she pointed out the way to open the wall, of course," he said impatiently. "Don't you know that was why she pressed those flowers? She meant us—me—to follow her. Follow her? God, I'd follow her through a thousand hells!"

HULDRICKSSON STEPPED beside him. He set a great hand upon the Irishman's shoulder.

"Ja!" he rumbled. "That was no *Troldkvinde,* no black witch, that *Jomfru!* She was a white virgin, *ja.* Well I know that this is Trolldom—but she will help me find my Helma! You go, and Olaf Huldricksson's arm you have with you—always; *ja,* ready to hold or to strike. Come!"

His hand fell from Larry's shoulder and gripped the Irishman's own. I reached down and picked up my emergency kit.

"Have your gun ready, Olaf!" said Larry. With Huldricksson at one end, O'Keefe at the other, both of them with automatics in hand, and Von Hetzdorp and I between them, we stepped over the threshold.

At our right, a few feet away, the passage ended abruptly in a square of polished stone, from which came the faint rose radiance of what Von Hetzdorp had called the "etheric lights." The roof of the place was less than two feet over O'Keefe's head. Behind us was the portal leading into the Chamber of the Pool.

We turned to the left to look down the tunnel's length—and each of us stiffened. A yard in front of us lifted a four-foot high, gently curved barricade, stretching from wall to wall—and beyond it was blackness; an utter and appalling blackness that seemed to gather itself from infinite depths and to be thrust back by the low barrier as a dike thrusts back the menacing sea threatening ever to overwhelm it. The rose-glow in which we stood was cut off by that blackness as though it had substance; it shimmered out to meet it, and was checked as though by a blow; indeed, so strong was the suggestion of sinister, straining force within the rayless opacity that I shrank back, and Von Hetzdorp with me. Not so O'Keefe. Olaf beside him, he strode to the wall and peered over. He beckoned us.

"Flash your pocket-light down there," he said to me, pointing into the thick darkness below us. The little electric circle quivered down as though afraid, and came to rest upon a surface that resembled nothing so much as clear, black ice. I ran the light across—here and there. The floor of the corridor was of stone, so smooth, so polished, that no man could have walked upon it; it sloped downward at a slowly increasing angle.

"We'd have to have non-skid chains and brakes on our feet to tackle that," mused Larry. Abstractedly he ran his hands over the edge on which he was leaning. Suddenly they hesitated and then gripped tightly.

"That's a queer one!" he exclaimed. His right palm was resting upon a rounded protuberance, on the side of which were three small circular indentations.

"A queer one—" he repeated—and pressed his fingers upon the circles. They gave under the pressure much, I thought, as an automatic punch does. O'Keefe's thrusting fingers sank deep, deeper, within the stone—

There was a sharp click; the slabs that had opened to let us through swung swiftly together; a curiously rapid vibration thrilled through us, a wind arose and passed over our heads—a wind that grew and grew until it became a whistling shriek, then a roar and then a mighty humming, to which every atom in our bodies pulsed in rhythm painful almost to disintegration!

The rosy wall dwindled in a flash to a point of light and disappeared!

Wrapped in the clinging, impenetrable blackness we were racing, dropping, hurling at a frightful speed—where?

And ever that awful humming of the rushing wind and the

lightning cleaving of the tangible dark—so, it came to me oddly, must the newly released soul race through the sheer blackness of outer space up to that Throne of Justice, where God sits high above all suns!

I felt Von Hetzdorp creep close to me; gripped my nerve and flashed my pocket-light; saw Larry standing, peering, peering ahead, and Huldricksson, one strong arm around his shoulders, bracing him. And then the speed began to slacken.

Millions of miles, it seemed, below the sound of the unearthly hurricane I heard Larry's voice, thin and ghostlike, beneath its clamor.

"Got it!" shrilled the voice. "Got it! Don't worry!"

The wind died down to the roar, passed back into the whistling shriek and diminished to a steady whisper. In the comparative quiet O'Keefe's tones now came in normal volume.

"Some little shoot-the-chutes, what?" he shouted. "Say—if they had this at Coney Island or the Crystal Palace! Press all the way in these holes and she goes top-high. Diminish pressure—diminish speed. The curve of this—dashboard—here sends the wind shooting up over our heads—like a wind-shield. What's behind you?"

I flashed the light back. The mechanism on which we were ended in another wall exactly similar to that over which O'Keefe crouched.

"Well, we can't fall out, anyway," he laughed. "Wish to hell I knew where the brakes were! Look out!"

We dropped dizzily down an abrupt, seemingly endless slope; fell—fell as into an abyss—then shot abruptly out of the blackness into a throbbing green radiance. O'Keefe's fingers must have pressed down upon the controls, for we leaped forward almost with the speed of light. I caught a glimpse of luminous immensities, on the verge of which we flew; of depths inconceivable, and flitting through the incredible spaces—gigantic shadows as of the wings of Israfel, which, are so wide, say the Arabs, the world can cower under them like a nestling—and then—again the dreadful blackness!

"What was that?" This from Larry, with the nearest approach to awe that I had yet heard from him he had yet shown.

"Trolldom!" croaked the voice of Olaf.

"*Gott!*" This from Von Hetzdorp. "What a space!

"Have you considered, Dr. Goodwin," he went on after a pause, "a curious thing? We know, or, at least, is it not that nine out of ten astronomers believe, that the moon was hurled out of this same region we now call the Pacific when the earth was yet like molasses; almost molten, I should say. And is it not curious that that which comes from the moon chamber needs the moon-rays to bring it forth; is it not? And is it not significant again that the stone depends upon the moon for operating? *Ja!* And last—such a space in mother earth as we just glimpsed, how else could it have been torn but by some gigantic birth—like that of the moon? *Hein!* I do not put forward these as statements of fact—no! But as suggestions—"

I started; there was so much that this might explain—an unknown element that responded to the moon-rays in opening the moon door; the blue Pool with its weird radioactivity, and the peculiar mystery within it that reacted to the same light stream—

"But if earth was then viscid, as it must have been, the scar would have closed without leaving trace; the torn sides have flowed together," I objected.

"All—but depending entirely upon how viscid, how fluid it was," he answered.

I grasped his idea. It was not inconceivable that a film had drawn over the world wound, a film of earth-flesh which drew itself over that colossal abyss after our planet had borne its satellite—that world womb did not close when her shining child sprang forth—it was possible; and all that we know of earth depth is four miles of her eight thousand.

What is there at the heart of earth? What of that radiant unknown element upon the moon mount Tycho? What of that element unknown to us as part of earth which is seen only in

the corona of the sun at eclipse and that we call coronium? Yet
the earth is child of the sun as the moon is earth's daughter.
And what of that other unknown element we find glowing
green in the far-flung nebulae—green as that we have just
passed through—and that we call nebulium? Yet the sun is child
of the nebulae as the earth is child of the sun and the moon is
child of earth.

How did Mme. Curie find radium but by searching in earth
for that other once sun mystery called helium? And what
miracles are there in coronium and nebulium which, as the
child of nebula and sun, we inherit? Yes—and in Tycho's enigma
which came from earth heart? And we were flashing down to
earth heart. And what miracles were hidden in earth heart?

CHAPTER X

THE END OF THE JOURNEY

"SAY, DOC!" IT was Larry's voice flung back at me. "I was
thinking about that frog. I think it was her pet. Damn me if I
see any difference between a frog and a snake, and one of the
nicest women I ever knew had two pet pythons that followed
her around like kittens. Not such a devilish lot of choice between
a frog and a snake—except on the side of the frog? What?
Anyway, any pet that girl wants is hers, I don't care if it's a
leaping twelve-toed lobster or a whale-bodied scorpion. Get
me?"

By which I knew that our remarks upon the frog-woman
were still bothering O'Keefe.

"He thinks of foolish nothings like the foolish sailor!" grunted
Von Hetzdorp, acid contempt in his words. "What are their
women to—this?" He swept out a hand. "And yet"—his tone
held an edge of mockery—"the biological factor is not one to
be ignored." He raised his voice. "At least, O'Keefe, you will

have a friend at whatever court we go to—that was plain—and it will be useful to us, *ja,* if you press your luck!"

The mockery had intensified, and into it had crept a thickness—a throaty note of sinister suggestiveness unmistakable. O'Keefe turned as though cut by a whiplash. But—

"You can't help being boche, can you, von Hetzdorp?" was all he said.

The German laughed and was silent. And crystallizing clearly in my mind came a thought that was, in essence, formulation of my dislike for him. I had seen Throckmartin, my friend, in the embrace of the Dweller, and Von Hetzdorp had seen Huldricksson's wife and child in the same dread enfolding—but I knew that there was all the difference between our points of view of those tragedies that there is between that of one who interestedly observes the struggles of a fly in the clutch of a spider and that of another who helplessly and in agony watches a beloved battling with death.

It was the modern German mind—observant, careful, admirably analytical, and—inhuman; a point of view not to be helped either by the boche or by the world which he has so curiously and deliberately set apart from himself.

The car seemed to poise itself for an instant, and then again dipped itself, literally, down into sheer space; skimmed forward in what was clearly curved flight, rose as upon a sweeping upgrade—and then began swiftly to slacken its fearful speed. I glanced at the illuminated dial of the watch on my wrist. It had been exactly twelve minutes since we had seen the roseate door fade into the blackness. But how far had we gone in those twelve minutes—scores of miles or hundreds of miles—there was no knowing.

Far ahead a point of light showed; grew steadily; we were within it—and softly all movement ceased. How acute had been the strain of our journey I did not realize until I tried to stand—and sank back, leg-muscles too shaky to bear my weight.* The

---

* It was then I noted that the car, for so I must call it, that had brought us to this

car rested in a slit in the center of a smooth walled chamber perhaps twenty feet square. The wall facing us was pierced by a low doorway through which we could see a flight of steps leading downward.

I glanced upward. The light streamed through an enormous oval opening, the base of which was twice a tall man's height from the floor. A curving flight of broad, low steps led up to it. And now it came to my steadying brain that there was something puzzling, peculiar, strangely unfamiliar about this light. It was silvery, shaded faintly with a delicate blue and flushed lightly with a nacreous rose; but a rose that differed from that of the terraces of the Pool Chamber as the rose within the opal differs from that within the pearl. In it were tiny, gleaming points like the motes in a sunbeam, but sparkling white like the dust of diamonds, and with a quality of vibrant vitality; they were as though they were alive. The light cast no shadows!

A little breeze came through the oval and played about us. It was laden with what seemed the mingled breath of spice flowers and pines. It was curiously vivifying, and in it the diamonded atoms of the light shook and danced.

Something flashed within the opening—fluttered and came to rest. A bird stood there regarding us; a bird as large as a pheasant, whose golden eyes were the color of the eyes of the maid of the rosy wall, and whose body was a floating, shimmering cloud of moonlight plumes as fairylike as those that veil the gigantic silver moths which guard, the fellahs say, the

---

place was shaped somewhat like one of the Thames punts. Its back must have fitted with the utmost nicety into the end of the passage upon which the inner doors of the Moon Pool Chamber had opened, for certainly when we stepped within it there had been no sign that it was other than part of the wall itself. But what, then, had happened to kill its radiance; to blot out the etheric lights set deep in its substance? And whence had come the two sides that linked it with the curved frontal barrier; where was its guiding mechanism? As to the latter, I remembered the *click* that had followed O'Keefe's pressure upon the little circles, and I could only conjecture that as the car moved away from the entrance these were slabs that slipped ingeniously into place, protecting those within from what would have been instant annihilating contact with the tunnel walls when the car ran close to them, or from pitching out when it skirted in the blackness, abysses such as that luminous green space that had sent each of our souls shivering back in awe.

secret shrine of Isis in the desert beyond the second cataract, and whose touch brings madness.

For a moment it looked at us, then slowly floated like a little shining cloud through the doorway. From without came a sudden sweet chiming as of tiny golden bells.

O'Keefe leaped over the low parapet to the floor; sprang to the portal; peered down.

"She sent that!" he said with conviction, turning to me. "She sent it to show the way!"

I caught a faint sardonic grin from Von Hetzdorp, stepped out of the car, the German following, and began to ascend the curved steps toward the oval opening, at the top of which O'Keefe and Olaf already stood. As they looked out I saw both their faces change—Olaf's with awe, O'Keefe's with half in-credulous amazement. I hurried to their side.

At first all that I could see was space—a space filled with the same coruscating effulgence that pulsed about me. I glanced upward, obeying that instinctive impulse of earth folk that bids them seek within the sky for sources of light. There was no sky—at least no sky such as we know—all was a sparkling nebulosity rising into infinite distances as the azure above the day-world seems to fill all the heavens—through it ran pulsing waves and flashing javelin rays that were like shining shadows of the aurora; echoes, octaves lower, of those brilliant arpeggios and chords that play about the poles. My eyes fell beneath its splendor; I stared outward.

And now I saw, miles away, gigantic luminous cliffs spring-ing sheer from the limits of a lake whose waters were of milky opalescence. It was from these cliffs that the spangled radiance came, shimmering out from all their lustrous surfaces. To left and to right, as far as the eye could see, they stretched—and they vanished in the auroral nebulosity on high!

"Look at that!" exclaimed Larry. I followed his pointing finger. On the face of the shining wall, stretched between two colossal columns, hung an incredible veil; prismatic, gleaming with all the colors of the spectrum. It was like a web of rainbows woven by the ringers of the daughters of the Jinni. In front of it and a little at each side was a semicircular pier, or, better, a plaza of what appeared to be glistening, pale-yellow ivory. At each end of its half-circle clustered a few low-walled, rose-stone structures, each of them surmounted by a number of high, slender pinnacles.

"Of a hugeness, that!" It was Von Hetzdorp speaking. "Have you considered that those precipices must from eight to ten miles away be, Dr. Goodwin? And, if so, how great must that so strange, prismatic curtain that we see so clearly be, eh? What hands could carve those columns between which it hangs? It is in my mind that we will carry back with us many new things, Dr. Goodwin—if we carry back at all—" he concluded slowly.

We looked at each other, I think, a bit helplessly—and back again through the opening. We were standing, as I have said, at its base. The wall in which it was set was at least ten feet thick, and so, of course, all that we could see of that which was without were the distances that revealed themselves above the outer ledge of the oval.

"Let's take a look at what's under us," said Larry.

He crept out upon the ledge and peered down, the rest of us following. We stared in utter silence. A hundred yards beneath us stretched gardens that must have been like those of many-columned Iram, which the ancient Addite King had built for his pleasure ages before the deluge, and which Allah, so the Arab legend tells, took and hid from man, within the Sahara, beyond all hope of finding—jealous because they were more beautiful than his in paradise. Within them flowers and groves of laced, fernlike trees, pillared pavilions nestled.

The trunks of the trees were of emerald, of vermilion, and of azure-blue, and the blossoms, whose fragrance was borne to us, shone like jewels. The graceful pillars were tinted delicately. I noted that the pavilions were double—in a way, two-storied—and that they were oddly splotched with circles, with squares,

Weird—weird beyond all telling—was the
exquisite head floating there in the air.

and with oblongs of—opacity; noted too that over many this
opacity stretched like a roof; yet it did not seem material; rather
was it—impenetrable shadow!

Down through this city of gardens ran a broad, shining green thoroughfare, glistening like glass and spanned at regular intervals with graceful, arched bridges. The road flashed to a wide square, where rose, from a base of that same silvery stone that formed the lip of the Moon Pool, a Titanic tower of seven terraces; and along it flitted objects that bore a curious resemblance to the shell of the Nautilus. Within them were—human figures! And upon tree-bordered promenades on each side walked others!

Far to the right we caught the glint of another emerald paved road.

And between the two the gardens grew sweetly down to the hither side of that opalescent water across which were the radiant cliffs and the curtain of mystery.

Thus it was that we first saw the city of the Dweller; blessed and accursed as no place on earth, or under or above earth has ever been—or, that force willing which some call God, ever again shall be!

"*Gott!*" whispered Von Hetzdorp. "Incredible!"

"Trolldom!" gasped Olaf Huldricksson. "It is Trolldom!"

"Listen, Olaf!" said Larry O'Keefe. "Cut out that Trolldom stuff! There's no Trolldom, or fairies, outside Ireland. Get that! And this isn't Ireland! And, buck up, professor!" This to Von Hetzdorp. "What you see down there are people—*just plain people.* And wherever there's people is where *I* live. Get me?"

"There's no way in but in—and no way out but out," said O'Keefe. "And there's the stairway. Eggs are eggs no matter how they're cooked—and people are just people, fellow travelers, no matter what dish they are in," concluded Larry. "Come on!"

With the three of us close behind him, he marched toward the entrance through which the white bird had floated.

Was Throckmartin out there in that strange place, I wondered—Throckmartin and his bride, Stanton and Thora—and Olaf's wife? And how would we find them—in what state? Was the Dweller *not* malign? A weird, inexplicable messenger carrying those on whom it set its seal to some unearthly paradise? No—this I could not believe.

But, whatever it was, I had found the place I had aimed for. My quest, my atonement was partly finished. Somewhere here, certainly, I was convinced, was my lost friend and those he loved—and the mate of Olaf Huldricksson.

CHAPTER XI

YOLARA, PRIESTESS OF THE SHINING ONE

"YOU'D BETTER HAVE this handy, Doc," O'Keefe paused at the head of the stairway and handed me one of the automatics he had taken from Von Hetzdorp.

"Shall I not have one also?" rather anxiously asked the latter.

"When you need it you'll get it," answered O'Keefe. "I'll tell you frankly, though, professor, that you'll have to show me before I trust you with a gun. You shoot too straight—from cover."

The flash of anger in the German's eyes turned to a cold consideration.

"You say always just what is in your mind, Lieutenant O'Keefe," he mused. *"Ja*—that I shall remember!" Later I was to recall this odd observation—and Von Hetzdorp was to remember, indeed.

IN SINGLE file, O'Keefe at the head and Olaf bringing up the rear, we passed through the portal. Before us dropped a circular shaft, into which the light from the chamber of the oval streamed liquidly; set in its sides, the steps spiraled, and down them we went, cautiously. The stairway ended in a circular well; silent—with no trace of exit! The rounded stones joined each other evenly—hermetically. Carved on one of the slabs was one of the five flowered vines. I pressed my fingers upon the calyxes, even as Larry had within the moon chamber.

A crack—horizontal, four feet wide—appeared on the wall; widened, and as the sinking slab that made it dropped to the level of our eyes, we looked through a hundred-feet-long rift in the living rock! The stone fell steadily—and we saw that it was a Cyclopean wedge set within the slit of the passageway. It reached the level of our feet and stopped. At the far end of this tunnel, whose floor was the polished rock that had, a moment before, fitted hermetically into its roof, was a low, narrow, triangular opening through which light streamed.

"Nowhere to go but out!" grinned Larry. "And I'll bet Golden Eyes is waiting for us with a taxi!" He stepped forward. We followed, slipping, sliding, along the glassy surface; and I, for one, had a lively apprehension of what our fate would be should that enormous mass rise before we had emerged! We reached the end; crept out of the narrow triangle that was its exit.

We stood upon a wide ledge carpeted with a thick yellow moss. I looked behind—and clutched O'Keefe's arm. The door through which we had come had vanished! There was only a precipice of pale rock, on whose surfaces great patches of the amber moss hung; around whose base our ledge ran, and whose summits, if summits it had, were hidden, like the luminous cliffs, in the radiance above us.

"Nowhere to go but ahead—and Golden Eyes hasn't kept her date!" laughed O'Keefe—but somewhat grimly.

We looked down. At the left the green roadway curved, and, at least thirty feet below us, swept on. Far off to the right it swerved again and continued as the glistening distant ribbon we had seen from the high oval. Within its loop, like a peninsula, its foot bathed by the lake, lay the gardened city. What was beyond the road we could not see for, all along its outer side, it was banked with solid masses of high-flung verdure.

We walked a few yards along the ledge and, rounding a corner, faced the end of one of the slender bridges. From this vantage point the oddly shaped vehicles were plain, and we could see they were, indeed, like the shell of the Nautilus and elfinly beautiful. Their drivers sat high upon the forward whorl. Their bodies were piled high with cushions, upon which lay women half-swathed in gay silken webs. From the pavilioned gardens smaller channels of glistening green ran into the broad way, much as automobile runways do on earth; and in and out of them flashed the fairy shells.

There came a shout from one. Its occupants had glimpsed us. They pointed; others stopped and stared; one shell turned and sped up a runway—and quickly over the other side of the bridge came a score of men. They were dwarfed—none of them more than five feet high, prodigiously broad of shoulder, clearly enormously powerful.

"*Trolde!*" muttered Olaf, stepping beside O'Keefe, pistol swinging free in his hand.

But at the middle of the bridge the leader stopped, waved back his men, and came toward us alone, palms outstretched in the immemorial, universal gesture of truce. He paused, scanning us with manifest wonder; we returned the scrutiny with interest. The dwarf's face was as white as Olaf's—far whiter than those of the other three of us; the features clean-cut and noble, almost classical; the wide set eyes of a curious greenish gray and the black hair curling over his head like that on some old Greek statue.

Dwarfed though he was, there was no suggestion of deformity about him. The gigantic shoulders were covered with a loose green tunic that looked like fine linen. It was caught in at the waist by a broad girdle studded with what seemed to be amazonites. In it was thrust a long curved poniard resembling the Malaysian kris. His legs were swathed in the same green cloth as the upper garment. His feet were sandaled.

My gaze returned to his face, and in it I found something subtly disturbing; an expression of half-malicious gaiety that underlay the wholly prepossessing features like a vague threat;

a mocking deviltry that hinted at entire callousness to suffering or sorrow; something of the spirit that was vaguely alien and disquieting.

He spoke—and, to my surprise, enough of the words were familiar to enable me clearly to catch the meaning of the whole. They were Polynesian, the Polynesian of the Samoans which is its most ancient form, but in some indefinable way—archaic. Later I was to know that the tongue bore the same relation to the Polynesian of today as does not that of Chaucer, but of the Venerable Bede, to modern English. Nor was this to be so astonishing, when with the knowledge came the certainty that it was from it the language we call Polynesian sprang.*

"From whence do you come, strangers—and how found you your way here?" said the green dwarf.

I waved my hand toward the cliff behind us. His eyes narrowed incredulously; he glanced at its drop, upon which even a mountain goat could not have made its way, and laughed.

"We came through the rock," I answered his thought. "And we come in peace," I added.

"And may peace walk with you," he said half-derisively—"if the Shining One wills it!"

He considered us again.

"Show me, strangers, where you came through the rock," he

---

* When one considers that in the unchanging East, speech persists almost unaltered in its form for centuries, that its flux in comparison with that of Occidental races is almost nil, it can readily be seen that the time-space between their forms and those of the Polynesian we knew must have been fully as great as these people claimed for it. Max Muller, the great philologist, has asserted that in three hundred years the tongue of the Tahitians has changed in only six inflections, and has added to itself only sixty new words, of which fifty-three are corruptions of traders' tongues. I have a very fair knowledge of the Polynesian, acquired of necessity in my explorations; Huldricksson spoke it well, and understood it better than he spoke it; O'Keefe had a working smattering. At the moment of my surprise I was uncertain about Von Hetzdorp—later I was to find him a master of it. In all that follows, I spare my readers the variations of our speech due to our differing attainments. I also translate into our own language and its idioms much of the necessarily untranslatable words and images with which we had to deal. I abridge as well the conversations to that which alone seems essential to the complete understanding of my narrative.—W.T.G.

commanded. We led the way to where we had emerged from the well of the stairway.

"It was here," I said, tapping the cliff.

"But I see no opening," he said suavely.

"It closed behind us," I answered; and then, for the first time, realized how incredible the explanation sounded. The derisive gleam passed through his eyes again. But he drew his poniard and gravely sounded the rock.

"You give a strange turn to our speech," he said. "It sounds strangely, indeed—as strange as your answers." He looked at us quizzically. "I wonder where you learned it! Well, all that you can explain to the *Afyo Maie*." His head bowed and his arms swept out in a wide salaam, "Be pleased to come with me!" he ended abruptly.

"In peace?" I asked.

"In peace," he replied—then slowly—"with me, at least."

"Oh, come on, Doc!" cried Larry. "As long as we're here let's see the sights. *Allons mon vieux!*" he called gaily to the green dwarf. The latter, understanding the spirit, if not the words, looked at O'Keefe with a twinkle of approval; turned then to the great Norseman and scanned him with admiration; reached out and squeezed one of the immense biceps.

"Lugur will welcome *you*, at least," he murmured as though to himself. He stood aside and waved a hand courteously, inviting us to pass. We reached the bridge again; he spoke two words to his men, who immediately lined up on each side of the arch, watching us as we walked between them with that same suggestion of expectant, malicious derision that I found so disquieting in their leader. We crossed. At the base of the span one of the elfin shells was waiting.

"Free ride in the subway patrol," whispered O'Keefe, grinning.

Beyond, scores of the shells had gathered, their occupants evidently discussing us in much excitement. The green dwarf waved us to the piles of cushions and then threw himself beside us. The vehicle started off smoothly, the now silent throng making way, and swept down the green roadway at a terrific pace and wholly without vibration, toward the seven-terraced tower.

As we flew along I tried to discover the source of the power, but I could not—then. There was no sign of mechanism, but that the shell responded to some form of energy was certain— the driver grasping a small lever which seemed to control not only our speed, but our direction.

"If you could only substitute these for the New York taxi— eh, Doc?" said O'Keefe, clearly enjoying himself.

We turned abruptly and swept up a runway through one of the gardens, and stopped softly before a pillared pavilion. I saw now that these were much larger than I had thought. The structure to which we had been carried covered, I estimated, fully an acre. Oblong, with its slender, varicolored columns spaced regularly, its walls were like the sliding screens of the Japanese— *shoji*. I had little time to note them, nor, to my regret, to satisfy my very eager curiosity as to the character of the trees and the bowering blossoms.

The green dwarf hurried us up a flight of broad steps flanked by great carved serpents, winged and scaled. He stamped twice upon mosaicked stones between two of the pillars, and a screen rolled aside, revealing an immense hall, scattered about with low divans on which lolled a dozen or more of the dwarfish men, dressed identically as he.

They sauntered up to us leisurely; the surprised interest in their faces tempered by the same inhumanly gay malice that seemed to be characteristic of all these people we had as yet seen.

"The *Afyo Maie* awaits them, Rador," said one.

So the green dwarf's name was Rador.

He nodded, beckoned us, and led the way through the great hall and into a smaller chamber whose far side was covered with the opacity I had noted from the aerie of the cliff. I examined the—blackness—with lively interest.

It had neither substance nor texture; it was not matter—and yet it suggested solidity; an entire cessation, a complete absorption of light; an ebon veil at once immaterial and palpable. I stretched, involuntarily, my hand out toward it, and felt it quickly drawn back.

"Do you seek your end so soon?" whispered Rador. "But I forget—you do not know," he added. "On your life touch not the blackness, ever. It—"

He stopped, for abruptly in the density a portal appeared; springing out of the shadow like a picture thrown by a lantern upon a screen. Through it was revealed a chamber filled with a soft, rosy glow. Rising from cushioned couches, a woman and a man regarded us, half leaning over a long, low table of what seemed polished jet, laden with flowers and unfamiliar fruits.

About the room—that part of it, at least, that I could see—were a few oddly shaped chairs of the same substance. On high, silvery tripods three immense globes stood, and it was from them that the rose glow emanated. At the side of the woman stood a smaller globe whose roseate gleam was tempered by quivering waves of blue.

"Enter Rador with the strangers!" a clear, sweet voice called.

Rador bowed deeply and stood aside, motioning us to pass. We entered, the green dwarf behind us, and out of the corner of my eye I saw the doorway fade as abruptly as it had appeared and again the dense shadow fill its place.

"Come closer, strangers. Be not afraid!" commanded the bell-toned voice.

We approached.

The woman, unimaginative scientist that I am, made the breath catch in my throat. Never have I seen a woman so beautiful as was Yolara of the Dweller's city—and none of so perilous a beauty. Her hair was of the color of the young tassels of the corn and coiled in a regal crown above her broad, white brows; her wide eyes were of gray that could change to a cornflower blue and in anger deepen to purple; gray or blue, they had little laughing devils within them, but when the storm of anger darkened them—they were not laughing, no!

The silken webs that half covered, half revealed her did not hide the ivory whiteness of her flesh nor the sweet curve of shoulders and breasts. But for all her amazing beauty, she was— sinister! There was cruelty about the curving mouth, and in the music of her voice—not conscious cruelty, but the more ter- rifying, careless cruelty of nature itself. And she exhaled an essence of vitality that made the nerves tingle toward her and shrink from her, too, as though from something abnormal.

The girl of the rose wall had been beautiful, yes! But her beauty was human, understandable. You could imagine her with a babe in her arms—but you could not so imagine this woman. About her loveliness hovered something unearthly. A sweet, feminine echo of the Dweller was Yolara, the Dweller's priest- ess—and as gloriously, terrifyingly evil!

CHAPTER XII

THE JUSTICE OF LORA

AS I LOOKED at her the man arose and made his way round the table toward us. For the first time my eyes took in Lugur. A few inches taller than the green dwarf, he was far broader, more filled with the suggestion of appalling strength.

The tremendous shoulders were four feet wide if an inch, tapering down to mighty thewed thighs. The muscles of his chest stood out beneath his tunic of red. Around his forehead shone a chaplet of bright-blue stones, sparkling among the thick curls of his silver-ash hair.

Upon his face pride and ambition were written large—and power still larger. All the mockery, the malice, the hint of callous indifference that I had noted in the other dwarfish men were there, too—but intensified, touched with the satanic.

The woman spoke again.

"Who are you strangers, and how came you here?" She turned to Rador. "Or is it that they do not understand our tongue?"

"One understands and speaks it—but very badly, O Yolara," answered the green dwarf.

"Speak, then, that one of you," she commanded.

But it was Von Hetzdorp who found his voice first, and I marveled at the fluency, so much greater than mine, with which he spoke.

"We came for different purposes. I to seek knowledge of a kind; he"—pointing to me—"of another. This man"—he looked at Olaf—"to find a wife and child."

The gray-blue eyes had been regarding O'Keefe steadily and with plainly increasing interest.

"And why did *you* come?" she asked him. "Nay—I would have him speak for himself, if he can," she stilled Von Hetzdorp peremptorily.

When Larry spoke it was haltingly, in the tongue that was strange to him, searching for the proper words.

"I came to help these men—and because something I could not then understand called me, O lady whose eyes are like forest pools at dawn," he answered; and even in the unfamiliar words there was a touch of the Irish brogue, and little merry lights danced in the eyes Larry had so apostrophized.

"I could find fault with your speech, but none with its burden," she said. "What forest pools are I know not, and the dawn has not shone upon the people of Lora these many *sais of laya*. But I sense what you mean!"

The eyes deepened to blue as she regarded him. I saw Lugur shift impatiently and send a none too pleasant look at O'Keefe. She smiled.

"Are there many like you in the world from which you come?" she asked softly. "Well, we soon shall—"

Lugur interrupted her almost rudely and glowering.

"Best we should know how they came hence," he growled.

She darted a quick look at him, and again the little devils danced in her wondrous eyes.

"Yes, that is true," she said. "How came you here?"

Again it was Von Hetzdorp who answered—slowly, considering every word.

"In the world above," he said, "there are ruins of cities not built by any of those who now dwell there. To some of us above these places called, and we sought for knowledge of the wise ones who made them and of those wise ones passed on. We were seeking, and we found a passageway. The way led us downward to a door in yonder cliff, and through it we came here."

"Then have you found what you sought!" spoke she. "For we are of those who built the cities. But this gateway in the rock—where is it?"

"After we passed, it closed upon us; nor could we after find trace of it," answered Von Hetzdorp.

The incredulity that had shown upon the face of the green dwarf fell upon theirs; on Lugur's it was clouded with a furious anger.

He turned to Raclor.

"I could find no opening, lord," thus the green dwarf quickly.

And there was so fierce a fire in the eyes of Lugur as he swung back upon us that O'Keefe's hand slipped stealthily down toward his pistol.

"Best it is to speak truth to Yolara, priestess of the Shining One, and to Lugur, the Voice," he cried menacingly.

"It is the truth," I interposed. "We came down the passage. At its end was a carved vine, a vine of five flowers"—the fire died from the red dwarf's eyes, and I could have sworn to a swift pallor. "I rested a hand upon these flowers, and a door opened. But when we had gone through it and turned, behind us was nothing but unbroken cliff. The door had vanished."

I had taken my cue from Von Hetzdorp. If he had eliminated the episode of car and Moon Pool, he had good reason, I had no doubt; and I would be as cautious. And deep within me something cautioned me to say nothing of my quest; to stifle all thought of Throckmartin—something that warned, peremptorily, finally, as though it were a message from Throckmartin himself!

"A vine with five flowers!" exclaimed the red dwarf. "Was it like this, say?"

He thrust forward a long arm. Upon the thumb of the hand was an immense ring, set with a dull-blue stone. Graven on the face of the jewel was the symbol of the rosy walls of the Moon Chamber that had opened to us their two portals. But cut over the vine were seven circles, one about each of the flowers and two larger ones covering, intersecting them.

"This is the same," I said; "but these were not there"—I indicated the circles.

The woman drew a deep breath and looked deep into Lugur's eyes.

"The sign of the Silent Ones!" he half whispered.

It was the woman who first recovered herself.

"The strangers are weary, Lugur," she said. "When they are rested they shall show us where the rocks opened."

I sensed a subtle change in their attitude toward us; a new intentness; a doubt plainly tinged with apprehension. What was it they feared? I wondered; and why had the symbol of the vine wrought the change? And who or what were the Silent Ones?

Yolara's eyes turned to Olaf, hardened, and grew cold gray. Subconsciously I had noticed that from the first the Norseman had been absorbed in his regard of the pair; had indeed never taken his gaze from them; had noticed, too, the priestess dart swift glances toward him.

Upon Olaf's face had been an early look of puzzlement, of uncertainty. Now this had changed to decision; clearly he had made his mind up about something. His gaze was fixed; he returned the woman's scrutiny fearlessly, a touch of contempt in the clear eyes—like a child watching a snake which he did not dread, but whose danger he well knew.

Under that look Yolara stirred impatiently, sensing, I know, its meaning.

"Why do you look at me so?" she cried.

An expression of bewilderment passed over Olaf's face.

"I do not understand," he said in English.

I caught a quickly repressed gleam in O'Keefe's eyes. He knew, as I knew, that Olaf must have understood. But did Von Hetzdorp?

I glanced at him. Apparently he did not. But why was Olaf feigning this ignorance?

"This man is a sailor from what we call the North," thus Larry haltingly. "He is crazed, I think. He tells a strange tale— of a something of white fire that took his wife and babe. We found him wandering where we were. And because he is strong we brought him with us. That is all, O lady whose voice is sweeter than the honey of the wild bees!"

"A shape of white fire?" she repeated eagerly.

"A shape of white fire that whirled beneath the moon, with the sound of little bells," answered Larry, watching her intently.

She looked at Lugur and laughed.

"Then he, too, is fortunate," she said. "For he has come to the place of his something of white fire—and tell him that he shall join his wife and child, in time; that *I* promise him."

Upon the Norseman's face there was no hint of comprehension, and at that moment I formed an entirely new opinion of Olaf's intelligence; for certainly it must have been a prodigious effort of the will indeed that enabled him, understanding, to control himself

"What does she say?" he asked.

Larry repeated.

An expression of gladness spread over his face.

"Good!" said Olaf. "Good!"

He looked at Yolara with well-assumed gratitude. Lugur,

who had been scanning his bulk, drew close. He felt the giant muscles which Huldricksson accommodatingly flexed for him.

"But he shall meet Valdor and Tahola before he sees those kin of his," he laughed mockingly. "And if he bests them, he shall meet me. After that—for reward—his wife and babe!"

A shudder, quickly repressed, shook the seaman's frame. The woman bent her supremely beautiful head.

"These two," she said, pointing to the German and to me, "seem to be men of learning. They may be useful. As for this man"—she smiled at Larry—"I would have him explain to me some things." She hesitated. "What 'hon-ey of'e wild bees-s' is." Larry had spoken the words in English, and she was trying to repeat them. "As for this man, the sailor, do as you please with him, Lugur; always remembering that I have given my word that he shall join that wife and babe of his!" She laughed sweetly, sinisterly. "And now—take them, Rador—give them food and water and let them rest till we shall call them again."

She stretched out a hand toward O'Keefe. The Irishman bowed low over it, raised it softly to his lips. There was a vicious hiss from Lugur; but Yolara regarded Larry with eyes now all tender blue.

"You please me," she whispered.

And the face of Lugur grew dark with passion.

We turned to go. The rosy, azure-shot globe at her side suddenly dulled. From it came a faint bell sound as of chimes far away. She bent over it. It vibrated, and then its surface ran with little waves of dull color; from it came a whispering so low that I could not distinguish the words—if words they were.

She spoke to the red dwarf.

"They have brought the three who blasphemed the Shining One," she said slowly. "Now it is in my mind to show these strangers the justice of Lora—that, perhaps, they may learn wisdom from it. What say you, Lugur?"

The red dwarf nodded, his eyes sparkling now with a malicious anticipation.

The woman spoke again to the globe. "Bring them here!"

And again it ran swiftly with its film of colors, darkened, and shone rosy once more. From without there came the rustle of many feet upon the rugs. Yolara pressed a slender hand upon the base of the pedestal of the globe beside her. Abruptly the light faded from all, and on the same instant the four walls of blackness vanished, revealing on two sides the lovely, unfamiliar garden through the guarding rows of pillars; at our backs soft draperies hid what lay beyond; before us, flanked by flowered screens, was the corridor through which we had entered, crowded now by the green dwarfs of the great hall.

The dwarfs advanced. Each, I now noted, had the same clustering black hair of Rador. They separated, and from them stepped three figures—a youth of not more than twenty, short, but with the great shoulders of all the males we had seen of this race; a girl of seventeen, I judged, white-faced, a head taller than the boy, her long, black hair disheveled, and clad in a simple white sleeveless garment that fell only to the knees; and behind these two a stunted, gnarled shape whose head was sunk deep between the enormous shoulders, whose white beard fell like that of some ancient gnome down to his waist, and whose eyes were a white flame of hate. The girl cast herself weeping at the feet of the priestess; the youth regarded her curiously.

"You are Songar of the Lower Waters?" murmured Yolara almost caressingly. "And this is your daughter and her lover?"

The gnome nodded, the flame in his eyes leaping higher.

"It has come to me that you three have dared blaspheme the Shining One, its priestess, and its Voice," went on Yolara smoothly. "Also that you have called out to the three Silent Ones. Is it true?"

"Your spies have spoken—and have you not already judged us?" The voice of the old dwarf was bitter.

A flicker shot through the eyes of Yolara, again cold gray. The girl reached a trembling hand up to the hem of her veils. She thrust it aside with her foot cruelly.

"Tell us why you did these things, Songar," she asked. "Why you did them, knowing full well what your—reward—would be."

The dwarf stiffened; he raised his withered arms, and his eyes blazed.

"Because evil are your thoughts and evil are your deeds," he cried. "Yours and your lover's, there"—he leveled a finger at Lugur. "Because of the Shining One you have made evil, too, and the greater wickedness you contemplate—you and he with the Shining One. But I tell you that your measure of iniquity is full; the tale of your sin near ended! Yea—the Silent Ones have been patient, but soon they will speak." He pointed at us. "A sign are they—a warning—harlot!" He spat the word.

In Yolara's eyes, grown black, the devils leaped unrestrained.

"Is it even so, Songar?" her voice caressed. "Now ask the Silent Ones to help you! They sit afar—but surely they will hear you." The sweet voice was mocking. "As for these two, they shall pray to the Shining One for forgiveness—and surely the Shining One will take them to its bosom! As for you—you have lived long enough, Songar! Pray to the Silent Ones, Songar, and pass out into the nothingness—you!"

She dipped down into her bosom and drew forth something that resembled a small cone of tarnished silver. She leveled it, a covering clicked from its base, and out of it darted a slender ray of intense green light.

It struck the old dwarf squarely over the heart, and swift as light itself spread, covering him with a gleaming, pale film. She clenched her hand upon the cone, and the ray disappeared; thrust it back into her breast and leaned forward expectantly; so Lugur and so the other dwarfs. From the girl came a low wail of anguish; the boy dropped upon his knees, covering his face.

For the moment the white beard stood rigid; then the robe that had covered him seemed to melt away, revealing all the knotted, monstrous body. And in that body a vibration began, increasing to incredible rapidity. It wavered before us like a reflection in a still pond stirred by a sudden wind. It grew and grew—to a rhythm whose rapidity was intolerable to watch and that still chained the eyes.

The figure grew indistinct, misty. Tiny sparks in infinite numbers leaped from it—like, I thought, the radiant shower of particles hurled out by radium when seen under the microscope. Mistier still it grew—and then there trembled before us for a moment a faintly luminous shadow which held, here and there, tiny sparkling atoms like those that pulsed in the light about us! The glowing shadow vanished, the sparkling atoms were still for a moment—and then they shot away, joining those dancing others.

Where the gnomelike form had been but a few seconds before—there was nothing!

O'Keefe drew a long breath, and I was sensible of a prickling along my scalp.

Yolara leaned toward us.

"You have seen," she said. Her eyes lingered tigerishly upon Olaf's pallid face. "Heed!" she whispered. She turned to the men in green, who were laughing softly among themselves.

"Take these two, and go!" she commanded.

"The justice of Lora," said the red dwarf. "The justice of Lora and the Shining One under Thanaroa!"

Upon the utterance of the last word I saw Von Hetzdorp start violently. The hand at his side made a swift, surreptitious gesture, so fleeting that I hardly caught it. The red dwarf stared at the German, and for the first time I saw complete amazement upon his face.

He glanced at Yolara, found her intent in thought, and as swiftly as had been Von Hetzdorp's action, returned it. I thought I saw the latter make an answering sign.

"Yolara," the red dwarf spoke, "it would please me to take this man of wisdom to my own place for a time. The giant I would have, too."

The woman awoke from her brooding; nodded.

"As you will, Lugur," she said. She beckoned Rador.

As he led us out I saw from the corner of my eye Olaf following quietly the German and the red dwarf. And again I wondered.

And as, shaken to the core, we passed out into the garden into the full throbbing of the light, I wondered if all the tiny sparkling diamond points that shook about us had once been men like Songar of the Lower Waters—and felt my very soul grow sick!

CHAPTER XIII

THE ANGRY, WHISPERING GLOBE

OUR WAY LED along a winding path between banked masses of softly radiant blooms, groups of feathery ferns whose plumes were starred with fragrant white and blue flowerets, slender creepers swinging from the branches of the strangely trunked trees bearing along their threads orchidlike blossoms both delicately frail and gorgeously flamboyant. There was no single species that I could name; although here and there I noted a characteristic that seemed familiar. Either, I thought, the flora was indigenous, a product of the peculiar conditions of the place, or else it was the result of long ages of hybridization, cross-pollenization, manipulations of the germ plasm itself.*

---

* The ferns illustrate the observation perfectly. These pteridophytes showed in their flowers unmistakable characteristics of the phanerogams amazing to the botanist and destructive of certain universally accepted theories of botanical science. I was to find that they, like the fruits, were the results of centuries of cultivation. Equally upsetting of the dictum that the origin of the pteridophytes was certainly not of the bryophytes were my discoveries among the giant mosses in the caverned road to the Sea of Crimson in our flight to the Silent Ones. For these were clearly nature's own work in which man had never a hand. But enough of this. I do not think it advisable to burden the narrative, written for the layman, with matter intelligible only to the comparatively few experts in my field of research. I shall therefore confine myself in my story to

The path we trod was an exquisite mosaic—pastel greens and pinks upon a soft gray base, garlands of nimbused forms like the flaming rose of the Rosicrucians held in the mouths of the flying serpents. Here and there in the boskage I caught a glimpse of moving figures.

The green dwarf hummed a merry little air, curiously gay and haunting, as he marched along. Larry, though, was as silent as I, walking with head bent, glancing neither to right nor left. A smaller pavilion arose before us, single-storied, front wide open.

Upon its threshold Rador paused, bowed deeply, and motioned us within. The chamber we entered was large, closed on two sides by screens of gray; at the back gay, concealing curtains. The low table of blue stone, dressed with fine white cloths, stretched at one side flanked by the cushioned divans.

At the left was a high tripod bearing one of the rosy globes we had seen in the house of Yolara; at the head of the table a smaller globe similar to the whispering one. Rador pressed upon its base, and two other screens slid into place across the entrance, shutting in the room.

He clapped his hands; the curtains parted, and two girls came through them. Tall and willow lithe, their bluish-black hair "bobbed" and falling in ringlets just below their white shoulders, their clear eyes of forget-me-not blue, and skins of extraordinary fineness and purity—they were singularly attractive. Each was clad in an extremely scanty bodice of silken blue, girdled above a kittle that came barely to their very pretty knees.

O'Keefe's absorption dropped from him on the instant; the sparkle in his eyes telling plainly that these charming images had banished, for the moment at least, the memories of that weird evanishment beneath the green ray of the Dweller's priestess.

The maidens returned our stares with interest—and now I

---

general descriptions of the flora of Muria, reserving technical discussion of it for my lectures and the publications of the International Association of Science.

noted that the uncanny deviltry written so large upon the faces of the dwarfs, limned so delicately upon that of Yolara, was here but a shadow. Present it certainly was, but tinctured, underlaid, with a settled wistfulness almost melancholy.

They gave me, I must admit, only a slight share of their attention; Larry the most of it. But that was natural, after all. I lack nearly a foot of his height, my eyes are spectacled, and although not more than half a score years older than Larry, science, alas, is a jealous mistress who, unlike Bellona, contrives in subtle ways to make her priests and lovers not too strongly attractive to mortal sirens who might lure them from her.

Their wistfulness fled; they laughed with little gleams of milky teeth—the laughter of careless youth—and Larry laughed with them. The green dwarf regarded all with his malice-tipped smile.

"Food and drink," he ordered.

They dropped back through the curtains.

"Do you like them?" he asked us.

"Some chickens!" said Larry. "They delight the heart," he translated for Rador.

The green dwarf's next remark made me gasp.

"They are yours," he said.

Before I could question him further upon this extraordinary statement the pair re-entered, bearing a great platter on which were small loaves, strange fruits, and three immense flagons of rock crystal—two filled with a slightly sparkling yellow liquid and the third with a purplish drink. I became acutely sensible that it had been hours since I had either eaten or drank. The yellow flagons were set before Larry and me, the purple at Rador's hand.

The girls, at his signal, again withdrew. I raised my glass to my lips and took a deep draft. The taste was unfamiliar but delightful.

Almost at once my fatigue disappeared. I realized a clarity of mind, an interesting exhilaration and sense of irresponsibil-

"We have looked upon the strange blossoming orbs
that circle the sun ye call Arcturus...."

ity, of freedom from care, that were oddly enjoyable. Larry
became immediately his old gay self.

Still there did not seem to be any of the characteristics of
alcohol in the drink. The bread was excellent, tasting like fine

wheat. The fruits were as unfamiliar as the wine, and seemed to have the quality of making one forget any desire for either flesh or vegetables. The green dwarf regarded us whimsically, sipping from his great flagon of rock crystal.

"Much do I desire to know of that world you came from," he said at last—"through the rocks," he added mischievously.

"And much do we desire to know of this world of yours, O Rador," I answered.

Should I ask him of the Dweller; seek from him a clue to Throckmartin? Again, clearly as a spoken command, came the warning to forbear, to wait. And once more I obeyed.

"Let us learn, then, from each other." The dwarf was laughing. "And first—are all above like you—drawn out"—he made an expressive gesture—"and are there many of you?"

"There are—" I hesitated, and at last spoke the Polynesian that means tens upon tens multiplied indefinitely—"there are as many as the drops of water in the lake we saw from the ledge where you found us," I continued; "many as the leaves on the trees without. And they are all like unvaryingly."

He considered skeptically, I could see, my remark upon our numbers.

"In Muria," he said at last, "the men are like me or like Lugur. Our women are as you see them—like Yolara or like those black-haired two who served you." He hesitated. "And there is a third; but only one."

Larry leaned forward eagerly.

"Brown-haired with glints of ruddy bronze, golden eyed, and lovely as a dream, with long, slender, beautiful hands?" he cried.

"Where saw you *her?*" interrupted the dwarf, starting to his feet.

"Saw her?" Larry recovered himself. "Nay, Rador, perhaps I only dreamed that there was such a woman."

"See to it, then, that you tell not your dream to Yolara," said the dwarf grimly. "For her I meant and her you have pictured is Lakla, the handmaiden to the Silent Ones, and neither Yolara nor Lugur, nay, nor the Shining One, love her overmuch, stranger."

"Does she dwell here?" Larry's face was alight.

The dwarf hesitated, glanced about him anxiously.

"If she does, Doc, we're going to beat it her way quick." Larry shot the words to me quickly.

"Nay," Rador was answering—"ask me no more of her." He was silent for a space. "And what do you who are as leaves or drops of water do in that world of yours?" he said, plainly bent on turning the subject.

"Keep off the golden-eyed girl, Larry," I interjected. "Wait till we find out why she's *tabu*."

"Love and battle, strive and accomplish and die; or fail and die," answered Larry—to Rador—giving me a quick nod of acquiescence to my warning in English.

"In that at least your world and mine differ little," said the dwarf.

"How great is this world of yours, Rador?" I spoke.

He considered me gravely.

"How great indeed I do not know," he said frankly at last. "The land where we dwell with the Shining One stretches along the white waters for—" He used a phrase of which I could make nothing. "Beyond this city of the Shining One and on the hither shores of the white waters dwell the *mayia ladala*—the common ones." He took a deep draft from his flagon. "There are, first, the fair-haired ones, the children of the ancient rulers," he continued. "There are, second, we the soldiers; and last, the *mayia ladala*, who dig and till and weave and toil and give our rulers and us their daughters, and dance with the Shining One!" he added.

"Who rules?" I asked.

"The fair haired, under the Council of Nine, who are under Yolara, the Priestess and Lugur, the Voice," he answered, "who are in turn beneath the Shining One!" There was a ring of bitter satire in the last.

"And those three who were judged?"—this from Larry.

"They were of the *mayia ladala,*" he replied, "like those two I gave you. But they grow restless. They do not like to dance with the Shining One—the blasphemers!" He raised his voice in a sudden great shout of mocking laughter.

In his words I caught a fleeting picture of the race—an ancient, luxurious, close-bred oligarchy clustered about some mysterious deity; a soldier class that supported them; and underneath all the toiling, oppressed hordes.

"And is that all?" asked Larry.

"No," he answered. "Beyond the Lower Waters, over the Black Precipices of Doul are the forests where lie the feathered serpents and the secrets they guard. The Black Precipices of Doul are hard to pass—but none can pass through the feathered serpents. And there is the Sea of Crimson where—" he stopped abruptly; drank and set down his flagon empty. Whatever the purple drink might be, it was loosening the green dwarf's tongue and neither of us cared to interrupt him.

"It is strange, strange indeed to be sitting with two who have newly come from that land that we were forced from so many *sais of laya* agone," he began again, half musingly, gone upon another tangent. "For we too came from your world—but how long, long ago! I have heard that the waters swept over us slowly, but dragging, ever dragging our land beneath them. And we sought refuge in the secret heart of our land, refusing to leave her. And at the last we made our way here—where was the Shining One and where had been others before us who had left behind them greater knowledge than we brought—and that was no little, strangers. And now the *laya* turn upon themselves. The tail of the serpent coils close to his fangs—" He took a great drink of the yellow liquid; his eyes flashed—

And without warning the globe beside us sent out an almost vicious note, Rador turned toward it, his face paling. Its surface crawled with whisperings—angry, peremptory!

"I hear!" he croaked, gripping the table, "I obey!"

He turned to us a face devoid for once of its malice.

"Ask me no more questions, strangers," he said. "And now, if you are done, I will show you where you may sleep and bathe."

He arose abruptly. We followed him through the hangings, passed through a corridor and into another smaller chamber, roofless, the sides walled with screens of dark gray. Two cushioned couches were there and a curtained door leading into an open, outer enclosure in which a fountain played within a wide pool of polished green stone. Its opalescent column rose high, and from it fell sprays of simmering, milky water.

"Your bath," said Rador. He dropped the curtain and came back into the room. He touched a carved flower at one side. There was a tiny sighing from overhead and instantly across the top spread a veil of blackness, impenetrable to light but certainly not to air, for through it pulsed little breaths of the garden fragrances. The room filled with a cool twilight, refreshing, sleep-inducing. The green dwarf pointed to the couches.

"Sleep!" he said. "Sleep and fear nothing. My men are on guard outside." He came closer to us, the old mocking gaiety sparkling in his eyes.

"But I spoke too quickly," he whispered. "Whether it is because the *Afyo Maie* fears their tongues—or—" he laughed at Larry. "The maids are *not* yours!" Still laughing he vanished through the curtains of the room of the fountain before I could ask him the meaning of his curious gift, its withdrawal and his most enigmatic closing remarks.

CHAPTER XIV

"THERE WAS CAIRILL MAC CAIRILL"

"**BACK IN THE** great old days of Ireland," thus Larry breaking into my thoughts raptly, the brogue thick, "there was Cairill mac Cairill—Cairill Swiftspear. An' Cairill wronged Keevan of Emhain Abhlach, of the blood of Angus of the great people when he was sleeping in the likeness of a pale reed. Then Keevan put this penance on Cairill—that for a year Cairill should wear his body in Emhain Ebhlach, which is the Land of Faery and for that year Keevan should wear the body of Cairill. And it was done.

"In that year Cairill met Emar of the Birds that are one white, one red, and one black—and they loved, and from that love sprang Ailill their son. And when Ailill was born he took a reed flute and first he played slumber on Cairill, and then he played old age so that Cairill grew white and withered; then Ailill played again and Cairill became a shadow—then a shadow of a shadow—then a breath; and the breath went out upon the wind!" He shivered. "Like the old gnome," he whispered, "that they called Songar of the Lower Waters!"

He shook his head as though he cast a dream from him. Then, all alert—

"But that was in Ireland ages agone. And there's nothing like that here, Doc!" He laughed. "It doesn't scare me one little bit, old boy. The pretty devil lady's got the wrong slant. When you've had a pal standing beside you one moment—full of life, and joy and power and potentialities, telling what he's going to do to make the world hum when he gets through killing boches, just running over with zip and pep of life, Doc—and the next instant, right in the middle of a laugh—a piece of boche shell takes off half his head and with it joy and power and all the rest of it"—his face twitched—"and when you see this happen a whole lot of times—well, old man, in the face of that mystery a disappearing act such as the devil lady treated us to doesn't make much of a dent. Not on me. But by the mighty brogans of Brian Boru—if we could only get some of that stuff and turn it on the Kaiser—oh, boy!"

He was silent, evidently contemplating the idea with vast pleasure. And as for me, at that moment my last doubt of Larry O'Keefe vanished, I saw that he did believe, really believed, in his banshees, his leprechawns and all the old dreams of the Gael—but only within the limits of Ireland.

In one drawer of his mind was packed all his superstition, his mysticism and what of weakness it might carry. But face him with any peril or problem and the drawer closed instantaneously, leaving a mind that was utterly fearless, incredulous and ingenious; swept clean of all cobwebs by as fine a skeptic broom as ever brushed a brain.

If there *are* actually fairies out of Ireland. Larry O'Keefe I now knew would be the very last man in the world to recognize them as such. His curious beliefs were, in a way, lightning rods— and I felt that he would need them all here—and grew suddenly warm with gladness that he had them.

"Some stuff!" Deepest admiration was in his voice. "Can you imagine half a dozen of us scooting over the boche batteries and the Heinies underneath all at once beginning to shake themselves to pieces! Wow!" His tone was rapturous.

"It's easy enough to explain, Larry," I answered. "The effect, that is—for what the green ray is made of I don't know, of course. But what it does, clearly, is stimulate atomic vibration to such a pitch that the cohesion between the particles of matter is broken and the body flies to bits—just as a fly-wheel does when its speed gets so great that the particles of which it is made can't hold together."

"Shake themselves to pieces is right, then!" he exclaimed.

"Absolutely right," I nodded. "Everything in Nature vibrates. And all matter—whether man or beast or stone or metal or vegetable—is made up of vibrating molecules, which are made up of vibrating atoms which are made up of truly infinitely small particles of electricity called electrons, and electrons, the base of all matter, are themselves perhaps only a vibration of the mysterious ether. Thomas Edison has said that when man knows how to harness this vibratory force, a block of wood one foot square will light all New York for a year. The force itself is called interatomic energy.

"There is no such thing as solid matter. The electrons that make up the atoms are as far apart in comparison to their mass as our earth is from the sun. In the last analysis we are all sieves of infinitesimal particles of electricity, each of which is held at the end of an invisible cord we call attraction, cohesion, affinity—something akin no doubt to that most mysterious of energies, gravitation.

"If a magnifying glass of sufficient size and strength could be placed over us we could see ourselves as these sieves—our space lattice, as it is called. And all that is necessary to break down the lattice, to shake us into nothingness, is some agent that will set our atoms vibrating at such a rate that at last they break the unseen cords and fly off.

"The green ray of Yolara is such an agent. It set up in the dwarf that incredibly rapid rhythm that you saw and—shook him to atoms!" *

"They had a gun on the west front—a seventy-five," said O'Keefe, "that broke the eardrums of everybody who fired it, no matter what protection they used. It looked like all the other seventy-fives—but there was something about its sound that did it. They had to recast it."

"It's practically the same thing," I replied. "By some freak its vibratory qualities had that effect. The deep whistle of the murdered Lusitania would, for instance, make the Singer Building shake to its foundations; while the Olympic did not affect the

---

* It is a matter of pride to me that upon so few known facts I was enabled to make so accurate an analysis of the vibratory ray; later observations of it only confirming my impromptu hypothesis. The substance emitting it was, of course, one of the radioactive group of elements—but with their potential destructivity raised to the nth degree. The X-ray burn, that terrible injury suffered by so many experimenters with radium and the Roentgen ray, resembles its action, but the effect of the latter is infinitely slow compared to the swift destruction wreaked by the green ray. The atrophy, or shrinking of tissue, caused by a long and careless exposure to the X-ray, is unquestionably a dissolution and rearrangement of atoms begun by the vibratory energy of the light. A remarkable example of this is one of America's greatest experts in radiology and the high frequency field. His left arm is the size of a six-year-old child's; the right immensely powerful. Bone, sinew, and muscle, all, of the left had dwindled away—a process taking ten years, where the almost exactly similar tissue destruction of the dwarf was practically instantaneous.

Singer at all but made the Woolworth shiver all through. This was because the dominant note of the Singer Building was that of the Lusitania's whistle and that of the Olympic the dominant note of the Woolworth. In each case they stimulated the atomic vibration of the particular building—"

I paused, aware all at once of an intense drowsiness. O'Keefe, yawning, reached down to unfasten his puttees.

"Lord, I'm sleepy!" he exclaimed. "Can't understand it—what you say—most—interesting—Lord!" he yawned again; straightened. "What made Reddy take such a shine to the von?" he asked.

"Thanaroa," I answered, fighting to keep my eyes open.

"What?"

"When Lugur spoke that name I saw Von Hetzdorp signal him. Thanaroa is, I suspect, the original form of the name of Tangaroa, the greatest god of the Polynesians. There's a secret cult to him in the islands. Von Hetzdorp may belong to it—he knows it any way. Lugur recognized the signal and despite his surprise answered it."

"The Heinie gave him the high sign, eh?" mused Larry. "How could they both know it?"

"The cult is a very ancient one. Undoubtedly it had its origin in the dim beginnings before these people migrated here," I replied. "It's a link—one—of the few links between up there and the lost past—"

"Trouble then," mumbled Larry. "Hell brewing! I smell it—Say, Doc, is this sleepiness natural? Wonder where my—gas mask—is—" he added, half incoherently.

But I myself was struggling now desperately against the dragged slumber pressing down upon me.

"Lakla!" I heard O'Keefe murmur, "Lakla of the golden eyes—no, Eilidh—the fair!" He made an immense effort, half raised himself, grinned faintly.

"Thought this was paradise when I first saw it, Doc," he sighed. "But I know now, if it is, no-man's land is the greatest place on earth for a honeymoon. They—they've got us, Doc—" He sank back. "Good luck, old boy, wherever you're going." His hand waved feebly. "Glad—knew—you. Hope—sees—you—'gain—"

His voice trailed into silence. Fighting, fighting with every fiber of brain and nerve against the sleep—I felt myself being steadily overcome. But before oblivion rushed down upon me I seemed to see upon the gray screened wall nearest the Irishman an oval of rosy light begin to glow; watched, as my falling lids inexorably fell, a flame-tipped shadow waver on it; thicken; condense—and there looking down upon Larry, her eyes great golden stars in which intensest curiosity and shy tenderness struggled, sweet mouth half smiling, was the girl of the Moon Pool's Chamber, the girl whom the green dwarf had named—Lakla; the vision Larry had invoked before that sleep which I could no longer deny had claimed him—

And did I see about and behind her a cloud of other eyes—not those phosphorescent saucers of the frog-woman's enormous eyes—*triangular*—pools of shining jet flecked with little rushing, flickering ruby flames.

Closer she came—closer—the eyes were over us.

Then oblivion indeed!

CHAPTER XV

YOLARA OF MURIA VS. THE O'KEEFE

I AWAKENED WITH all the familiar, homely sensation of a shade having been pulled up in a darkened room. I thrilled with a wonderful sense of deep rest and restored resiliency. The ebon shadow had vanished from above and down into the room was pouring the silvery light. From the fountain pool came a mighty splashing and shouts of laughter. I jumped over and drew the curtain. O'Keefe and Rador were swimming a wild race; the dwarf like an otter, outdistancing and playing around the Irishman at will.

Then, suddenly, I was conscious of an odd surprise; exactly what I suppose a man must feel who goes to sleep believing that he will either never awaken or, if he does, in extremely unusual situation and upon awakening finds not only everything the same but really much pleasanter. Had that overpowering sleep—and now I confess that my struggle against it had been largely inspired by fear that it was the abnormal slumber which Throckmartin had described as having heralded the approach of the Dweller before it had carried away Thora and Stanton—had that sleep been after all nothing but natural reaction of tired nerves and brains?

And that last vision of the golden-eyed girl bending over Larry—and the little cloud of flame-flecked eyes shaped like lance points? Had they also been delusions of an overstressed mind? Well, they might have been, I could not tell. At any rate, I decided, I would speak about them to O'Keefe once we were alone again—and then giving myself up to the urge of buoyant well-being I shouted like a boy, stripped and joined the two in the Pool. The water was warm and I felt the unwonted tingling of life in every vein increase; something from it seemed to pulse through the skin, carrying a clean vigorous vitality that toned every fiber. Tiring at last, we swam to the edge and drew ourselves out. The waters, I then noted, had another peculiar quality—almost at once they dried or were absorbed. The green dwarf quickly clothed himself and Larry rather carefully donned his uniform.

"The *Afyo Maie* has summoned us, Doc," he said. "We're to—well—I suppose you'd call it breakfast with her. After that, Rador tells me, we're to have a session with the Council of Nine. I suppose Yolara is as curious as any lady of—the upper world, as you might put it—and just naturally can't wait," he added.

He gave himself a last shake, patted the automatic hidden under his left arm, whistled cheerfully.

"After you, my dear *Alphonse*," he said to Rador, with a low bow. The dwarf laughed, bent in an absurd imitation of Larry's mocking courtesy and started ahead of us to the house of the priestess. When he had gone a little way on the orchid-walled path I whispered to O'Keefe:

"Larry, when you were falling off to sleep—did you think you saw anything?"

"See anything!" he grinned. "Doc, sleep hit me like a Hun shell. I thought they were pulling the gas on us. I—I had some intention of bidding you tender farewells," he continued, half sheepishly. "I think I did start 'em, didn't I?"

"And I appreciated them," I nodded. "But did you see anything?"

"No!" he almost shouted. "I tell you I was hit by that sleep like a fly swatted by Goliath. But wait a minute—" he hesitated. "I had a queer sort of dream—"

"What was it?" I asked, eagerly.

"Well," he answered, slowly, "I suppose it was because I'd been thinking of Golden Eyes. Anyway, I thought she came through the wall and leaned over me—yes, and put one of those long white hands of hers on my head—I couldn't raise my lids—but in some queerish way I could see her. Then it got real dreamish. She had eyes all about her; a whole little cloud of them—"

"Like these, Larry," I asked. I drew a pencil from my pocket and sketched the high triangles of flame-flecked blackness I had seen in my own vision.

"How did you know that!" he cried, in utter amazement. Rador turned back toward us. I slipped the paper in my pocket.

"Later," I answered. "Not now. When we're alone."

But through me went a little glow of reassurance. Whatever the maze through which we were moving; whatever of menacing evil lurking there—the Golden Girl was clearly watching over us; watching with whatever unknown powers she could muster. It had been no dream, that vision; and as certain as I was of that, just as certain was I that nothing malign lay hidden in the Golden Girl, nothing of menace to us, only good. And I wished sincerely that I could think the same of the lovely witch whose summons we were obeying!

We passed the pillared entrance. In the great hall were the same green dwarfs, this time introduced to us by a variety of names. Each saluted, throwing the right hand high above the head. We went through a long, bowered corridor and stepped before a door that seemed to be sliced from a monolith of pale jade—high, narrow, set in a wall of opal.

Rador stamped twice and the same supernally sweet, silver bell tones of—yesterday, I must call it, although in that place of eternal day the term is meaningless—bade us enter. The door slipped aside. The chamber was small, the opal walls screening it on three sides, the black opacity covering it, the fourth side opening out into a delicious little walled garden, a mass of the fragrant, luminous blooms and delicately colored fruit. Facing it was a small table of reddish wood and from the omnipresent cushions heaped around it arose to greet us—Yolara.

Larry drew in his breath with an involuntary gasp of admiration and bowed low. My own admiration was as frank—and the priestess was well pleased with our homage.

She was swathed in the filmy, half-revelant webs, now of palest blue. The corn-silk hair was caught within a wide-meshed golden net in which sparkled tiny brilliants, like blended sapphires and diamonds. Her own azure eyes sparkled as brightly as they, and I noted again in their clear depths the half-eager approval as they rested upon O'Keefe's lithe, well-knit figure and his keen, clean-cut face. The high-arched, slender feet rested upon soft sandals whose gauzy withes laced the exquisitely formed leg to just below the dimpled knee.

"Some giddy wonder!" exclaimed Larry, looking at me and placing a hand over his heart. "Put her on a New York roof and she'd empty Broadway. Dramatic sense too well developed though for comfort. Soft pedal on that stuff—I don't want anymore of those Songar matinees. Take the cue from me, Doc."

He turned to Yolara, whose face was somewhat puzzled.

"I said, O lady whose shining hair is a web for hearts, that in our world your beauty would dazzle the sight of men as would a little woman sun!" he said, in the florid imagery to which the tongue lends itself so well.

A tiny flush stole up through the translucent skin. The blue eyes softened and she waved us toward the cushions. Black-haired maids stole in, placing before us the fruits, the little loaves and a steaming drink somewhat the color and odor of chocolate. I was conscious of outrageous hunger.

"What are you named, strangers?" she asked.

"This man is named Goodwin," said O'Keefe. "As for me, call me Larry.

"Nothing like getting acquainted quick," he said to me—but kept his eyes upon Yolara as though he were voicing another honeyed phrase. And so she took it, for: "You must teach me your tongue," she said.

"Then shall I have two words where now I have one to tell you of your loveliness," he answered her.

"And also that'll take time," he spoke to me. "Essential occupation out of which we can't be drafted to make these fun loving folk any Roman holiday. Get me!"

"*Larree,*" mused Yolara. "I like the sound. It is sweet—" and indeed it was as she spoke it.

"And what is your land named, *Larree?*" she continued. "And Goodwin's?" She caught the sound perfectly.

"MY LAND, O lady of loveliness, is two—Ireland and America; his but one—America."

She repeated the two names—slowly, over and over. We seized the opportunity to attack the food; halting half guiltily as she spoke again.

"Oh, but you are hungry!" she cried. "Eat then." She leaned her chin upon her hands and regarded us, whole fountains of questions brimming up in her eyes.

"How is it, *Larree,* that you have two countries and Goodwin but one?" she asked, at last unable to keep silent longer.

"I was born in Ireland; he in America. But I have dwelt long in his land and my heart loves each," he said.

She nodded, understandingly.

"Are all the men of Ireland like you, *Larree!* As all the men here are like Lugur or Rador? I like to look at you," she went on, with naïve frankness. "I am tired of men like Lugur and Rador. But they are strong," she added, swiftly. "Lugur can hold up twenty in his two arms and raise six with but one hand."

We could not understand her numerals and she raised white fingers to illustrate.

"That is little, O lady, to the men of Ireland," replied O'Keefe. "Lo, I have seen one of my race hold up ten times twenty of our—what call you that swift thing in which Rador brought us here?"

"*Corial,*" said she.

"Hold up ten times twenty of our *corials* with but two fingers—and these *corials* of ours—

"*Coria,*" said she.

"And these *coria* of ours are each greater in weight than ten of yours. Yea, and I have seen another with but one blow of his hand raise hell!

"And so I have," he murmured to me. "And both at Forty-Second and Fifth Avenue, N.Y.—U.S.A."

Yolara considered all this with manifest doubt.

"Hell?" she inquired at last. "I know not the word."

"Well," answered O'Keefe. "Say Muria then. In many ways they are, I gather, O heart's delight, one and the same."

Now the doubt in the blue eyes was strong indeed. She shook her head.

"None of our men can do *that!*" she answered, at length. "Nor do I think you could, *Larree.*"

"Oh, no," said Larry easily. "I never tried to be that strong. I fly," he added, casually.

Lakla, Handmaiden to the Silent Ones

The priestess rose to her feet, gazing at him with startled eyes.

"Fly!" she repeated incredulously. "Like a *Zitia?* A bird?"

Larry nodded—and then seeing the dawning command in her eyes, went on hastily.

"Not with my own wings, Yolara. In a—a *corial* that moves through—what's the word for air, Doc—well, through this—" He made a wide gesture up toward the nebulous haze above us. He took a pencil and on a white cloth made a hasty sketch of an airplane. "In a—a *corial* like this—" She regarded the sketch gravely, thrust a hand down into her girdle and brought forth a keen-bladed poniard; cut Larry's markings out and placed the fragment carefully aside.

"That I can understand," she said.

"Remarkably intelligent young woman," muttered O'Keefe. "Hope I'm not giving anything away—but she had me."

"Do you have a God in Ireland and America?" she asked. Larry nodded. "What is he called?" she continued.

"He is called the Prince of Peace," answered Larry, and his tone was curiously reverent. "But a false god challenged him and placed a yoke upon his people; and so he has gone to battle that peace may come again to his world where now there is no peace."

She considered this.

"Is your god winning?" she asked.

"He surely is!" Larry's conviction was so profound that it impressed her, clearly.

"Does your god dwell with you, like—" She hesitated. "Or afar, like Thanaroa?"

"He dwells in the heart of each of his followers, Yolara," answered the Irishman gravely.

"Yes, so does Thanaroa—but—" she hesitated again, skeptically. "He must have been afar when that other god put the yoke on his people," she concluded. "Now the Shining—" and again she caught herself.

"But what are your women like, *Larree?* Are they like me? And how many have loved you?"

"In all Ireland and America there is none like you, Yolara," he answered. "And take that any way you please," he whispered in English. She took it, it was evident, as it most pleased her.

"Do you have goddesses?" she asked.

"Every woman in Ireland and America, is a goddess," he answered.

"Now *that* I do not believe." There was both anger and mockery in her eyes. "I know women, *Larree*—and if that were so there would be no peace for men."

"There isn't!" said O'Keefe. The anger died out and she laughed, sweetly, understandingly.

"And which goddess do you worship, *Larree?*"

"You!" said Larry O'Keefe, boldly.

"Larry! Larry!" I whispered. "Be careful. It's high explosive."

But the priestess was laughing—little trills of sweet bell notes; and pleasure was in each note.

"You are indeed bold, *Larree*," she said, "to offer me your worship. Yet am I pleased by your boldness. Still—Lugur is strong; and you are not of those who—what did you say—have tried. And your wings are not here—*Larree!*"

Again her laughter rang out. The Irishman flushed; it was touché for Yolara!

"Fear not for me with Lugur," he said, grimly. "Rather fear for him!"

The laughter died; she looked at him searchingly; approval again in her eyes; a little enigmatic smile about her mouth—so sweet and so cruel.

"Well—we shall see," she murmured. "You say you battle in your world. With what?"

"Oh, with this and with that," answered Larry, airily. "We manage—"

"Have you the *Keth*—I mean that with which I sent Songar into the nothingness?" she asked swiftly.

"See what's she's driving at?" O'Keefe spoke to me, swiftly. "Well I do! Gray matter in that lady's head. But here's where the O'Keefe lands.

"I said," he turned to her, "O voice of silver fire, that your spirit is high even as your beauty—and searched out men's souls as does your loveliness their hearts. And now listen, Yolara, for what I speak is truth"—into his eyes came the far-away gaze; into his voice the Irish softness—"Lo, in my land of Ireland, this many of your life's length agone—see"—he raised his ten fingers, clenched and unclenched them times twenty—"the mighty men of my race, the Taitha-da-Dainn, could send men out into the nothingness even as do you with the *Keth*. And this they did by their harpings, and by words spoken—words of power, O Yolara, that have their power still—and by pipings and by slaying sounds.

"There was Cravetheen who played swift flames from his harp, flying flames that ate those they were sent against. And there was Dalua, of Hy Brasil, whose pipes played away from man and beast and all living things their shadows—and at last played them to shadows too, so that wherever Dalua went his shadows that had been men and beast followed like a storm of little rustling leaves; yea, and Bél the Harper, who could make women's hearts run like wax and men's hearts flame to ashes and whose harpings could shatter strong cliffs and bow great trees to the sod—"

His eyes were bright, dream filled; she shrank a little from him, faint pallor on the perfect skin.

"And they could make as well as destroy, those men of Ireland," he said. "There was Ulad of the Dreams. And Ulad took a sprig of fair white blossoms and warmed it on his heart and blew upon it—and what had been but flowers stood rosy before him—a woman, Fand the Lovely. But Fand sinned against Ulad, and lo! he breathed upon her again, and again she was but white blossoms that the wind took and scattered! I say to you, Yolara, that these things were and are—in Ireland." His voice rang strong. "And I have seen men as many as those that are in your great chamber this many times over"—he clenched his hands once more, perhaps a dozen times—"blasted into nothingness before your *Keth* could even have touched them.

Yea—and rocks as mighty as those through which we came lifted up and shattered before the lids could fall over your blue eyes. And this is truth, Yolara—all truth! Stay—have you that little cone of the *Keth* with which you destroyed Songar?"

She nodded, gazing at him, fascinated, fear and puzzlement contending.

"Then use it." He took a vase of crystal from the table, placed it on the threshold that led into the garden. "Use it on this—and I will show you."

"I will use it upon one of the *ladala*—" she began eagerly.

The exaltation dropped from him; there was a touch of horror in the eyes he turned to her; her own dropped before it.

"It shall be as you say," she said hurriedly. She drew the shining cone from her breast; leveled it at the vase. The green ray leaped forth, spread over the crystal, but before its action could even be begun, a flash of light shot from O'Keefe's hand, his automatic spat and the trembling vase flew into fragments. As quickly as he had drawn it, he thrust the pistol back into place and stood there empty handed, looking at her sternly. From the anteroom came shouting, a rush of feet.

Yolara's face was white, her eyes strained—but her voice was unshaken as she called to the clamoring guards:

"It is nothing—go to your places!"

But when the sound of their return had ceased she stared tensely at the Irishman—then looked again at the shattered vase;

"It is true!" she cried, "but see, the *Keth* is—alive!"

I followed her pointing ringer. Each broken bit of the crystal was vibrating, shaking its particles out into space. Broken it the bullet of Larry's had—but not released it from the grip of the disintegrating force. The priestess's face was triumphant.

"But what matters it, O shining urn of beauty—what matters it to the vase that is broken what happens to its fragments?" asked Larry, gravely—and pointedly.

The triumph died from her face and for a space she was silent; brooding.

"Next," whispered O'Keefe to me. "Lots of surprises in the little box; keep your eye on the opening and see what comes out."

We had not long to wait. There was a sparkle of anger about Yolara, something too of injured pride. She clapped her hands; whispered to the maid who answered her summons, and then sat back regarding us, maliciously.

"You have answered me as to your strength—but you have not proved it; answered me as to your God—and left me doubtful indeed; but the *Keth* you *have* answered. Now answer this!" she said.

She pointed out into the garden. I saw a flowering branch suddenly bend and snap as though a hand had broken it—but no hand was there! Saw then another and another bend and break, a little tree sway and fall—and closer and closer to us came the trail of snapping boughs while down into the garden poured the silvery light revealing—nothing! Now a great ewer beside a pillar rose swiftly in air and hurled itself crashing at my feet. Cushions close to us swirled about as though in the vortex of a whirlwind.

And unseen hands held my arms in a mighty clutch fast to my sides, another gripped my throat and I felt a needle-sharp poniard point pierce my shirt, touch the skin just over my heart.

"Larry!" I cried, despairingly. I twisted my head; saw that he too was caught in this grip of the invisible. But his face was calm, even amused.

"Keep cool, Doc!" he said. "Remember—she wants to learn the language!"

Now from Yolara burst chime upon chime of mocking laughter. She gave a command—the hands loosened, the poniard withdrew from my heart; suddenly as I had been caught I was free—and unpleasantly weak and shaky.

"Have you *that* in Ireland, *Larree!*" cried the priestess—and once more trembled with laughter.

"A good play, Yolara." His voice was as calm as his face. "But they did that in Ireland even before Dalua piped away his first man's shadow. There's a tree there, Yolara, with little red berries and it's called the rowan tree. And if you take the berries and squeeze them on your eyes and hands when the moon is just so, there's nobody can see you, at all. It's old in Ireland, Yolara! And in Goodwin's land they make ships—*coria* that go on water—so you can pass by them and see only sea and sky; and those water *coria* are each of them many times greater than this whole palace of yours."

But the priestess laughed on.

"It did get me a little," whispered Larry. "That wasn't quite up to my mark. But, God! If we could find it out and take it back to the front!"

"Not so, *Larree!*" Yolara gasped, through her laughter. "Not so! Goodwin's cry betrayed you!"

Her good humor had entirely returned; she was like a mischievous child pleased over some successful trick; and like a child she cried—"I'll show you!"—signaled again; whispered to the maid who, quickly returning, laid before her a long metal case. Yolara took from her girdle something that looked like a small pencil, pressed it and shot a thin stream of light for all the world like an electric flash, upon its hasp. The lid flew open. Out of it she drew three flat, oval crystals, faint rose in hue. She handed one to O'Keefe and one to me.

"Look!" she commanded, placing the third before her own eyes. I peered through the stone and instantly there leaped into sight, out of thin air—six grinning dwarfs! Each was covered from top of head to soles of feet in a web so tenuous that through it their bodies were plain. The gauzy stuff seemed to vibrate—its strands to run together like quicksilver. I snatched the crystal from my eyes and—the chamber was empty! Put it back—and there were the grinning six!

Yolara gave another sign and they disappeared, even from the crystals.

"It is what they wear, *Larree*," explained Yolara, graciously. "It is something that came to us from—the ancient ones. But we have so few"—she sighed—"and the secret of their making is well-nigh lost—it is difficult to make"—she hesitated—"but almost are we upon the verge of refinding its ease."

"Such treasures must be two-edged swords, Yolara," commented O'Keefe. "For how know you that one within them creeps not to you with hand eager to strike?"

"There is no danger," she said indifferently. "I am the keeper of them—and I know always where they are. Besides, they cannot pass through the blackness. When one wears them and tries to pass, the darkness sucks the light out of him as thirsty ground does water! And at last he is naught but one of those shadows of which you speak, *Larree*—although the robe itself is not harmed. I will have one of the *ladala* don one and show you," she added, brightly.

"No! No!" cried O'Keefe. She regarded him, amused.

"And now no more," abruptly. "You two are to appear before the council at a certain time—but fear nothing. You, Goodwin, go with Rador about our city and increase your wisdom. But you. *Larree*, await me here in my garden—" she smiled at him, provocatively—maliciously, too. "For shall not one who has resisted a world of goddesses be given all chance to worship when at last he finds his own?"

She laughed—whole heartedly and was gone. And at that moment I liked Yolara better than ever I had before and—alas—better than ever I was to in the future.

I noted Rador standing outside the open jade door and started to go, but O'Keefe caught me by the arm.

"Wait a minute," he urged. "About Golden Eyes—you were going to tell me something—it's been on my mind all through that little sparring match."

I told him of the vision that had passed through my closing lids. He listened gravely and then laughed.

"Hell of a lot of privacy in this place!" he grinned. "Ladies who can walk through walls and others with regular invisible cloaks to let 'em flit wherever they please. Oh, well, don't let it get on your nerves, Doc. Remember—everything's natural! That robe stuff is just camouflage of course. But Lord, if we could only get a piece of it!"

"The material simply admits all light-vibrations, or perhaps curves them, just as the opaque screens cut them off," I answered. "A man under the X-ray is partly invisible; this makes him wholly so. He doesn't register, as the people of the motion-picture profession say."

"I doped that out myself as soon as I had my first peep," he said. "But you want to keep remembering—it's all natural! Just keep saying that to yourself. They've got a bag of tricks and they keep pulling them. When we get on to 'em all we'll be all right—just as we were with the Huns."

I began to be irritated—why this repeated warning to me, who knew only fact?

"And as for their Shining One—Say!" Larry snorted. "I'd like to set the O'Keefe banshee up against it. I'll bet that old resourceful Irish body would give it the first three bites and a strangle hold and wallop it before it knew it had 'em."

Rador beckoned me.

"I'm glad Golden Eyes is on the job, no matter how unconventional her visits are—but I wish she'd show her hand soon," sighed Larry.

Then the mercurial Celtic mind went back to that other picture he had drawn.

"If our banshee ever takes it into its head to land here to help me out instead of ushering me out—Wow! Boy! Howdy!"

I heard him still chuckling gleefully over this vision as I passed along the opal wall with the green dwarf, bound for my first excursion.

Would I come across any trace of Throckmartin? Did I dare even to hint to Rador the real reason we had invaded this enigmatic land?

CHAPTER XVI

THE LOVELY LAND OF
LURKING HATE

AS I REACHED Rador I looked at my watch, which I had taken the precaution to wind before preparing for sleep. It had then been eleven o'clock of the morning in our world outside. Now the watch registered four—but whether we had slept five hours or seventeen or twenty-nine I had no means of knowing. Rador scanned the dial with much interest; drew from his girdle a small disk, and compared the two.

His had thirteen divisions and, beneath the circle marking them, another circle divided into smaller spaces. About each circle a small glowing point moved. What he held was, in principle, a watch the same as mine—but I could not know upon what system their time recording was based.*

---

* Later I was to find that reckoning rested upon the extraordinary increased luminosity of the cliffs at the time of full moon on earth—this action, to my mind, being linked either with the effect of the light streaming globes upon the Moon Pool, whose source was in the shining cliffs, or else upon some mysterious affinity of their radiant element with the flood of moonlight on earth—the latter, most probably, because even when the moon must have been clouded above, it made no difference in the phenomenon. Thirteen of these shining forth constituted a *laya*, one of them a *lat*. Ten was *sa;* ten times ten times ten a *said*, or thousand; ten times a thousand was a *sais*. A *sais* of *laya* was then literally ten thousand years. What we would call an hour was by them called a *va*. The whole time system was, of course, a mingling of time as it had been known to their remote, surface-dwelling ancestors, and the peculiar determining factors in the vast cavern.

Unquestionably there is a subtle difference, between time as we know it and time in this subterranean land—its progress there being slower. This, however, is only in accord with the well-known doctrine of relativity, which predicates both space and time as necessary inventions of the human mind to orient itself to the conditions under which it finds itself. I tried often to measure this difference, but could never do so to my entire satisfaction. The closest I can come to it is to say that an hour of our time is the equivalent of an hour and five-eighths in Muria. For further information upon

"Two *va* we have before the council sits," he said, thrusting the disk back in his girdle. "As a man of learning you are to be shown whatever of ours may interest you—while the *Afyo Maie* sits with that of yours which certainly interests her," he said, maliciously. "But this I warn you—how are you named, stranger?"

"Goodwin," I answered.

"Goodwin!" he repeated as excellently as had Yolara. "This I must warn you, Goodwin—that I will answer you all I may, but some things I must not and you shall know by my silence what these are."

On fire with eagerness I hurried on. A shell was awaiting us. I paused before entering it to examine the polished surface of runways and great road. It was obsidian—volcanic glass of pale emerald, unflawed, translucent, with no sign of block or juncture. It was, indeed, as though it had been poured molten, and then gone over as carefully as a jeweler would a gem. I examined the shell.

"What makes it go?" I asked Rador. At a word from him the driver touched a concealed spring and an aperture appeared beneath the control-lever, of which I have spoken in a preceding chapter. Within was a small cube of black crystal, through whose sides I saw, dimly, a rapidly revolving, glowing ball, not more than two inches in diameter. Beneath the cube was a curiously shaped, slender cylinder winding down into the lower body of the Nautilus whorl.

"Watch!" said Rador. He motioned me into the vehicle and took a place beside me. The driver touched the lever; a stream of coruscations flew from the ball down into the cylinder. The shell started smoothly, and as the tiny torrent of shining particles increased it gathered speed.

"The *corial* does not touch the road," explained Rador. "It is

---

this matter of relativity the reader may consult any of the numerous books upon the subject.

lifted so far"—he held his forefinger and thumb less than a sixteenth of an inch apart—"above it."

And perhaps here is the best place to explain the activation of the shells or *coria*.

The force utilized was atomic energy. Passing from the whirling ball the ions darted through the cylinder to two bands of a peculiar metal affixed to the base of the vehicles somewhat like skids of a sled. Impinging upon these they produced a partial negation of gravity, lifting the shell slightly, and at the same time creating a powerful repulsive force or thrust that could be directed backward, forward, or sidewise at the will of the driver. The creation of this energy and the mechanism of its utilization were, briefly, as follows:

> [Dr. Goodwin's lucid and exceedingly comprehensive description of this extraordinary mechanism has been deleted by the Executive Council of the International Association of Science as too dangerously suggestive to scientists of the Central European Powers with which we are at war. It is allowable, however, to state that his observations are in the possession of experts in this country, who are, unfortunately, hampered in their research not only by the scarcity of the radioactive elements that we know, but also by the lack of the element or elements unknown to us that entered into the formation of the fiery ball within the cube of black crystal. Nevertheless, as the principle is so clear, it is believed that these difficulties will ultimately be overcome.—J.B.K., President, I.A. of S.]

The wide, glistening road was gay with the *coria*. They darted in and out of the gardens; within them the fair-haired, extraordinarily beautiful women on their cushions were like princesses of Elfland, caught in gorgeous fairy webs, resting within the hearts of flowers. In some shells were flaxen-haired, dwarfish men of Lugur's type; sometimes black-polled brother officers of Rador; often raven-tressed girls, plainly handmaidens of the women; and now and then beauties of the lower folk went by with one of the blond dwarfs—and then it was plain indeed what their relations were.

Among those who walked along the paralleling promenade were none of the fair-haired. And the haunting wistfulness that underlay the thin film of gaiety on the faces and in the eyes of the black-haired folk, and its contrast with the sinisterly sweet malice, the sheer, unhuman exuberance of life written upon the fair-haired, made something deep, deep, within me tremble with indefinable repulsion.

We swept around the turn that made of the jewel-like roadway an enormous horseshoe and, speedily, upon our right the cliffs through which we had come in our journey from the Moon Pool began to march forward beneath their mantels of moss. They formed a gigantic abutment, a titanic salient. It had been from the very front of this salient's invading angle that we had emerged; on each side of it the precipices, faintly glowing, drew back and vanished into distance.

At the bridge-span we had first crossed, Rador stopped the *corial,* beckoning me to accompany him. We climbed the arch and stood once more upon the mossy ledge. Half a score of the dwarfs were cutting into the cliff face, using tools much resembling our own pneumatic drills, except that they had no connection with any energizing machinery. The drills bit in smoothly but slowly. I imagined that their power was supplied by the same force that ran the *coria,* and asked Rador. He nodded.

"They search for your disappearing portal," he grinned, mischievously. I thought of the depth of that monstrous slice of solid stone that had dropped before us and over whose top we had passed through the hundred-foot tunnel and I felt fairly certain that they would not soon penetrate to the well of the stairway that it concealed and to which the Golden Girl had led us. And I was equally sure the art that had covered this entrance so amazingly had provided at the same time a screen for the oval, high above, through which our eyes had first beheld the city of the Shining One.

Somewhat grimly I asked Rador why they did not use the green ray to disintegrate the rock—as it had the body of Sangar. He answered that they did use it—but sparingly.

Out from the sparkling mists stretched two hands,
enormously long, utterly unhuman....

There were two reasons for this, he went on to explain: first, that, in varying degrees, all the rock walls resisted it; the shining cliffs on the opposite side of the White Waters completely. And, second, that when it was used it was at the risk of very dangerous rock falls. There were, it appeared, lines of non-re-sistance in the cliffs—faults, I suppose—which, under the *Keth*, disintegrated instantaneously. These lines of non-resistance could not be mapped out beforehand and were likely to bring enormous masses of the resistant portion tumbling down, exactly, I gathered, as a structure of cemented stone would tumble if the cement should abruptly crumble into dust.

They seldom used the ray, therefore, for tunneling or blasting rock in *situ*. The resistant qualities of the barriers were probably due to the presence of radioactive elements that neutralized the vibratory ray whose essence was, of course, itself radioactive.

The slender, graceful bridges under which we skimmed ended at openings in the up-flung, far walls of verdure. Each had its little garrison of soldiers. Through some of the openings a rivulet of the green obsidian river passed. These were roadways to the farther country, to the land of the *ladala*, Rador told me; adding that none of the lesser folk could cross into the pavilioned city unless summoned or without pass.

We turned the bend of the road and flew down that further emerald ribbon we had seen from the great oval. Before us rose the shining cliffs and the lake. A half-mile, perhaps, from these the last of the bridges flung itself. It was more massive and about it hovered a spirit of ancientness lacking in the other spans; also its garrison was larger and at its base the tangent way was guarded by two massive structures, somewhat like blockhouses, between which it ran. Something about it aroused in me an intense curiosity.

"Where does that road lead, Rador?" I asked.

"To the one place above all of which I may not tell you, Goodwin," he answered. And again I wondered—and into my wonder burst a thought. Did the road lead to Throckmartin and those others the Dweller had made its prey? How could I find out?

We skimmed slowly out upon the great pier. Far to the left was the prismatic, rainbow curtain between the Cyclopean pillars. On the white waters graceful shells—lacustrian replica of the Elf chariots—swam, but none was near that distant web of wonder.

"Rador—what is that?" I asked.

"It is the veil of the Shining One!" he answered slowly.

Was the Shining One that which we named the Dweller?

"*What* is the Shining One?" I cried, eagerly. Again he was silent. Nor did he speak until we had turned on our homeward way.

And lively as my interest, my scientific curiosity, were—I—was conscious suddenly of acute depression. Beautiful, wondrously beautiful, this place was—and yet in its wonder dwelt a keen edge of menace, of unease—of inexplicable, inhuman wo; as though in a secret garden of God a soul should sense upon it the gaze of some lurking spirit of evil which some way, somehow, had crept into the sanctuary and only bided its time to spring.

CHAPTER XVII

THE LEPRECHAWN

THE SHELL CARRIED us straight back to the house of Yolara. We stood again before the tenebrous wall where first we had faced the priestess and the Voice. And as we stood, again the portal appeared with all its disconcerting, magical abruptness; Rador drew aside; I entered; once more the entrance faded.

But now the scene was changed. Around the jet table were grouped a number of figures—Lugur, Yolara beside him; seven others—all of them fair-haired and all men save one who sat at the left of the priestess—an old, old woman, how old I could not tell, her face bearing traces of beauty that must once have been as great as Yolara's own, but now ravaged, in some way awesome; through its ruins the fearful, malicious gaiety shining out like a spirit of joy held within a corpse!

Larry was not present. I wondered why, but as I wondered he entered. He sent me a cheerful grin, and Yolara darted a glance at him that was—revelant. Lugur saw it, too, and read it aright, for his face darkened. Began then our examination, for such it was. And as it progressed I was more and more struck by the change in the O'Keefe. All flippancy was gone, rarely did his sense of humor reveal itself in any of his answers. He was like a cautious swordsman, fencing, guarding, studying his opponent; or rather, like a chess-player who keeps sensing some far-reaching purpose in the game; alert, contained, watchful. Always he stressed the power of our surface races, their multitudes, their solidarity.

Their questions were myriad. What were our occupations? Our system of government? How great were the waters? The land? Intensely interested were they in the world war, querying minutely into its causes; its possible outcome. Lugur was curiously silent, but at some of our answers I caught his sneer and saw behind it—Von Hetzdorp! In our weapons their interest was avid. And they were exceedingly minute in their examination of us as to the ruins which had excited our curiosity; their position and surroundings—and if others than ourselves might be expected to find and pass through their entrance!

At this I shot a glance at Lugur. He did not seem unduly interested. I wondered if the German had told him as yet of the girl of the rosy wall of the Moon Pool Chamber and the real reasons for our search. Then I answered as briefly as possible—omitting all reference to these things. The red dwarf watched me with unmistakable amusement—and I knew Von Hetzdorp *had* told him. But clearly Lugur had kept his information even from Yolara; and as clearly she had spoken to none of that episode when O'Keefe's automatic had shattered the *Keth*-smitten vase. And again I felt that sense of deep bewilderment—of helpless search for clue to all the tangle.

For two hours we were questioned and then the priestess called Rador and let us go.

Larry was somber as we returned. Rador soon left us.

"One thing's sure," Larry remarked, almost inconsequentially, "we've got to beat Von Hetzdorp to it. Didn't see anything of a lady named Lakla in your trip around the bazaars, did you?"

I shook my head. He walked about the room, uneasily.

"Hell's brewing here all right," he said at last, stopping before me. "I can't make out just the particular brand—that's all that bothers me. We're going to have a stiff fight, that's sure. What I want to do quick is to find the Golden Girl, Doc. Haven't seen her on the wall lately, have you?" he queried, hopefully fantastic.

"Laugh if you want to," he went on, "But she's our best bet. It's going to be a race between her and the O'Keefe banshee— but I put my money on her. I had a queer experience while I was in that garden, after you'd left." His voice grew solemn, "Did you ever see a leprechawn, Doc?" I shook my head again, as solemnly. "He's a little man in green," said Larry. "Oh, about as high as your knee. I saw one once—in Carntogher Woods. And as I sat there, half asleep, in Yolara's garden, the living spit of him stepped out from one of those bushes, twirling a little shillalah.

" 'It's a tight box ye're gettin' in, Larry *avick*,' said he, 'but don't ye be downhearted, lad.'

" 'I'm carrying on,' said I, 'but you're a long way from Ireland,' I said, or thought I did.

" 'Ye've a lot o' friends there,' he answered. 'An' where the heart rests the feet are swift to follow. Not that I'm sayin' I'd like to live here, Larry,' said he.

" 'I know where my heart is now,' I told him. 'It rests on a girl with golden eyes and the hair and swan-white breast of Eilidh the Fair—but me feet don't seem to get me to her.' I said."

The brogue thickened.

"An' the little man in green nodded his head an' whirled his shillalah.

" 'It's what I came to tell ye,' says he. 'Don't ye fall for the

Bhean-Nimher, the serpent woman wit' the blue eyes; she's a daughter of Ivor, lad—an' don't ye do nothin' to make the brown-haired colleen ashamed o' ye, Larry O'Keefe. I knew yer great, great grandfather an' his before him, aroon,' says he, 'an' wan o' the O'Keefe failin's is to think their hearts big enough to hold all the wimmen o' the world. A heart's built to hold only wan permanently, Larry,' he says, 'an' I'm warnin' ye a nice girl don't like to move into a place all cluttered up wid another's washin' an' mendin' an' cookin' an' other things pertainin' to general wife work. Not that I think the blue-eyed wan is keen for mendin' an' cookin'!' says he.

" 'You don't have to be comin' all this way to tell me that,' I answer.

" 'Well, I'm just a tellin' you,' he says. 'Ye've got some rough knocks comin', Larry. In fact ye're in for a very devil of a time. But, remember that ye're the O'Keefe,' says he. 'An' while the *bhoys* are all wid ye, *avick,* ye've got to be on the job yourself.'

" 'I hope,' I tell him, 'that the O'Keefe banshee can find her way here in time—that is, if it's necessary, which I hope it won't be.'

" 'Don't ye worry about that,' says he. 'Not that she's keen on leavin' the ould sod, Larry. The good ould soul's in quite a state o' mind about ye, aroon. I don't mind tellin' ye, lad, that she's mobilizin' all the clan an' if she *has* to come for ye, *avick,* they'll be wid her an' they'll sweep this joint clean before ye go. What they'll do to it'll make the Big Wind look like a summer breeze on Lough Lene! An' that's about all Larry. We thought a voice from the green isle would cheer ye. Don't fergit that ye're the O'Keefe—an' I say it agin—all the *bhoys* are wid ye. But we want t' kape bein' proud o' ye, lad!'

"An' I looked again and there was only a bush waving."

There wasn't a smile in my heart—or if there was it was a very tender one. Subconscious visions, or whatever it had been, he meant every word, and I was curiously touched.

"Lord, I'd like to have a cigarette," he said. "Spill me a little scientific dope, old dear. What is this place, anyway?"

"Well," I said. "I think it's the matrix of the moon."

"The what!" he exclaimed, with almost ludicrous amazement. I told him of Von Hetzdorp's suggestion and my ideas upon it, as I have related them, somewhat fragmentarily, in another chapter.

"Any real evidence for that?" he asked. I assured him that there was.

"That," I continued, "would explain these enormous, caverned spaces—scar tissue of the world, permeated with gigantic spaces as human scar tissue is often permeated with lesions beneath the scarified surface. Now these people we have encountered are undoubtedly, as poor Throckmartin divined, the remnants of that lost and ancient race that built the Nan-Matal and similar Pacific structures. Undoubtedly they were forced below as their continent subsided. And here the green dwarf's statement that they made their way here where was the Shining One and 'where others before us had been' is highly suggestive."

"Odd lads, those dwarfs," said Larry. "They look like folk who started out to be gods and somebody's hand pushed them down while they were still soft!"

The characterization was so apt I started.

"However—" said O'Keefe. "Pardon me, Doc. Go on—it just occurred to me."

"This race that they found," I went on, "or rather its remnants, its relics or only its monuments, must have been immeasurably more ancient even than they. Indeed, it is legitimate to doubt whether they had ever reached the surface of our planet. And while on this point I would call your attention to the fact that the legend that their most distant ancestors were born within and issued from deep earth caverns is no uncommon one, not only among primitive peoples, but others who once, at least, had a high culture.

"What happened here I cannot of course tell. It may be that a condition prevailed analogous to that of the Mayans and Aztecs. The Mayans were the great race of Central America.

They developed a marvelous civilization; attained a high command of art and science, were unsurpassed—and are even today—as builders, were extraordinary astronomers and their calendar is now one of the wonders of the scientific world.

"Pestilence and famine destroyed them. Down upon their last few survivors came the Aztecs, far, far lower in all knowledge. But they took what they found and upon it built that civilization so amazingly complex in its mingled wickedness and good, darkest barbarism and true enlightenment, that the Spaniards, under Cortez, wantonly annihilated."

He nodded.

"Just as the Aztecs picked up some, but not nearly all, of the art and science of the Mayans—so these may have done from that great people who preceded them here, Larry. That they knew nothing of the existence of the passage from the Chamber of the Moon Pool proves that they have lost much of the ancient knowledge—if, indeed, they ever possessed it.

"On the other hand, Yolara, it was clear, knows of the sinister excursions of the Dweller into the outer world—"

"But knowing that, she must also know how the thing you saw comes out," he objected. "Besides, the place of the Moon Pool was clearly known to the builders of Nan-Tauach, who were, apparently, the forefathers of these."

"I admit that it is puzzling," I answered. "Still—neither Yolara nor Lugur *did* know. Perhaps the hidden road was made by the earliest of their buried kind, and the secret lost. Or it may be it was built by some of that race they found"—I had a flash of intuition—"to keep watch upon them and upon the Shining One, who may have escaped some way, somehow, their own control!"

Larry shook his head, perplexedly.

"There's some sort of scrap brewing all right," he observed. "Maybe you're right. What the devil are the 'Silent Ones?'—and where is that Golden Girl who led us—Lakla, the handmaiden." His eyes grew soft and far away.

"Ask rather where is Throckmartin and his and where the wife of Olaf." I answered, a little bruskly.

"I'm going to bed," he said abruptly. "Keep an eye on the wall, Doc!"

CHAPTER XVIII

"ALLONS, ENFANTS DE LA PATRIE!"

BETWEEN THE SEVEN sleeps that followed, Larry and I saw but little of each other. Yolara sought him more and more. Thrice we were called before the council; once we were at a great feast, whose splendors and surprises I can never forget. Largely I was in the company of Rador. Together we two passed the green barriers into the dwelling-place of the *ladala*.

And here I felt the atmosphere of hostility, of brooding calamity, stiffen into a definitely unpleasant reality. We went among them, but never could I force my mind through the armor of their patent hate for Rador, or at least, for what he represented.

They lived in homes—if homes the pavilions could be called—that were lesser replicas of those within the city. Those who supplied the necessities and luxuries of their rulers worked in what were, in a fashion, community houses of wood and stone.

They seemed provided with everything needful for life. But everywhere was an oppressiveness, a *gathering together* of hate, that was spiritual rather than material—as tangible as the latter and far, far more menacing!

"They do not like to dance with the Shining One," was Rador's constant and only reply to my efforts to find the cause.

Once I had concrete evidence of the mood. Glancing behind me, I saw a white, vengeful face peer from behind a tree-trunk, a hand lift, a shining dart speed from it straight toward Rador's back. Instinctively I thrust him aside. He turned upon me angrily. I pointed to where the little missile lay, still quivering, on the ground. He gripped my hand.

"That some day I will repay!" he said. I looked again at the thing. At its end was a tiny cone covered with a glistening, gelatinous substance.

Rador pulled from a tree beside us a fruit somewhat like an apple.

"Look!" he said. He dropped it upon the dart—and at once, before my eyes, in less than ten seconds, the fruit had rotted away!

"That's what would have happened to Rador but for you, friend!" he said.

Still another curious incident I must record here. I had been commenting upon the scarcity of bird-life. The only avian species I had seen so far had been a few gaily colored, tiny, songless creatures. I mentioned, unthinkingly, the golden-eyed bird that had greeted us. He gave evidence of perturbation indeed at this. He asked where we had seen it. On guard again. I told him that it had appeared when we emerged from the cliff.

"Tell that not to Yolara, nor to Lugur! And warn *Larree*," he said, earnestly.

I asked why. He shook his head. And then, softly, his thoughts clearly finding unconscious vent in words.

"Have the Silent Ones still the power—even as she says? Is the old wisdom yet strong? Almost do I believe—and it comes to me that I would be glad to believe—and what said Songar? That these strangers—"

He broke off and once more fell into silence.

I cite these two happenings for the light they cast upon that which I have still to tell.

Come now between this and the prelude to the latter half of the tremendous drama whose history this narrative is—interlude, rather, between what has gone before and the second curtain soon to rise so amazingly—only scattering and necessarily fragmentary observations.

First—the nature of the ebon opacities, blocking out the spaces between the pavilion-pillars or covering their tops like roofs. These were magnetic fields, light absorbers, negativing the vibrations of radiance; literally screens of electric force which formed as impervious a barrier to light as would have screens of steel.

They instantaneously made night appear in a place where no night was. But they interposed no obstacle to air or to sound. They were extremely simple in their inception—no more miraculous than is glass, which, inversely, admits the vibrations of light, but shuts out those coarser ones we call—air—and, partly, those others which produce upon our auditory nerves the effects we call sound.

Briefly, their mechanism was this:

[For the same reason that Dr. Goodwin's exposition of the mechanism of the atomic engines was deleted, his description of the light-destroying screens has been omitted by the Executive Council. The benefits of such a discovery to the armed forces still in the field are obvious. Added to this danger is the amazing simplicity of their construction. It can be confidently predicted that these screens will shortly be in use on the seas as protection against submarines and as cover for infantry attacks on land by Allied forces.—J.B.K., President, I.A. of S.]

There were two favored classes of the *ladala*—the soldiers and the dream-makers. The dream-makers were the most astonishing social phenomena. I think, of all. Denied by their circumscribed environment the wider experiences of us of the outer world, the Murians had perfected an amazing system of escape through the imagination.

The dream-makers were recruited from the *ladala*, and must have been extremely powerful—far more so than the vulgar fortune-tellers of earth, because to a certain extent the sleep visions they induced were their own—or were they?

At any rate, they led a precarious life, because if their patrons were annoyed by unpleasant sleep experiences they suffered for it either by death or by cruel beatings. At the one feast I attended I saw them summoned to the side of half-drunken women and men to ply their mysterious profession.

And before the sixth sleep I myself was induced by Rador to call upon one. I remember slipping straight out of this consciousness straight into another—visions of a young world—nightmare figures—steaming jungles—monsters—a bestial shaggy woman beast whom I, also a beast, loved brutally. But enough!

They were intensely musical. Their favorite instruments were double flutes; immensely complex pipe-organs; harps, great and small. They had another remarkable instrument made up of a double octave of small drums which gave forth percussions remarkably disturbing to the emotional centers.

Their development of music was, indeed, as decadent—if that be the right word to use—as the activities of the dream-makers. They were—I quote an extraordinary phrase of O'Keefe's—"jazz-jag hounds!"

It was this love of music that gave rise to one of the few truly humorous incidents of our caverned life. Larry came to me—it was just after our fourth sleep, I remember.

"Come on to a concert," he said.

We skimmed off to one of the bridge garrisons. Rador called the twoscore guards to attention; and then, to my utter stupefaction, the whole company, O'Keefe leading them, roared out the "Marseillaise." *"Allons, enfants de la patrie!"* they sang—in a closer approach to the French than might have been expected ten or fifty miles below France level. *"Marchons! Marchons!"* they bellowed.

Larry quivered with suppressed mirth at my paralysis of surprise.

"Taught 'em that for Von Hetzdorp's benefit!" he gasped. "Wait till that boche hears it. He'll blow up. I've got 'em going on 'Tipperary' and that great Yank trench-song:

> "Here come the doughboys,
> The dirt behind their ears;
> Here come the doughboys.
> Their pay is in arrears."

And the dwarfs joined in musingly, following the words as closely as they could. It was irresistibly funny; and in my laughter I forgot for the moment my forebodings.

"Just wait until you hear Yolara lisp a pretty little thing I taught her," said Larry as we set back for what we now called home. There was an impish twinkle in his eyes.

And I did hear. For it was not many minutes after that the priestess condescended to command me to come to her with O'Keefe.

"Show Goodwin how much you have learned of our speech, O lady of the lips of honeyed flame!" murmured Larry.

She hesitated; smiled at him and then from that perfect mouth, out of the exquisite throat, in the voice that was like the chiming of little silver bells, she trilled a melody familiar to me indeed:

> "She's only a bird in a gilded cage,
> A bee-yu-tiful sight to see—"

And so on to the bitter end. I did not dare to look at O'Keefe; with utmost difficulty I controlled the spasm that shook me.

"She thinks it's a love-song," said Larry when we had left. "It's only part of a repertoire I'm teaching her. Honestly, Doc, it's the only way I can keep my mind clear when I'm with her," he went on earnestly. "She's a devil-ess from hell—but a wonder. Whenever I find myself going I get her to sing that, or 'Take back your gold!' and I'm back again—*pronto*—with the right perspective! *Pop* goes all the mystery! 'Hell!' I say, 'she's only a woman!'"

Through those seven sleeps there was no sign either of Olaf or of Von Hetzdorp, Always, when we asked Yolara, she said that they were both well and content. Nor was there sign of the Golden Girl—although Larry told me that he dreamed of her, and sometimes I turned quickly, feeling her eyes upon me.

And ever the passion light in the eyes of the priestess grew stronger, more perilous, when she looked upon Larry O'Keefe— and steadily the face of Lugur grew more forbidding.

Then at last came the summons to that tragic interlude which was to be the curtain-raiser to the dread, the incredible, the glorious finale of our adventure.

CHAPTER XIX

THE AMPHITHEATER OF HELL

FOR HOURS THE black-haired folk had been streaming across the bridges, flowing along the promenade by scores and by hundreds, drifting down toward the gigantic seven-terraced temple whose interior I had never as yet seen, and from whose towering exterior, indeed, I had always been kept far enough away—unobtrusively, but none the less decisively—to prevent any real observation. The structure, I had estimated, nevertheless, could not reach less than a thousand feet above its silvery base, and the diameter of its circular foundation was about the same.

I wondered what it was that was bringing the *ladala* into Lora, and where were they vanishing. All of them were flower-crowned with the luminous, lovely blooms—old and young, slender, mocking-eyed girls, dwarfed youths, mothers with their babes, gnomed oldsters—on they poured, silent for the most part and sullen—a sullenness that held acid bitterness even as their subtle, half-sinister, half-gay malice seemed tempered into little keen-edged flames, oddly, menacingly defiant.

There were many of the green-clad soldiers along the way,

and the garrison of the only bridge span I could see had certainly been doubled.

WONDERING STILL, I turned from my point of observation and made my way back to our pavilion, hoping that Larry, who had been with Yolara for the past two hours, had returned. Hardly had I reached it before Rador came hurrying up, in his manner a curious exultance, mingled with what in any one else I would have called a decided nervousness.

"Come!" he commanded before I could speak. "The council has made decision—and *Larree* is awaiting you."

"What has been decided?" I panted as we sped along the mosaicked path that led to the house of Yolara. "And why is Larry awaiting me?"

And at his answer I felt my heart pause in its beat and through me race a wave of mingled panic and eagerness; panic born of the memory of that which I had seen in the cabin of the *Southern Queen,* and eagerness that what I had set forth to seek I was at last to find.

"The Shining One dances!" had answered the green dwarf. "And you are to worship!

"Lugur was against it," he whispered as we went swiftly on. "The Shining One's Voice said 'No,' but the Shining One's priestess said 'Yes'; and the council thought at last, and as usual, as she did. What the Shining One may think, friend Goodwin, I do not know"—he shot a mocking glance at me—"but Yolara with you, there is no fear that you will join the dance," he added hastily, and obviously with reassuring intention.

What was this dancing of the Shining One, of which so often he had spoken? And in it, what was there for us of the deadly, inexplicable danger that had blasted Throckmartin and his and destroyed the wife and child of Olaf? Would we meet at this ceremony, whatever it was, those I had come here to find?

Whatever my forebodings, Larry evidently had none.

"Great stuff!" he cried, when we had met in the great antechamber, now empty of the dwarfs. "We're invited to the show—reserved seats and all the rest of it. Hope it will be worth seeing—have to be something damned good, though, to catch me, after what I've seen of shows at the front," he added.

And remembering, with a little shock of apprehension, that he had no knowledge of the Dweller beyond my poor description of it—for there are no words actually to describe what that miracle of interwoven glory and horror was—I wondered what Larry O'Keefe would say and do when he did behold it!

Rador began to show impatience.

"Come!" he urged. "There is much to be done—and the time grows short!"

He led us to a tiny fountain room, in whose miniature pool the white waters were concentrated, pearl-like and opalescent in their circling rim.

"Bathe!" he commanded; and set the example by stripping himself and plunging within. We followed. I experienced the peculiar stimulation that these waters always gave. They seemed to sparkle through every nerve and muscle. Only a minute or two did the green dwarf allow us, and he checked us as we were about to don our clothing—and let me note that we had long been provided with all necessary garments to replace our own. And I would, indeed, gladly have donned the outer costume of the place, save that Larry had clung to his uniform; and so I kept also to my knickerbockers, my stockings, and my canvas shoes, compromising, however, with a Murian tunic above them in the place of my American shirt.

Then, to my intense embarrassment, without warning, two of the black-haired girls entered, bearing robes of a peculiar dull-blue hue. At our manifest discomfort Rador's bellow of laughter roared out. He took the garments from the pair, motioned them to leave us, and, still laughing, threw one around me. Its texture was soft, but decidedly metallic—like some blue metal spun to the fineness of a spider's thread. The garment buckled tightly at the throat, was girdled at the waist, and, below this cincture, fell to the floor, its folds being held together by a half-dozen looped cords; from the shoulders a hood resembling a monk's cowl.

Rador cast this over my head; it completely covered my face, but was of so transparent a texture that I could see, though somewhat mistily, through it. Finally he handed us both a pair of long gloves of the same material and high stockings, the feet of which were gloved—five-toed.

And again his laughter rang out at our manifest surprise.

"The priestess of the Shining One does not altogether trust the Shining One's Voice," he said at last. "And these are to guard against any sudden—errors. And fear not, Goodwin," he went on kindly. "Not for the Shining One itself would Yolara see harm come to *Larree* here—nor, because of him, to you. But I would not stake much on her heart toward the Double Tongue whom Lugur has claimed—nor to the great white one. And for the last I am sorry, for him I do like well."

"Are they to be with us?" asked Larry eagerly.

"They are to be where we go," replied the dwarf soberly. "For Double Tongue there is no more peril than for you—Lugur stands with him—but for the other—"

He was silent. Grimly Larry reached down and drew from his uniform his automatic. He popped a fresh clip into the pocket fold of his girdle. The pistol he slung high up beneath his arm-pit. Now O'Keefe had cautioned me against revealing my weapon, and had, up till now, kept his own concealed.

"When we do need 'em, we're certain to have a bunch of odds against us, Doc," he had said. "And the element of surprise will be mighty valuable to us. Keep 'em under cover till we have to use 'em; then shoot straight!"

Therefore I wondered why Larry was showing his hand. The green dwarf looked at the weapon curiously. O'Keefe tapped it, and as he spoke I understood.

"Listen, Rador," he said. "I like you, and I believe you like us."

The dwarf nodded emphatically.

"This," said Larry, "slays quicker than the *Keth*—I take it so no harm shall come to the blue-eyed one whose name is Olaf. If I should raise it—be you not in its way, Rador!" he added significantly.

The dwarf nodded again, his eyes sparkling. He thrust a hand out to both of us.

"A change comes," he said. "What it is I know not, nor how it will fall. But this remember—Rador is more friend to you than you yet can know. And now let us go!" he ended abruptly.

He led us, not through the entrance, but into a sloping passage ending in a blind wall; touched a symbol graven there, and it opened, precisely as had the rosy barrier of the Moon Pool Chamber. And, just as there, but far smaller, was a passage end, a low curved wall facing a shaft, not black as had been that abode of living darkness, but faintly luminescent. Rador leaned over the wall.

O'Keefe winked at me. The mechanism clicked and started; the door swung shut; the sides of the car slipped into place, and we swept swiftly down the passage; overhead the wind whistled; Rador turned toward us.

"Have no fear—" he began, and then, for the green dwarf was keen, was aware without doubt of our lack of surprise. He started again to speak—shrugged his shoulders, and turned his back. Our speed was great and the journey not long. In a few moments the moving platform began to slow down. It stopped in a closed chamber no larger than itself.

Rador scanned the wall before him, and then, finding what he sought, although I could see nothing on its smooth surface, drew his poniard and struck twice with its hilt. Immediately a panel moved away, revealing a space filled with faint, misty blue radiance. And at each side of the opened portal stood four of the dwarfish men, gray-headed, old, clad in a flowing garment of white; each pointing toward us a short silver rod.

Rador drew from his girdle a ring and held it out to the first dwarf. He examined it, lowered his rod, handed it to the one beside him, and not until each had examined the ring did each lower his curious weapon; containers of that terrific energy they called the *Keth*, I thought; and later was to know that I had been right.

We stepped out; the doors closed behind us. The place was weird enough. Its pave was a greenish-blue stone resembling lapis lazuli. On each side were high pedestals holding carved figures of the same material. There were perhaps a score of these, but in the mistiness I could not make out their outlines. A droning, rushing roar beat upon our ears; filled the whole cavern.

"I smell the sea," said Larry suddenly.

And then I, too, realized that the tang of ocean was strong. I felt its moisture upon my face and hands. Rador spoke again to the leader of—the priests—as I now began to think them. Four leading the way and four following us, we marched forward. The floor arose gradually, and the rushing roar grew louder, the sea breath stronger.

And now the roaring became deep-toned, clamorous, and close in front of us a rift opened. Twenty feet in width, it cut the cavern floor and vanished into the blue mist on each side. The priests leading us knelt, Rador imitating them; O'Keefe nudged me, and we, too, dropped to our knees. We arose and went forward. Before us the cleft was spanned by one solid slab of rock not more than two yards wide. It had neither railing nor other protection.

The four leading priests marched out upon it one by one, and we followed. In the middle of the span they stopped and again we knelt. Ten feet beneath us was a torrent of blue sea-water racing with prodigious speed between polished walls. It gave the impression of vast depth. It roared as it sped by, and far to the right was a low arch through which it disappeared. It was so swift that its surface shone like polished blue steel, and from it came the blessed, *our worldly*, familiar ocean breath that strengthened my soul amazingly and made me realize how earth-sick I was. Larry, too, drew himself up, drawing deep breaths. Rador uttered a curious phrase—it loses in translation its peculiar picturesqueness.

"The Holy Cord of the Naval of the Great Waters!" is the closest I can come to it.

Whence came the stream, I marveled, forgetting for the moment as we passed on again, all else. Were we closer to the surface of earth than I had thought, or was this some mighty stream falling through an opening in sea floor. Heaven alone knew how many miles above us, losing itself in deeper abysses beyond these? How near and how far this was from the truth I was to learn—and never did truth come to man in more dreadful guise!

The roaring fell away, the blue haze lessened. In front of us stretched a wide flight of steps, huge as those which had let us into the courtyard of Nan-Tauach through the ruined sea-gate. We scaled it; it narrowed; from above light poured through a still narrower opening. Side by side Larry and I passed out of it.

How can I describe what I saw? Two things there are before which I falter—to picture that temple of the Shining One as it first met our eyes in all its incredible immensity, and what happened there; and that thing to come to pass, that twilight of the gods, in the abode of the Silent Ones on the Sea of Crimson. But I must attempt it, knowing full well that it is impossible to make clear one-tenth of their grandeur, their awfulness, their soul-shaking terror.

We had emerged upon an enormous platform of what seemed to be glistening ivory. It stretched before us for a hundred yards or more and then shelved gently into the white waters. Opposite—not a mile away—was that prodigious web of woven rainbows Rador had called the curtain of the Shining One. There it shone in all its unearthly grandeur, on each side of the Cyclopean pillars, as though a mountain should stretch up arms raising between them a fairy banner of auroral glories—in front the curved, similar sweep of the pier with its clustered, gleaming temples.

Before that brief, fascinated glance was done, there dropped upon my soul a sensation as of brooding weight intolerable; a spiritual oppression as though some vastness was falling, pressing, stilling me. I turned—and Larry caught me as I reeled.

"Steady! Steady, old man!" he whispered.

At first all that my staggering consciousness could realize was an immensity, an immeasurable uprearing, that brought with it the same throat-gripping vertigo as comes from gazing downward from some great height—then a blur of white faces—intolerable shinings of hundreds upon thousands of eyes—huge, incredibly huge, a colossal amphitheater of jet, a stupendous semicircle held within its mighty arc the ivory platform on which I stood.

It reared itself almost perpendicularly hundreds of feet up into the sparkling heavens, and thrust down on each side its ebon bulwarks—like monstrous paws. Now, the giddiness from its sheer greatness passing, I saw that it was indeed an amphitheater, sloping slightly backward tier after tier, and that the white blur of faces against its blackness, the gleaming of countless eyes, were those of myriads of the people who sat silent, flower-garlanded, their gaze focused upon the rainbow curtain and sweeping over me like a torrent—tangible, appalling!

Five hundred feet beyond, the smooth, high retaining wall of the amphitheater raised itself—above it the first terrace of the seats, and above this, dividing the tiers for another half a thousand feet upward, set within them like a panel, was a dead-black surface in which shone faintly with a bluish radiance a gigantic disk; above it and around it a cluster of innumerable smaller ones.

On each side of me, bordering the platform, were scores of small pillared alcoves; a low wall stretching across their fronts; delicate, fretted grills shielding them, save where in each lattice an opening stared—it came to me that they were like those stalls in ancient Gothic cathedrals wherein for centuries had kneeled paladins and people of my own race on earth's fair face. And within these alcoves were gathered, score upon score, the elfin beauties, the dwarfish men, of the fair-haired folk. At my right, a few feet from the opening through which we had come, a passageway led back between the fretted stalls. Halfway between us and the massive base of the amphitheater a dais rose. Up the platform to it a wide ramp ascended; and on ramp and dais and along the center of the gleaming platform down to where it kissed the white waters, a broad ribbon of the radiant flowers lay like a fairy carpet.

On one side of this dais, meshed in a silken web that hid no line or curve of her sweet body, white flesh gleaming through its folds, stood Yolara; and opposite her, crowned with a circlet of flashing blue stones, his mighty body stark bare, was Lugur!

O'Keefe drew a long breath; Rador touched my arm and, still dazed, I let myself be drawn into the aisle and through a corridor that ran behind the alcoves. At the back of one of these the green dwarf paused, opened a door, and motioned us within.

Entering, I found that we were exactly opposite where the ramp ran up to the dais—and that Yolara was not more than fifty feet away. She glanced at O'Keefe and smiled. I noted her extraordinary exhilaration—her eyes ablaze with little dancing points of light; her body that seemed to palpitate, the rounded delicate muscles beneath the translucent skin to run with little eager waves; she seemed—what is the word the Scotch use?— fey! Suddenly Larry whistled softly.

"There's Von Hetzdorp!" he said.

I looked where he pointed. Opposite us sat the German; clothed as we were, leaning forward, his eyes eager behind his glasses; but if he saw us he gave no sign.

"And there's Olaf!" said O'Keefe.

Beneath the carved stall in which sat the German was an aperture. Unprotected by pillars, or by grills, opening clear upon the platform, near it stretched the trail of flowers up to the great dais which Lugur the Voice and Yolara the Priestess guarded. Nor was Olaf clad as we. His mighty torso covered with a white tunic stuffed into his old dungarees, his feet bare, he sat immobile, staring out toward the prismatic veil, and in his eyes, even at that distance, I could see a flare of consuming hatred. So he sat alone, and my heart went out to him.

O'Keefe's face softened.

"Bring him here," he said to Rador.

The green dwarf was looking at the Norseman, too, a shade of pity upon his mocking face. He shook his head.

"Wait!" he said. "You can do nothing now—and it may be there will be no need to do anything," he added; but I could feel that there was little of conviction in his words.

CHAPTER XX

THE MADNESS OF OLAF

YOLARA DREW HERSELF up; threw her white arms high. From the mountainous tiers came a mighty sigh; a ripple ran through them. And upon the moment, before Yolara's arms fell, there issued, apparently from the air around us, a peal of sound that might have been the shouting of some playful god hurling great suns through the net of stars. It was like the deepest notes of all the organs in the world combined in one; summoning, majestic, cosmic!

It held within it the thunder of the spheres rolling through the infinite, the birth-song of suns made manifest in the womb of space; echoes of creation's supernal chord! It shook the body like a pulse from the heart of the universe—pulsed—and died away.

On its death came a blaring as of all the trumpets of conquering hosts since the first Pharaoh led his swarms—triumphal, compelling! Alexander's clamoring hosts, brazen-throated wolf-horns of Caesar's legions, blare of trumpets of Genghis Khan and his golden horde, clangor of the locust levies of Tamerlane, bugles of Napoleon's armies—war-shout of all earth's conquerors! And it died!

Fast upon it, a throbbing, muffled tumult of harp sounds, mellownesses of myriads of wood horns, the subdued sweet shrilling of multitudes of flutes, Pandean pipings—inviting, carrying with them the calling of waterfalls in the hidden places, rushing brooks and murmuring forest winds—calling, calling, languorous, lulling, dripping into the brain like the very honeyed essence of sound.

And after them a silence in which the memory of the music seemed to beat, to beat, ever more faintly, through every quivering nerve.

From me all fear, all apprehension, had fled. In their place was nothing but joyous anticipation, a supernal freedom from even the shadow of the shadow of care or sorrow; not now did anything matter—Olaf or his haunted, hate-filled eyes; Throckmartin or his fate—nothing of pain, nothing of agony, nothing of striving nor endeavor nor despair in that wide outer world that had turned suddenly to a troubled dream.

And in that moment, as the muscles of my face grew rigid with inhuman emotion, in my subconsciousness stirred understanding of that element in the Murians that had so perplexed me—for what to those who experienced in such sounds the emotions of universal Nature herself could be either the joys or sorrows of mankind? And yet—

My eyes sought the crowded tiers, sensing there in multitudinous form the same reaction of those stupendous vibrations that had so shaken me—and yet—again that furtive doubt—

Once more the first great note peeled out! As once more it died, from the clustered spheres a kaleidoscopic blaze shot as though drawn from the majestic sound itself. The many-colored rays darted across the white waters and sought the face of the irised veil. As they touched, it sparkled, flamed, wavered, and shook with fountains of prismatic color.

The light increased—and in its intensity the silver air darkened. Faded into shadow that white mosaic of flower-crowned faces set in the amphitheater of jet, and vast shadows dropped upon the high-flung tiers and shrouded them. But on the skirts of the rays the fretted stalls in which we sat with the fair-haired ones blazed out, iridescent, like jewels.

I was sensible of an acceleration of every pulse; a wild stimulation of every nerve. I felt myself being lifted above the world—close to the threshold of the high gods—soon their essence and their power would stream out into me! I glanced at Larry. His face was transformed—he was like Balder the Beautiful—wonderful as one of those olden half gods of his own beloved isle! His eyes were—wild—with life! And Yolara—I cannot describe her—but as her face turned toward his I saw in the joy of her own eyes infernal allure and a passion withering.

I looked at Olaf—and in his face was none of this—only hate, and hate, and hate.

The peacock waves streamed out over the waters, cleaving the seeming darkness, a rainbow path of glory. And the veil flashed as though all the rainbows that had ever shone were burning within it. Again the mighty sound pealed.

Into the center of the veil the light drew itself, grew into an intolerable brightness—and with a storm of tinklings, a tempest of crystalline notes, a tumult of tiny chimings, through it sped—the Shining One!

Straight down that radiant path, its high-flung plumes of feathery flame shimmering, its coruscating spirals whirling, its seven globes of seven colors shining above its glowing core, it raced toward us. The hurricane of bells of diamond glass were jubilant, joyous. I felt O'Keefe grip my arm; Yolara threw her white arms out in a welcoming gesture; I heard from the tiers a sigh of rapture—and in it a poignant, wailing undertone of agony!

And over the waters, down the light stream, to the end of

the ivory pier, flew the Shining One. Through its crystal pizzicati drifted inarticulate murmurings—deadly sweet, stilling the heart and setting it leaping madly.

For a moment it paused, poised itself, and then came whirling down the flower path to its priestess, slowly, ever more slowly. It passed Olaf—and I saw his hands clench until the knuckles whitened; saw his mighty chest swell with the terrific restrained impulse to leap out upon it!

It passed—hovered for a moment between the woman and the dwarf, as though contemplating them; turned to her with its storm of tinklings softened, its murmurings infinitely caressing. Bent toward it, Yolara seemed to gather within herself pulsing waves of power; she was terrifying; gloriously, maddeningly evil; and as gloriously, maddeningly heavenly! Aphrodite and the Virgin! Tanith of the Carthaginians and St. Bride of the Isles! Succubus and Angel! A queen of hell and a princess of heaven—in one!

Only for a moment did that which we had called the Dweller and that these named the Shining One, pause. It swept up the ramp to the dais, rested there, slowly turning, plumes and spirals lacing and unlacing, throbbing, pulsing. Now its nucleus grew plainer, stronger—human in a fashion, and all inhuman; neither man nor woman; neither god nor devil; subtly partaking of all. Nor could I doubt that whatever if was, within that shining nucleus was something sentient; something that had will and energy, and in some awful, supernormal fashion—intelligence!

Another trumpeting—a sound of stones opening—a long, low wail of utter anguish—something moved shadowy in the river of light, and slowly at first, then ever more rapidly, shapes swam through it. There were half a score of them—girls and youths, women and men. And I knew that these were sacrifices thrust out to the god. As they drew on, the Shining One poised itself, regarded them. They drew closer, and in the eyes of each and in their faces was the bud of that strange intermingling of emotions, of joy and sorrow, ecstasy and terror, that I had seen in full blossom on Throckmartin's.

The Thing began again its murmurings—now infinitely caressing, coaxing—like the song of a siren from some witched star! And the bell sounds rang out—compellingly, calling—calling—calling—

I saw Olaf lean far out of his place; saw, half-consciously, at Lugur's signal, three of the dwarfs creep in and take place, unnoticed, behind him. But in the fire of my interest the sight was burned instantaneously from my mind.

Now the first of the swift figures rushed upon the dais—and paused. But only for a moment. It was the girl who had been brought before Yolara, when the gnome named Sangar was driven into the nothingness! With all the quickness of light a spiral of the Shining One stretched out and encircled her.

At its touch there was an infinitely dreadful shrinking and, it seemed, a simultaneous hurling of herself into its radiance. And as it wrapped its swirls around her, permeated her—the crystal chorus burst forth—tumultuously; through and through her the radiance pulsed. Began then that infinitely dreadful, but infinitely glorious, rhythm they called the dance of the Shining One. And as the girl swirled within its sparkling mists, another and another flew into its embrace, until, at last, the dais was an incredible vision; a mad star's Witches' Sabbath, *phantasmagoric Macaberesque;* an altar of white faces and bodies gleaming through living flame; transfused with rapture insupportable and horror that was hellish—and ever, radiant plumes and spirals expanding, the core of the Shining One waxed—growing greater—as it consumed, as it drew into and through itself the life-force of these lost ones!

So they spun there, interlaced, souls caught in the monstrous web—and there began to pulse from them life, vitality, as though the very essence of nature was filling us. Dimly I recognized that what I was beholding was vampirism inconceivable! The banked tiers chanted. The mighty sounds pealed forth!—it was a Saturnalia of demigods—Yolara transformed beyond semblance of earth—her beauty flaring out into unholy and devilish, and at once holy and wondrous fulfillment impossible to tell—

Whirling, murmuring, bell-notes storming, the Shining One began to pass from the dais down the ramp, still embracing, still interwoven with those who had thrown themselves into its spirals. They drew along with it as though half carried; in dreadful dance; white faces sealed—forever—into that semblance of those who held within linked God and devil—I covered my eyes!

And the Shining One passed—passed on—was beside Olaf—

I heard a gasp from O'Keefe; opened my eyes and sought his; saw the madness depart from them as he strained forward. Olaf had leaned far out, and as he did so two of the dwarfs beside him caught him, and whether by design or through his own swift, involuntary movement, thrust him half into the Dweller's path. The Dweller paused in its gyrations—seemed to watch him. The Norseman's face was crimson, his eyes blazing. He threw himself back and, with one mad, defiant shout, gripped one of the dwarfs about the middle and sent him hurtling through the air, straight at the radiant thing! A whirling mass of legs and arms, the dwarf flew—then in mid-flight stopped as though some gigantic invisible hand had caught him, and—was dashed—it came to me as one would dash a great spider, with prodigious force, down upon the platform not a yard from the Shining One!

And like a broken spider he moved—feebly—once, twice. From the Dweller shot a shimmering tentacle—touched him— recoiled. Its crystal tinklings changed into an angry chiming. From all about—jeweled stalls and jet peak—came a sigh of incredulous horror.

And all the while those dead-alive, who had danced with the Shining One, turned slowly within its sparkling mist—faces devoid of all human semblance—turning, slowly turning, in its coruscating net—*chatoyant*—like fireflies in gleaming, swirling mist—God!

"God!" The echo of my invocation came from O'Keefe. "Olaf threw him short!" But I knew that was not what had stopped his flight!

Lugur, his face gray, all exaltation gone from it, leaped forward. On the instant Larry was over the low barrier between the pillars, rushing to the Norseman's side. And even as they ran there was another wild shout from Olaf, and he hurled himself out, straight at the throat of the Dweller!

But before he could touch the Shining One, now motion-less—and never was the thing more horrible than then, with the purely human suggestion of surprise plain in its poise—Larry had struck him aside.

I tried to follow—and was held by Rador. He was trembling—but not with fear. In his face was incredulous hope, inexplicable eagerness.

"Wait!" he said. "Wait!"

The Shining One stretched out a slow spiral, and as it did so I saw the bravest thing man has ever witnessed. Instantly O'Keefe thrust himself between it and Olaf, pistol out. The tentacle touched him, and the dull blue of his robe flashed out into blinding, intense azure light. From the automatic in his gloved hand came three quick bursts of flame straight into the Thing. The Dweller drew back; the bell-sounds swelled angrily.

And all that time its prey, unheeding, white faces transfig-ured—turned—turned slowly on its radiant web—can I ever forget!

Then I saw Lugur pause—his hand darted up, and in it was one of the silver *Keth* cones. But before he could flash it upon the Norseman, Larry had unlooped his robe, thrown its fold over Olaf, and, holding him with one hand away from the Shining One, thrust with the other his pistol into the dwarf's stomach. His lips moved, but I could not hear what he said. But Lugur seemed to understand, for his hand dropped.

Now Yolara was there—all this had taken barely more than five seconds. She thrust herself between the three men and the apparition, of which she was priestess. She spoke to it—and the wild buzzing died down; the gay crystal tinklings burst forth again. The Thing murmured to her—began to whirl—faster, faster—passed down the ivory pier, out upon the waters, bearing with it, meshed in its light, the sacrifice—swept on ever more swiftly, triumphantly—and vanished; turning, turning, with its ghastly crew, through the Veil!

Abruptly the polychromatic path snapped out. The silver light poured in upon us. From all the amphitheater arose a clamor, a shouting. Von Hetzdorp, his eyes staring, was leaning out, listening. Unrestrained now by Rador, I vaulted the wall and rushed forward. But not before I had heard the green dwarf murmur:

"There is something stronger than the Shining One! Two things—yea—a strong heart—and hate!"

Olaf, panting, eyes glazed, trembling, shrank beneath my hand.

"The devil that took my Helma!" I heard him whisper. "The Shining Devil!"

"Both these men," Lugur was raging, "they shall dance with the Shining One. And this one, too." He pointed at me malignantly.

"This man is mine," said the priestess, and her voice was icily menacing. She rested her hand on Larry's shoulder. "He shall not dance. No—nor his friend. I have told you I care not for this one!" She pointed to Olaf.

"Neither this man, nor this," said Larry, his pistol still pressed against Lugur, "shall be harmed. This is my word, Yolara!"

She looked at him.

"Even so," she said quietly, "my lord!"

Lugur's eyes grew hellish, and I saw Von Hetzdorp stare at O'Keefe with a new and curiously speculative interest.

"I have said it!" She turned to Lugur. "What can you do?" she added quite insolently.

He raised his arms as though to strike her. Her hand swept to her bosom. Larry's pistol prodded him rudely enough.

"No rough stuff now, kid!" said O'Keefe in English. The red dwarf quivered, turned—caught a robe from a priest standing by, and threw it over himself. The *ladala*, shouting, gesticulating, fighting with the soldiers, were jostling down from the tiers of jet.

"Come!" commanded Yolara—her eyes rested upon Larry. "Your heart is great, indeed—my lord!" she murmured; and her voice was very sweet. "Come!"

"This man comes with us, Yolara," said O'Keefe, pointing to Olaf.

"Bring him," she said. "What you have done—and what may come from what you have done, I know not." She laughed. "But compared to what I think that will be—this man is but a straw in a torrent. So bring him—only tell him to look no more upon me as before!" she added fiercely.

Beside her the three of us passed along the stalls, where sat the fair-haired, now silent, at gaze, as though in the grip of some great doubt. Silently Olaf strode beside me. Rador had disappeared. Down the stairway, through the hall of turquoise mist, over the rushing sea-stream we went and stood beside the wall through which we had entered. The white-robed ones had fled.

Yolara pressed; the portal opened. We stepped upon the car; Yolara took the lever; the walls flashed by—and dazed, troubled, I, at least, more than half-incredulous as to the reality of it all, we sped through the faintly luminous corridor to the house of the priestess.

And as we sped I, too, wondered what it was that Olaf had done—and what was to come of it.

But one thing I wondered about no more, sick at heart and soul the truth had come to me—no more need to search for Throckmartin. Behind that Veil, in the lair of the Dweller, dead-alive like those we had just seen swim in its shining train was he, and Edith, Stanton and Thora and Olaf Huldricksson's wife.

CHAPTER XXI

"THE *LADALA* ARE AWAKE!"

NO WORD WAS spoken during the swift journey. The webs that clothed Yolara streamed out behind her like little filmy pennons; she stared ahead, strangely *exalté*, brows drawn in one delicate line above eyes now deepest blue. O'Keefe watched her, and from his beauty-loving soul one could see admiration creep up and stand at gaze. Upon Olaf's grim face a shade of greater grimness fell; his jaw hardened. Whatever Larry's change of heart might be, I thought, it found no echo in the Norseman's breast.

The car came to rest; the portal opened; Yolara leaped out lightly, beckoned and flitted up the corridor. She paused before an ebon screen. At a touch it vanished, revealing an entrance to a small blue chamber, glowing as though cut from the heart of some gigantic sapphire; bare, save that in its center, upon a low pedestal, stood a great globe fashioned from milky rock-crystal; upon its surface were faint tracings as of seas and continents, but, if so, either of some other world or of this world in immemorial past, for in no way did they resemble the mapped coast lines of our earth.

Poised upon the globe, rising from it out into space, locked in each other's arms, lips to lips, were two figures, a woman and a man, so exquisite, so lifelike, that for the moment I failed to realize that they, too, were carved of the crystal. And before this shrine—for nothing else could it be, I knew—three slender cones raised themselves: one of purest white flame, one of opalescent water, and the third of—moonlight! There was no mistaking them, the height of a tall man each stood—but how water, flame, and light were held so evenly, so steadily in their spire-shapes, I could not tell.

Before this shrine Yolara bowed lowly—once, twice, thrice. She turned to O'Keefe. Nor by slightest look or gesture betrayed she knew others were there than he. The blue eyes wide, searching, unfathomable, she drew close; put white hands on his shoulders, looked down into his very soul—and I saw a shadow dim their azure brilliance.

"Not yet," she whispered. "Not yet—is your heart mine!" She was silent again for a space, regarding him.

"My lord," at last she murmured. "Now listen well—for I, Yolara, offer you three things—myself, and the Shining One, and the power that is the Shining One's—yea, and still a fourth thing that is all three—power over all upon that world from whence ye came! These, my lord, ye shall have. I swear it"—she turned toward the altar—uplifted her arms—"by Siya and by Siyana, and by the flame, by the water, and by the light!"

She bent toward him once more, drew still closer.

"Not yet is that heart of yours mine!" she repeated softly. "Yet shall it be! And that, too, I swear by Siya and by Siyana, and by the flame, by the water, and by the light!"

Her eyes grew purple dark. "And let none dare to take you from me! Nor ye go from me unbidden!" she whispered fiercely.

And then swiftly, still ignoring us, she threw her arms about O'Keefe, pressed her white body to his breast, lips raised, eyes closed, seeking his. O'Keefe's arms tightened around her, his head dropped lips seeking, finding hers—passionately! From Olaf came a deep indrawn breath that was almost a groan. But not in *my* heart could I find blame for the Irishman!

The priestess opened eyes now all misty blue, thrust him back, stood regarding him. O'Keefe, face dead-white, raised a trembling hand to his face.

"And thus have I sealed my oath, O my lord!" she whispered. For the first time she seemed to recognize our presence, stared at us a moment, and then through us, turned to O'Keefe.

"Go, now!" she said. "Soon Rador shall come for you. Then—well, after that let happen what will!"

She smiled once more at him—so sweetly; turned toward the figures upon the great globe; sank upon her knees before them. Quietly we crept away; in utter silence we passed through the anteroom, still deserted; found the head of the mosaicked path, and, still silent, made our way to the little pavilion. But as we passed along we heard a tumult from the green roadway; shouts of men, now and then a woman's scream. Through a rift in the garden I glimpsed a jostling crowd on one of the bridges; green dwarfs struggling with the *ladala*—and all about droned a humming as of a giant hive disturbed!

Larry threw himself down upon one of the divans, covered his face with his hands, dropped them to catch in Olaf's eyes troubled reproach, looked at me.

"*I* couldn't help it," he said, half defiantly—half-miserably. "God, what a woman! I *couldn't* help it!" He walked about the room restlessly. "What do you suppose she meant by offering me that shining devil they worship in this cross-section of beautiful hell?" he demanded, halting. "And what did she mean about 'power over all the world?'"

"Larry," I said. "Why didn't you tell her you didn't love her—then?"

He gazed at me—the old twinkle back in his eye.

"Spoken like a scientist, Doc!" he exclaimed. "I suppose if a burning angel struck you out of nowhere and threw itself about you, you would most dignifiedly tell it you didn't want to be burned. For God's sake, don't talk nonsense, Goodwin!" he ended, almost peevishly.

"But if it was a bad angel—a beautiful devil—*djaevelsk*—and she should come to you—and you knew her a devil, and your soul the price of her kisses—would you kiss or slay her?" Thus Olaf, heavily, sadly. Larry glanced at him, troubled.

"Evil! Evil!" The Norseman's voice was deep, nearly a chant. "All here is of evil: Trolldom and Helvede it is, *ja!* And that she *djaevelsk* of beauty—what is she but harlot of that shining devil they worship. I, Olaf Huldricksson, know what she meant when she held out to you power over all the world, *ja!*—as if the world had not devils enough in it now!"

"What?" The cry came from both O'Keefe and myself at once.

"*Ja!*" said Olaf. "I have heard. I have listened to that *Trolde* Lugur and to Von Hetzdorp. They did not know I could understand them—no! I crept about and listened. And I know, *ja!* Evil! All evil that woman—and Helvede snarling at these gates—mad to be loosed on our world above!"

"We'd better just forget why I kissed the lady and hear what Olaf's got to say, Doc," said O'Keefe.

"It was when the woman, the wonder-witch, broke—*ad-sprede*—the oldster—" began Olaf. He stopped, peering down the path—made a gesture of caution, relapsed into sullen silence. There were footsteps on the path, and into sight came Rador—but a Rador changed. Gone was every vestige of his mockery; his face all serious, curiously solemn, he saluted O'Keefe and Olaf with that salute which, before this, I had seen given only to Yolara and to Lugur. There came from far-away a swift quickening of the tumult—died away. He shrugged mighty shoulders.

"The *ladala* are awake!" he said. "So much for what two brave men can do!" He paused thoughtfully. "Bones and dust jostle not each other for place against the grave wall!" he added oddly. "But if bones and dust have revealed to them that they still— live—"

He stopped abruptly, eyes seeking the globe that bore and sent forth speech.*

---

* I find that I have neglected to explain the working of these interesting mechanisms that were telephonic, dictaphonic, telegraphic in one. I must assume that my readers are familiar with the receiving apparatus of wireless telegraphy, which must be tuned by the operator until its own vibratory quality is in exact harmony with the vibrations—the extremely rapid impacts—of those short electric wave-lengths we call Hertzian, and which carry the wireless messages. I must assume also that they are familiar with the elementary fact of physics that the vibrations of light and sound are interchangeable. The hearing-talking globes utilize both these principles, and with consummate simplicity. The light with which they shone was produced by an atomic "motor" within their base, similar to that which activated the merely illuminating globes. The composition of the phonic spheres gave their surfaces an acute sensitivity and resonance. In conjunction with its energizing power, the metal set up what is called a "field of force," which linked it with every particle of its kind no matter how

"The *Afyo Maie* has sent me to watch over you till she summons you," he announced clearly. A vestige of raillery flitted over his face. "There is to be a—feast. You, *Larree,* you, Goodwin, are to come. I remain here with—Olaf."

"No harm to him!" broke in O'Keefe sharply. Rador touched his heart, his eyes.

"By the Ancient Ones, and by my love for you, and by what you twain did before the Shining One—I swear it!" he answered. O'Keefe, satisfied, thrust him his hand.

Rador clapped palms; a soldier came round the path, in his grip a long flat box of polished wood. The green dwarf took it, dismissed him, threw open the lid.

"Here is your apparel for the feast, *Larree,*" he said, pointing to the contents.

O'Keefe stared, reached down and drew out a white, shimmering, softly metallic, long-sleeved tunic, a broad, silvery girdle, leg swathings of the same argent material, and sandals that seemed to be cut out from silver. He made a quick gesture of angry dissent.

"Nay, *Larree!*" whispered the dwarf. "Wear them—I counsel it—I pray it—ask me not why?" he went on swiftly, looking again at the globe.

O'Keefe, as I, was impressed by his earnestness. The dwarf made a curiously expressive pleading gesture. O'Keefe abruptly took the garments; passed into the room of the fountain.

"What is the feast, Rador?" I asked. "The Shining One dances not again?" I added.

"No," he said. "No"—he hesitated—"it is the usual feast that

---

distant. When vibrations of speech impinged upon the resonant surface its rhythmic light-vibrations were broken, just as a telephone transmitter breaks an electric current. Simultaneously these light-vibrations were changed into sound—on the surfaces of all spheres tuned to that particular instrument. The "crawling" colors which showed themselves at these times were literally the voice of the speaker in its spectrum equivalent. While usually the sounds produced required considerable familiarity with the apparatus to be understood quickly, they could, on occasion, be made startlingly loud and clear—as I was soon to realize—W.T.G.

follows the—sacrament! Lugur—and Double Tongue, who came with you, will be there," he added slowly.

"Lugur—" I gasped in astonishment. "After what happened—he will be there?"

"Perhaps because of what happened, Goodwin, my friend," he answered—his eyes again full of malice; "and there will be others—friends of Yolara—friends of Lugur—and perhaps another"—his voice was almost inaudible—"one whom they have not called—" He halted, half-fearfully, glancing at the globe; put finger to lips and spread himself out upon one of the couches.

"Strike up the band"—came O'Keefe's voice—"here comes the hero!"

The curtains parted and he strode into the room. I am bound to say that the admiration in Rador's eyes was reflected in my own, and even, if involuntarily, in Olaf's. For in the gleaming silver garb the Irishman was truly splendid. Long, lithe, clean-limbed, his keen, dark face smiling, he shone in contrast with Rador, and would, I knew, be among those other dwarfish men as was Cuchullin, son of Lerg and beloved of the Dark Queen Scathach, among the Pictish trolls.

"A son of Siyana!" whispered Rador. "A child of Siya—"Who, I wondered, were these twain whose names had been uttered so holily by Yolara and now by the green dwarf—with far, far more reverence than they spoke of the Shining One?* The green

---

* I have no space here even to outline the eschatology of this people, nor to cata-logue their pantheon. Siya and Siyana typified worldly love. Their ritual was, how-ever, singularly free from those degrading elements usually found in love-cults. Their youthful priests and priestesses were selected from the most beautiful children of the ruling class, and at the age of nineteen the girls, and at the age of twenty-one the youths were automatically released from their service, taking, if they desired, mates. Priests and priestess of all cults dwelt in the immense seven-terraced structure, of which the jet amphitheater was the water side. The symbol, icon, representation, of Siya and Siyana—the globe and the up-striving figures—typified earthly love, feet bound to earth, but eyes among the stars. Hell or heaven I never heard formulated, nor their equivalents; unless that existence in the Shining One's domain could serve for either. Over all this was Thanaroa, remote, unheeding, but still maker and ruler of all an absentee First Cause personified! Thanaroa seemed to be the one article of be-lief in the creed of the soldiers—Rador, with his reverence for the Ancient Ones, was

dwarf knelt, took from his girdle-pouch a silk-wrapped something, unwound it—and, still kneeling, drew out a slender poniard of gleaming white metal, hilted with the blue, scintillating stones; stretching out a long arm he thrust it into O'Keefe's girdle; then gave him again the rare salute. Before he could rise the tripod globe chimed; swam with its film of racing colors; whispered. The dwarf listened.

"I hear!" he said. Its humming stopped, the crawling colors stilled. "You know the way." He turned to O'Keefe and to me. He followed us to the head of the pathway.

"Now," he said grimly, "let the Silent Ones show their power—if they still have it!"

And with this strange benediction perplexing me, we passed on.

"For God's sake, Larry." I urged as we approached the house of the priestess, "you'll be careful!"

He nodded—but I saw with a little deadly pang of apprehension in my heart a puzzled, lurking doubt within his eyes.

There were many guards about the place—far more than I had ever seen before. They stood at attention along the bowered path, and just before we reached the portal of the palace, a dozen of them, manifestly awaiting us, stepped forward, saluted, then formed on each side of us a guard of honor.

As we ascended the serpent steps Von Hetzdorp suddenly appeared. The blue robes were gone; he was clothed in gay green tunic and leg-swathings—and odd enough he looked in them, with his owl-rimmed spectacles and his pointed Teutonic beard. He gave a signal to our guards—and I wondered what influence the German had attained, for promptly, without question, they drew aside. At me he smiled amiably.

"It is good to see you again, Dr. Goodwin," he said. "No

---

an exception. Whatever there was, indeed, of high, truly religious impulse among the Murians, this far, High God had. I found this exceedingly interesting, because it had long been my theory—to put the matter in the shape of a geometrical formula—that the real attractiveness of gods to man increases uniformly according to the square of their distance.—W.T.G.

doubt you have been observing much. You and I will have much to say to each other—yes?"

Friendly as were the words, in them was something furtively menacing.

"Have you found your friends yet?" he went on—and now I sensed something more deeply sinister in him. "No! It is too bad! Well, don't give up hope. I have an idea Olaf will find his wife before you find Professor Throckmartin, *ja!*" His lips curled in a vulpine grin—what was the man hinting, what was he driving at? He turned to O'Keefe.

"Lieutenant, I would like to speak to you—alone!"

"I've no secrets from Goodwin," answered O'Keefe.

"So?" queried Von Hetzdorp suavely. He bent, whispered to Larry.

The Irishman started, eyed him with a certain shocked incredulity, then turned to me.

"Just a minute, Doc!" he said, and I caught the suspicion of a wink. They drew aside, out of ear-shot. The German talked rapidly. Larry was all attention. Von Hetzdorp's earnestness became intense; O'Keefe interrupted—appeared to question. Von Hetzdorp glanced at me and as his gaze shifted from O'Keefe, I saw a hot flame of rage and horror blaze up in the latter's eyes. At last O'Keefe appeared to consider gravely; nodded as though he had arrived at some decision, and Von Hetzdorp, fairly beaming with delight and satisfaction, thrust his hand to him. And only I could have noticed Larry's shrinking, his microscopic hesitation before he took it, and his involuntary movement, as though to shake off something unclean, when the clasp had ended.

Von Hetzdorp, without another look at me, turned and went quickly within. The guards took their places, and we passed on to face whatever it was that fate held for us. I looked at Larry inquiringly.

"Don't ask a thing now, Doc!" he said tensely. "Wait till we get home. But we've got to get damned busy and quick—I'll tell you that now—"

CHAPTER XXII

THE TEMPTING OF LARRY

WE PAUSED BEFORE thick curtains, through which came the faint murmur of many voices. They parted; out came two—ushers, I suppose, they were—in cuirasses and kilts that reminded me somewhat of chain-mail—the first armor of any kind here that I had seen. They held open the folds, bowed, and as we entered fell in behind us.

The chamber, on whose threshold we stood, was far larger than either anteroom or hall of audience. Not less than three hundred feet long and half that in depth, from end to end of it ran two huge semicircular tables, paralleling each other, divided by a wide aisle, and heaped with flowers, with fruits, with viands unknown to me, and glittering with crystal flagons, beakers, goblets of as many hues as the blooms. And on the gay-cushioned couches that flanked the tables, lounging luxuriously, were scores of the fair-haired ruling class.

Their eyes were turned upon us, and there rose a little buzz of admiration, oddly mixed with a half-startled amaze, as their gaze fell upon O'Keefe in all his silvery magnificence. Everywhere the light-giving globes sent their roseate radiance.

The cuirassed dwarfs led us through the aisle. Within the arc of the inner half-circle was another glittering board, an oval. But of those seated there, facing us—I had eyes for only one—Yolara! She swayed up to greet O'Keefe—and she was like one of those white lily maids, whose beauty Hoang-Ku, the sage, says made the Gobi first a paradise, and whose lusts later the burned-out desert that it is. She held out hands to Larry, and on her face was passion—unashamed, unhiding.

She was Circe—but Circe conquered. Webs of filmiest white clung to the rose-leaf body—like rosy morning mists about a nymph of Diana. Twisted through the corn-silk hair a threaded circlet of pale sapphires shone; but they were pale beside

Yolara's eyes. O'Keefe bent, kissed her hands, something more than mere admiration flaming from him. She saw—and, laughing, drew him down beside her.

It came to me that of all, only these two, Yolara and O'Keefe, were in white—and I wondered; then with a stiffening of nerves ceased to wonder as there entered—Lugur! He was all in scarlet, and as he strode forward the voices were still; a silence fell—a tense, strained silence.

His gaze turned upon Yolara, rested upon O'Keefe, and instantly his face grew—dreadful—there is no other word than that for it. Satan, losing heaven and finding an usurper on his throne in hell, could have held in his eyes no more of devilish malignity. It flashed through my mind, fancifully, that his face was like the pitch-black cloud hovering over a volcano's crater lit by the crimson flames below!

I had not noticed Von Hetzdorp, but now I saw him lean forward from the center of the table, near whose end I sat, touch Lugur, and whisper to him swiftly. With an appalling effort the red dwarf controlled himself; his rage slowly gave way to a sinister saturninity, coldly malefic as the rage had been hotly menacing. He saluted the priestess ironically, I thought; took his place at the further end of the oval. And now I noted that the figures between were the seven of that council of which the Shining One's priestess and Voice were the heads. The tension relaxed, but did not pass—as though a storm-cloud should turn away, but still lurk, threatening.

My gaze ran back. This end of the room was draped with the exquisitely colored, graceful curtains looped with gorgeous garlands. Between curtains and table, where sat Larry and the nine, a circular platform, perhaps ten yards in diameter, raised itself a few feet above the floor, its gleaming surface half-covered with the luminous petals, fragrant, delicate.

On each side, below it, were low carven stools. The curtains parted and softly entered girls bearing their flutes, their harps, the curiously emotion-exciting, octaved drums. They sank into their places. They touched their instruments; a faint, languorous measure throbbed through the rosy air.

The stage was set! What was to be the play?

Now about the tables passed other dusky-haired maids, fair bosoms bare, their scanty kirtles looped high, pouring out the wines for the feasters. And gradually into the voices of these crept the olden recklessness, the gaiety—but Lugur sat silent, brooding; his face like that of some fallen god; and I sensed behind the prisoning bars of his calm a monstrous striving of evil, struggling to be free.

My eyes sought O'Keefe. Whatever it had been that Von Hetzdorp had said, clearly it now filled his mind—even to the exclusion of the wondrous woman beside him. His eyes were stern, cold—and now and then, as he turned them toward the German, filled with a curious speculation. Yolara watched him, frowned, gave a low order to the Hebe behind her.

The girl disappeared, entered again with a ewer that seemed cut of amber. The priestess poured from it into Larry's glass a clear liquid that shook with tiny sparkles of light. She raised the glass to her lips, handed it to him. Half-smiling, half-abstractedly, he took it, touched his own lips where hers had kissed; drained it. A nod from Yolara and the maid refilled his goblet.

At once there was a swift transformation in the Irishman. His abstraction vanished; the watchfulness, the sternness fled; his eyes sparkled. He looked upon Yolara with seemingly a new vision; leaned caressingly toward her; whispered. Her blue eyes flashed triumphantly; her chiming laughter rang. She raised her own glass—but within it was not that clear drink that filled Larry's! And again he drained his own; and, lifting it, filled once more, caught the baleful eyes of Lugur, and raised the glass to him mockingly.

I watched him anxiously; noted that Von Hetzdorp, too, was leaning forward apprehensively. Yolara swayed close—alluring, tempting. And wildly, ever more wildly, gay grew Larry. Whatever that drink, I thought, cold fear gathering at my heart, it was too potent for him. And this Circe—again the thought came to me—why was this Circe, whom I had thought tamed, leading him into—drunkenness! And where was that strength of the O'Keefe upon which I had so leaned?

He arose, face all reckless gaiety, rollicking deviltry.

"A toast!" he cried in English, "to the Shining One—and may the hell where it belongs soon claim it!"

He had used their own word for their god—all else had been in his own tongue, and so, fortunately, they did not understand. But the intent of the contempt in his action they did recognize—and a dead, a fearful silence fell upon them all. Lugur's eyes blazed, little sparks of crimson in their green. Yolara reached up, caught at O'Keefe. He seized the soft hand; caressed it; his gaze grew far away, somber.

"The Shining One." He spoke low, as though to himself. "An' now again I see the faces of those who dance with it. It is the Fires of Mora—come, God alone knows how—from Erin—to this place. The Fires of Mora!" He contemplated the hushed folk before him; and then from his lips came that weirdest, most haunting of the lyric legends of Erin—the Curse of Mora:

"The fretted fires of Mora blew o'er him in the night;
He thrills no more to loving, nor weeps for past delight.
For when those flames have bitten, both grief and joy take flight—
For when those flames have bitten, both joy and grief take flight!"

Again Yolara tried to draw him down beside her; and once more he gripped her hand. His eyes grew fixed—he crooned:

"And through the sleeping silence his feet must track the tune,
When the world is barred and speckled with silver of the moon—
When the world is barred and speckled with silver of the moon."

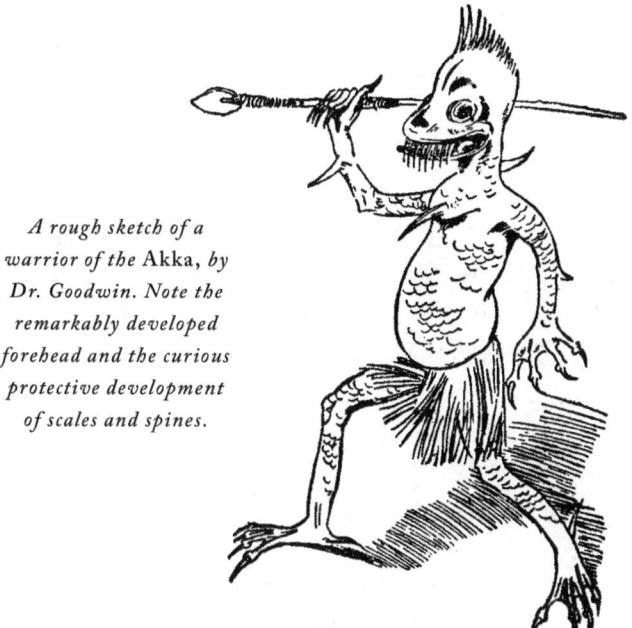

A rough sketch of a warrior of the Akka, *by Dr. Goodwin. Note the remarkably developed forehead and the curious protective development of scales and spines.*

He stood, swaying, for a moment, and then, laughing, let the priestess have her way; drained again the glass.

And now my heart was cold, indeed—for what hope was there left—with Larry mad, wild drunk!

The silence was unbroken—elf women and dwarfs glancing furtively at each other. But now Yolara arose, face set, eyes flashing gray.

"Hear you, the council, and you, Lugur—and all who are here!" she cried. "Now I, the priestess of the Shining One, take, as is my right, my mate. And this is he!" She pointed down upon Larry. He glanced up at her roguishly.

"Can't quite make out what you say, Yolara," he muttered thickly. "But say anything—you like—I love your voice!" He laughed, glanced at Lugur, now upon his feet, forced calmness gone, volcano-seething. "Don't be such a skeleton at the feast, old dear!" cried O'Keefe. "Everybody's merry and bright here—sure—everybody's merry and bright!"

I turned sick with dread. Yolara's hand stole softly upon the Irishman's curls caressingly. He drew it down; kissed it.

"You know the law, Yolara," Lugur's voice was flat, deadly. "You may not mate with other than your own kind. And this man is a stranger—a barbarian—food for the Shining One!" Literally, he spat the phrase.

"No, not of our kind—Lugur—higher!" Yolara answered serenely. "Lo, higher even than the Ancient Ones—a son of Siya and of Siyana!"

"A lie!" roared the red dwarf. "A lie!"

"The Shining One revealed it to me!" said Yolara sweetly. "And if ye believe not, Lugur—go ask of the Shining One if it be not truth!"

There was bitter, nameless menace in those last words—and whatever their hidden message to Lugur, it was potent. He stood, choking, face hell-shadowed—Von Hetzdorp leaned out again, whispered. The red dwarf bowed, now wholly ironically; resumed his place and his silence. And again I wondered, icy-hearted, what was the power the German had so to sway Lugur—what was it that he had said to O'Keefe?—and what plots and counterplots were hatching in that unscrupulous brain?

"What says the council?" Yolara demanded, turning to them.

Only for a moment they consulted among themselves. Then the woman, whose face was a ravaged shrine of beauty, spoke.

"The will of the priestess is the will of the council!" she answered.

Defiance died from Yolara's face; she looked down at Larry tenderly. He sat swaying, crooning. She clapped her hands, and one of the cuirassed dwarfs strode to her.

"Bid the priests come," she commanded, then turned to the silent room. "By the rites of Siva and Siyana, Yolara takes their son for her mate," she said; and again her hand stole down possessingly, serpent soft, to the drunken head of the O'Keefe.

The curtains parted widely. Through them filed, two by two,

twelve hooded figures clad in flowing robes of the green one sees in forest vistas of opening buds of dawning spring. Of each pair one bore clasped to breast, a globe of that milky crystal I had seen in the sapphire shrine-room; the other a harp, small, shaped somewhat like the ancient clarsach of the Druids.

Two by two they stepped upon the raised platform, placed gently upon it each their globe; and two by two crouched behind them. They formed now a star of six points about the petaled dais, and, simultaneously, they drew from their faces the covering cowls.

I half-rose from my feet—youth and maidens these of the fair-haired; all young; and youths and maids more beautiful than any of those I had yet seen—for upon their faces was little of that disturbing mockery to which I have been forced so often, because of the deep impression it made upon me, to refer. The ashen-gold of the maiden priestesses' hair was wound about their brows in shining coronals. The pale locks of the youths were clustered within circlets of translucent, glimmering gems like moonstones. And then, crystal globe alternately before and harp alternately held by youth and maid, they began to sing.

What was that song, I do not know—nor ever shall. Archaic, ancient beyond thought, it seemed—not with the ancientness of things that for uncounted ages have been but wind-driven dust. Rather was it the ancientness of the golden youth of the world, love lilts of earth younglings, with light of newborn suns drenching them, chorals of young stars mating in space; murmurings of April gods and goddesses. A languor stole through me. The rosy lights upon the tripods began to die away, and as they faded the milky globes gleamed forth brighter, ever brighter. Yolara rose, stretched a hand to Larry, led him through the sextuple groups, and stood face to face with him in the center of their circle.

The rose-light died; all that immense chamber was black, save for the circle of the glowing spheres. Within this their milky radiance grew brighter—brighter. The song whispered away. A throbbing arpeggio dripped from the harps, and as the notes pulsed out, up from the globes, as though striving to follow, pulsed with them tips of moon-fire cones, such as I had seen before Yolara's altar. Weirdly, caressingly, compellingly the harp notes throbbed in repeated, re-repeated theme, holding within itself the same archaic golden quality I had noted in the singing. And over the moon flame pinnacles rose higher!

Yolara lifted her arms; within her hands were clasped O'Keefe's. She raised them above their two heads and slowly, slowly drew him with her into a circling, graceful, step, tendrilings, delicate as the slow spiralings of twilight mist upon some still stream.

As they swayed the rippling arpeggios grew louder, and suddenly the slender pinnacles of moon fire bent, dipped, flowed to the floor, crept in a shining ring around those two—and began to rise, a gleaming, glimmering, enchanted barrier—rising, ever rising—hiding them!

With one swift movement Yolara unbound her circlet of pale sapphires, shook loose the waves of her silken hair. It fell, a rippling, wondrous cascade, veiling both her and O'Keefe to their girdles—and now the shining coils of moon fire had crept to their knees—was circling higher—higher.

And ever despair grew deeper in my soul!

What was that! I started to my feet, and all around me in the blackness I heard startled motion. From without came a blaring of trumpets, the sound of running men, loud murmurings. The tumult drew closer. I heard cries of "Lakla! Lakla!" Now it was at the very threshold and within it, oddly, as though—punctuating—the clamor, a deep-toned, almost abysmal, booming sound—thunderously bass and reverberant.

Abruptly the harpings ceased; the moon fires shuddered, fell, and began to sweep back into the crystal globes; Yolara's swaying form grew rigid, every atom of it seeming to be listening with intensity so great that it was itself like clamor. She threw aside the veiling cloud of hair, and in the gleam of the last retreating spirals I saw her face glare out like some old Greek mask of tragedy.

The sweet lips that, even at their sweetest could never lose their delicate cruelty, had no sweetness now. They were drawn into a square—inhuman as that of the Medusa; in her eyes were the fires of the pit, and her hair seemed to writhe like the serpent locks of that Gorgon, whose mouth she had borrowed; all her beauty was transformed into a nameless thing—hideous, inhuman, blasting! If this was the true soul of Yolara springing to her face, then, I thought, God help us in very deed!

I wrested my gaze away to O'Keefe. All drunkenness gone, himself again, he was staring down at that hellish sight, and in his eyes were loathing and horror unutterable. So they stood— and the light fled.

Only for a moment did the darkness hold. With lightning swiftness the blackness that was the chamber's other wall vanished. Through a portal, open between gray screens, the silver sparkling light poured.

And through the portal marched, two by two, incredible, nightmare figures—frog-men, giants, taller by nearly a yard than even tall O'Keefe! Their enormous saucer eyes were irised by wide bands of green-flecked red, in which the phosphorescence flickered like cold flames. Their long muzzles, lips half-open in monstrous grin, held rows of glistening, slender, lancet sharp fangs. Over the glaring eyes arose a horny helmet, a carapace of black and orange scales, studded with foot-long lance-headed horns.

They lined themselves like soldiers on each side of the wide table aisle, and now I could see that this horny armor covered shoulders and backs, ran across the chest in a knobbed cuirass, and at wrists and heels jutted out into curved, murderous spurs. The webbed hands and feet ended in yellow, spade-shaped claws. A short kilt of the same pale amber stones that I had seen upon the apparition of the Moon Pool Chamber's wall hung about their swollen middles.

They carried spears, ten feet, at least, in length, the heads of which were pointed cones, glistening with that same covering, from whose touch of swift decay I had so narrowly saved Rador.

They were grotesque, yes—more grotesque than anything I had ever seen or dreamed, and they were—terrible! Half-hysterically there came into my mind a phrase that O'Keefe himself might have used: "What a sight for Larry to open his eyes upon on the morning after!"

In all the chamber there was now no sound. Yolara's hellish face had changed no whit; nor had O'Keefe's eyes left it.

And then, quietly, through the ranks of the frog-men came—a girl! Behind her, enormous pouch at his throat swelling in and out menacingly, in one paw a treelike, spike-studded mace, a frog-man, huger than any of the others, guarding. But of him I caught but a fleeting, involuntary impression—all my gaze was for the girl.

For it was she who had pointed out to us the way from the peril of the Dweller's lair on Nan-Tauach. And as I gazed at her, I marveled that ever could I have thought the priestess more beautiful. Turning, I saw Larry's own gaze leave Yolara for her; saw him stiffen, and to his eyes rush joy incredible and an utter abasement of shame.

And from all about came murmurs—edged with anger, half-incredulous, tinged with fear:

"Lakla!"

"Lakla!"

"The handmaiden to the Silent Ones!"

CHAPTER XXIII

"THESE MEN THE SILENT ONES SUMMON!"

THROUGH THE GROTESQUE ranks of the frog-men she paced and halted close beside me. From firm little chin to dainty buskined feet she was swathed in the soft metallic robes; these of a dull, almost coppery hue. The left arm was hidden, the right free and gloved, the gloving disappearing high in the shoulder folds. Wound tight about the arm was one of the vines of the sculptured wall and of Lugur's circled signet-ring. Thick, a vivid green, its five tendrils ran between her fingers, sketching out five flowered heads that gleamed like blossoms cut from gigantic, glowing rubies.

So she stood for a moment, contemplating Yolara, from whose visage the mask had fled, leaving, it is true, a face still seared with rage and hate, but human. Drawn perhaps by my gaze, she dropped her eyes upon me; golden, translucent, with tiny flecks of amber in their aureate irises, the soul that looked through them was as far removed from that flaming out of the priestess's as zenith is above nadir.

I noted the low, broad brow, the proud little nose, the tender mouth, and the soft—sunlight—glow that seemed to transfuse the delicate skin. And suddenly in the eyes dawned a smile—sweet, friendly, a touch of roguishness, profoundly reassuring in its all humanness. I felt my heart expand as though freed from fetters, a recrudescence of confidence in the essential reality of things—as though in nightmare the struggling consciousness should glimpse some familiar face and know the terrors with which it strove were but dreams. And involuntarily I smiled back at her.

She raised her head and looked again at Yolara, contempt and a certain curiosity in her gaze; at O'Keefe—and through the softened eyes drifted swiftly a shadow of sorrow, and on its fleeting wings deepest interest, and hovering over that a naïve approval as reassuringly human as had been her smile. She spoke, and her voice, deep-timbred, soft gold as was Yolara's all silver, was subtly the synthesis of all the golden glowing beauty of her.

"The Silent Ones have sent me, O Yolara," she said. "And this is their command to you—that ye deliver to me to bring before them three of the four strangers who have found their way here. This man they summon"—she pointed to O'Keefe—"and this"—her hand almost touched me—"and that yellow-haired one who seeks his mate and babe"—and how knew she of Olaf's quest, I wondered. "But for him there who plots with Lugur"—she pointed at Von Hetzdorp, and I saw Yolara start—"they have no need. Into his heart the Silent Ones have looked; and Lugur and you may keep him, Yolara!"

There was honeyed venom in the last words; and let me write here that truly angelic as Lakla might look and on occasion be, great as was her heart and high her spirit, she was very human indeed; feminine through and through, and therefore not disdainful, when they served her, either of woman's guile or woman's needle tongue.

Yolara was herself again; now only the edge of shrillness on her voice revealed her wrath as she answered the handmaiden.

"And whence have the Silent Ones gained power to command, *choya?*"

This last, I knew, was a very vulgar word; I had heard Rador use it in a moment of anger to one of the serving maids, and it meant, approximately, "kitchen girl," "scullion." Beneath the insult and the acid disdain, the blood rushed up under Lakla's ambered ivory skin. Her hand clenched, and I thought I saw writhe the vine that braceleted her arm.

"Yolara"—her voice was calm—"of no use is it to question me. I am but the messenger of the Silent Ones. And one thing only am I bidden to ask you—do you deliver to me the three strangers?"

Lugur was on his feet; eagerness, sardonic delight, sinister anticipation thrilling from him—and my same glance showed Von Hetzdorp, crouched, biting his fingernails, glaring at the Golden Girl.

"No!" Yolara fairly spat the word. "No! Now by Thanaroa and by the Shining One, no!" Her eyes blazed, her nostrils were wide, in her fair throat a little pulse beat angrily. "You, Lakla—take you *my* message to the Silent Ones. Say to them that I keep this man"—she pointed to Larry—"because he is mine.

Say to them that I keep the yellow-haired one and him"—she pointed to me—"because it pleases me.

"Tell them that upon their mouths I place my foot, so!"—she stamped upon the dais viciously—"and that in their faces I spit!"—and her action was hideously snakelike. "And say last to them, you handmaiden, that if *you* they dare send to Yolara again, she will feed you to the Shining One! Now—go!"

The handmaiden's face was white.

"Not unforeseen by the three was this, Yolara," she replied. "And did you speak as you have spoken, then was I bidden to say this to you." Her voice deepened. "Three *tal* have ye to take counsel, Yolara. And at the end of that time three things must ye have determined—either to do or not to do: first, send the strangers to the Silent Ones; second, give up, ye and Lugur and all of ye, that dream ye have of conquest of the world without; and, third, foreswear the Shining One! And if ye do not one and all these things, then are ye done, your cup of life broken, your wine of life spilled. Yea, Yolara, for ye and the Shining One, Lugur and the Nine and all those here and their kind shall pass! This say the Silent Ones, 'Surely shall all of ye pass and be as though never had ye been!'"

Now a gasp of rage and fear arose from all those around me—but the priestess threw back her head and laughed loud and long. Into the silver sweet chiming of her laughter clashed that of Lugur—and after a little the nobles took it up, till the whole chamber echoed with their mirth. O'Keefe, lips tightening, moved toward the handmaiden, and almost imperceptibly, but peremptorily, she waved him back.

"Those are great words—great words indeed, *choya*," shrilled Yolara at last; and again Lakla winced beneath the word. "Lo, for *laya* upon *laya*, the Shining One has been freed from the three; and for *laya* upon *laya* they have sat helpless, rotting. Now I ask you again—whence comes their power to lay their will upon me, and whence comes their strength to wrestle with the Shining One and the beloved of the Shining One?"

Swiftly the Thing upreared, more and more of it
drawing into sight as the head of horror mounted—
until it stood above us like a scaled tower.

And again she laughed—and again Lugur and all the fair-
haired joined in her laughter.

Into the eyes of Lakla I saw creep a doubt, a wavering; as
though deep within her the foundations of her own belief were
none too firm.

She hesitated, turning upon O'Keefe eyes in which rested
more than suggestion of appeal! And Yolara saw, too, for she
flashed with triumph, stretched a finger toward the handmaid-
en.

"Look!" she cried. "Look! Why, even *she* does not believe!"
Her voice grew silk of silver—merciless, cruel. "Now am I
minded to send another answer to the Silent Ones. Yea! But

not by *you*, Lakla; by these"—she pointed to the frog-men, and, swift as light, her hand darted into her bosom, bringing forth the little shining cone of death.

But before she could level it, dart the *Keth* upon her, the Golden Girl had released that hidden left arm and thrown over her face a fold of the metallic swathings. Swifter than Yolara, she raised the arm that held the vine—and now I knew this was no inert blossoming thing. It was alive! It writhed down her arm, and with its five rubescent flower heads thrust itself out toward the priestess—vibrating, quivering held in leash only by the light touch of the handmaiden at its very end.

From the swelling throat pouch of the monster behind her came a succession of the reverberant boomings I had heard when the little tendrils of moon flame began to shrink back to the crystal globes. The frog-men wheeled, raised their lances, leveled them at the throng. Around the reaching ruby flowers a red mist swiftly grew.

The silver cone dropped from Yolara's rigid fingers; her eyes grew stark with horror; all her unearthly loveliness fled from her; she stood pale-lipped, face shrunken, shorn of beauty by that one gesture of Lakla's as Samson was of his strength by the first clip of Delilah's shears. The handmaiden dropped the protecting veil—and now it was she who laughed.

"It would seem, then, Yolara, that there *is* a thing of the Silent Ones ye fear!" she said. "Well—the kiss of the *Yekta* I promise you in return for the embrace of your Shining One."

She looked at Larry, long, searchingly, and suddenly again with all that effect of sunlight bursting into dark places, her smile shone upon him. She nodded, half gaily; looked down upon me again, the little merry light dancing in her eyes; waved her hand to me.

She spoke to the giant frog-man. He wheeled behind her as she turned, facing the priestess, club upraised, fangs glistening. His troop moved not a jot, spears held high. And Lakla began to pass, slowly—almost, I thought, tauntingly—and as she reached the portal Larry leaped from the dais.

"Alanna!" he cried. "You'll not be leavin' me just when I've found you!"

In his excitement he spoke in his own tongue, the velvet brogue appealing. Lakla turned—and well it was that she did, for her Gargantuan follower boomed a war-note and swept the great mace over his horned head, whirling it downward as the Irishman rushed forward.

There was a sharp cry from the handmaiden, and he halted the club not a foot from O'Keefe's black hair.

The Irishman looked him up and down, stretched out his hand, and patted the scaled arm approvingly, as one would a dog.

"Good boy," he said; "good boy! But I wouldn't harm a hair of her sweet head for all the jewels in all the crowns the kings of Ireland ever wore. Let me by!"

The monster's enormous eyes, direct on Larry, were unblinking, but from the huge throat came a puzzled croak. He turned toward the Golden Girl—as though expecting some order.

The handmaiden contemplated O'Keefe, hesitant, unquestionably longingly, irresistibly, like a child making up her mind whether she dared or dared not take a delectable something offered her.

"I go with you," said O'Keefe, this time in her own speech. A glimmer of a smile passed through her eyes. "Come on, Doc!" He reached out a hand to me.

But now Yolara spoke. Life and beauty had flowed back into her face, and in her purple eyes all her hosts of devils were gathered.

"Do you forget what I promised you before Siya and Siyana? Or what I promised you should you turn from me! And do you think that you can leave me—*me*—as though I were a *choya*—like *her*." She pointed to Lakla. "Do you—"

"Now, listen, Yolara," Larry interrupted almost plaintively. "No promise has passed from me to you—and why would you hold me?" He passed unconsciously into English. "Be a good sport, Yolara," he urged. "You *have* got a very devil of a temper, you know, and so have I; and we'd be really awfully uncomfortable together. And why don't you get rid of that devilish pet of yours, and be good!"

She looked at him, puzzled. Von Hetzdorp leaned over, translated to Lugur. The red dwarf smiled maliciously, drew near the priestess; whispered to her what was without doubt as near as he could come in the Murian to Larry's own very colloquial phrases.

Yolara stiffened, her lips writhed.

"Hear me, Lakla!" she cried, her voice vibrant with determination unshakable. "Now would I not let you take this man from me were I to dwell ten thousand *laya* in the agony of the *Yekta's* kiss. This I swear to you—by Thanaroa, by my heart, and by my strength—that should you try to take him, or should he try to go with you, then shall I slay both him and you with the *Keth,* though the *Yekta* you carry blast me; and may my strength wither, my heart rot in my breast, and Thanaroa forget me if I do not this thing!"

"Listen, Yolara—" began O'Keefe again.

"Be silent, you!" It was almost a shriek. And her hand again sought in her breast for the cone of rhythmic death.

Lugur touched her arm, whispered again. The glint of guile shone in her eyes; she laughed softly, relaxed.

"The Silent Ones, Lakla, bade you say that they—allowed—me three *tal* to decide," she said suavely. "Go now in peace, Lakla, and say that Yolara has heard, and that for the three *tal* they—allow—her she will take council."

The handmaiden hesitated, a vague apprehension, a hint of doubt in her face.

"The Silent Ones have said it," she answered at last. "Stay you here, strangers"—the long lashes drooped as her eyes met O'Keefe's and a hint of blush was in her cheeks—"stay you here, strangers, till then. But, Yolara, see you on that heart and strength you have sworn by that they come to no harm—else that which you have invoked will come upon you swiftly indeed—and that *I* promise you," she added.

Their eyes met, clashed, burned into each other—black flame from Abaddon and golden flame from Paradise.

"Remember!" said Lakla, and passed through the portal. The gigantic frog-man boomed a thunderous note of command, his grotesque guards turned and, slowly, eyes menacing, followed their mistress; and last of all passed out the monster with the mace.

CHAPTER XXIV

LARRY'S DEFIANCE

A CLAMOR AROSE from all the chamber; stilled in an instant by a motion of Yolara's hand. She stood silent, regarding O'Keefe with something other now than the blind wrath of her threat to him; something half regretful, half beseeching. But the Irishman's control was gone.

"Yolara"—his voice shook with rage, and he threw caution to the wind—"now hear *me*. I go where I will and when I will. Here shall we stay until the time *she* named is come. And then we follow her, whether you will or not. And if any should have thought to stop us—tell them of that flame that shattered the vase," he added grimly.

The wistfulness died out of her eyes, leaving them cold.

"Is it so?" she answered. "Now it is in my mind that much may happen ere then. Perchance you and those others may dance with the Shining One, or perchance one of those hidden men that I showed you may visit you, or it may be that I myself will slay ye—and not so swiftly, *Larree*."

"And is that so," he said, slipping back into English, "and is that so? A promise means as much to you as it does to Potsdam Bill—some little scrap-of-paper scrapper, aren't you?" And now, the breath of danger having blown upon him, back came his old, alert careless, whimsical self. "Before that sweet little pet of yours"—he spoke now in her own tongue—"that you name the Shining One, dances with *us*, Yolara, many shall wither under that swift flame I showed you; and as for you—think whether *you* may not feel it, too, before you have a chance to slay; and as for those hidden ones of yours, Yolara, know you that I have *anui*"—he used the Murian for spirit, the Polynesian *ani*—"who will warn me long, long before they can don those robes that hide them."

A SPARKLE came into his eyes. "Lo, Yolara, even before you can command them, shall you hear the voice of my spirit—and it is this—" He threw back his head, and from his throat pulsed the wo-laden, sobbing cry, raising steadily into the heart-shaking, shuddering wail that I had heard on the deck of the *Suwarna;* louder and ever louder it wailed, died away into the soul-broken sobbing, and faltered out into silence!

Upon those listening, sensitive as they were to sound, the effect of the high-pitched keening was appalling; it was gruesome enough to me. There was startled movement, a panic rush from the tables to the portal; even Lugur's face was gray; the priestess's eyes stark wide; in Von Herzdorp's I saw ungrudging admiration.

"And when you hear that, Yolara," thus O'Keefe, "know that my spirit is near, and think well before you send your hidden ones, or come yourself."

No answer made the priestess to him.

She turned to the white-faced nobles.

"What Lakla has said, the council must consider, and at once," said she. "Now, friends of mine, and friends of Lugur, must all feud, all rancor, between us end." She glanced swiftly at Lugur. "The *ladala* are stirring, and the Silent Ones threaten. Yet fear not—for are we not strong under the Shining One? And now—leave us."

She waited until the last of the fair-haired had withdrawn.

Her hand dropped to the table, and she gave, evidently, a signal, for in marched a dozen or more of the green dwarfs.

"Take these two to their place," she commanded, pointing to us. "But wait—" She turned to the whispering globe, touched its control; its light broke, swam with the film of rushing colors.

"Rador," she spoke upon it, "the two strangers come to you. Guard them and the third named Olaf as you would your life. And—listen well, Rador—if you do not, and if they should escape you, then before you die shall you beg me for what shall seem to you *laya* upon *laya* to throw you to the Shining One!"

The green dwarfs clustered about us. Without another look at the priestess O'Keefe marched beside me, between them, from the chamber. But glancing round, I saw pain writhe beneath the frozen anger on her face—and in silence she and Lugur and the council and Von Hetzdorp watched us as we passed through the portals. And it was not until we had reached the pillared entrance that Larry spoke.

"I hated to talk like that to a woman, Doc," he said, "and a pretty woman, at that. But first she played me with a marked deck, and then not only pinched all the chips, but drew a gun on me. What the hell!—she nearly had me—*married*—to her, I don't know what the stuff was she gave me; but, take it from me, if I had the recipe for that brew I could sell it for a thousand dollars a jolt at Forty-Second and Broadway.

"One jigger of it, and you forget there is a trouble in the world; three of them, and you forget there *is* a world. You'll admit, Doc, that it wasn't the kind of thing for a lady to pull on an unsuspecting guest, won't you? Hardly cricket—what? No excuse for it, Doc; and I don't care what *you* say or what Lakla may say—it wasn't my fault, and I don't hold it up against myself for a damn."

"I must admit that I'm a bit uneasy about her threats," I said, ignoring all this. He stopped abruptly.

"What're you afraid of?"

"Mostly," I answered dryly, "I have no desire to dance with the Shining One!"

"Listen to me, Goodwin." He took up his walk impatiently. "Cut the bated-breath approach you use whenever you talk about that bunch of animated fireworks. I've seen stuff at the front that had it beaten a mile—and that took more people when it moved off, too. Can the slow and dirgeful music, won't you? Now I'm going to tell you something—you won't be hurt, will you?"

"No," I said.

"I've all the love and admiration for you in the world; but this place has got your nerve. Hereafter one Larry O'Keefe, of Ireland and the little old U.S.A., leads this party. Nix on the tremolo stop, nix on the superstitions! I'm the works. Get me?"

"Yes, I get you!" I exclaimed testily enough. "But to use your own phrase, kindly *can* the repeated references to superstitions."

"Why should I?" He was almost wrathful. "I'm going to be frank with you, Goodwin. You scientific people are such slaves to fact that when you meet a new one that isn't in your own neat little catalogue you either pass it by with the haughty air or hold up your hands in wonder and scream.

"You build up whole philosophies on the basis of things you never saw, and you scoff at people who believe in other things that you think *they* never saw and that don't come under what you label scientific. You talk about paradoxes—why, your scientist, who thinks he is the most skeptical, the most materialistic aggregation of atoms ever gathered at the exact mathematical center of Missouri, has more blind faith than a dervish, and more credulity, more superstition, than a cross-eyed smoke beating it past a country graveyard in the dark of the moon!"

"Larry!" I cried, a little dazed and more than a little indignant.

"Olaf's no better," he said. "But I can make allowances for him. He's a sailor. No, sir. What this expedition needs is a man without superstition. And remember this. The leprechawn promised that I'd have full warning before anything happened. And if we do have to go out, we'll see that banshee bunch clean up before we do, and pass in a blaze of glory. And don't forget it. And hereafter—I'm—in—charge!"

By this time we were before our pavilion; and neither of us in a very amiable mood, I'm afraid. Rador was awaiting us, and, to my surprise, cold indeed was his greeting. He took us from our guard, placed a whistle to his lips, and down the paths came a score of his own men.

"Let none pass in here without authority—and let none pass out unless I accompany them," he ordered bruskly. "Summon one of the swiftest of the *coria* and have it wait in readiness," he added, as though by afterthought.

But when we had entered and the screens were drawn together his manner changed; all eagerness, he questioned us. Briefly we told him of the happenings at the feast, of Lakla's dramatic interruption, and of what had followed.

"Three *tal*," he said musingly, "three *tal* the Silent Ones have allowed—and Yolara agreed." He sank back, silent and thoughtful.*

"Ja!" It was Olaf. *"Ja!* I told you the Shining Devil's mistress was all evil. *Ja!* Now I begin again that tale I started when he came"—he glanced toward the preoccupied Rador. "And tell him not what I say should he ask. For I trust none here in Trolldom, save the *Jomfrau*—the White Virgin!"

"After the oldster was *adsprede*"—Olaf once more used that expressive Norwegian word for the dissolving of Songar—"I knew that it was a time for cunning, craft. I said to myself, 'If they think I have no ears to hear, they will speak; and it may be I will find a way to save my Kelma and Dr. Goodwin's friends, too.' *Ja,* and they did speak. When I left that place with the red devil and the German, they made many signs.

"The red *Trolde* asked the German how came it he was a worshiper of Thanaroa." I could not resist a swift glance of triumph toward O'Keefe. "And the German," rumbled Olaf, "said that all his people worshiped Thanaroa and now fought against the other nations that denied him. He said that his ruler was high priest of Thanaroa, and because the other nations had

---

* A *tal* in Muria is the equivalent of thirty hours of earth surface time.—W.T.G.

defied him his people had taken up arms to make them bow their necks to him. *Ja!* And Lugur believed—for Lugur he worships Thanaroa more, much more than the Shining Devil. *Ja!*

"And then we had come to Lugur's palace. They put me in rooms, and there came to me men who rubbed and oiled me and loosened my muscles. The next day I wrestled with a great dwarf they called Valdor. He was a mighty man, and long we struggled, and at last I broke his back. And Lugur was pleased, so that I sat with him at feast and with the German, too. And again, not knowing that I understood them, they talked.

"The German had gone fast and far. No longer was there talk of his ruler, his Kaiser, but of Lugur as emperor of the Germans, and Von Hetzdorp under him. They spoke of the green light that shook life from the oldster; and Lugur said that the secret of it had been the Ancient Ones' and that the council had not too much of it. But Von Hetzdorp said that among his race were many wise men who could make more once they had studied it.

"Then he spoke of the robes that protected from the Shining Devil. Lugur told him of the priests who make them and of the earth they dig that coats them. Then said the German that his wise men would make many for themselves, in case the Shining Devil should ever grow too strong, and that Lugur and he and his nation would give the Shining Devil all the rest of the world to eat, so that Lugur and he and all the Germans should always be mighty as he was when the Shining Devil ate up those who cast themselves into it.

"And the next day I wrestled with a great dwarf named Tahola, mightier far than Valdor. Him I threw after a long, long time, and his back also I broke. Again Lugur was pleased, saying that now was I worthy to be slain by him. And again we sat at table, he and the German and I. This time they spoke of something these *Trolde* have which opens up a *Svaelc*—abysses into which all in its range drops up into the sky!"

"What!" I exclaimed.

"I know about them," said Larry. "Wait!"

"Lugur had drunk much," went on Olaf. "He was boastful. The German pressed him to show this thing. After a while the red one went out and came back with a little golden box. He and the German went into the garden. I followed them. There was a *lille Hoj*—a mound—of stones in that garden on which grew flowers and trees.

"Lugur pressed upon the box, and a spark no bigger than a sand grain leaped out and fell beside the stones. Lugur pressed again, and a blue light shot from the box and lighted on the spark. The spark that had been no bigger than a grain of sand grew and grew as the blue struck it. And then there was a sighing, a wind rush—and the stones and the flowers and the trees were not. They were *forsvinde*—vanished!

"Then Lugur, who had been laughing, grew quickly sober; for he thrust the German back—far back. And soon down into the garden came tumbling the stones and the trees, but broken and shattered, and falling as though from a great height. And Lugur said that of this something they had much, for its making was a secret handed down by their own forefathers and not by the Ancient Ones.

"They feared to use it, he said, for a spark thrice as large as that he had used would have sent all that garden falling upward and might have opened a way to the outside before—he said just this—'before we are ready to go out into it!'

"The German questioned much, but Lugur sent for more drink and grew merrier and threatened him, and the German was silent through fear. Thereafter I listened when I could, and little more I learned, but that little enough. *Ja!* Lugur is hot for conquest; so Yolara and so the council. They tire of it here, and the Silent Ones make their minds not too easy, no, even though they jeer at them! And this they plan—to rule our world with their Shining Devil that Lugur says has grown strong enough to fare forth.

"Already have they tunneled upward at that place they call the Lower Waters, and that I think is under Ponape itself. There was to be their gathering-place to sweep out upon the earth. But now Von Hetzdorp has told Lugur of the passage through which we came, and Lugur and he now plan to open that.

"The *ladala* they will almost utterly destroy before they go, except the soldiers and the dream makers. They talk of 'sealing' the Silent Ones within their Crimson Sea, but—and this is point of trouble—they fear that if they do it they may pull down all this place they call Muria. Those who speak against it say— The Silent Ones can have no power on earth, never have they had it. And it may be that we shall not do well under the sun; perhaps we may wish to return—and let the haven be open in case of our need.'

"Lugur would burn all bridges behind him; destroying all. But not so Yolara. And Von Hetzdorp would not, because he would keep what is here for Germany and in his heart, too, he laughs at the Silent Ones and he schemes to—*smadre*—smash all these people. Yet has he played upon Lugur by promising him that his own people will cast aside their rulers and will muster to Lugur and that Lugur as Kaiser and the Shining Devil as Earth God shall rule all the world for Thanaroa—and under his whisperings Lugur begins to forget even Thanaroa!"

The Norseman was silent for a moment; then, voice deep, trembling—

"Trolldom is awake; Helvede crouches at Earth Gate whining to be loosed into a world already devil ridden! And we are but three!"

CHAPTER XXV

THE COUNCIL'S DECISION

I FELT THE blood drive out of my heart. But Larry's was the fighting face of the O'Keefes of a thousand years. Rador glanced at him, arose, stepped through the curtains; returned swiftly with the Irishman's uniform.

"Put it on," he said, bruskly; again fell back into his silence and whatever O'Keefe had been about to say was submerged in his wild and joyful whoop. He ripped from him glittering tunic and leg swathings.

"Richard is himself again!" he shouted; and each garment, as he donned it, fanned his old devil-may-care confidence to a higher flame. The last scrap of it on, he drew himself up before us.

"Bow down, ye divils!" he cried. "Bang your heads on the floor and do homage to Larry the First, Emperor of Great Britain, Autocrat of all Ireland, Scotland, England, and Wales, and adjacent waters and islands! Kneel, ye scuts, kneel."

"Larry," I cried, "are you going crazy!"

"Not a bit of it," he said. "I'm that and more if Herr von Hetzdorp keeps his promise. Whoop! Bring forth the royal jewels an' put a whole new bunch of golden strings in Tara's harp an' down with the Sassenach forever! Whoop!"

He did a wild jig.

"Lord how good the old togs feel," he grinned. "The touch of 'em has gone to my head. But it's straight stuff I'm telling you about my empire."

He laughed again; then sobered.

"Not that it's not serious enough at that. A lot that Olaf's told us I've surmised from hints dropped by Yolara. But I got the full key to it from the von himself when he stopped me just before—before"—he reddened—"well, before I acquired that brand-new brand of souse. Do you remember, Goodwin, away back in the Moon Pool Chamber that the German made a very curious remark about being certain that I always spoke what was in my mind—and that he'd remember it.

"Funny, funny psychology—the German. He made a picture of me in his mind—a little innocent, frank, truthful, and impulsive Larry O'Keefe; always saying right out just what I thought and with no more subterfuge or guile about me than there is hair under John D.'s wig! That's the picture he carried in his neat German mind—and by the shade of Genseric the Vandal let me be any different if I dared!

"Maybe he had a hint—maybe he just surmised—that I knew a lot more than I did. And he thought Yolara and I were going to be loving little turtle doves. Also he figured that Yolara had a lot more influence with the Unholy Fireworks than Lugur. Also she could be more easily handled. All this being so, what was the logical thing for the Hun to do? Sure, you get me, Steve! Throw down Lugur and make an alliance with me! So *he* calmly offered to ditch the red dwarf if *I* would deliver Yolara. My reward from the All Highest was to be said emperorship! Can you beat it? Good Lord!"

He went off into a perfect storm of laughter. But not to me in the light of what Germany has done and has proved herself capable, did this thing seem at all absurd; rather in it I sensed the dawn of catastrophe colossal.

"But how would they get to Germany—how carry the Shining One—"

"Oh that's all worked out," answered Larry, airily. "There's a Hun warship hiding down there in the Carolines somewhere. It got away from Kiaochow before the Japs took it. The von knows where it is. Also he has a nice little wireless rigged up on one of the Nan-Matal islets.

With that boat equipped with the *Keth*—and Fritz confided to me that they had apparatus that could sweep it over a fifty-mile range—and a few of those gravity-destroying bombs Olaf described—

"Gravity-destroying bombs!" I gasped.

"Sure! The little fairy that sent the trees and stones kiting up—Von Hetzdorp licked his lips over *them*. What they do is to cut off gravity, just about as the shadow screens cut off light—and consequently whatever's in their range just naturally goes shooting up toward the moon." He sobered. "I admit I'm a bit

scared about them, Doc! Anyway with those two things and—
oh, yes, gentle, invisible soldiers walking around assassinating
all the leaders of the rest of the world—well, *bingo* for all the
rest of our world, Goodwin!

"And take it from me old chap, it's not a dream. We've got
to beat Von Hetzdorp and all the rest of 'em to it, Goodwin,"
he ended, solemnly enough.

"But the Shining One?" I began.

"Yolara's to nurse the sweet little thing," he said. "It'll follow
her like a lamb, Von Hetzdorp says—and there's something
about that I don't understand at all—"

"Something? I don't understand a bit of it," I interrupted,
almost testily.

"No," he grinned. "I don't mean what it is—I mean how it's
controlled—oh, well, I'll bet Lakla knows all about it. And I'll
bet we'll damned soon be hearing her tell us," he ended grimly.

"But Larry," I exclaimed, stupidly enough I confess. "You
shook hands with Von Hetzdorp on it."

"Oh, the ingenuous, the unsuspecting childlike mind of
science," he intoned, piously. "Old dear—aren't you spoofing
me? Why, Doc, just as I'd make love to Hecate at the gates of
Hades if it would find me the way to the Golden Girl, I'd
kiss—yes, actually kiss—Von Hetzdorp if it would give me one
more minute to block a game like this. It's bad medicine for
our old world, Doc, whichever way you look at it. And as Olaf
says—there's only three of us!

"Not that I mind Fireworks," he concluded. "If I had Fireworks outside I could finish it—with one splash of a down-town
New York high-pressure fire hose. But the other stuff—*are the
goods!*"

For once his courage, his unquenchable confidence, found
no echo within me. Not lightly, as he, did I hold that dread
mystery the Dweller—and a vision passed before me, a vision
of an Apocalypse undreamed by the Evangelist.

A vision of the Shining One swirling into our world, a monstrous, glorious framing pillar of incarnate, eternal Evil—of peoples passing through its radiant embrace into that hideous, unearthly life-in-death which I had seen enfold the sacrifices— of armies trembling into dancing atoms of diamond dust beneath the green ray's rhythmic death—of cities rushing out into space upon the wings of that other demoniac force which Olaf had watched at work—of a haunted world through which the assassins of the Dweller's court stole invisible, carrying with them every passion of hell—of the rallying to the Thing of every sinister soul and of the weak and the unbalanced, mystics and carnivores of humanity alike; for well I knew that, once loosed, not even Germany could hold this devil-god for long and that swiftly its blight would spread!

And then a world that was all colossal reek of cruelty and terror; a welter of lusts, of hatreds and of torment; a chaos of horror in which the Dweller waxing ever stronger, the ghastly hordes of those it had consumed growing ever greater, wreaked its inhuman will!

At the last a ruined planet, a cosmic plague, spinning through the shuddering heavens; its verdant plains, its murmuring forests, its meadows and its mountains manned only by a count- less crew of soulless, mindless dead-alive, their shells illumined with the Dweller's infernal glory—and flaming over this vam- pirized world like a flare from some hell far, infinitely far, beyond the reach of man's farthest flung imagining—the Dweller!

Panic gripped my throat; strangled me. My science could not help—what god or gods could? Olaf had turned to ancient Thor and Odin—O'Keefe's faith was in—banshees! A glimmer of laughter came to me; lifted me out of my fear.

Rador jumped to his feet; smiled amiably at us; walked to the whispering globe. He bent over its base; did something with its mechanism; beckoned to us. The globe swam rapidly, faster than ever I had seen it before. A low humming arose, changed into a murmur and then from it I heard Lugur's voice clearly.

"It is to be war then?"

There was a chorus of assent—from a council I thought.

"I will take the tall one named—*Larree.*" It was the priestess's voice. "After the three *tal,* you may have him, Lugur, to do with as you will."

"No!" it was Lugur's voice again, but with a rasp of anger. "All three must die."

"He shall die," again Yolara. "But I would that first he see Lakla die—and that she know what is to happen to him."

"No!" I started—for this was Von Hetzdorp. "Now is no time, Yolara, for one's own desires. This is my council. At the end of the three *tal* Lakla will come for our answer. Your men will be in ambush and they will slay her and her escort quickly with the *Keth.* But not till that is done must the three be slain—and then quickly. With Lakla dead we shall go forth to the Silent Ones—and I promise you that I will find the way to destroy them!"

"It is well!" It was Lugur.

"It is well, Yolara." It was a woman's voice, and I knew it for that old one of ravaged beauty. "Cast from your mind whatever is in it for this stranger—either of love or hatred. In this the council is with Lugur and the man of wisdom."

There was a silence. Then came the priestess's voice, sullen but—beaten.

"It is well!"

"Let the three be taken now by Rador to the temple and given to the High Priest Sator"—thus Lugur—"until what we have planned comes to pass."

Rador gripped the base of the globe; abruptly it ceased its spinning. He turned to us as though to speak and even as he did so its bell note sounded peremptorily and on it the color films began to creep at their accustomed pace.

"I hear," the green dwarf whispered. But now we could no longer distinguish the words. He listened.

"They shall be taken there at once," he said, at last, gravely. The globe grew silent.

He stepped toward us. Larry had drawn his automatic; Olaf and I followed their example. We faced the green dwarf defiantly.

"You have heard," he said, smiling faintly.

"Not on your life, Rador," said Larry, "Nothing doing!" And then in the Murian's own tongue. "We follow Lakla, Rador. And you lead the way." He thrust the pistol close to the green dwarf's side.

Rador did not move. But his eyes gleamed their approval as they looked up into the Irishman's determined ones.

"Of what use, *Larree?*" he said, quietly. "Me you can slay—but in the end you will be taken. Life is not held so dear in Muria that my men out there or those others who can come quickly will let you by—even though you slay many. And in the end they will overpower you."

There was a trace of irresolution in O'Keefe's face.

"And," said Rador, "if I let you go I dance with the Shining One—or worse!"

O'Keefe's pistol hand dropped.

"You're a good sport, Rador, and far be it from me to get you in bad," he said. "Take us to the temple—when we get there— well, your responsibility ends, doesn't it?"

The green dwarf nodded; on his face a curious expression— was it relief? Or was it profound emotion higher than this?

Whatever it was he turned curtly.

"FOLLOW," HE said. We passed out of that gay little pavilion that had come to be home to us even in this alien place. The guards stood at attention.

"You, Sattoya, stand by the globe," he ordered one of them. "Should the *Afyo Maie* ask, say that I am on my way with the strangers even as she has commanded."

We passed through the lines to the *corial* standing like a great shell at the end of the runway leading into the green road.

"Wait you here," he said curtly to the driver. The green dwarf ascended to his seat, sought the lever and we swept on—on and out upon the glistening obsidian.

Then Rador turned and laughed.

"Larree," he cried, "I love you for that spirit of yours! And did you think that Rador would carry to the temple prison a man who would take the chances of death upon his own shoulders to save him? Or you, Goodwin, who saved him from the rotting death? For what did I take the *corial* or lift the veil of silence that I might hear what threatened you—"

Laughing again into our amazed faces he swept the *corial* to the left, away from the temple approach.

"I am done with Lugur and with Yolara and the Shining One!" cried Rador. "My hand is for you three and for Lakla and those to whom she is handmaiden!"

The shell leaped forward; seemed to fly.

"Whence go we, Rador?" I gasped in his ear.

"Straight to that bridge that guards the way to the Crimson Sea," he shouted, "and pray whatever gods you worship that we pass it before ever Yolara finds whence our way has led!"

CHAPTER XXVI

THE CASTING OF THE SHADOW

NOW WE WERE flying down toward that last span whose ancientness had set it apart from all the other soaring arches. The shell's speed slackened; we approached warily.

"We pass there?" asked O'Keefe.

The green dwarf nodded, pointing to the right where the bridge ended in a broad platform held high upon two gigantic piers, between which ran a spur from the glistening road. Platform and bridge were swarming with men-at-arms; they crowded the parapets, looking down upon us curiously but with no evidence of hostility. Rador drew a deep breath of relief.

"We don't have to break our way through, then?" There was disappointment in the Irishman's voice.

"No use, *Larree!*" Smiling, Rador stopped the *corial* just beneath the arch and beside one of the piers. "Now listen well. They have had no warning, hence does Yolara still think us on the way to the temple. This is the gateway of the Portal—and the gateway is closed by the Shadow. Once I commanded here and I know its laws. This must I do—by craft persuade Serku, the keeper of the gateway, to lift the Shadow; or raise it myself. And that will be hard and it may well be that in the struggle life will be stripped of us all. Yet is it better to die fighting than to dance with the Shining One!"

"*Ja!*" It was Olaf, eyes again ice glinting as he clutched one of Rador's broad shoulders. "*Ja!* Well, it is to die fighting—but I would slay Lugur before I die!"

"And so you may, strong one," laughed the green dwarf. "For here Lugur will surely come when the alarm is given; and they will try to save us for a slower death. And now—see to those flame tubes of yours—and follow my lead—for too long have we waited here."

He swept the shell around the pier. Opened a wide plaza paved with the volcanic glass, but black as that down which we had sped from the Chamber of the Moon Pool. It shone like a mirrored lakelet of jet; on each side of it arose what at first glance seemed towering bulwarks of the same ebon obsidian; at second revealed themselves as structures hewn and set in place by men; polished faces pierced by dozens of high, narrow windows each ovaled with exquisite intaglios of feathered serpent and the flower snake that Lakla had called the Yekla and with whose kiss she had threatened Yolara.

Down each façade a stairway fell, broken by small landings on which a door opened; they dropped to a broad ledge of grayish stone edging the lip of this midnight pool and upon it also fell two wide flights from either side of the bridge platform. Along all four stairways the guards were ranged; and here and there against the ledge stood the shells—in a curiously comforting resemblance to parked motors in our own world.

The somber walls, bulked high; curved and ended in two obelisked pillars from which, like a tremendous curtain stretched a barrier of that tenebrious gloom which, though weightless as shadow itself, I now knew to be as impenetrable as the veil between life and death. In this murk, unlike all others I had seen, I sensed movement, a quivering, a tremor constant and rhythmic; not to be seen yet caught by some subtle sense; as though through it beat a swift pulse of—black light.

In the center of the pit of glittering darkness, poised over the depths that were like some frozen spring upwelling from inky Styx itself, we hung for a moment watching.

The green dwarf turned the *corial* slowly to the edge at the right; crept cautiously on toward where, not more than a hundred feet from the barrier, a low, wide entrance opened in the fort. Guarding its threshold stood two guards, armed with broadswords, double handed, terminating in a wide lunette mouthed with murderous fangs. These they raised in salute and through the portal strode a dwarf huge as Rador, dressed as he and carrying only the poniard that was the badge of office of Muria's captaincy.

"Ho, Rador!" he hailed, merrily. "Why hover without when within are cheer and welcome?"

The green dwarf swept the shell expertly against the ledge; leaped out.

"Greeting, Serku!" he answered. "I was but looking for the *coria* of Lakla."

"Lakla!" exclaimed Serku. "Why, the handmaiden passed with her *Akka* nigh a *va* ago!"

"Passed!" The astonishment of the green dwarf was so real that half was I myself deceived. "You let her *pass?*"

"Certainly I let her pass—" But under the green dwarf's stern gaze the truculence of the guardian faded. "Why should I not?" he asked, apprehensively.

"Because Yolara commanded otherwise," answered Rador, coldly.

"There came no command to me." Little beads of sweat stood out on Serku's forehead. "Else would I surely have obeyed—"

"Serku," interrupted the green dwarf swiftly, "truly is my heart wrung for you. This is a matter of Yolara and of Lugur and the council; yes, even of the Shining One! And the message was sent—and the fate, mayhap, of all Muria rested upon your obedience and the return of Lakla with these strangers to the council. Now truly is my heart wrung, for there are few I would less like to see dance with the Shining One than you, Serku," he ended, softly.

Livid now was the gateway's guardian, his great frame shaking.

"Come with me and speak to Yolara," he pleaded. "There came no message—tell her—"

"Wait, Serku!" There was a thrill as of inspiration in Rador's voice. "This *corial* is of the swiftest—Lakla's of the slowest. With Lakla scarce a *va* ahead we can reach her before she enters the Portal. Lift you the Shadow—we shall bring her back and this will I do for you, Serku."

Doubt tempered Serku's panic.

"Why not go alone Rador, leaving the strangers here with me?" he asked—and I thought not unreasonably.

"Nay then." The green dwarf was brusk. "Lakla will not return unless I carry to her these men as evidence of our good faith. There is strife brewing, Serku, battle between Muria and the Silent Ones—nor have I time to explain more with Lakla now a *va* away. Come—we will speak to Yolara and she shall judge you—" He started away—but Serku caught his arm.

"No, Rador, no!" he whispered, again panic stricken. "Go

you—as you will. But bring her back! Speed Rador!" He sprang toward the entrance. "I lift the Shadow—"

Into the green dwarf's poise crept a curious, almost a listening, alertness. He leaped to Serku's side.

"I go with you," I heard. "Some little I can tell you—" They were gone.

"Fine work!" muttered Larry. "Nominated for a citizen of Ireland when we get out of this, one Rador of—"

The Shadow trembled—shuddered into nothingness; the obelisked outposts that had held it framed a ribbon of roadway, high banked with verdure, vanishing in green distances.

And then from the portal sped a shriek, a death cry! It cut through the silence of the ebon pit like a whimpering arrow. Before it had died down the stairways came pouring the guards. Those at the threshold raised their swords and peered within. Abruptly Rador was between them. One dropped his hilt and gripped him—the green dwarf's poniard flashed and was buried in his throat. Down upon Rador's head swept the second blade. A flame leaped from O'Keefe's hand and the sword seemed to fling itself from its wielder's grasp—another flash and the soldier crumpled. Rador threw himself into the shell, darted to the high seat—and straight between the pillars of the Shadow we flew!

There came a crackling, a shadow as of vast wings flinging down upon us. The *corial's* flight was checked as by a giant's hand. I was hurled forward into Olaf and O'Keefe, tumbled beneath the front whorl. The shell swerved sickeningly; there was an oddly metallic splintering; it quivered; shot ahead. Dizzily I picked myself up and looked behind.

The Shadow had fallen—but too late, a bare instant too late. And shrinking as we fled from it, still it seemed to strain like some fettered Afrit from Eblis, throbbing with wrath, seeking with every malign power it possessed to break its bonds and pursue. Not until long after were we to know that it had been the dying hand of Serku, groping out of oblivion, that had cast it after us as a fowler upon an escaping bird.

"Snappy work, Rador!" It was Larry speaking. "But they cut the end off your bus all right!

I glanced back, a full quarter of the hindward whorl was gone, sliced off cleanly. Rador noted it with anxious eyes.

"That is bad," he said, "but not too bad perhaps. We cannot tell yet. All depends upon how closely Lugur and his men can follow us."

He raised a hand to O'Keefe in salute.

"But to you, *Larree,* I owe my life—not even the *Keth* could have been as swift to save me as was that death flame of yours—friend!"

The Irishman waved an airy hand, relapsing into his own tongue.

"You're doing your bit yourself, old thing," he remarked; Rador caught the meaning. "Fluke," Larry murmured to me. "Aimed at the beggar's head and went high. Reputation maker—the shot you never meant. What happened?" He turned again to Rador.

"Serku"—the green dwarf drew from his girdle the blood-stained poniard—"Serku I was forced to slay. Even as he raised the Shadow the globe gave the alarm. Lugur follows with twice ten times ten of his best. Serku drew his blade upon me—and I killed—" He hesitated. "Though we have escaped the Shadow it has taken toll of our swiftness. May we reach the Portal before it closes upon Lakla—but if we do not—" He paused again. "Well—I know a way—but it is not one I am gay to follow—*no!*"

He snapped open the aperture that held the ball framing within the dark crystal; peered at it anxiously. I crept to the torn end of the *corial.* How, I wondered, could the Shadow have first held, then shorn with such unbelievable energy. The edges were crumbling, disintegrated. They powdered in my fingers like dust. Mystified still, I crept back where Larry, sheer happiness pouring from him, was whistling softly and polishing up his automatic. His gaze fell upon Olaf's grim, sad face and softened.

"Buck up, Olaf!" he said. "We've got a good fighting chance. Once we link up with Lakla and her crowd I'm betting that we get your wife—never doubt it! The baby—" he hesitated awkwardly. The Norseman's eyes filled; he stretched a hand to the O'Keefe.

"The *Yndling*—she is of *de Dode*," he half whispered, "of the blessed dead. For her I have no fear and for her vengeance will he given me. *Ja!* But mine *Hustru*, my Helma—she is of the dead-alive—like those we saw whirling like leaves in the light of the Shining Devil—and I would that she too were of *de Dode*—and at rest. I do not know how to fight the Shining Devil—no!"

His heart's bitter despair welled up in his voice.

"Olaf," Larry's voice was gentle. "We'll come out on top—I know it. And I hope, and I do believe, Olaf, that we'll get your wife out of it all right. But there's one thing you must remember: All this stuff that seems so strange and—and, well, sort of supernatural, is just a lot of tricks we're not hep to as yet. Don't fall for it, Olaf! That's what they're hoping we'll do. They want to get our nerve. They're just like the Huns with their *schrecklichkeit*.

"What you call the Shining Devil isn't any devil or spook or anything of the kind. Why, I've seen men shell shocked or gassed who acted just as queerly as those you saw; and the gassed ones looked a lot more hellish. Afterward they were all right again—some of them. Why, Olaf, suppose you took a Fijian and set him suddenly down in London with autos rushing past, sirens blowing, Archies popping, a dozen boche planes dropping bombs and the search-lights shooting all over the sky—wouldn't he think he was among thirty-third degree devils in some exclusive circle of hell? Sure he would! And yet everything he saw would be natural—just as natural as all this is, once we get the answer to it. Not that we're Fijians, of course, but the principle is the same."

The Norseman considered this; nodded gravely.

"*Ja!*" he answered at last. "And at least we can fight. That is why I have turned to Thor of the battles, *ja!* And *one* have I hope in for mine Helma—the white maiden. Since I have turned to the old gods it has been made clear to me that I shall slay Lugur and that the Heks, the evil witch Yolara, shall also die. But I would talk with the white maiden."

"All right," said Larry, "but just don't be afraid of what you don't understand, Olaf. I could lie on my back in a field in Ireland and dream in an hour more things of this sort than these people could show us in a million years! There's another thing"—he hesitated, nervously—"there's another thing that may startle you a bit when we meet up with Lakla—her—er—frogs!"

"Like the frog-women we saw on the wall?" asked Olaf.

"YES," WENT on Larry, rapidly. "It's this way—I figure that the frogs grow rather large where she lives, and they're a bit different too. Well, Lakla's got a lot of 'em trained. Carry spears and clubs and all that junk—just like trained seals or monkeys or so on in the circus. Probably a custom of the place. Nothing queer about that, Olaf. Why, hell, people have all kinds of pets—armadillos and snakes and rabbits, kangaroos and elephants and tigers. Look what you can do with chimpanzees—make 'em almost human; even teach 'em to smoke and drink. Lakla was probably up against it for help and specialized in frogs; probably an extr'ordinary intelligent frog—that's all there is to it. Just didn't want you to be startled."

Remembering how the frog-woman had stuck in Larry's mind from the outset, I wondered whether all this was not more to convince himself than Olaf.

"Why I remember a nice girl in Paris who had four pet pythons—" he went on.

But I listened no more, for now I was sure of my surmise. I busied myself taking note of the rapidly changing aspect of the country through which we were running. The road had begun to thrust itself through high-flung, sharply pinnacled masses and rounded outcroppings of rock on which clung patches of the amber moss.

The trees had utterly vanished, and studding the moss carpeted plains were only clumps of a willowy shrub from which hung, like grapes, clusters of white waxen blooms. The light too had changed; gone were the dancing, sparkling atoms and the silver had faded to a soft, almost ashen grayness. Ahead of us marched a rampart of coppery cliffs, rising like all these mountainous walls we had seen, into the immensities of haze. Something long drifting in my subconsciousness turned to startled realization. The speed of the shell was slackening! The aperture containing the ionizing mechanism was still open; I glanced within. The whirling ball of fire was not dimmed, but its coruscations, instead of pouring down through the cylinder, swirled and eddied and shot back as though trying to re-enter their source. Rador nodded grimly.

"The Shadow takes its toll," he said.

We topped a rise—Larry gripped my arm.

"Look!" he cried, and pointed. Far, far behind us, so far that the road was but a glistening thread, a score of shining points came speeding.

"Lugur and his men," said Rador.

"Can't you step on her?" asked Larry.

"Step on her?" repeated the green dwarf, puzzled.

"Give her more speed; push her," explained O'Keefe.

Rador looked about him. The coppery ramparts were close, not more than five of our miles distant; in front of us the plain lifted in a long rolling swell, and up this the *corial* essayed to go—with a terrifying lessening of speed. Faintly behind us came shoutings, and we knew that Lugur drew close. Nor anywhere was there sign of Lakla nor her frog-men—the *Akka*.

Now we were halfway to the crest; the shell barely crawled and from beneath it came a faint hissing; it quivered and I knew that its base was no longer held above the glassy surface but rested on it.

"One last chance!" exclaimed Rador. He pressed upon the control lever and wrenched it from its socket. Instantly the sparkling ball expanded, whirling with prodigious rapidity and sending a cascade of coruscations into the cylinder. The shell rose; leaped through the air; the dark crystal split into fragments; the fiery ball dulled; died—but upon the impetus of that last thrust we reached the crest. Poised there for a moment I caught a glimpse of the road dropping down the side of an enormous moss-covered bowl-shaped valley whose sharply curved sides ended abruptly at the base of the towering barrier.

Then down the steep, hissing over the obsidian, powerless to guide or to check the shell, we plunged in a meteor rush straight for the annihilating adamantine breasts of the cliffs!

Now the quick thinking of Larry's air training came to our aid. As the rampart reared close he threw himself upon Rador; hurled him and himself against the side of the flying whorl. Under the shock the finely balanced machine, almost floating in air through its projectile speed, swerved from its course. It struck the soft, low bank of the road, shot high in air, bounded on through the thick carpeting, whirled like a dervish and fell upon its side. Shot from it, we rolled for yards but the moss saved broken bones or serious bruise.

"Quick!" cried the green dwarf. He seized an arm, dragged me to my feet, began running to the cliff base not a hundred feet away. Beside us raced O'Keefe and Olaf. At our left was the black road. It stopped abruptly—was cut off by—a slab of polished crimson stone a hundred feet high, and as wide, set within the coppery face of the barrier. On each side of it stood pillars, cut from the living rock and immense, almost, as those which held the rainbow veil of the Dweller. Across its face weaved unnameable carvings—but I had no time for more than a glance. The green dwarf gripped my arm again.

"QUICK!" HE cried again. "The handmaiden has passed!"

At the right of the Portal ran a low wall of shattered rock. Over this we raced like rabbits. Hidden behind it was a narrow path. Crouching, Rador in the lead, we sped along it; three hundred, four hundred yards we raced—and the path ended in a *cul de sac!* To our ears was borne a louder shouting. O'Keefe peered over the wall.

"Here they come," he announced.

The first of the pursuing shells had swept over the lip of the great bowl, poised for a moment as we had and then, and not as we had, began a cautious descent. Within it, scanning the slopes, I saw Lugur.

"A little closer and I'll get him!" whispered Larry viciously. He raised his pistol.

His hand was caught in a mighty grip; Rador, eyes blazing, stood beside him.

"No!" rasped the green dwarf. He heaved a shoulder against one of the boulders that formed the pocket. It rocked aside, revealing a slit of an entrance.

"In!" ordered he, straining against the weight of the stone. O'Keefe, weapon in hand, slipped through, Olaf at his back, I following. With a lightning leap the green dwarf was beside me, the huge rock missing him by a hairbreadth as it swung into place!

We were in Cimmerian darkness. I felt for my pocket-flash and recalled with distress that I had left it behind with my medicine kit when we fled from the gardens. But Rador seemed to need no light.

"Grip hands!" he ordered. A palm shot into mine.

"It's me, professor," laughed O'Keefe. A great paw touched my side, fell into my other hand, and I knew this for Olaf's. We crept, single file, holding to each other like children, through the black. At last the green dwarf paused.

"Await me here," he whispered. "Do not move. And for your lives—be silent!"

And he was gone.

CHAPTER XXVII

DRAGON WORM AND
MOSS DEATH

FOR A SMALL eternity—to me at least—we waited. Then as silent as ever the green dwarf returned.

"It is well," he said, some of the strain gone from his voice. "Grip hands again, and follow."

"Wait a bit, Rador," this was Larry. "If Lugur's going to follow us in here why not let Olaf and me go back to the opening and pick them off as they come in? We could hold the lot—and in the mean time you and Goodwin could go after Lakla for help."

"Lugur knows the secret of the Portal—if he dare use it," answered the captain, with a curious indirection. "And now that they have challenged the Silent Ones I think he will dare. Also he will find our tracks—and it may be that he knows this hidden way."

"Well, for God's sake!" O'Keefe's appalled bewilderment was almost ludicrous. "If he knows all that, and you knew all that, why in hell didn't you let me click him when I had the chance?"

"*Larree,*" the green dwarf was grave and oddly humble. "It seemed good to me, too—at first. And then I heard a command, heard it clearly, to stop you—that Lugur die not now, lest a greater vengeance fail!"

"Command? From whom?" The Irishman's voice distilled out of the blackness the very essence of bewilderment.

"I thought," Rador was whispering—"I thought it came from the Silent Ones!"

"Superstition!" groaned O'Keefe in utter exasperation. "Always superstition! What can you do against it!"

"Never mind, Rador." His sense of humor came to his aid. "It's too late now anyway. Where do we go from here, old dear?" he laughed.

"We tread the path of one I am not fain to meet," answered Rador. "But if meet we must, point the death tubes at the pale shield he bears upon his throat and send the flame into the flower of cold fire that is its center—nor look into his eyes!"

Again Larry gasped, and I with him.

"It's getting too deep for me, Doc," he muttered, dejectedly. "Can you make head or tail of it?"

"No," I answered, shortly enough, "but Rador fears something and that's his description of it."

"Sure," he replied, "only it's a code I don't understand." I could feel his grin.

"All right for the flower of cold fire, Rador, and I won't look into his eyes," he went on cheerfully. "But hadn't we better be moving?"

"Come!" said the soldier; again hand in hand we went blindly on.

O'Keefe was muttering to himself.

"Flower of cold fire! Don't look into his eyes! Some joint! Damned superstition." Then he chuckled and caroled, softly:

"Oh, mama, pin a cold rose on me;
Two young frog-men are in love with me;
Shut my eyes so I can't see."

"Sh!" Rador was warning; he began whispering. "Lugur for a little time will be perplexed. He will not open the Portal until he must. They will find the *corial* and search. They will follow our tacks. Beyond the moving stone is naught but bare rock; there will be no tacks there but neither will there be hiding place. They will seek the entrance and they will find it. Then Lugur will send after us there a force of his men and with his others will pass through the Portal to beat for us.

"For half a *va* we go along a way of death. From its peril we pass into another against whose dangers I can guard you. But in parts this is in view of the roadway and it may be that Lugur will see us. If so we must fight as best we can. If we pass these two roads safely, then is the way to the Crimson Sea clear nor need we fear Lugur nor any. And there is another thing—that Lugur does not know—when he opens the Portal the Silent Ones will hear and Lakla and the *Akka* will be swift to greet its opener."

"Rador," I asked, "how know you all this?"

"The handmaiden is my own sister's child," he answered, quietly.

O'Keefe drew a long breath.

"Uncle," he remarked casually in English, "meet the man who's going to be your nephew!" And thereafter, except in grave moments he never addressed the green dwarf except by the avuncular title, which Rador, humorously enough, apparently conceived to be one of respectful endearment.

For me a light broke. Plain now was the reason for his fore-knowledge of Lakla's appearance at the feast where Larry had so narrowly escaped Yolara's spells; plain the determining factor that had cast his lot with ours, and my confidence despite his discourse of mysterious perils, experienced a remarkable quickening. Speculation as to the marked differences in pigmentation and appearance of niece and uncle was dissipated by my consciousness that we were now moving in a dim half light. We were in a fairly wide tunnel. Not far ahead the gleam filtered, pale yellow like sunlight sifting through the leaves of autumn poplars. And as we drew closer to its source I saw that it did indeed pass through a leafy screen hanging over the passage end. This Rador drew aside cautiously, beckoned us and we stepped through.

At first thought it appeared to be a tunnel cut through soft green mold. Its base was a flat strip of pathway a yard wide from which the walls curved out in perfect cylindrical form, smoothed and evened with utmost nicety. Thirty feet wide they were at their widest, then drew toward each other with no break in their symmetry; they did not close. Above was, roughly, a ten-foot rift, ragged edged, through which poured light like that in the heart of pale amber, a buttercup light shot through with curiously evanescent bronze shadows. Under the feet the path gave with a resiliency like hard rubber or well-rolled turf. It was ridged—rippled—the ripples a foot apart and flanked by deep, sharp indentations, clean cut as though drilled. Just such a tunnel, it came to me, as would be made by a huge metal ball belted with a long, toothed strip and sent rolling with terrific force through some compressible material such, for instance, as sphagnum moss.

"Quick!" commanded Rador, uneasily and set off at a sharp pace.

Sphygnum moss—why had that image come to me? Ah—so that was why! For now, my eyes becoming more accustomed to the strange light, I saw that the tunnel's walls were of moss. In it I could trace fringe leaf and curly leaf, pressings of enormous bladder caps (Physcomitrium), immense splashes of what seemed to be the scarlet-crested Cladonia, traceries of huge moss veils, crushings of teeth (peristome) gigantic; spore cases brown and white, saffron and ivory, hot vermilions and cerulean blues, pressed into an astounding mosaic by some Titanic force.

Among them the hepatics, that higher form which only a few daring souls had ventured to put forth as a link between the Bryophyta and the Angiospermae, or flowering plants, predominated. And I noted dozens upon dozens of species utterly strange, utterly unknown upon earth even among the fossils. Their hugeness, their giantism, filled me with awe and a fire of curiosity. I burned with eagerness to examine them minutely.

"Hurry!" It was Rador calling. I had lagged behind and reluctantly I turned my mind from those tempting walls, luring me to stop and study them; whose spell, indeed, already had slowed my pace. Hurriedly I rejoined the others; resolutely I kept my eyes at my feet, maintaining my place in the file.

And down the corridor swept ever tiny gusts, overladen with

unfamiliar, oddly fragrant odors; some so pronounced as to produce a trifle of light headedness—almost as though surcharged with oxygen.

Rador quickened the pace to a half-run; we were climbing; panting. The tunnel was no longer straight, it was—sinuous. Dispossessing the picture of the rolling ball came another of a long, flexible cylinder being forced through the luxuriant growth. The amber light grew stronger; the rift above us wider. The tunnel curved; on the left a narrow cleft appeared. The green dwarf leaped toward it, thrust us within, pushed us ahead of him up a steep rocky fissure—well nigh, indeed, a chimney. Up and up this we scrambled until my lungs were bursting and I thought I could climb no more. The crevice ended; we crawled out and sank, even Rador, upon a little, leaf-carpeted clearing circled by lacy-tree ferns.

Gasping, legs aching, we lay prone, relaxed, drawing back strength and breath. Rador was first to rise. Thrice he bent low as in homage, then—

"Give thanks to the Ancient Ones—for their power has been over us!" he exclaimed.

Dimly I wondered what he meant. Something about the fern leaf at which I had been staring aroused me. I leaped to my feet and ran to its base. This was no fern, no! It was fern moss! The largest of its species I had ever found in tropic jungles had not been more than two inches high, and this was—twenty feet! The scientific fire I had experienced in the tunnel returned uncontrollable. I parted the fronds, gazed out, froze with sheer wonder.

My outlook commanded a vista of miles—and that vista! A *Fata Morgana* of plantdom! A *Scheherezade's* garden of enchantment! A land of flowered sorcery!

Forests of tree-high mosses spangled over with blooms of every conceivable shape and color; cataracts and clusters, avalanches and nets of blossoms in pastels, in dulled metallics, in gorgeous flamboyant hues; some of them phosphorescent and shining like living jewels; some sparkling as though with dust of opals, of sapphires, of rubies and topazes and emeralds; thickets of convolvuli like the trumpets of the seven archangels of Mara, king of illusion, which are shaped from the bows of splendors arching his highest heaven!

And moss veils like banners of a marching host of Titans, pennons and bannerets of the sunset; gonfalons of the jinn; webs of faery; oriflammes of elfland!

Springing up through that polychromatic flood myriads of pedicles—slender and straight as spears, or soaring in spirals, or curving with undulations gracile as the white serpents of Tanit in ancient Carthaginian groves—and all surmounted by a fantasie of spore cases in shapes of minaret and turret, domes and spires and cones, caps of Phrygia and bishops' mitres, shapes grotesque and unnameable—shapes delicate and lovely!

They hung high poised, nodding and swaying—like goblins hovering over *Titania's* court; cacophony of Cathay accenting the *Flower Maiden* music of "Parsifal"; *bizarrerie* of the angled, fantastic beings that people the Javan pantheon watching a bacchanal of houris in Mohammed's paradise!

Down upon it all poured the amber light; dimmed in the distances by huge, drifting darkenings lurid as the flying mantles of the hurricane.

And through the light, like showers of jewels, myriads of birds, darting, dipping, soaring and still other myriads of gigantic, shimmering butterflies.

As I gazed, breath strangled with awe, a sound began to come to us, reaching out like the first faint susurrus of the incoming tide; sighing, sighing, growing stronger—now its mournful whispering quivered all about us, shook us—then passing like a Presence, died away in far distances.

"The Portal!" said Rador. "Lugur has entered!"

He, too, parted the fronds and peered back along our path. Peering with him we saw the barrier through which we had come stretching verdure-covered walls for miles three or more away. Like a mole burrow in a garden stretched the trail of the tunnel; here and there we could look down within the rift at its top; far off in it I thought I saw the glint of spears.

"They come!" whispered Rador. "Quick! We must not meet them here!"

And then—

"Holy St. Brigid!" gasped Larry.

From the rift in the tunnel's continuation, nigh a mile beyond the cleft through which we had fled, lifted a crown of horns—of tentacles—erect, alert, of mottled gold and crimson; lifted higher—and from a monstrous scarlet head beneath them blazed two enormous, oblold eyes their depths wells of purplish phosphorescence; higher still—noseless, earless, chinless; a livid, worm mouth from which a slender scarlet tongue leaped like playing flames! Slowly it rose—its mighty neck cuirassed with gold and scarlet scales from whose polished surfaces the amber light glinted like flakes of fire; and under this neck shimmered something like a palely luminous silvery shield, guarding it. More and more it drew into sight as the head of horror mounted—and in the shield's center, full ten feet across, glowing, flickering, pulsating, shining out—coldly, was a rose of white flame, a "flower of cold fire" even as Rador had said.

Now swiftly the Thing upreared, standing like a scaled tower a hundred feet above the rift, its eyes scanning that movement I had seen along the course of its lair. There was a hissing; the crown of horns fell, whipped and writhed like the tentacles of an octopus; the towering length dropped back.

"Quick!" gasped Rador and through the fern moss, along the path and down the other side of the steep we raced.

Behind us for an instant there was a rushing as of a torrent, a far-away, faint, agonized screaming—silence!

"No fear *now* from those who followed," whispered the green dwarf, pausing.

"Sainted St. Patrick!" O'Keefe gazed ruminatively at his automatic. "An' he expected me to *kill* that with *this*. Well, as

Fergus O'Connor said when they sent him out to slaughter a wild bull with a potato knife: 'Ye'll niver rayilize how I appreciate the confidence ye show in me!'"

"What was it, Doc?" he asked.

"The dragon worm!" Rador said.

"It was Helvede Orm—the hell worm!" groaned Olaf.

"There you go again—" blazed Larry; but the green dwarf was hurrying down the path and swiftly we followed, Larry muttering, Olaf mumbling behind me, and I myself so engrossed by memory pictures of the Thing and my entire respect for Rador's courage in invading its corridor, that for long I was insensible to the botanical wonders I was passing.

The green dwarf was slowing; signaling us for caution. He pointed through a break in a grove of fifty-foot cedar mosses— we were skirting the glassy road! Scanning it we found no trace of Lugur and wondered whether he too had seen the worm and had fled. Quickly we passed on; drew away from the *coria* path. The mosses began to thin; less and less they grew, giving way to low clumps that barely offered us shelter. Unexpectedly another screen of fern moss stretched before us. Slowly Rador made his way through it and stood hesitating.

The scene in front of us was oddly weird and depressing; in some indefinable way—dreadful. Why, I could not tell, but the impression was plain; I shrank from it. Then, self-analyzing, I wondered whether it could be the uncanny resemblance the heaps of curious mossy fungi scattered about had to beast and bird—yes, and to man—that was the cause of it. Our path ran between a few of them. To the left they were thick. They were viridescent, almost metallic hued—verd-antique. Curiously indeed were they like distorted images of dog and deerlike forms, of birds—of *dwarfs* and here and there the simulacra of the giant frogs! Spore cases, yellowish green, as large as mitres and much resembling them in shape protruded from the heaps. My repulsion grew.

Rador turned to us a face whiter far than that with which he had looked upon the dragon worm.

"Now for your lives," he whispered, "tread softly here as I do—and speak not at all!"

He stepped forward on tiptoe, slowly, with utmost caution. We crept after him; passed the heaps beside the path—and as I passed my skin crept and I shrank and saw the others shrink too with that un-nameable loathing; nor did the green dwarf pause until he had reached the brow of a small hillock a hundred yards beyond. And he was trembling.

"Now what the hell are we up against?" muttered O'Keefe.

The green dwarf stretched a hand; stiffened; gazed over to the left of us beyond a lower hillock upon whose broad crest lay a file of the moss shapes. They fringed it, their miters having a grotesque appearance of watching what lay below. And now I saw that the glistening road lay below—and from it came a shout! A dozen of the *coria* were there, filled with Lugur's men and in one of them Lugur himself, laughing wickedly.

There was a rush of soldiers and up the low hillock raced a score of them toward us.

"Run!" shouted Rador.

"Not much!" grunted O'Keefe—and took swift aim at Lugur. The automatic spat; Olaf's echoed. Both bullets went wide, for Lugur, still laughing threw himself into the protection of the body of his shell. But following the shots, from the file of moss heaps on the crest, came a series of muffled explosions. Under the pistols' concussions the mitred caps had burst and instantly all about the running soldiers grew a cloud of tiny, glistening white spores—like a little cloud of puff-ball dust many times magnified. Through this cloud I glimpsed their faces, stricken with an agony I could not fathom.

Some turned to fly, but before they could take a second step stood rigid.

The spore cloud drifted and eddied about them; rained down on their heads and half bare breasts, covered their garments—and swiftly they began to change! Their features grew indistinct—merged! The glistening white spores that covered them turned to a pale yellow, grew greenish, spread and swelled, darkened. The eyes of one of the soldiers glinted for a moment—and then were covered by the swift growth!

Where but a few moments before had been men were only grotesque heaps, swiftly melting, swiftly rounding into the semblance of the mounds that lay behind us—and already beginning to take on their gleam of ancient viridescence!

The Irishman was gripping my arm fiercely; the pain brought me back to my senses.

"Olaf's right," he gasped. "This *is* hell! I'm sick." And he was, frankly and without restraint. Lugur and his others awakened from their nightmare; piled into the *coria,* wheeled, raced away.

"On!" said Rador thickly. "Two perils have we passed—the Silent Ones watch over us!"

Soon we were again among the familiar and so unfamiliar moss giants. I knew what I had seen and this time Larry could not call me—superstitious. In the jungles of Borneo I had examined that other swiftly developing fungus which wreaks the vengeance of some of the hill tribes upon those who steal their women; gripping with its microscopic hooks into the flesh; sending quick, tiny rootlets through the skin down into the capillaries, sucking life and thriving and never to be torn away until the living thing it clings too has been sapped dry. Here was but another of the species in which the development's rate was incredibly accelerated. Some of this I tried to explain to O'Keefe as we sped along, reassuring him.

"But they, turned to moss before our eyes!" he said.

Again I explained, patiently. But he seemed to derive no comfort at all from my assurances that the phenomena were entirely natural and explicable and, aside from their more terrifying aspect, of peculiar interest to the botanist.

"I know," was all he would say. "But suppose one of those things had burst while we were going through—God!"

I was wondering how I could with comparative safety study

the fungus when Rador stopped; in front of us was again the road ribbon.

"Now is all danger passed," he said.

"The way lies open and Lugur has deliberately fled—"

There was a flash from the road. It passed me like a little lariat of light. It struck Larry squarely between the eyes, spread over his face and drew itself within!

"Down!" cried Rador, and hurled me to the ground. My head struck sharply; I felt myself grow faint; Olaf fell beside me; I saw the green dwarf draw down the O'Keefe; he collapsed limply, face still, eyes staring. A shout—and from the roadway poured a host of Lugur's men; I could hear Lugur bellowing.

There came a rush of little feet; soft, fragrant draperies brushed my face; dimly I watched Lakla bend over the Irishman.

She straightened—her arms swept out and the writhing vine, with its tendriled heads of ruby bloom, five flames of misty incandescence, leaped into the faces of the soldiers now close upon us. It darted at their throats, striking, coiling, and striking again; coiling and uncoiling with incredible rapidity and flying from leverage points of throats, of faces, of breasts like a great green spring endowed with consciousness, volition and hatred—and those it struck stood rigid as stone with faces masks of inhuman fear and anguish; and those still unstricken fled.

Another rush of feet—and down upon Lugur's forces poured the frog-men, their booming giant leading, thrusting with their lances, tearing and rending with talons and fangs and spurs.

Against that onrush the dwarfs could not stand. They raced for the shells; I heard Lugur shouting, menacingly—and then Lakla's voice, pealing like a golden bugle of wrath.

"Go, Lugur!" she cried. "Go that you and Yolara and your Shining One may die together! Death for you, Lugur—death for you all! Remember Lugur—death!"

There was a great noise within my head—no matter. Lakla was here—Lakla here—but too late—Lugur had outplayed us; moss death nor dragon worm had frightened him away—he had crept back to trap us—Lakla had come too late—Larry was dead—Larry! But I had heard no banshee wailing—and Larry had said he could not die without that warning—no, Larry was not dead. So ran the turbulent current of my mind.

A horny arm lifted me; two enormous, oddly gentle saucer eyes were staring into mine; my head rolled; I caught a glimpse of the Golden Girl kneeling beside the O'Keefe.

The noise in my head grew thunderous—was carrying me away on its thunder—swept me into soft, blind darkness.

CHAPTER XXVIII

THE CRIMSON SEA

I WAS IN the heart of a rose pearl, swinging, swinging; no, I was in a rosy dawn cloud, pendulous in space. Consciousness flooded me; in reality I was in the arms of one of the man frogs, carrying me as though I were a babe, and we were passing through some place suffused with glow enough like heart of pearl or dawn cloud to justify my awakening vagaries.

Just ahead walked Lakla in earnest talk with Rador, and content enough was I for a time to watch her. She had thrown off the metallic robes; her thick braids of golden brown with their flame glints of bronze were twined in a high coronal meshed in silken net of green; little clustering curls escaped from it, clinging to the nape of the proud white neck, shyly kissing it. From her shoulders fell a loose, sleeveless garment of shimmering green belted with a high golden girdle; skirt folds dropping barely below the knees.

She had cast aside her buskins, too, and the slender, high-arched feet were sandaled. She walked like one of Diana's nymphs, free, floating, delicately graceful, but with none of that serpent touch entwined in the least of Yolara's movements. Between the buckled edges of her kirtle I caught gleams of translucent ivory as exquisitely molded, as delectably rounded, as those revealed so naïvely beneath the hem.

Something was knocking at the doors of my consciousness—some tragic thing. What was it? Larry! Where was Larry? I remembered; raised my head abruptly; saw at my side another frog-man carrying O'Keefe, and behind him Olaf, step instinct with grief, following like some faithful, wistful dog who has lost a loved master. Upon my movement the monster bearing me halted, looked down inquiringly, uttered a deep, booming note that held the quality of interrogation.

Lakla turned; the clear, golden eyes were sorrowful, the sweet mouth pale; but her loveliness, her gentleness, that undefinable synthesis of all her tender self that seemed always to circle her with an atmosphere of lucid normality, lulled my panic. She spoke, and her words were as reassuringly matter of fact as though chosen for that purpose.

"Does your head pain you much?" she asked.

I lifted it gingerly; beyond a slight soreness there seemed little amiss.

"Drink this," she commanded, holding a small vial to my lips.

Its contents were aromatic, unfamiliar but astonishingly effective, for as soon as they passed my lips I felt a surge of strength; consciousness was restored.

"Larry!" I cried. "Is he dead?"

Lakla shook her head; her eyes were troubled.

"No," she said; "but he is like one dead—and yet unlike—"

"Put me down," I demanded to my bearer.

He tightened his hold; round eyes upon the Golden Girl. She spoke—in sonorous, reverberating monosyllables—and I was set upon my feet; I leaped to the side of the Irishman. He lay limp, with a disquieting, abnormal sequacity, as though every bone and muscle were utterly flaccid; the antithesis of the rigor mortis, thank God, but terrifyingly toward the other end of its arc; a syncope I had never known or heard. The flesh was stone cold; the pulse barely perceptible, long intervaled; the respiration undiscoverable; there were no nervous reflexes or reactions; the pupils of the eyes were enormously dilated; it was as though life had been drawn from every nerve.

"What did this?" I asked.

Lakla shook her head, looking at Rador, the trouble in her eyes deepening.

"At first I thought it was the *Keth* that was cast, but—" The green dwarf hesitated.

"A light flashed from the road. It struck his face and seemed to sink in," I said.

"I saw," answered Rador; "but what it was I know not; and I thought I knew all the weapons of our rulers." He glanced at me curiously. "Some talk there has been that the stranger who came with you, Double Tongue, was making new death tools for Lugur," he ended.

Von Hetzdorp! The German at work already in this storehouse of devastating energies, fashioning the weapons for his plots! The Apocalyptic vision swept back upon me, and I resolved that this quick blossoming of dread possibilities I had foreseen should be destroyed before it fruited—aye, and Von Hetzdorp destroyed with it.

"He is not dead." Lakla's voice was poignant. "He is not dead; and the Three have wondrous healing. They can restore him if they will—and they will, they *will!*" For a moment she was silent. "Now their gods help Lugur and Yolara," she whispered; "for come what may, whether the Silent Ones be strong or weak, if he dies, surely will I fall upon them with my *Akka* and I will slay those two with the *Yekta* death—with my own hands—yea, though I, too, perish!"

"Yolari and Lugur shall both die." Olaf's eyes were burning. "But Lugur is mine to slay."

That pity I had seen before in Lakla's eyes when she looked upon the Norseman banished the white wrath from them. She turned, half hurriedly, as though to escape his gaze, fastened upon her with hope-poised yearning on uplifted palms of appeal. He sighed, dropped behind.

"The white maiden *knows*," he murmured. "Not yet does she will to speak, and until she speaks I will not despair—no!"

Lakla glanced behind.

"**WALK WITH** us," she said to me, "unless you are still weak."

I shook my head, gave a last look at O'Keefe; there was nothing I could do; I stepped beside her. She thrust a white arm into mine protectingly, the wonderfully chiseled hand with its long, tapering fingers catching about my wrist; my heart glowed toward her.

"Soon we walk no more," she said. "When the Portal called, we sped back, my *Akka* and I, leaving the bearers behind. They wait for us, not far ahead. Are you strong enough?" she asked anxiously. "Or shall I call Ork to carry you again?"

I shook my head vigorously.

"Your medicine is potent, handmaiden," I answered. "And the touch of your hand would give me strength enough, even had I not drunk it." I added in Larry's best manner.

Her eyes danced, trouble flying.

"Now, that was well spoken for such a man of wisdom as Rador tells me you are," she laughed; and a little pang shot through me. Could not a lover of science present a compliment without it always seeming to be as unusual as plucking a damask rose from a cabinet of fossils? Ah, well, as I have said, those who swear allegiance to Minerva must expect the suspicion of Aphrodite.

Mustering my philosophy, I smiled back at her. Again I noted that broad, classic brow, with the little tendrils of slurring bronze caressing it, the tilted, delicate, nut-brown brows that gave a curious touch of innocent *diablerie* to the lovely face—flower-like, pure, high-bred, a touch of roguishness, subtly alluring, sparkling over the maiden Madonna-ness that lay ever like a delicate, luminous suggestion beneath it; the long, black, curling lashes—the tender, rounded, bare left breast—

"What is wisdom, O maiden, but clear seeing and understanding?" I replied. "And never has my wisdom, such as it is, seen clearer than when I look upon your countenance."

A little flush sped over her face. Rador laughed.

"I have always liked you," she murmured naïvely, enchantingly embarrassed, "since first I saw you in that place where the Shining One goes forth into your world. And I am glad you like—you like my medicine as well as that you carry in the black box that you left behind," she added swiftly.

"How know you of that, Lakla?" I gasped.

"Oft and oft I came to him there, and to you, while you lay sleeping. How call you him?" She paused.

"LARRY!" I said.

"Larry!" she repeated it excellently. "And you?"

"Goodwin," said Rador.

I bowed quite as though I were being introduced to some charming young lady met in that old life now seemingly eons removed.

"Yes—Goodwin," she said. "Oft and oft I came. Sometimes I thought you saw me. And he—did he not dream of me sometimes?" she asked wistfully.

"He did," I said, "and watched for you." Then amazement grew vocal. "But how came you?" I asked.

"By a strange road," she answered, "to see that all was well with *him*—and to look into his heart; for I feared Yolara and her beauty. But I saw that she was not in his heart." A blush burned over her, turning even the little bare breast rosy. "It is a strange road," she went on hurriedly. "Many times have I followed it and watched the Shining One bear back its prey to the blue pool; seen the woman *he* seeks"—she made a quick gesture toward Olaf—"and a babe cast from her arms in the last pang of her mother love; seen another woman throw herself into the Shining One's embrace to save a man she loved; and I could not help!" Her voice grew deep, thrilled. "The friend, it comes to me, who drew you here, Goodwin!"

Unable to speak, I stared at her in stark astonishment.

"Well," she said, "*you* must pass upon that road, too, Goodwin; and *he,* if he live, to see what you must—the Silent Ones are speaking to me, and by that I know he *shall* live." Her face was rapt, with that expression that Delphi's pythoness must have borne, listening to the whispers of Apollo. "But not *he*—not the great one you call Olaf; he may not pass upon it," she murmured, and again the pity welled up in the eyes of gold.

She was silent, walking as one who sees visions and listens to voices unheard by others. Rador made a warning gesture; I crowded back my questions, glanced about me. We were passing over a smooth strand, hard packed as some beach of long-thrust-back ocean. It was like crushed garnets, each grain stained deep red, faintly sparkling. On each side were distances, the floor sketching away into them bare of vegetation—stretching on and on into infinitudes of rosy mist, even as did the space above.

Flanking and behind us marched the giant batrachians, fivescore of them at least, black scale and crimson scale lustrous and gleaming in the rosaceous radiance; saucer eyes, shining circles of phosphorescence, green, purple, red; spurs clicking as they crouched along with a gait at once grotesque and formidable.

Ahead the mist deepened into a ruddier glow; through it a long, dark line began to appear—the mouth I thought of the caverned space through which we were going; it was just before us; over us—we stood bathed in a flood of rubescence!

A sea stretched before us—a crimson sea, gleaming like that lost lacquer of royal coral and the Flame Dragon's blood which Fu S'cze set upon the bower he built for the sun maiden he had stolen—that going toward it she might think it the sun itself rising over the summer seas. Unmoved by wave or ripple, it was placid as some deep woodland pool when night rushes up over the world.

About it was no hint of stagnancy, no unpleasant suggestion

of tide of blood. Rather it seemed molten—or as though some hand great enough to rock earth had distilled here from conflagrations of autumn sunsets their naming essences.

A fish broke through, large as a shark, blunt-headed, flashing bronze, ridged and mailed as though with serrate plates of armor. It leaped high, shaking from it a sparkling spray of rubies; dropped and shot up a geyser of fiery gems.

Across my line of vision, moving stately over the sea, floated a half globe, luminous, diaphanous, its iridescence melting into turquoise, thence to amethyst, to orange, to scarlet shot with rose, to vermilion, a translucent green, thence back into the iridescence; behind it four others, and the least of them ten feet in diameter, and the largest no less than thirty. They drifted past like bubbles blown from froth of rainbows by pipes in mouths of Titans' young. Then from the base of one arose a tangle of shimmering strands, long, slender whiplashes that played about and sank slowly again beneath the crimson surface.

I gasped—for the fish had been a ganoid—that ancient, armored form that was perhaps the most intelligent of all life on our planet during the Devonian era, but which for age upon age had vanished, save for its fossils held in the embrace of the stone that once was their soft bottom beds; and the half-globes were *Medusae*, jelly-fish—but of a size, luminosity, and color unheard of.

Now Lakla cupped her mouth with pink palms and sent a clarion note ringing out. The ledge on which we stood continued a few hundred feet before us, falling abruptly, though from no great height to the Crimson Sea; at right and left it extended in a long semicircle. Turning to the right whence she had sent her call, I saw rising a mile or more away, veiled lightly by the haze, a rainbow, a gigantic prismatic arch, flattened, I thought, by some quality of the strange atmosphere. It sprang from the ruddy strand, leaped the crimson tide, and dropped three miles away upon a precipitous, jagged upthrust of rock frowning black from the lacquered depths.

And surmounting a higher ledge beyond this upthrust a huge dome of dull gold. Cyclopean, striking eyes and mind with something unhumanly alien, baffling; sending the mind groping, as though across the deserts of space, from some far-flung star, should fall upon us linked sounds, coherent certainly, meaningful surely, vaguely familiar—yet never to be translated into any symbol or thought of our own particular planet.

This sea of crimson lacquer, with its floating moons of luminous color—this bow of prismed light leaping to the weird isle crowned by the anomalous, aureate—excrescence—the half human batricians—the elf land through which we had passed, with all its hidden wonders and terrors—I felt the foundations of my cherished knowledge shaking. Was this all a dream? Was this body of mine lying somewhere, fighting a fevered death, and all these but images floating through the breaking chambers of my brain? My knees shook; involuntarily I groaned.

Lakla turned, looked at me anxiously, slipped a soft arm behind me, held me till the vertigo passed.

"Patience," she said. "The bearers come. Soon you shall rest."

I looked; down toward us from the bow's end were leaping swiftly another score of the frog-men. Some bore litters, high, handled, not unlike palanquins—

"Asgard!" Olaf stood beside me, eyes burning pointing to the arch. "Bifrost Bridge, sharp as sword edge, over which souls go to Valhalla. And *she*—she is a valkyr—a sword maiden, *ja!*"

I gripped the Norseman's hand. It was hot, and a pang of remorse shot through me. If this place had so shaken *me*, how must it have shaken Olaf, who had neither my armor of science nor Larry's protecting belief that outside of Ireland could occur only wholly natural phenomena. As soon as we reached wherever we were going, Olaf must be cared for—surely only his obsessing grief and his fixed idea of vengeance could have carried him so far!

And it was with relief that I watched him, at Lakla's gentle command, drop humbly into one of the litters and lie back, eyes closed, as two of the monsters raised its yoke to their scaled shoulders. Nor was it without further relief that I myself lay back on the soft velvety cushions of another.

The cavalcade began to move. Lakla had ordered O'Keefe placed beside her, and she sat, knees crossed Orient fashion, leaning over the pale head on her lap, the white, tapering fingers straying fondly through his hair.

Presently I saw her reach up, slowly unwind the coronal of her tresses, shake them loose, and let them fall like a veil over her and him.

Her head bent low; I heard a soft sobbing—I turned away my gaze, lorn enough in my own heart, God knew!

CHAPTER XXIX

THE THREE SILENT ONES

THE ARCH WAS closer—and in my awe as I looked upon it I forgot for the moment Larry and aught else. For this was no rainbow, no thing born of light and mist, no Bifrost Bridge of myth—no! It was a flying arch of stone, stained with flares of Tyrian purples, of royal scarlets, of blues dark as the Gulf Stream's ribbon, sapphires soft as midday May skies, splashes of chromes and greens—a palette of giantry, a bridge of wizardry; a hundred, nay, a thousand, times greater than that of Utah which the Navaho call Nonnegozche and worship, as well they may, as a god, and which is itself a rainbow in eternal rock.

It sprang from the ledge and winged its prodigious length in one low arc over the sea's crimson breast, as though in some ancient paroxysm of earth it had been hurled molten, crystallizing into that stupendous span and still flaming with the fires that had molded it.

Closer we came and closer, while I watched spellbound; now we were at its head, and the litter-bearers swept upon it. All of five hundred feet wide it was, surface smooth as a city road, sides low walled, curving inward as though in the jetting-out of its making the edges of the plastic rock had curled.

On and on we sped; the high thrusting precipices upon which the bridge's far end rested, frowned close; the enigmatic, dully shining dome loomed ever greater. Now we had reached that end; were passing over a smooth plaza whose level door was enclosed, save for a rift in front of us, by the fanged tops of the black cliffs.

From this rift stretched another span, half a mile long, perhaps, widening at its center into a broad platform, continuing straight to two massive gates set within the face of the second cliff wall like panels, and of the same dull gold as the dome rising high beyond. And this smaller arch passed over a pit, an abyss, of which the outer precipices were the rim holding back from the pit the red flood.

We were rapidly approaching; now upon the platform, my bearers were striding closely along the side; I leaned far out—a giddiness seized me! I gazed down into depth upon vertiginous depth; an abyss indeed—an abyss dropping to world's base like that in which the Babylonians believed writhed Talaat, the serpent mother of Chaos; a pit that shuck down into earth's heart itself. It was as though I were looking over the edge of a world into illimitable space.

Now, what was that—distance upon unfathomable distance below? A stupendous glowing like the green fire of life itself. What was it like? I had it! It was like the corona of the sun in eclipse—that other burgeoning of unknown elements that makes of our luminary when moon veils it an incredible blossoming of splendors in the black heavens.

And strangely, strangely, it was like the Dweller's beauty when with its dazzling spiralings and whirlings it raced amid its storm of crystal bell sounds!

The abyss was behind us; we had paused at the gilden portals; they swung inward. A wide corridor filled with soft light was before us, and on its threshold stood—bizarre, yellow gems gleaming, huge muzzle wide in what was evidently meant for a smile of welcome—the woman frog of the Moon Pool wall. And from behind her leaped a frog-child, black and scarlet as were our guards, who with little croakings and boomings of joy jumped into the arms of the giant who had led us—he who had gone before Lakla at Yolara's interrupted feast, and whose beastly club had so narrowly missed scattering the brains of O'Keefe.

Lakla raised her head; swept back the silken tent of her hair and gazed at me with eyes misty from weeping. The frog-woman crept to her side; gazed down upon Larry; spoke—*spoke*—to the Golden Girl in a swift stream of the sonorous, reverberant monosyllables; and Lakla answered her in kind. The webbed digits swept over O'Keefe's face, felt at his heart; she shook her head and moved with extraordinary rapidity ahead of us up the passage. The golden gates closed.

Still borne in the litters we went on, winding, ascending until at last they were set down in a great hall carpeted with soft fragrant rushes and into which from high narrow slits streamed the crimson light from without.

I jumped over to Larry; there had been no change in his condition; still the terrifying limpness, the slow, infrequent pulsation. Rador and Olaf—and the fever now seemed to be gone from him—came and stood beside me, silent.

"I go to the Three," said Lakla. "Wait you here." She passed through a curtaining; nor one word did we utter until she returned, standing there about the body of the man whom each of us, in his own fashion, loved well. Then as swiftly as she had gone she came through the hangings; tresses braided, a swathing of golden gauze about her.

"Rador," she said, "bear you Larry—for into your heart the Silent Ones would look. And fear nothing," she added at the green dwarf's disconcerted, almost fearful start.

Rador bowed, started to lift O'Keefe; was thrust aside by Olaf.

"No," said the Norseman; "I will carry him."

He lifted Larry like a child against his broad breast. The dwarf glanced quickly at Lakla; she nodded.

"Come!" she commanded, and held aside the folds.

Of that journey I have few memories. I only know that we went through corridor upon corridor; successions of vast halls and chambers, some carpeted with the rushes, others with rugs into which the feet sank as into deep, soft meadows; glimpses of things carved, things wrought and woven; brilliant screens of feathers; great tapestries and odd, unfamiliar, thronelike seats; divans like giants' beds; spaces illumined by the rubrous light, and spaces in which softer lights held sway.

We paused before a slab of the same crimson stone as that the green dwarf had called the Portal, and upon its polished surface, even as they had upon it, weaved the unnameable symbols. The Golden Girl pressed upon its side; it slipped softly back; a torrent of opalescence gushed out of the opening—and as one in a dream I entered.

We were, I knew, just under the dome; but for the moment, caught in the flood of radiance, I could see nothing. It was like being held within a fire opal—so brilliant, so flashing, was it. I closed my eyes, opened them; the lambency cascaded from the vast curves of the globular walls; in front of me was a long, wide opening in them, through which, far away, I could see the end of the wizards' bridge and the ledged opening of the cavern through which we had come; against the light from within beat the crimson light from without—and was checked as though by a barrier.

I felt Lakla's touch; turned.

A hundred paces away was a dais, its rim raised a yard above the floor. From the edge of this rim streamed upward a steady, coruscating mist of the opalescence, veined even as was that of the Dweller's shining core and shot with milky shadows like curdled moonlight; up it stretched like a wall.

Over it, from it, down upon me, gazed three faces—two

clearly male, one a woman's. At the first I thought them statues, and then the eyes of them gave the lie to me; for the eyes were alive, terribly, and if I could admit the word—*supernaturally*—alive.

They were thrice the size of the human eye and triangular, the apex of the angle upward; black as jet, pupilless, filled with tiny, leaping red flames; and they were the eyes of that little cloud I had seen hovering about Lakla in what I had then thought to be a singularly vivid dream.

Over them were foreheads, not as ours—high and broad and visored; their sides drawn forward into a vertical ridge, a prominence, an upright wedge, somewhat like the visored heads of some of the great lizards—and the heads, long, narrowing at the back, were fully twice the size of mankind's!

Upon the brows were caps—and with a fearful certainty I knew that they were not caps—long, thick strands of gleaming, yellow, feathered scales thin as sequins! Sharp, curving noses like the beaks of the giant condors; mouths thin, austere; long, powerful, pointed chins; the—*flesh*—of the faces white as whitest marble; and wreathing up to them, covering all their bodies, the shimmering, curdled, misty fires of opalescence!

Olaf stood rigid; my own heart leaped wildly. What—what were these beings?

I forced myself to look again—and from their gaze streamed a current of reassurance, of will—nay, of intense spiritual strength. I saw that they were not fierce, not ruthless, not inhuman, despite their strangeness; no, they were kindly, in some unmistakable way, benign and sorrowful—so sorrowful! I straightened, gazed back at them fearlessly. Olaf drew a deep breath, gazed steadily, too, the hardness, the despair wiped from his face.

Now Lakla drew closer to the dais; the three pairs of eyes searched hers, the woman's with an ineffable tenderness; some message seemed to pass between the Three and the Golden Girl. She bowed low, turned to the Norseman.

"Place Larry there," she said softly—"there at the feet of the Silent Ones."

SHE POINTED into the radiant mist; Olaf started, hesitated, stared from Lakla to the Three, searched for a moment their eyes—and something like a smile drifted through them. He stepped forward, lifted O'Keefe, set him squarely within the covering light. It wavered, rolled upward, swirled about the body, steadied again—and within it there was no sign of Larry!

Again the mist wavered, shook, and seemed to *climb* higher, hiding the chins, the beaked noses, the brows of that incredible Trinity—but before it ceased to climb I thought I saw the yellow, feathered heads bend; sensed a movement as though they lifted something.

The mist fell; the eyes gleamed out again, inscrutable.

And groping out of the radiance, pausing at the verge of the dais, leaping down from it, came Larry, laughing, filled with life, blinking as one who draws from darkness into sunshine. He saw Lakla, sprang to her, gripped her in his arms.

"Lakla!" he cried. *"Mavourneen!"*

Swiftly she slipped from his embrace, blushing, glancing at the Three shyly, half-fearfully. And again I saw the tenderness creep into the inky, flame-shot orbs of the woman being; and a tenderness in the others, too—as though they regarded some well-beloved child.

"Doc," shouted Larry, catching me by the hand, "what hit me? Say—I've had some dream—and where are we?"

Lakla touched his arm and proceeded to answer his question.

"You lay in the arms of Death, Larry," she said. "And the Silent Ones drew you from him. Do homage to the Silent Ones, Larry, for they are good and they are mighty!"

She turned his head with one of the long, white hands—and he looked into the faces of the Three; looked long, was shaken even as had been Olaf and myself; stiffened under that same wave of power and of—of—what can I call it?—*holiness* that streamed from them.

Then for the first time I saw real awe mount into his face. Another moment he stared—and dropped upon one knee and bowed his head before them as would a worshiper before the shrine of his saint. And—I am not ashamed to tell it—I joined him; and with us knelt Lakla and Olaf and Rador.

We bent there, my heart as full of thanksgiving and of confidence as a child who has passed through nightmare land into safe fireside haven. I looked up—the eyes of the Trinity were soft, the leaping flames within them quiet, the black depths filled with tenderness.

Then the mist of fiery opal swirled up, covering them.

And with a long, deep, joyous sigh Lakla took Larry's hand, drew him to his feet, and silently we followed them out of that hall of wonder.

But why, in going, did the thought come to me that from where the Three sat throned they ever watched the cavern mouth that was the door into their abode; and looked down ever into the unfathomable depth in which glowed and pulsed that mystic flower, colossal, awesome, of green flame that had seemed to me fire of life itself?

CHAPTER XXX

SPECULATION

I HAD SLEPT soundly and dreamlessly; I wakened quietly in the great chamber into which Rador had ushered O'Keefe and myself after that culminating experience of crowded, nerve-racking hours—the facing of the weird Three.

I remembered the drowsiness that had come upon me as tension relaxed beneath the reassurance, the calm that had flowed from them; how sleepily I had partaken of the food and drink served by marvelously deft fingers of frog-women; the unwonted gravity of Larry listening to Rador's tale of the little paralyzing lariat of light and of his suspicions regarding Von

Hetzdorp's part in it; the O'Keefe's troubled silence as he contemplated, even as had I, the possibilities brought so close by this revelation of the German's energy; the shy quietness of Lakla, her heart so plainly filled with happiness that there was no corner left for even shadow of apprehension; the beginnings of Larry's eager questioning as to the Silent Ones; the half-wistful distress of the handmaiden's obvious evasions that had so quickly stilled him, and the almost embarrassed haste with which she bundled us off to bed in care of the green dwarf, who, after seeing us comfortably installed on two of the enormous cushion-covered divans, had taken Olaf as company for himself.

Much to my relief Larry had, by that time, revealed himself as weary too, tumbling well-nigh rudely off to sleep with only a muttered: "Sleep tight, Doc!"

Now, lying gazing upward at the high-vaulted ceiling, I heard his voice:

"They look like birds." Evidently he was thinking of the Three; a silence—then: "Yes, they look like birds—and they look, and it's meaning no disrespect to them I am at all, they look like *lizards*"—another silence—"and they look like some sort of gods, and, by the good sword-arm of Brian Boru, they look human, too! And it's *none* of them they are either, so what—what the—what the sainted St. Bridget are they?" Another short silence, and then in a tone of awed and absolute conviction: "That's it, sure! That's what they are—it all hangs in—they couldn't be anything else—"

He gave a whoop; a pillow shot over and caught me across the head.

"Wake up!" shouted Larry. "Wake up, ye seething cauldron of fossilized superstitions! Wake up, ye bogy-haunted man of scientific unwisdom!"

Under pillow and insults I bounced to my feet, filled for a moment with quite real wrath; he lay back, roaring with laughter, and my anger was swept away.

"If I hadn't known already that it's a real two-fisted man you are, Doc, I'd know it now!" he gasped. "And I needed something heavy to wake you up. Here I've been lying and soliloquizing for the last half-hour, and you sleeping like a mermaid on the top of a wave; although in all candor, Doc, if any mermaid slept like you, she'd have no difficulty in getting a job as a fog-buoy."

This last annoyed me greatly, because I have habituated myself to sleeping silently, my explorations having taken me into many regions where it would be the height of folly to seek slumber unless one were absolutely sure that slumber could give no signal of one's whereabouts. His solemn disclaimer of seriousness upon my anxious queries and my explanation of the reason for them relieved me therefore greatly.

"Doc," he said, very seriously, after this, "I know who the Three are!"

"Yes?" I queried, with studied sarcasm.

"Yes?" he mimicked. "Yes! Ye—ye—" He paused under the menace of my look, grinned. "Yes, I know," he continued. "They're of the Tuatha Dé, the old ones, the great people of Ireland, *that's* who they are!"

I knew, of course, of the Tuatha Dé Danann, the tribes of the god Danu, the half-legendary, half-historical clan who found their home in Erin some four thousand years before the Christian era, and who have left so deep an impress upon the Celtic mind and its myths. Mighty necromancers they were supposed to be, skilled in all charms, lords of the forces of nature. They destroyed the fierce Firbolgs, all but annihilated the Formarians—the latter, legend has it, by their wizardry.

Exist they certainly did, although one is permitted to doubt their accredited powers. History is inclined to place them as migrants from Greece—although some also place them as an advanced race of the middle stone age—and to attribute their disappearance to the invasion of Ireland by the Milesians. But the legends of Ireland will not have it that they were conquered; they say that the Tuatha Dé withdrew into the fairy mounds, where they still dwell, and through which is the way to Tir n'Óg, their paradise.

Whatever they were and wherever they went no ancients ever stamped themselves so strongly upon the imagination of a race as these have upon the Gaels.

"Yes," said Larry again, "the Tuatha Dé—the Ancient Ones who had spells that could compel Mananan, who is the spirit of all the seas, and Keithor, who is the god of all green living things, and even Hesus, the unseen god, whose pulse is the pulse of all the firmament; yes, an' Orchil too, who sits within the earth an' waves with the shuttle of mystery her three looms of birth an' life an' death—even Orchil would weave as they commanded!"

He was silent—then:

"These are of them—the mighty ones—why else would I have bent my knee to them as I would have to the spirit of my dead mother? Why else would Lakla, whose gold-brown hair is the hair of Eilidh the Fair, whose mouth is the sweet mouth of Deirdre, an' whose soul walked with mine ages agone among the fragrant green myrtle of Erin, serve them?" he whispered, eyes full of dream.

"Have you any idea how they got here?" I asked, not unreasonably.

"I haven't thought about that," he replied somewhat testily. "But at once, me excellent man o' wisdom, a number occur to me. One of them is that this little party of three might have stopped here on their way to Ireland, an' for good reasons of their own decided to stay a while; an' another is that they might have come here afterward, havin' got wind of what those rats out there were contemplating and have stayed on the job till the time was ripe to save Ireland from 'em; the rest of the world, too, of course," he added magnanimously, "but Ireland in particular. And do any of those reasons appeal to ye?"

I shook my head.

"Well, what do *you* think?" he asked wearily.

"I think," I said cautiously, "that we face an evolution of highly intelligent beings from ancestral sources radically removed from those through which mankind ascended. These half-human, highly developed batrachians they call the *Akka*, prove that evolution in these caverned spaces has certainly pursued one different path than on earth. The Englishman, Wells, once wrote an imaginative and very entertaining book concerning an invasion of earth by Martians, and he made his Martians enormously specialized cuttlefish. There was nothing inherently improbable in Wells's choice. Man is the ruling animal of earth today solely by reason of a series of accidents; under another series spiders or ants, or even elephants, could have become the dominant race, and man have stopped at the mud-puppy stage—or before.

"What *I* think, since you have asked me, Larry O'Keefe," I went on, "is that the Three are of a race which came up from a lizard form. I am swayed in this by the shape of the forehead, with its vertical wedge; the—well, I suppose I may call it hirsutage—of thin, feathered scales—the feather of the bird is, you may take this as determined, only a development of the scale of its reptilian ancestors. Finally, I take into consideration the large, sharp, beaked nose, with its entirely birdlike suggestion—and the bird's beak is as much a modification of saurian form as are its feathers.

"Finally, I think that the race to which the Three belong never appeared on earth's surface; that their development took place here unhindered through hundreds of thousands of years, during which, because of its chaotic condition, any higher intelligences could not have existed on the surface of our planet. If this is true, the structure of their brains, and therefore their reactions and potentialities must be different from ours. Hence their knowledge and command of energies unfamiliar to us— and hence, also, the grave question whether they may not have an entirely different sense of justice, of values—and that is rather terrifying!" I concluded.

"That last sort of knocks your argument, Doc," he said. "They had sense of justice enough to help me out—and certainly they know love—for I saw the way they looked at Lakla; and sorrow—for there was no mistaking that in their faces."

"I consider that a frivolous objection, Larry," I answered, a bit nonplused, nevertheless.

"There was that feeling of awe; I bent my knee to them," he said stubbornly. "I can't see any O'Keefe kneeling to anything whose greatgrandfather was a lizard!"

"Great Scott, man!" I cried. "Do you believe in angels?"

"Yes—Lakla," he grinned.

"No," I said, "in heavenly angels?"

"Well—" He hesitated. "Yes, I do," half-defiantly.

"And where do you think angels come from?"

"Well—I don't know; I think there's one of them now who used to be my mother," he replied softly.

"Ah!" I pressed the point home. "And you'd kneel to *her?*"

"*Would* I!" he exclaimed.

"Well," I cried triumphantly, "is there anymore shock to the reason in supposing that a lizard could develop slowly into one of these Three than there is in supposing a human being can, in a twinkling, turn into a winged and shining shape of glory!"

And the minute I said it I was sorry—one should never argue an abstract question from the factors of the personal; I realized the full tactlessness of my remark. Larry flushed.

"I don't quite like your comparison, Doc," he said stonily. "I'd have knelt to my mother *any time.*"

"Oh, Larry," I cried, "I *am* sorry!"

The resentment died away, his eyes twinkled.

"You scientists are an inhuman lot—sometimes," he said. "That's why I *like you* to be superstitious now and then—it shows you're not fossilized!"

"O'Keefe," I answered sternly, "in this I'm not at all—superstitious. I am wholly materialistic. I see before us unfamiliar evolutionary forms which, because of that unhuman evolution, possess powers and wisdom which, though entirely natural, may well fill us with wonder and unease. That is all."

But he shook his head again.

"No," he replied. "I hold to my own idea. They're of the old people. The little leprechawn knew his way here, an' I'll bet it was they who sent the word. An' if the O'Keefe banshee comes here—which save the mark!—I'll bet she'll drop in on the Silent Ones for a social visit before she an' her clan get busy. Well, it'll make her feel more at home, the good old body. No, Doc, no," he concluded, "I'm right; it all fits in too well to be wrong."

I made a last despairing attempt.

"Is there anything anywhere in Ireland that would indicate that the Tuatha Dé ever looked like the Three?" I asked—and again I had spoken most unfortunately.

"Is there?" he shouted. "Is there? By the kilt of Cormack Maccormack, I'm glad ye reminded me. It was worryin' me a little meself. There was Daghda, who could put on the head of a great fish an' the body of a giant boar, and cleave the waves an' tear to pieces the birlins of any who came against Erin; an' there was Rinn, the son of Eochaidh Iuil, who walked about Tara Hill, with his head an eagle's head, huge with flaming red eyes, an' a body of pale, whispering rushes; an' there was Keevan Honeymouth—"

How many more of the metamorphoses of the old people I might have heard, I do not know, for the curtains parted and in walked Rador.

"You have rested well," he smiled. "I can see. The hand-maiden bade me call you. You are to eat with her in her garden."

O'Keefe was hustling into his clothes.

"Can you swim in that red stuff out there, uncle?" he asked.

"Don't you ever try it, *Larree*," Rador was plainly appalled. "There's a pool here—I'll show it to you. In the mean time—" He spun out through the hangings—returning a moment later with two man-frogs carrying basins filled with clear water. Into these we dipped our hands and faces. Larry, splashing and rubbing vigorously, had not dismissed from his mind the subject I had thought closed.

"No, Doc," he spluttered, "we're in right. The Three are a slice of the old isle. *They're* here for a purpose and we're here for a purpose. I knew it the minute I set eyes on Lakla. Just remember—there's nothing outside of Ireland that ain't natural, and it's as natural for Ireland to have all the fairies, the *sidh*, as it would be unnatural for any other place to have 'em. Say, is my hair fairly decent? Ireland's the oldest country in the world—an' her heart's the youngest. That's why the fairies love her, an' why they won't go anywhere else.

"Lord! I wish I had a brush. Lakla must have one, though, look how she keeps her hair—don't get me wrong, old dear. The leprechawn said the *bhoys* are rooting for us. Everything natural—we're in right with the right people. Four of 'em—an' all Irish, God bless 'em! On your way, Rador!"

He pushed the laughing green dwarf ahead of him; the frog-men blinked and followed. Down long corridors we trod and out upon a gardened terrace as beautiful as any of those of Yolara's city; bowered, blossoming, fragrant, set high upon the cliffs beside the domed castle. A table, as of milky jade, was spread at one corner, but the Golden Girl was not there. A little path ran on and up, hemmed in by the mass of verdure, I looked at it longingly; Rador saw the glance; interpreted it and led me up the stepped, sharp slope into a rocky embrasure.

Here I was above the foliage, and everywhere the view was clear. Below me stretched the incredible bridge, with the frog people hurrying back and forth upon it. A pinnacle at my side hid the abyss. My eyes followed the cavern ledge. Above it the rock rose bare, but at the ends of the semicircular strand a luxuriant vegetation began, stretching from the crimson shores back into far distances. Of browns and reds and yellows, like an autumn forest, was the foliage, with here and there patches of dark-green, as of conifers. Five miles or more, on each side, the forests swept, and then were lost to sight in the haze.

I turned and faced an immensity of crimson waters, unbroken, a true sea, if ever there was one. A little breeze blew—the first real wind I had encountered in the hidden places; under it the surface, that had been as molten lacquer, rippled and dimpled. Little waves broke with a spray of rose-pearls and rubies. The giant Medusae drifted—stately, luminous, kaleidoscopic elfin moons.

Far down, peeping around a jutting tower of the cliff, I saw dipping, with the motion of the waves, a floating garden. The flowers, too, were luminous—indeed sparkling—gleaming brilliants of scarlet and vermilions lighter than the flood on which they lay, mauves and odd shades of reddish-blue. They glimmed and shone like a little lake of jewels.

A thought with me since our flight claimed utterance.

"Rador," I said, "if it is permissible to tell—how did Lakla, who is your sister's child, come to be handmaiden to the Three?"

"I can tell you that now, Goodwin," he answered. "I told you that of the Murians there are the black-haired, who are the *ladala,* and the soldiers from them; and the fair-haired, who are the rulers. From among the *ladala,* never from among the rulers, there is born once in two generations a girl baby whose eyes are golden; whose hair, even as a babe, is like that of Lakla's, and who is in other ways—different.

"Now there are some who say that this child is of a strain that was among us before—before we found this land and which was destroyed, for a certain reason, by the fair-haired. And there are others who say that the Silent Ones have something to do with it. Whatever the reason, by an ancient pact with the Three, this child, when it is but three months old, is carried here and given to the handmaiden who then serves. She it is who rears and instructs it, and when the child is fourteen *laya* old she takes the place of that handmaiden who has cared for it."

"And what becomes of the other one?" I asked.

"**SHE—GOES!**" **HE** answered. "She has the right, if she will, to choose a mate from the *ladala.* But none has done so. It is said that as reward—and perhaps because she is no more like the Murians than the Three—she is taken to that land of wonder beyond the black precipices of Dual. Or it may be that she goes where those who are the race of the Silent Ones dwell—I do not know."

"And where is that?" I asked. He shook his head.

"Lakla comes!" he said. "Let us go down."

It was a shy Lakla who came slowly around the end of the path and, blushing furiously, held her hands out to Larry. And the Irishman took them, placed them over his heart, kissed them with a tenderness that had been lacking in the half-mocking, half-fierce caresses he had given the priestess. She blushed deeper, holding out the tapering fingers—then pressed them to her own heart.

"I like the touch of your lips, Larry," she whispered. "They warm me here"—she pressed her heart again—"and they send little sparkles of light through me." Her brows tilted perplexed-ly, accenting the nuance of *diablerie,* delicate and fascinating, that they cast upon the flower face.

"Do you?" whispered the O'Keefe fervently. "Do you, Lakla?" He bent toward her. She caught the amused glance of Rador; drew herself aside half-haughtily.

"Rador," she said, "is it not time that you and the strong one, Olaf, were setting forth?"

"Truly it is, handmaiden," he answered respectfully enough—yet with a current of laughter under his words. "But as you know the strong one, Olaf, wished to see his friends here before we were gone—and he comes even now," he added, glancing down the pathway, along which came striding the Norseman.

As he faced us I saw that a transformation had been wrought in him. Gone was the pitiful seeking, and gone too the hope. About him was implacable resolution, stony determination like one who knows the worst and has consecrated body and soul to meet and destroy it. The set lines softened as he looked at the Golden Girl and bowed low to her. He thrust a hand to O'Keefe and to me.

"There is to be battle," he said. "I go with Rador to call the armies of these frog people. As for me—Lakla has spoken. There is no hope for—for mine Helma in life, but there is hope that we destroy the Shining Devil and give mine Helma peace. And with that I am well content, *ja!* Well content!" He gripped our hands again. "We will fight!" he muttered. *"Ja!* And I will have vengeance!" The sternness returned; and with a salute Rador and he were gone.

Two great tears rolled from the golden eyes of Lakla.

"Not even the Silent Ones can heal those the Shining One has taken," she said. "He asked me—and it was better that I tell him. It is part of the Three's—*punishment*—but of that you will soon learn," she went on hurriedly. "Ask me no questions now of the Silent Ones. I thought it better for Olaf to go with Rador, to busy himself, to give his mind other than sorrow upon which to feed."

CHAPTER XXXI

THE WOOING OF LAKLA

UP THE PATH came five of the frog-women, bearing platters and ewers. Their bracelets and anklets of jewels were tinkling; their middles covered with short kirtles of woven cloth studded with the sparkling ornaments.

And here let me say that if I have given the impression that the *Akka* are simply magnified frogs, I regret it. Froglike they are, and hence my phrase for them—but as unlike the frog, as we know it, as man is unlike the chimpanzee. Springing, I hazard, from the stegocephalia, the ancestor of the frogs, these batrachians followed a different line of evolution and acquired the upright position just as man did his from the four-footed folk.

The great staring eyes, the shape of the muzzle were froglike, but the highly developed brain had set upon the head and shape of it vital differences. The forehead, for instance, was not low, flat, and retreating—its frontal arch was well defined. The head was, in a sense, well shaped, and with the females the great horny carapace that stood over it like a fantastic helmet was much modified, as were the spurs that were so formidable in the male; coloration was different also. The torso was upright; the legs a little bent, giving them their crouching gait—but I wander from my subject.*

They set their burdens down. Larry looked at them with interest.

"You surely have those things well trained, Lakla," he said.

"Things!" The handmaiden arose, eyes flashing with indignation. "You call my *Akka* things!"

"Well," said Larry, a bit taken aback, "what do you call them?"

"My *Akka* are a *people*," she retorted. "As much a people as your race or mine. They are good and loyal, and they have speech and arts, and they slay not, save for food or to protect themselves. And I think them beautiful, Larry, *beautiful!*" She stamped her foot. "And you call them—*things!*"

Beautiful! These? Yet, after all, they were, in their grotesque fashion. And to Lakla, surrounded by them, from babyhood, they were not strange, at all. Why shouldn't she think them beautiful? The same thought must have struck O'Keefe, for he flushed guiltily.

"I think them beautiful, too, Lakla," he said remorsefully. "It's my not knowing your tongue too well that traps me. Truly, I think them beautiful—I'd tell them so, if I knew their talk."

Lakla dimpled, laughed—spoke to the attendants in that strange speech that was unquestionably a language; they bridled, looked at O'Keefe with fantastic coquetry, clacked and boomed softly among themselves.

---

* The *Akka* are viviparous. The female produces progeny at five-year intervals, never more than two at a time. They are monogamous, like certain of our own *Ranidae*. Pending my monograph upon what little I had time to learn of their habits and customs, the curious will find entertainment and instruction in Brandes and Schvenichen's *Brulpfleige der Schwanzlosen Batrachier*, p. 305: and Lilian V. Sampson's "Unusual Modes of Breeding Among Anura," Amer. Nat. XXXIV, 1900.

"They say they like you better than the men of Muria," laughed Lakla.

"Did I ever think I'd be swapping compliments with lady frogs!" he murmured to me. "Buck up, Larry—keep your eyes on the captive Irish princess!" he muttered to himself.

"Rador goes to meet one of the *ladala* who is slipping through with news," said the Golden Girl as we addressed ourselves to the food. "Then, with Nak, he and Olaf go to muster the *Akka*—for there will be battle, and we must prepare. Nak," she added, "is he who went before me when you were dancing with Yolara, Larry." She stole a swift, mischievous glance at him. "He is headman of all the *Akka*."

"How comes the messenger through?" I asked. "Can he open the Portal?"

"No, but there are other ways, she answered, "although perilous—like that you took."

"I should think with what's brewing outside they would be guarded," said Larry.

"No," replied Lakla, almost indifferently. "Not many would dare take them; not many could pass over them unscathed. And there are always the guards at the gateway of the bridge there that none may pass. To come in force to be feared, they must go through the Portal, and it will give us warning. Besides—it will take all of four *tals* for them to plan and prepare—and during that time we will also have prepared."

"Just what forces can we muster against them when they come, darlin'?" said Larry.

"Darlin'?"—the Golden Girl had caught the caress of the word—"what's that?"

"It's a little word that means Lakla," he answered. "It does—that is, when I say it; when *you* say it, then it means Larry."

"I like that word," mused Lakla.

"You can even say Larry darlin'!" suggested O'Keefe.

"Larry darlin'!" said Lakla. "When they come we shall have first of all my *Akka*—"

"Can they fight, *mavourneen?*" interrupted Larry.

"Can they fight! My *Akka!*" Again her eyes flashed. "They will fight to the last of them—with the spears that give the swift rotting, covered, as they are, with the jelly of those *Sadda* there—" She pointed through a rift in the foliage, across which, on the surface of the sea, was floating one of the moon globes— and now I know why Rador had warned Larry against a plunge there. "With spears and clubs and with teeth and nails and spurs—they are a strong and brave people, Larry—darlin', and though they hurl the *Keth* at them, it is slow to work upon them, and they slay even while they are passing into the nothingness!"

"And have we none of the *Keth?*" he asked.

"No"—she shook her head—"none of their weapons have we here, although it was—it was the Ancient Ones who shaped them."

"But the Three are of the Ancient Ones?" I cried, "Surely they can tell—"

"No," she said slowly. "No—there is something to be told you—and soon; and then the Silent Ones say you will understand. *You*, especially, Goodwin, who worship wisdom."

The raptness vanished, her eyes cleared.

"Then," said Larry, "we have the *Akka;* and we have the four men of us, and among us three guns and about a hundred cartridges—an'—an' the power of the Three—but what about the Shining One, Fireworks—"

"I do not know." Again the indecision that had been in her eyes when Yolara had launched her defiance crept back. "The Shining One is strong—and he has his—slaves!"

"Well, we'd better get busy good and quick!" the O'Keefe's voice rang. But Lakla, for some reason of her own, would pursue the matter no further. The trouble fled from her eyes—they danced.

"Larry darlin'!" she murmured. "I like the touch of your lips—"

"You do?" he whispered, all thought flying of anything but the beautiful, provocative face so close to his. "Then, *acushla*, you're goin' to get acquainted with 'em! Turn your head. Doc!" he said.

And I turned it. There was quite a long silence, broken by an interested, soft outburst of gentle boomings from the serving frog-maids. I stole a glance behind me. Lakla's head lay on the Irishman's shoulder, the golden eyes misty sun-pools of love and adoration; and the O'Keefe, a new look of power and strength upon his clear-cut features, was looking down into them with that look which rises only from the heart touched for the first time with that true, all-powerful love, which is the pulse of the universe itself, the real music of the spheres of which Plato dreamed, the love that is stronger than death itself, immortal as the high gods and the true soul of all that mystery we call life.

Then Lakla raised her hands, pressed down Larry's head, kissed him between the eyes, drew herself with a trembling little laugh from his embrace.

"My mate!" she murmured, the golden voice throbbing.

"The future Mrs. Larry O'Keefe, Goodwin," said Larry to me a little unsteadily.

I took their hands—and Lakla kissed me!

She turned to the booming—*smiling*—frog-maids; gave them some command, for they filed away down the path. Suddenly I felt, well, a little superfluous.

"If you don't mind," I said, "I think I will go up the path there again and look about."

But they were looking at each other again, unheeding—and I stole away, up to the embrasure where Rador had taken me. The movement of the batrachians over the bridge had ceased. Dimly, at the far end, I saw a cluster, ant sized, and supposed it to be the garrison that guarded it. I sent my mind past the entrance, back into the elf land of giant moss and blossomings, wondering wistfully whether I might ever study its wonders.

My thoughts flew back to Lakla and to Larry. What was to be the end?

If we won, if we were able to pass from this place, could the Golden Girl live in our world? A product of these caverns with their atmosphere and light that seemed in some subtle way to be both food and drink—how would she react to the unfamiliar foods and the atmosphere and light of outer earth? Further, here, so far as I was able to discover, there were no malignant bacilli; what immunity could Lakla have then to those microscopic evils without, which only long ages of sickness and death have bought for us a modicum of protection? I began to be oppressed. Surely they had been long enough by themselves. I descended the path.

Stepping softly, not to embarrass them, I heard Larry.

"It's a green land, *mavourneen*. And the sea rocks and dimples around it—blue as the heavens, green as the isle itself, and foam horses toss their white manes, and the great, clean winds blow over it, and the sun shines down on it like your eyes, *acushla*—"

"And are you a king of Ireland, Larry darlin'?" Thus Lakla. I decided I might make my presence known.

They sat, one of her white arms about Larry's neck, his hands caressing the silken webs of her hair.

"I was just tellin' the future Mrs. O'Keefe about her future home," he said half sheepishly. And looking into his eyes I stifled the apprehensions that I have noted.

Lakla arose, delicately, delightfully disconcerted.

"Soon," she said, "I must wait upon the Three. They have a message for you."

We turned to go—and around the corner of the path I caught another glimpse of what I have called the lake of jewels. I pointed to it.

"Those are lovely flowers, Lakla," I said. "I have never seen anything like them in the place from whence we come."

She followed my pointing finger—laughed.

"Come," she said, "let me show you them."

She ran down an intersecting way, we following; came out of it upon a little ledge close to the brink, three feet or more I suppose about it. The Golden Girl's voice ran out in a high-pitched, tremulous, throbbing call.

The lake of jewels stirred as though a breeze had passed over it; stirred, shook, and then began to move swiftly, a shimmering torrent of shining flowers down upon us! She called again, the movement became more rapid; the gem blooms streamed closer—closer, wavering, shifting, winding—at our very feet. Above them hovered a little radiant mist; a faint, oddly disturbing perfume wafted up, checking subtly the heart beat. The Golden Girl leaned over; called softly, and up from the sparkling mass shot a green vine whose heads were five flowers of flaming ruby—shot up, flew into her hand and coiled about the white arm, its quintette of lambent blossoms—regarding us!

It was the thing Lakla had called the *Yekta;* that with which she had threatened the priestess; the thing that carried the dread of death—and the Golden Girl was handling it like a rose!

I gasped, Larry swore—I looked at it more closely. It was a hydroid, a development of that strange animal-vegetable that, sometimes almost microscopic, waves in the sea depths like a cluster of flowers paralyzing its prey with the mysterious force that dwells in its blossom heads!

"Put it down, Lakla," the distress in O'Keefe's voice was deep. Lakla laughed mischievously, caught the real fear for her in his eyes; opened her hand, gave another faint call—and back it flew to its fellows.

"Why, it wouldn't hurt me, Larry!" she expostulated. "I feed them—the *Yekta.*"

"I don't like it," he said hoarsely.

She sighed, gave another sweet, prolonged call. The lake of gems—rubies and amethysts, mauves and scarlet-tinged blues—wavered and shook even as it had before—and swept swiftly back to that place whence she had drawn them!

Then, with Larry and Lakla walking ahead, white arm about

his brown neck; the O'Keefe still expostulating, the hand-maiden laughing merrily, we passed through her bower to the domed castle.

Glancing through a cleft I caught sight again of the far end of the bridge; noted among the clustered figures of the garrison a movement, a flashing of green fire like marsh-lights on spear tips; wondered idly what it was, and then, other thoughts crowding in, followed along, head bent, behind the pair who had found in what was Olaf's hell, their true paradise.

CHAPTER XXXII

THE COMING OF YOLARA

"NEVER WAS THERE such a girl!" Thus Larry, dreamily, leaning head in hand on one of the wide divans of the chamber where Lakla had left us, pleading service to the Silent Ones.

"An', by the faith and the honor of the O'Keefes, an' by my dead mother's soul may God do with me as I do by her!" he whispered fervently.

I told him what Rador had revealed to me regarding the handmaiden and her origin. He nodded, showing no surprise whatever.

"Sure," he said. "It's as I told you. The Silent Ones are of the Tuatha Dé, an' they send to Ireland for the colleens. They won't have anything to do with the crowd here. Lakla's Irish—no doubt of it. Maybe she comes from one of the fairy hills—or maybe the handmaidens come straight from Tir n'Óg. One of my own ancestors married a girl of the green people, an' the O'Keefes have long been kin to the *Sidh*—that's why I can see the leprechawns, and why the banshee is so faithful. Why not, when she's one of the family?"

He considered.

"They probably bring them in as changelings," he decided. "They do that in Ireland to this day. An' if she thinks her frogs

are beautiful, why beautiful they are! An' if she wants to take
'em with her, why by the *Lia Fail* take 'em she shall, if every
circus man in the United Kingdom complains to the king that
we're minin' the business!"

He relapsed into open-eyed dreaming.

I walked about the room, examining it—the first opportunity I had gained to inspect carefully any of the rooms in the
abode of the Three. It was octagonal, carpeted with the thick
rugs that seemed almost as though woven of soft mineral wool,
faintly shimmering, palest blue. I paced its diagonal; it was fifty
yards; the ceiling was arched, and either of pale rose metal or
metallic covering; it collected the light from the high, slitted
windows, and shed it, diffused, through the room.

Around the octagon ran a low gallery not two feet from the
floor, balustraded with slender pillars, close set; broken at opposite curtained entrances over which hung thick, dull-gold
curtainings giving the same suggestion of metallic or mineral
substance as the rugs. Set within each of the eight sides, above
the balcony, were colossal slabs of lapis lazuli, inset with graceful but unplaceable designs in scarlet and sapphire blue.

There was the great divan on which mused Larry; two smaller
ones; half a dozen low seats and chairs carved apparently of
ivory and of dull soft gold. Touching these I found that they
gave an impression of warmth, indeed of living warmth, as
though they were infused with a slow, mild electric current—or
rather as though one touched a warm hand, so full of vitality
was the sensation communicated.

Most curious were tripods, strong, pike-like legs of golden
metal four feet high, holding small circles of the lapis intaglios
with one curious symbol somewhat resembling the ideographs
of the Chinese.

There was no dust—nowhere in these caverned spaces had
I found this constant companion of ours in the world overhead.
My eyes caught a sparkle from a corner. Pursuing it I found
upon one of the low seats a flat, clear crystal oval, remarkably

like a lens. I took it and stepped up on the balcony. Standing on tiptoe I found I commanded from the bottom of a window slit a view of the bridge approach. Scanning it I could see no trace of the garrison there, nor of the green spear flashes. I placed the crystal to my eyes—and with a disconcerting abruptness the cavern mouth leaped before me, apparently not a hundred feet away; decidedly the crystal was a very excellent lens—but where were the guards?

I peered closely. Nothing! But now against the aperture I saw a score or more of tiny, dancing sparks. An optical illusion, I thought, and turned the crystal in another direction. There were no sparklings there. I turned it back again—and there they were. And what were they like? Realization came to me—they were like the little, dancing, radiant atoms that had played for a time about the emptiness where had stood Sanger of the Lower Waters before he had been shaken into the nothingness! And that green light I had noticed—the *Keth!*

A cry on my lips, I turned to Larry—and the cry died as the heavy curtainings at the entrance on my right undulated, parted as though a body had slipped through, shook and parted again and again—with the dreadful passing of unseen things!

"Larry!" I cried. "Here! Quick!"

He leaped to his feet, gazed about wildly—and disappeared! Yes—vanished from my sight like the snuffed flame of a candle or as though something moving with the speed of light itself had snatched him away!

Then from the divan came the sounds of struggle, the hissing of straining breaths, the noise of Larry cursing. The pillows flew about as though the raging ghosts of a pair of panthers were tossing them. I leaped over the balustrade, drawing my own pistol—was caught in a pair of mighty arms, my elbows crushed to my sides, drawn down until my face pressed close against a broad, hairy breast—and through that obstacle—formless, shadowless, transparent as air itself—I could still see the battle on the divan!

Now there were two sharp reports; the struggle abruptly ceased. From a point not a foot over the great couch, as though oozing from the air itself, blood began to drop, faster and ever faster, pouring out of nothingness.

And out of that same air, now a dozen feet away, leaped the face of Larry—bodyless, poised six feet above the floor, blazing with rage—floating weirdly, uncannily to a hideous degree, in vacancy.

His hands flashed out—armless; they wavered, appearing, disappearing—swiftly tearing something from him. Then there, feet hidden, stiff on legs that vanished at the ankles, striking out into vision with all the dizzy abruptness with which he had been stricken from sight was the O'Keefe, a smoking pistol in hand.

And ever that red stream trickled out of vacancy and spread over the couch, dripping to the floor.

I made a mighty movement to escape; was held more firmly—and then close to the face of Larry, flashing out with that terrifying instantaneousness even as had his, was the head of Yolara, as devilishly mocking as I had ever seen it, the cruelty shining through it like delicate white flames from hell—and beautiful!

"Stir not! Strike not—until I command!" She flung the words beyond her, addressed to the invisible ones who had accompanied her; whose presences I sensed filling the chamber. The floating, beautiful head, crowned high with corn-silk hair, darted toward the Irishman. He took a swift step backward. The gray eyes of the priestess deepened toward purple; sparkled with malice.

"So," she said. "So, *Larree*—you thought you could go from me so easily!" She laughed softly. "In my hidden hand I hold the *Keth* cone," she murmured. "Before you can raise the death tube I can smite you—and will. And consider, *Larree,* if the handmaiden, the *choya* comes, I can vanish—so"—the mocking head disappeared, burst forth again—"and slay her with the

Keth—or bid my people seize her and bear her to the Shining One! And anger me not too much, *Larree,* else may I grow wroth and let the *Keth* loose upon you—come what may," she ended darkly.

I saw tiny beads of sweat stand out on O'Keefe's forehead, and knew he was thinking not of himself, but of Lakla.

"What do you want with me, Yolara?" he asked hoarsely.

"Nay," came the mocking voice. "Not Yolara to you, *Larree*— call me by those sweet names you taught me—Honey of the Wild Bee-e-s, Net of Hearts—"Again her laughter tinkled.

"What do you want with me?" his voice was strained, the lips rigid.

"Ah, you are afraid, *Larree.*"There was diabolic jubilation in the words. "What should I want but that you return with me? Why else did I creep through the lair of the dragon worm and pass the path of perils but to ask you that? And the *choya* guards you not well." Again she laughed. "We came to the cavern's end and there were her *Akka.* And the *Akka* can see us—as shadows. But it was my desire to surprise you with my coming, *Larree,*" the voice was silken. "And I feared that they would hasten to be first to bring you that message to delight in your joy. And so, *Larree,* I loosed the *Keth* upon them—and gave them peace and rest within the nothingness. And the portal below was open—almost in welcome!"

Once more the malignant, silver pealing of her laughter.

"What do you want with me?"There was loathing in his eyes, but plainly he strove for control.

"Want!" the silver voice hissed, grew calm. "Do not Siya and Siyana grieve that the rite I pledged them is but half done—and do they not desire it finished? And am I not beautiful? More beautiful than your *choya?*"

The fiendishness died from the eyes; they grew blue, won-drous; the veil of invisibility slipped down from the neck, the shoulders, half revealing the gleaming breasts. And weird, weird beyond all telling was that exquisite head and bust floating there in air—and beautiful, sinisterly beautiful beyond all telling, too. So even might Lilith, the serpent woman, have shown herself tempting Adam!

"And perhaps," she said; "perhaps I want you because I hate you; perhaps because I love you—or perhaps for Lugur or perhaps for the Shining One."

"And if I go with you?" He said it quietly.

"Then shall I spare the handmaiden—and—who knows?— take back my armies that even now gather at the portal and let the Silent Ones rot in peace in their abode—from which they had no power to keep me," she added venomously.

"You will swear that, Yolara; swear to go without harming the handmaiden?" he asked eagerly. The little devils danced in her eyes. I wrenched my face from the smothering contact.

"Don't trust her, Larry!" I cried—and again the grip choked me.

"Is that devil in front of you or behind you, old man?" he asked quietly, eyes never leaving the priestess. "If he's in front I'll take a chance and wing him—and then you scoot and warn Lakla."

But I could not answer; nor, remembering Yolara's threat, would I had I been able.

"Decide quickly!" There was cold threat in her voice. And then—

The curtains toward which O'Keefe had slowly, step by step, drawn close, opened. They framed the handmaiden! The face of Yolara changed into that gorgon mask that had transformed it once before at sight of the Golden Girl. In her blind rage she forgot to cast the occulting veil. Her hand darted like a snake out of the folds; poising itself with the little silver cone aimed at Lakla.

But before it was wholly poised, before the priestess could loose its force, the handmaiden was upon her. Swift as the lithe white wolfhound she leaped, and one slender hand gripped Yolara's throat, the other the wrist that lifted the quivering death; white limbs wrapped about the hidden ones. I saw the golden head bend, the hand that held the *Keth* swept up with a vicious jerk; saw Lakla's teeth sink into the wrist—the blood spurt forth and heard the priestess shriek. The cone fell, bounded toward me; with all my strength I wrenched free the hand that held my pistol, thrust it against the pressing breast and fired.

The clasp upon me relaxed; a red rain stained me; at my feet a little pillar of blood jetted; a hand thrust itself from nothingness, clawed—and was still.

Now Yolara was down, Lakla meshed in her writhings and fighting like some wild mother whose babes are serpent menaced. Over the two of them, astride, stood the O'Keefe, a pike from one of the high tripods in his hand—thrusting, parrying, beating on every side as with a broadsword against poniard-clutching hands that thrust themselves out of vacancy striving to strike him; stepping here and there, always covering, protecting Lakla with his own body even as a cave-man of old who does battle with his mate for their lives.

The sword-club struck—and on the floor lay the half body of a dwarf, writhing with vanishments and reappearings of legs and arms. Beside him lay the shattered tripod from which Larry had wrenched his weapon. I flung myself upon it, dashed it down to break loose one of the remaining supports, struck in midfall one of the unseen even as his dagger darted toward me! The seat splintered, leaving in my clutch a golden bar. I jumped to Larry's side, guarding his back, whirling it like a staff; felt it crunch once—twice—through unseen bone and muscle.

At the door was a booming. Into the chamber rushed a dozen of the frog-men. While some guarded the entrances, others leaped straight to us, and forming a circle about us, began to strike with talons and spurs at unseen things that screamed and sought to escape. Now here and there about the blue rugs great stains of blood appeared; heads of dwarfs, torn arms and gashed bodies, half occulted, half revealed. And at last the priestess lay silent, vanquished, white body gleaming with that uncanny—fragmentariness—from her torn robes. The O'Keefe reached down, drew Lakla from her. Shakily, Yolara rose to her feet, panting, the hatred in her eyes, the hellish mask of her face no whit softened. The handmaiden, face still blazing with wrath, stepped before her; with difficulty she steadied her voice.

"Yolara," she said, "you have defied the Silent Ones, you have desecrated their abode, you came to slay these men who are the guests of the Silent Ones and me, who am their handmaiden—why did you do these things?"

"I came for him!" gasped the priestess; she pointed to O'Keefe.

"Why?" asked Lakla.

"Because he is pledged to me," replied Yolara, all the devils that were hers in her face. "Because he wooed me! Because he is mine!"

"That is a lie!" The handmaiden's voice shook with rage. "It is a lie! But here and now he shall choose, Yolara. And if you he choose, you and he shall go forth from here unmolested—for Yolara, it is his happiness that I most desire, and if you are that happiness—you shall go together. And now, Larry, choose!"

Swiftly she stepped beside the priestess; swiftly wrenched the last shreds of the hiding robes from her.

There they stood—Yolara with but the filmiest net of gauze about her wonderful body; gleaming flesh shining through it; serpent woman—and wonderful, too, beyond the dreams even of Phidias—and hell fire glowing from the purple eyes.

And Lakla, like a girl of the Vikings, like one of those warrior maids who stood and fought for dun and babes at the side of those old heroes of Larry's own green isle; translucent ivory lambent through the rents of her torn draperies, and in the wide, golden eyes flaming wrath, indeed—not the diabolic flames of the priestess but the righteous wrath of some soul that looking out of paradise sees vile wrong in the doing.

"Lakla," the O'Keefe's voice was subdued, hurt, "there is no choice. I love you and only you—and have from the moment I saw you. It's not easy—this. God, Goodwin, I feel like an utter cad," he flashed at me. "There is no choice, Lakla," he ended, eyes steady upon hers.

The priestess's face grew deadlier still.

"What will you do with me?" she asked.

"Keep you," I said, "as hostage."

O'Keefe was silent; the Golden Girl shook her head.

"Well would I like to," her face grew dreaming, "but the Silent Ones say—*no;* they bid me let you go, Yolara—"

"The Silent Ones," the priestess laughed. *"You,* Lakla, I surmise. You fear, perhaps, to let me tarry here too close!"

Storm gathered again in the handmaiden's eyes; she forced it back.

"No," she answered, "the Silent Ones so command—and for their own purposes. Yet do I think, Yolara, that you will have little time to feed your wickednesses—tell that to Lugur—and to your Shining One!" she added slowly.

Mockery and disbelief rode high in the priestess's pose. "Am I to return alone—like this?" she asked.

"Nay, Yolara, nay; you shall be accompanied," said Lakla, "and by those who will guard—and watch—you well. They are here even now."

The hangings parted, and into the chamber came Olaf and Rador—and paused in blank amazement.

"You—traitor!" hissed the priestess to the green dwarf. "Be sure that *you* shall not dance with the Shining One!"

He gazed at her, face stern, immovable; listened to Lakla's swift explanation.

"She shall be guarded—well!" was all he said. The priestess bit her lips, turned and met the fierce hatred and contempt in the eyes of the Norseman—and for the first time lost her bravado.

"Let not him go with me," she gasped—her eyes searched the floor frantically.

"He goes with you," said Lakla, and threw about Yolara a

swathing that covered the exquisite, alluring body. "And you shall pass through the Portal, not skulk along the path of the worm!"

She bent to Rador, whispered to him; he nodded; she had told him, I supposed, the secret of its opening.

"Come," he said, and with the ice-eyed giant behind her, Yolara, head bent, passed out of those hangings through which, but a little before, unseen, triumph in her grasp, she had slipped.

Then Lakla came to the unhappy O'Keefe, rested her hands on his shoulders, looked deep into his eyes.

"*Did* you woo her, even as she said?" she asked.

The Irishman flushed miserably.

"I did not," he said. "I was pleasant to her, of course, because I thought it would bring me quicker to you, darlin'."

She looked at him doubtfully; then—

"I think you must have been *very*—pleasant!" was all she said—and leaning, kissed him forgivingly straight on the lips. An extremely direct maiden was Lakla, with a truly sovereign contempt for anything she might consider nonessentials; and at this moment I decided she was wiser even than I had thought her.

The O'Keefe's face was sheepish; then admiration blazed up in it. He caught her hands.

"Lord, but it was a brave thing to do," he cried. "You leaped like the white hound of Maev the Huntress, and you fought like Scathach of the Misty Isle who taught Cuchullin battle!"

"You were in danger, Larry," she answered, "and better that I die than live without you, darlin'."

"You bet you're Irish!" muttered the O'Keefe, hugging her to him rapturously. "An' with you beside me, an' the family banshee scoutin' ahead, I could be a king in Erin—if I wanted to take it from George, God bless him, which I don't."

"What is that you say in your strange tongue?" asked the Golden Girl.

"I said there was no other girl like you in the whole world, nor ever was!" said Larry.

He stepped toward me, stumbled, feet vanishing; reached down and picked up something that in the grasping turned his hand to air.

"One of the cloaks of invisibility," he said to me. "There must be quite a lot of 'em about—a little bit shopworn, 'tis true, but still damned useful."

There was a ghastly rattling at my feet; half the head of one of Yolara's men raised itself from nothingness; beat twice upon the floor in a last death throe; fell back. Lakla shivered, grew white; gave a command to the frog-men still on guard. They moved about; lifting the unseen folds; revealing now in full stark rigidity dwarf after dwarf.

Lakla had been right—her *Akka* were thorough fighters.

She called, and to her came the frog-woman who was her attendant. To her the handmaiden spoke, pointing to the batrachians who stood, paws and forearms melted beneath the robes they had gathered. She took them and passed out—more grotesque than ever, shattering into streaks of vacancies, reappearing with flickers of shining scale and yellow gems as the torn pennants of invisibility fluttered about her.

The frog-men reached down, swung each a dead dwarf in her arms, and filed, booming, away.

And feeling in my pocket, I drew out a little silver cone, caught and slipped there by me unconsciously as it rolled from Yolara's hand—and knew then for what her mad eyes had been searching.

Decidedly the priestess's visit had added to our weapons, no matter how unpleasant her call had been.

CHAPTER XXXIII

IN THE LAIR OF
THE DWELLER

IT IS WITH marked hesitation that I begin his chapter, because in it I must deal with an experience so contrary to every known law of physics as to seem impossible. Until this time, barring, of course, the mystery of the Dweller, I had encountered nothing that was not susceptible of naturalistic explanation; nothing, in a word, outside the domain of science itself; nothing that I would have felt hesitancy in reciting to my colleagues of the International Association of Science. Amazing, unfamiliar—*advanced*—as many of the phenomena were, still they lay well within the limits of what we have mapped as the possible; in regions, it is true, still virgin to the mind of man, but toward which that mind is steadily advancing.

But this—well, I confess that I have a theory that *is* naturalistic; but so abstruse, so difficult to make clear within the short confines of the space I have to give it, so dependent upon conceptions that even the highest-trained scientific brains find difficult to grasp, that I despair.

I can only say that the thing occurred; that it took place in precisely the manner I am about to narrate, and that I *experienced* it.

Yet, injustice to myself, I must open up some paths of preliminary approach toward the heart of the perplexity. And the first path is the realization that our world, *whatever* it is, is certainly not the world as we see it! Regarding this I shall refer to a discourse upon Gravitation and the Principle of Relativity," by the distinguished English physicist, Dr. A.S. Eddington, which I had the pleasure of hearing him deliver before the Royal Institution.[*]

---

[*]   Reprinted in full in *Nature*, in which those sufficiently interested may peruse it.—

I REALIZE, of course, that it is not true logic to argue—"The world is not as we think it is—therefore everything we think impossible is possible in it." Even if it *be* different, it is governed by *law*. The truly impossible is that which is outside law, and as nothing can be outside law, the impossible *cannot* exist.

The crux of the matter then becomes our determination whether what we think is impossible may or may not be possible under laws still beyond our knowledge.

I hope that you will pardon me for this somewhat academic digression, but I felt it was necessary, and it has, at least, put me more at ease. And now to resume.

We had watched, Larry and I, the frog-men throw the bodies of Yolara's assassins into the crimson waters. As vultures swoop down upon the dying, there came sailing swiftly to where the dead men floated, dozens of the luminous globes. Their slender, varicolored tentacles whipped out; the giant iridescent bubbles *climbed* over the cadavers. And as they touched them there was the swift dissolution, the melting away into putrescence of flesh and bone that I had witnessed when the dart touched fruit that time I had saved Rador—and upon this the Medusae gorged; pulsing lambently; their wondrous colors shifting, changing, glowing stronger; elfin moons now indeed, but satellites whose glimmering beauty was fed by death; alembics of enchantment whose glorious hues were sucked from horror.

Sick, I turned away—O'Keefe as pale as I passed back into the corridor that had opened on the ledge from which we had watched; met Lakla hurrying toward us. Before she could speak there throbbed faintly about us a vast sighing. It grew into a murmur, a whispering, shook us—then passing like a presence, died away in far distance.

"The Portal has opened," said the handmaiden. A fainter sighing, like an echo of the other, mourned about us. "Yolara is gone," she said, "the Portal is closed. Now must we hasten—for the Three have ordered that you, Goodwin, and Larry and I go

W.T.G.

upon that strange road of which I have spoken, and which Olaf may not take lest his heart break—and we must return ere he and Rador cross the bridge."

Her hand sought Larry's; we passed down to a chamber in which stood a table, bearing one of the crystal ewers and goblets. From the former she poured a ruddy liquid; held a glass to me. Mischievously she kissed the lip of that she reached to Larry, and turning it he drank from the spot her mouth had touched. A weariness that I had not known was in me vanished away as I drank; I felt fortified, alert, eager—and in the O'Keefe's brightening eyes I read that he, too, had drawn to himself new force.

"Drink deep," said the handmaiden, and poured the goblets full again. "The road is strange indeed—even to me who have followed it often—and you will need all your strength to hold you steady upon it!"

But now, quaffing that second glass, I felt that there was no road that I could not travel.

"Come!" said Lakla, and we walked on; down and down through hall after hall, flight upon flight of stairways. Deep, deep indeed we must be beneath the domed castle—Lakla paused before a curved, smooth breast of the crimson stone rounding gently into the passage. She pressed its side; it revolved; we entered; it closed behind us.

The room, the—hollow—in which we stood was faceted like a diamond; and like a cut brilliant its sides glistened—though dully. Its shape was a deep oval, and our path dropped down to a circular, polished base, roughly two yards in diameter. Glancing behind me I saw that in the closing of the entrance there had been left no trace of it save the steps that led from where that entrance had been—and as I looked these steps *turned*, leaving us isolated upon the circle, only the faceted walls about us—and in each of the gleaming faces the three of us reflected—dimly. It was as though we were within a diamond egg whose graven angles had been turned *inward*.

But the oval was not perfect; at my right a screen cut it—a screen that gleamed with fugitive, fleeting luminescences—stretching from the side of our standing place up to the tip of the chamber; slightly convex and crisscrossed by millions of fine lines like those upon a spectroscopic plate, but with this difference—that within each line I sensed the presence of multitudes of finer lines, dwindling into infinitude, ultra-microscopic, traced by some instrument compared to whose delicacy our finest tool would be as a crowbar to the needle of a micrometer.

A foot or two from it stood something like the standee of a compass, bearing, like it, a cradled dial under whose crystal ran concentric rings of prisoned, lambent vapors, faintly blue. From the edge of the dial jutted a little shelf of crystal, a keyboard, in which were cut eight small cups.

Within these cups the handmaiden placed her tapering fingers. She gazed down upon the disk; pressed a digit—and the screen behind us slipped noiselessly into another angle.

"PUT YOUR arm around my waist, Larry, darlin', and stand close," she murmured. "You, Goodwin, place your arm over my shoulder."

Wondering, I did as she bade; she pressed other fingers upon the shelf's indentations—three of the rings of vapor spun into intense light; raced around each other; from the screen behind us grew a radiance that held within itself all spectrums—not only those seen, but those *unseen* by man's eyes. It waxed and waxed, brilliant and ever more brilliant, all suffusing, passing through me as day streams through a window pane!

The enclosing facets burst into a blaze of coruscations, and in each sparkling panel I saw our images, shaken and torn like pennants in a whirlwind. I turned to look—was stopped by the handmaiden's swift command: "Turn not—on your life!"

The radiance behind me grew; was a rushing tempest of light in which I was but the shadow of a shadow. I heard, but not with my ears—nay, with *mind* itself—a vast roaring; an *ordered* tumult of sound that came hurling from the outposts of space; approaching—rushing—hurricane out of the heart of the cosmos—closer, closer. It wrapped itself about us with un-earthly mighty arms.

And brilliant, ever more brilliant, streamed the radiance through us.

The faceted walls dimmed; in front of me they melted, di-aphanously, like a gelatinous wall in a blast of flame; through their vanishing, under the torrent of driving light, the unthink-able, impalpable tornado, I began to move, slowly—then ever more swiftly!

Still the roaring grew; the radiance streamed—ever faster we went. Cutting down through the length, the *extension* of me, dropped a wall of rock, foreshortened, clenched close; I caught a glimpse of the elfin gardens; they whirled, contracted, dwindled into a thin—*slice*—of color that was a part of me; another wall of rock shrinking into a thin wedge through which I flew, and that at once took its place within me like a card slipped beside those others!

Flashing around me, and from Lakla and O'Keefe, were nimbuses of flickering scarlet flames. And always the steady hurling forward—appallingly mechanical.

Another barrier of rock—a gleam of white waters incorpo-rating themselves into my—*drawing out*—even as were the flowered moss lands, the slicing, rocky walls—still another rampart of cliff, dwindling instantly into the vertical plane of those others. Our flight checked; we seemed to hover within, then to sway onward—slowly, cautiously.

A mist danced ahead of me—a mist that grew steadily thinner. We stopped, wavered—the mist cleared.

I looked out into translucent, green distances; shot with swift, prismatic gleamings; waves and pulsings of luminosity like midday sun glow through green, tropic waters; dancing, scintil-lating veils of sparkling atoms that flew, hither and yon, through depths of nebulous splendor!

And Lakla and Larry and I were, I saw, like shadow shapes upon a smooth breast of stone twenty feet or more above the surface of this place—a surface spangled with tiny white blossoms gleaming wanly through creeping veils of phosphorescence like smoke of moon fire. We were shadows—and yet we had substance; we were incorporated with, a part of, the rock—and yet we were living flesh and blood; we stretched—nor will I qualify this—we stretched through mile upon mile of space that weirdly enough gave at one and the same time an absolute certainty of immense horizontal lengths and a vertical concentration that contained nothing of length, nothing of space whatever; we stood there upon the face of the stone—and still we were here within the faceted oval before the screen of radiance!

"Steady!" It was Lakla's voice—and not beside me there, but at my ear close before the screen. "Steady, Goodwin! And—see!"

The sparkling haze cleared. Enormous reaches stretched before me. Shimmering up through them, and as though growing in some medium thicker than air, was mass upon mass of verdure—fruiting trees and trees laden with pale blossoms, arbors and bowers of pallid blooms, like that sea fruit of oblivion—grapes of Lethe—that cling to the tide-swept walls of the caverns of the Hebrides.

Through them, beyond them, around and about them, drifted and eddied a horde—great as that with which Tamerlane swept down upon Rome, vast as the myriads which Genghis Khan rolled upon the califs—men and women and children—clothed in tatters, half nude and wholly naked; slant-eyed Chinese, sloe-eyed Malays, islanders black and brown and yellow, fierce-faced warriors of the Solomons with grizzled locks fantastically bedizened; Papuans, feline Javas, Dyaks of hill and shore; hook-nosed Phoenicians, Romans, Straight-browed Greeks, and Vikings centuries beyond their lives; scores of the black-haired Murians; white faces of our own Westerners—men and women and children—drifting, eddying—each stamped with that mingled horror and rapture, eyes filled with ecstasy and terror entwined, marked by God and devil in embrace—the seal of the Shining One—the dead-alive; the lost ones!

The loot of the Dweller!

Soul-sick, I gazed. They lifted to us visages of dread; they swept down toward us, glaring upward—a bank against which other and still other waves of faces rolled, were checked, paused; until as far as I could see, like billows piled upon an evergrowing barrier, they stretched beneath us—staring—staring!

Now there was a movement—far, far away; a concentrating of the lambency; the dead-alive swayed, oscillated, separated— forming a long lane against whose outskirts they crowded with avid, hungry insistence.

First only a luminous cloud, then a whirling pillar of splendors through the lane came—the Shining One. As it passed, the dead-alive swirled in its wake like leaves behind a whirlwind, eddying, twisting; and as the Dweller raced by them, brushing them with its spiralings and tentacles, they shone forth with unearthly, awesome gleamings—like vessels of alabaster in which wicks flare suddenly. And when it had passed they closed behind it, staring up at us once more.

The Dweller paused beneath us.

Out of the drifting ruck swam the body of Throckmartin! Throckmartin, my friend, to find whom I had gone to the pallid moon door; my friend whose call I had so laggardly followed. On his face was the Dweller's dreadful stamp; the lips were bloodless; the eyes were wide, lucent, something like pale phosphorescence gleaming within them—and soulless.

He stared straight up at me, unwinking, unrecognizing. Pressing against his side was a woman, young and gentle, and lovely—lovely even through the mask of horror and joy that lay upon her face. And her wide eyes, like Throckmartin's, gleamed with the lurking, unholy fires. She pressed against him closely; though the hordes kept up the faint churning, these two kept ever together, as though bound by unseen fetters.

And I knew the girl for Edith, his wife, who in vain effort to save him had cast herself into the Dweller's embrace!

"Throckmartin!" I cried. "Throckmartin! I'm here! Courage, man!"

Did he hear? I know now, of course, he could not.

But then I waited—hope striving to break through the nightmare hands that gripped my heart.

Their wide eyes never left me. There was another movement about them, others pushed past them; they drifted back, swaying, eddying—and still staring were lost in the awful throng.

Vainly I strained my gaze to find them again, to force some sign of recognition, some awakening of the clean life we know from them. But they were gone. Try as I would I could not see them—nor Stanton and the northern woman named Thora who had been the first of that tragic party to be taken by the Dweller.

"Throckmartin!" I cried again, despairingly. My tears blinded me.

I felt Lakla's light touch.

"Steady," she commanded, pitifully. "Steady, Goodwin. You cannot help them—now! Steady and—watch!"

Below us the Shining One had paused—spiraling, swirling, vibrant with all its transcendent, devilish beauty; had paused and was contemplating us. Now I could see clearly that nucleus, that core shot through with flashing veins of radiance, that ever-shifting shape of glory through the shroudings of shimmering, misty plumes, throbbing lacy opalescences, vaporous spiralings of prismatic fantom fires. Steady over it hung the seven little moons of amethyst, of saffron, of emerald and azure and silver, of rose of life and moon white. They poised themselves like a diadem—calm, serene, immobile—and down from them into the Dweller, piercing plumes and swirls and spirals, ran countless tiny strands, radiations, finer than the finest spun thread of spider's web, gleaming filaments through which seemed to run—*power*—from the seven globes; like—yes, that was it—miniatures of the seven torrents of moon flame that poured through the septichromatic, high crystals in the Moon Pool's chamber roof.

Swam out of the coruscating haze the Dweller's—face!

Both of man and of woman it was—like some ancient, androgynous deity of Etruscan fanes long dust, and yet neither woman nor man; human and unhuman; seraphic and sinister, benign and malefic—and still no more of these four than is flame, which is beautiful whether it warms or devours, or wind whether it feathers the trees or shatters them, or the wave which is wondrous whether it caresses or kills.

Subtly, undefinably it was of our world and of one not ours. Its lineaments flowed from another sphere, took fleeting familiar form—and as swiftly withdrew whence they had come; something amorphous, unearthly—as of unknown, unheeding, unseen gods rushing through the depths of star-hung space; and still of our own earth, with the very soul of earth peering out from it, caught within it—and in some—unholy—way debased.

It had eyes—eyes that were now only shadows darkening within its luminosity like veils falling, and falling, *opening* windows into the unknowable; deepening into softly glowing blue pools, blue as the Moon Pool itself; then flashing out, and this only when the—face—bore its most human resemblance, into twin stars large almost as the crown of little moons; and with that same baffling suggestion of peep-holes into a world untrodden, alien, perilous to man!

And once more the tempest of mingled terror and joy, of ineffable yearning to leap into the radiant folds, of insupportable urge to flee from them that Throckmartin had described, and that I had felt in the temple of jet, swept through me.

"Steady!" came Lakla's voice; her body leaned against mine.

I gripped myself, my brain steadied, I looked again. And I saw that of body, at least body as we know it, the Shining One had none—nothing but the throbbing, pulsing core streaked with lightning veins of rainbows; and around this, never still, sheathing it, the swirling, glorious veilings of its hell and heaven born radiance.

So the Dweller stood—and gazed.

Then up toward us swept a reaching, questing spiral!

Under my hand Lakla's shoulder quivered; Dead-Alive and their master vanished—I danced, flickered, *within* the rock; felt a swift sense of shrinking, of withdrawal; slice upon slice the carded walls of stone, of silvery waters, of elfin gardens slipped from me as cards are withdrawn from a pack, one by one— slipped, wheeled, flattened and lengthened out as I passed through them and they passed from me.

Gasping, shaken, weak, I stood *all* within the faceted oval chamber; arm still about the handmaiden's white shoulder; Larry's hand still clutching her girdle.

The roaring, impalpable gale from the cosmos was retreating to the outposts of space—was still; the intense, streaming, flooding radiance lessened—died.

"Now have you beheld," said Lakla, "and well you trod the road. And now shall you hear, even as the Silent Ones have commanded, what the Shining One is—and how it came to be."

The steps flashed back; the doorway into the chamber opened.

Larry as silent as I—we followed her through it.

CHAPTER XXXIV

IN THE BEGINNING

AND THAT INEXPLICABLE journey is the experience I have been so loath to describe. Moving slowly on behind the O'Keefe and the love he had found so strangely, my mind was threaded with thoughts in which they had no part at all.

Then remembering that I must have still other experiences before me which would command all my poise and entire clarity of reasoning, I decided to put for the time the whole matter from me. I felt myself being withdrawn from those set limits of science within which only is mental safety, surety of judgment.

We had reached what I knew to be Lakla's own boudoir, if I may so call it. Smaller than any of the other chambers of the domed castle in which we had been, its intimacy was revealed not only by its faint fragrance but by its high mirrors of polished silver and various oddly wrought articles of the feminine toilet that lay here and there; things I afterward knew to be the work of the artisans of the *Akka*—and no mean metal workers were they. One of the window slits dropped almost to the floor, and at its base was a wide, comfortably cushioned seat commanding a view of the bridge and of the cavern ledge. To this the hand-maiden beckoned us; sank upon it, drew Larry down beside her and smiling witchingly motioned me to sit close to him.

"Now this," she said, "is what the Silent Ones have commanded me to tell you two: To you, Larry, that knowing you may weigh all things in your mind and answer as your spirit bids you a question that the Three will ask—and what that is I know not," she murmured, "and I, they say, must answer, too—and it—frightens me!"

The great golden eyes widened; darkened with dread; she sighed, shook her head impatiently; leaned over to me:

"And to you, Goodwin," she went on, "that you may understand; and understanding carry to your own world, if so it be that you attain it, a new wisdom and a warning; and be not afraid, they say, to speak, for what they utter through me is truth, truth more eternal than that sun of yours which I so long to see, and may, perhaps, never behold—" She paused wistfully.

"Not like us, and never like us," she spoke low, wonderingly, "the Silent Ones say were they. Nor were those from which they sprang like those from which we have come; although like these last they were born, lived and died; and like us now they live and die—but they pass only when they will it! Ancient, ancient beyond thought are the *Taithu*, the race of the Silent Ones. Far, far below this place where now we sit, close to earth heart itself were they born; and there they dwelt for time upon time, *laya* upon *laya* upon *laya*—with others, not like them, some of which have vanished time upon time agone, others that still dwell—below—in their—cradle.

"It is hard"—she hesitated—"hard to tell this—that slips through my mind—because I know so little that even as the Three told it to me it passed from me for lack of place to stand upon," she went on, quaintly. "Something there was of time when earth and sun were but cold mists in the—the heavens— something of these mists drawing together, whirling, whirling, faster and faster—drawing as they whirled more and more of the mists—growing larger, growing warm—forming at last into the globes they are, with others spinning around the sun— something of regions within this globe where vast fire was prisoned and bursting forth tore and rent the young orb—of one such bursting forth that sent what you call moon flying out to company us and left behind those spaces whence we now dwell—and of—of life particles that here and there below grew into the race of the Silent Ones, and those others—but not the *Akka* which, like you, they say came from above—and all this I do not understand—do you, Goodwin?" she appealed to me.

I nodded—for what she had related so fragmentarily was in reality an excellent approach to See's theory of a coalescing nebula contracting into the sun and its planets, as against the older hypothesis of Laplace which explained our planetary system as rings of molten matter thrown off by the whirling sun, forming into balls, cooling down to a habitable crust but still, our world at least, possessing a core of liquid fires held rigid by that crust.

Astonishing was the recognition of the theory, this time *contra*. See with his hypothesis of capture by earth, of the

hurling out of our moon in a cataclysm of earth and the reference to the life particles, which is, of course, the idea of Arrhenius, the great Swede, of life starting on earth through the
dropping upon portions favorable to their development of
similar minute, life *spores*, propelled through space by the driving
power of light and, encountering as I have said, favorable environment here, developing through the vast ages into man and
every other living thing we know.*

Nor was it incredible that in the ancient nebula that was the
matrix of our solar system similar, or rather *dissimilar* particles
in all but the subtle essence we call life, might have become
entangled and, resisting every cataclysm as they had resisted
the absolute zero of outer space, found in these caverned spaces
their proper environment to develop into the race of the Silent
Ones and—only *they* could tell what else!

"I understand," I replied, "and although it is all very—marvelous—still, I believe."

There was gratitude and—relief in the face Lakla turned to
me; some amazement in O'Keefe's.

"It really squares with what you know, does it, Doc?" he asked.

"It does," I answered shortly.

"All right then," said he. "If you say it's all right—all right;
I'm prepared for anything—now. Go on—darlin'," he whispered
to Lakla.

"They say," the handmaiden's voice was now surer, "they say
that in their—cradle—near earth heart they grew; grew un-
troubled by the turmoil and disorder which flayed the surface
of this globe, although then they knew not that there was aught
beside the place in which they dwelt. And they say it was a
place of light and that strength came to them from earth

---

* Professor Svante August Arrhenius, in his "Worlds in the Making"—the con-
ception that life is universally diffused, constantly emitted from all habitable worlds
in the form of spores which traverse space for years and ages, the majority being
ultimately destroyed by the heat of some blazing star, but some few finding a resting-
place on globes which have reached the habitable stage.—W.T.G.

heart—strength greater than you and those from which you sprang ever derived from sun.

"At last, ancient, ancient beyond all thought they say again, was this time—they began to know, to—to—realize—themselves. And wisdom came ever more swiftly. Up from their cradle, because they did not wish to dwell longer with those— others—they came and found this place.

"When all the face of earth was covered with waters in which lived only tiny, hungry things that knew naught save hunger and its satisfaction, *they* had attained the wisdom that enabled them to make paths such as we have just traveled and to look out upon those waters! And *laya* upon *laya* thereafter, time upon time, they went upon the paths and watched the flood recede; saw great bare flats of steaming ooze appear on which crawled and splashed larger things which had grown from the tiny hungry ones; watched the flats rise higher and higher and green life begin to clothe them; saw mountains uplift and vanish.

"Ever the green life waxed and the things which crept and crawled grew greater and took ever different forms; until at last came a time when the steaming mists lightened and the things which had begun as little more than tiny hungry mouths were huge and monstrous, so huge that the tallest of my *Akka* would not have reached the knee of the smallest of them.

"But in none of these, in none, was then—realization—of themselves, say the Three; naught but hunger driving, always driving them to still its crying.

"So for time upon time the race of the Silent Ones took the paths no more, placing aside the half thought that they had of making their way to earth face even as they had made their way from beside earth heart. They turned wholly to the seeking of wisdom—and after other time on time they attained that which killed even the faintest shadow of the half-thought. For they crept far within the mysteries of life and death, they mastered the illusion of space, they lifted the veils of creation and of its

They stood bravely waiting as the radience grew
brighter and the dread Dweller swept closer....

twin destruction, and they stripped the covering from the
flaming jewel of truth—but when they had crept within those
mysteries they bid me tell you, Goodwin, they found ever other
mysteries veiling the way; and after they had uncovered the
jewel of truth they found it to be a gem of infinite facets and

therefore not wholly to be read before eternity's unthinkable end!

"And for this they were glad—because now throughout eternity might they and theirs pursue knowledge over ways illimitable.

"They conquered light—light that sprang at their bidding from the nothingness that gives birth to all things and in which all things that are, have been and shall be lie; light that streamed through their bodies cleaning them of all dross; light that was food and drink; light that carried their vision afar or bore to them images out of space opening many windows through which they gazed down upon life on thousands upon thousands of the rushing worlds; light that was the flame of life itself and in which they bathed, ever renewing their own. They set radiant lamps within the stones and of black light they wove the sheltering shadows and the shadows that slay.

"Arose from this people those Three—the Silent Ones. They led them all in wisdom so that in the Three grew—pride. And the Three built them this place in which we sit and set the Portal in its place and withdrew from their kind to go alone into the mysteries and to map alone the facets of truth jewel.

"Then there came here the ancestors of the—*Akka;* tribes of them, not as they are now, and glowing but faintly within them the spark of—self-realization. And the *Taithu* seeing this, did not slay them. But they took the ancient, long untrodden paths and looked forth once more upon earth face. Now on the land were vast forests and a chaos of green life. On the shores things scaled and fanged, fought and devoured each other and in the green life moved bodies great and small that slew, and ran from those that would slay.

"They searched for the passage through which the *Akka* had come and closed it. Then the Three took them and brought them here; and taught them and blew upon the spark until it burned ever stronger and stronger and in time they became much as they are now—my *Akka*.

"The Three took council after this and said—'We have strengthened spirit in these until it has become articulate; shall we not *create* spirit?'" Again she hesitated, her eyes rapt, dreaming; her gaze once more that of the pythoness through whom Apollo is whispering. "The Three are speaking," she murmured. "They have my tongue—"

And certainly, with an ease and rapidity as though she were but a voice through which minds far more facile, more powerful poured their thoughts, she spoke. At the change of person in her phrases I felt a faint, an uncanny crepitation. Larry started, stretched out a hand toward her lips; I drew it back quickly; anxiety written plain on his face he restrained himself. In some vague way I felt that she was speaking now our own tongue, so fluent was she, so clean cut the images from her words, so clear the abstractions not possible in her own speech, and borne in upon my understanding with no slightest labor of translation; the thought impinging upon consciousness and being absorbed by it—*liquidly*. Still I knew it was not our speech; could not be; rather was it our *thought*.

"Yea," she said, the golden voice vibrant, "the sin of pride was ours, and pride and wisdom such as ours are perilous comrades, ye who are named Goodwin, and who also in your way pursue knowledge. We said that the spirit we would create should be of the spirit of life itself, speaking to us with the tongues of the far-flung stars, of the winds, of the waters and of all upon and within these. Upon that universal matrix of matter, that mother of all things that you name the ether we labored. Think not that her wondrous fertility is limited by what ye see on earth or what has been on earth from its beginning. Infinite, infinite are the forms the mother bears and countless are the energies that are part of her.

"By our wisdom we had fashioned many windows out of our abode and through them we stared into the faces of myriads of worlds. We have looked upon the blossoming orbs that circle the sun ye call Arcturus, the crystal-clear globes that girdle Betelgeuse, the fantom spheres that diadem Aldebaran, the worlds of cool misty flame that swim within that ye name the Pleiades, and upon others, countless, countless others and upon them all were the children of ether even as they themselves were her children.

"Watching we learned, and learning we formed that ye term the Dweller, that those without name—the Shining One. Within the Universal Mother we shaped it, to be a voice to tell us her secrets, a thing of glory to go before us lighting the mysteries, a guide and an interpreter. Out of the ether we fashioned it, giving it the soul of light that still ye know not nor perhaps ever may know, and with the essence of life that ye saw blossoming deep in the abyss and that is the pulse of earth heart we filled it And we wrought with pain and with love, with yearning and with fierce, scorching pride and from our travail came the Shining One—our child!

"There is an energy beyond and above ether, a purposeful, sentient force that laps like an ocean the furthest-flung star, that transfuses all that ether bears, that sees and speaks and feels in us and in you, that is incorporate in beast and bird and reptile, in tree and grass and all living things, that sleeps in rock and stone, that finds sparkling tongue in jewel and star and in all dwellers within the firmament. And this ye call consciousness!

"Your forefathers knew this when they worshiped spirits of wood and stream, of wave and torrent and mountain, of fire and air; for their eyes were younger and saw clearer, and what to them appeared these spirits were pools and billows and wavelets of the ocean of consciousness moving within all these things and in that sea rests all experience, all knowledge that has been and is of things created from birth of eternity.

"We crowned the Shining One with the seven orbs of light which are the channels between it and the sentient flood we sought to make articulate, the portals through which flow its currents and so flowing, become choate, vocal, self-realizant within our child.

"But as we shaped, there passed some of the essence of our pride; in giving will we had given power, perforce, to exercise that will for good or for evil, to speak or to be silent, to tell us what we wished of that which poured into it through the seven orbs or to withhold that knowledge itself; and in forging it from the immortal energies we had endowed it with their indifference; open to all consciousness it held within it the pole of utter joy and the pole of utter wo with all the arc that lies between; all the ecstasies of the countless worlds and suns and all their sorrows; all that ye symbolize as gods and all ye symbolize as devils—not negativing each other, for there is no such thing as negation, but holding them together, balancing them, encompassing them, pole upon pole!"

So *this* was the explanation of the entwined emotions of joy and terror that had changed so appallingly Throckmartin's face and the faces of all the Dweller's slaves!

CHAPTER XXXV

THE MIGHTY EPIC OF A LOST WORLD

THE HANDMAIDEN'S EYES grew bright, alert, again; the brooding passed from her face; the golden voice that had been so deep sought its own familiar pitch.

"I listened while the Three spoke to you," she said. "Now the shaping of the Shining One had been a long, long travail and time had flown over the world without *laya* upon *laya*. For a space the Shirting One was content to dwell here; to be fed with the foods of light; to open the eyes of the Three to mystery upon mystery and to read for them facet after facet of the gem of truth. Yet as the tides of consciousness flowed through it they left behind shadowings and echoes of their burdens; and the Shining One grew stronger, always stronger *of itself within itself*. Its will strengthened and now not always was it the will of the Three; and the pride that was woven in the making of it waxed, while the love for them that its creators had set within it waned.

"Not ignorant were the *Taithu*, of the work of the Three. First there were a few, then more and more who coveted the Shining One and who would have had the Three share with them the knowledge it drew in for them. But the Three, in their pride, would not.

"There came a time when its will was now *all* its own, and it rebelled, turning its gaze to the wider spaces beyond the Portal, offering itself to the many there who would serve it; tiring of the Three, their control and their abode.

"NOW THE Shining One has its limitations, even as we. Over water it can pass, through air and through fire; but pass it cannot through rock or metal. So it sent a message—how I know not—to the *Taithu* who desired it, whispering to them the secret of the Portal. And when the time was ripe they opened the Portal and the Shining One passed through it to them; nor would it return to the Three though they commanded, and when they would have forced it they found that it had hived and hidden a knowledge that they could not overcome.

"Yet by their arts the Three could have shattered the seven shining orbs and stilled its life, sending it back to that from which they had drawn it; but they would not because—they loved it!

"Those to whom it had gone built for it that place I have just shown you, and they bowed to it and drew wisdom from it. But ever they turned more and more from the ways in which the *Taithu* had walked—for it seemed that which came to the Shining One through the seven orbs had less and less of good and more and more of the power you call evil. Knowledge it gave and understanding, yes; but not that which, clear and serene, lights the paths of right wisdom, rather were they flares pointing the dark roads that lead to—to the ultimate evil!

"Not all of the race of the Three followed the counsel of the

Shining One. There were many, many, who would have none
of it nor of its power and who saw clearly the peril threatening.
So were the *Taithu* split; and in this place where there had been
none, came hatred, fear and suspicion. Those who pursued the
ancient ways went to the Three and pleaded with them to
destroy their work—and they would not, for still they loved it;
sitting lonely, mourning in their place like those from whom a
best beloved has run.

"Stronger grew the Dweller's pride, darker its power and less
and less did it lay before its worshipers—for now so they had
become—the fruits of its knowledge; and it grew—restless—
turning its gaze upon earth face even as it had turned it from
the Three. It whispered to the *Taithu* to take again the paths
and look out upon the world. Lo! above them was no longer
sea but a great fertile land on which dwelt an unfamiliar race,
skilled in arts, seeking and finding wisdom—mankind! Mighty
builders were they; vast were their cities and huge their temples
of stone.

"They called their lands Muria and they worshiped a god
Thanaroa whom they imagined to be the maker of all things,
dwelling far away, careless, indifferent, as to the fate of his
creations. They worshiped as closer gods, not indifferent but to
be prayed to and to be propitiated, the moon and the sun. Two
kings they had, each with his council and his court. One was
high priest to the moon and the other high priest to the sun.

"The mass of this people were black haired, but the sun king
and his nobles were ruddy with hair like mine; and the moon
king and his followers were like Yolara—or Lugur. And this,
the Three say, Goodwin, came about because for time upon
time the law had been that whenever a ruddy haired or ashen-
tressed child was born of the black haired it became dedicated
at once to either sun god or moon god, later wedding and
bearing children only to their own kind. Until at last from the
black haired came no more of the light-locked ones, but the
ruddy ones, being stronger, still arose from them."

She paused, running her long fingers through her own

bronze-flecked ringlets. Selective breeding this with a vengeance, I thought; an ancient experiment in heredity which of course would in time result in the stamping out of the tendency to depart from type that lies in all organisms; resulting, obviously, at last in three fixed forms of black haired, ruddy haired, and silver haired—but this, with a shock of realization it came to me, was also an accurate description of the dark-polled *ladala*, their fair-haired rulers and of the golden-brown tressed Lakla!

How—questions began to stream through my mind; silenced by the handmaiden's voice.

"Above, far, far above the abode of the Shining One," she said, "was their greatest temple, holding the shrines both of sun and moon. All about it were other temples hidden behind mighty walls, each enclosing its own space and squared and ruled and standing within a shallow lake; the sacred city, the city of the gods of this land—"

"It is the Nan-Matal that she is describing," I thought.

"Out upon all this looked the *Taithu* who were now but the servants of the Shining One as it had been the messenger of the Three," she went on. "When they returned the Shining One spoke to them, promising them dominion over all that they had seen, yea, *under it* dominion of all earth itself and later perhaps of other earths. With all of mankind their slaves!

"In the Shining One had grown craft, cunning; knowledge to gain that which it desired. Therefore it told its *Taithu*—and mayhap told them truth—that not yet was it time for *them* to go forth; that slowly must they pass into that outer world, for they had sprung from heart of earth and that even it, the Shining One itself, lacked power to swirl unaided into and through the above. Then it counseled them, instructing them what to do. They hollowed the chamber wherein first I saw you, cutting their way to it that path down which from it you sped.

"It revealed to them that the force that is within moon flame is kin to the force that is within it, for the chamber of its birth was the chamber too of moon birth and into it went the subtle essences and powers that flow in that earth child; and it taught them how to make that which fills what you call the Moon Pool whose opening is close behind its veil hanging upon the gleaming cliffs.

"When this was done it taught them how to make and how to place the seven lights through which moon flame streams into Moon Pool—the seven lights that are kin to its own seven orbs even as its fires are kin to moon fires—and which would open for it a path that it could tread. And all this the *Taithu* did, working so secretly that neither those of their race whose faces were set against the Shining One nor the busy men above knew aught of it.

"When it was done they moved up the path, clustering within the Moon Pool Chamber. Moon flame streamed through the seven globes, poured down upon the pool; they saw mists arise, embrace and become one with the moon flame—and then up through Moon Pool, drawn by the seven torrents, shaping itself within the mists of light, whirling, radiant—the Shining One!

"Almost free, almost loosed upon the world it coveted!

"Again it counseled them, and they pierced the passage whose portal you found first; set the fires within its stones that they might breathe of their light, and revealing themselves to the moon king and his priests spake to them even as the Shining One had instructed.

"Now was the moon king filled with fear and amaze when he looked upon the *Taithu*, shrouded with protecting mists of light in Moon Pool Chamber, and heard their words. Yet, being crafty, he thought of the power that would be his if he heeded and how quickly the strength of the sun king would dwindle. So he and his made a pact with the Shining One's messengers.

"When next the moon was round and poured its flames down upon Moon Pool, *Taithu* gathered there again, watched the child of the Three take shape within the pillars, speed away—and out! They heard a mighty shouting, a tumult of terror, of awe and of worship; a silence; a vast sighing—and they waited, wrapped in their mists of light for they feared to follow nor were they near the paths that would have enabled them to look without.

"Another tumult—and back came the Shining One, murmuring with joy, pulsing, triumphant and clasped within its vapors a man and woman, ruddy haired, golden eyed, in whose faces rapture and horror lay side by side—gloriously, hideously. And still holding them it danced above the Moon Pool and—sank!

"Now must I be brief. *Lat* after *lat* the Shining One went forth, returning with its sacrifices. And stronger after each it grew—and gayer and more cruel. Ever when it passed with its prey toward the pool, the *Taithu* who watched felt a swift, strong intoxication, a drunkenness of spirit, streaming from it to them. And the Shining One forgot what it had promised them of dominion—and in this new evil delight they too forgot. And by this, more and more, they became its slaves—even as it had planned.

"Athirst for this poison the Shining One distilled from the flame of life within those it embraced, they built for it the great temple opposite the Veil where you watched it dance. Then here by compact with the moon king they carried throng upon throng of the black haired, set them in the places beyond the green roadway and drew from them the brides and bridegrooms of that which had become their god; rejoicing in the soul drunkenness with which it flooded them when the Shining One took the offerings. Further, their god counseled them, so that the *Taithu* who would have washed away their evil could not prevail.

"The outer land was torn with hatred and open strife. The moon king and his kind, through the guidance of the evil *Taithu* and the favor of the Shining One, had become powerful and the sun king and his were darkened. And the moon priests preached that the child of the Three was the moon god itself come to dwell with them. Many believed, saying:

" 'They can show us a god, but the sun king can show none. Further when he appears he warms our spirits with a fire that makes us even as gods. And does not the moon pass before the sun in the heavens and shadow him? Nor can the sun forbid it. Therefore shall we worship the moon god!'

"Yet were there many who hated the moon king and the ways of the Dweller. Battles there were and the whole land sickened. It was at this time that the evil *Taithu* set in place the pale stone whose keys are the moon rays and which you opened—set it there that all who doubted might see the moon summon its spirit; but more than that to guard the Moon Pool against those whose doubts could not be stilled and who might creep in seeking to destroy. For only when the moon was full, all of its silver radiance streaming upon earth, could the Shining One draw strength to pass forth; at all other times it dwelt below, the Moon Pool Chamber was free of it and bold, determined men might well enter, close its Portal and shatter the spheres of power.

"Now suddenly vast tides arose and when they withdrew they took with them great portions of this country. And the land itself began to sink. Then said the moon king that the moon had called to ocean to destroy because wroth that another than he was worshiped. The people believed and there was wide slaughter. When it was over there was no more a sun king nor any of the ruddy haired folk; slain were they, slain down to the babe at breast.

"But still the tides swept higher; still dwindled the land!

"As it shrank multitudes of the fleeing people were led through Moon Pool Chamber and carried here. They were what now are called the *ladala,* and they were given place and set to work; and they thrived. Came too many of the fair haired; and they were given dwellings. They sat beside the evil *Taithu;* they became drunk even as they with the dancing of the Shining One; they learned—not all, only a little part but that little enough—of their arts. And ever the Shining One danced more gaily out there within the black amphitheater; grew ever stronger—and ever the hordes of its slaves behind the Veil increased.

"Nor did the *Taithu* who clung to the old ways check this—they could not. By the sinking of the land above their own spaces were imperiled. Shattered mountains crashed through and there were quaking as though its eternal walls strove to march upon each other. All of their strength and all of their wisdom it took to keep this land from perishing; nor had they help from those others mad for the poison of the Shining One; and they had no time to deal with them nor the earth race with whom they had foregathered.

"At last came a slow, vast tide. It roiled even to the bases of the walled islets of the city of the gods—and within these now were all that were left of my people on earth face.

"I am of those people," she paused, looking at me proudly, "one of the daughters of the sun king whose seed is still alive in the *ladala!*"

As Larry opened his mouth to speak she waved a silencing hand.

"This tide did not recede," she went on. "And after a time this remnant, the moon king leading them, joined those who had already fled below. The rocks became still, the quakings ceased and now those Ancient Ones who had been laboring could take breath. And anger grew within them as they looked upon the work of their evil kin. Again they sought the Three—and the Three now knew what they had done and their pride was humbled. They would not slay the Shining One themselves, for still they loved it; but they instructed these others how to undo their work; how also they might destroy the evil *Taithu* were it necessary.

"Armed with the wisdom of the Three they went forth—but now the Shining One was strong indeed. They could not slay it!

"Nay, it knew and was prepared; they could not even pass beyond its veil nor seal its abode. Ah, strong, strong, mighty of will, full of craft and cunning had the Shining One become. So they turned upon their kind who had gone astray and made them perish, to the last. The Shining One came not to the aid of its servants—though they called; for within its will was the thought that they were of no further use to it; that it would rest awhile and dance with them—who had so little of the power and wisdom of its *Taithu* and therefore no reins upon it. And while this was happening black haired and fair haired ran and hid and were but shaking vessels of terror.

"The Ancient Ones took council. This was their decision; that they would go from the gardens before the Silver Waters— leaving, since they could not kill it, the Shining One with its worshipers. They sealed the mouth of the passage that leads to the Moon Pool Chamber and they changed the face of the cliff so that none might tell where it had been. But the passage itself they left open—having foreknowledge I think, of a thing that was to come to pass in the far future—perhaps it was your journey here, my Larry and Goodwin—verily I think so.

"For the last time they went to the Three—to pass sentence upon them. They found them broken, their wisdom dulled with sorrow. And this was the doom they put upon the Three—that here they should remain, alone, among the *Akka,* served by them, until that time dawned when they would have strength and will to destroy the evil they had created—and even now— loved; nor might they seek death, nor follow their judges until this had come to pass. This was the doom they put upon the Three for the wickedness that had sprung from their pride, and they strengthened it with their arts that it might not be broken.

"Then they passed—to a far land they had chosen where the Shining One could not go, beyond the black precipices of Doul that guard the place of wonders and are in turn guarded by the winged serpents, a green land—"

"Ireland!" interrupted Larry, with conviction. "I knew it."

"Since then time upon time had passed," she went on, un- heeding. "The people called this place Muria after their sunken land and soon they forgot where was the portal the *Taithu* had sealed. The moon king became the Voice of the Dweller and always with the Voice is a beautiful woman of the moon king's kin who is its priestess. The Shining One is kinder to his priestess than to his Voice; and so really the woman rules. Long have they dwelt here and many have been the *ladala* who have danced—before the tiers of jet, upon the ivory dais, and passed in the Shining One's train over the Silvery Waters and through the Veil.

"And many have been the journeys upward of the Shining One, through the Moon Pool—returning with still others in its coils.

"Long has it watched the world swarm with man—and now again is it grown restless, longing for the wider spaces. It has spoken to Yolara and to Lugur even as it did to the dead *Taithu*, promising them dominion. And it has grown even stronger, drawing to itself power to go far on the moon stream where it wills from the Moon Pool Chamber. Thus was it able to seize your friend, Goodwin, and Olaf's wife and babe—and many more. Yolara and Lugur plan to open ways to earth face; to depart with their court and under the Shining One grasp the world!

"But now is the *va* about to strike when it will be settled whether the Shining One shall rule—or whether the Three shall destroy it!

"And this is the tale the Silent Ones bade me tell you—and it is done."

Breathlessly I had listened to the stupendous epic of a long-lost world. Now I found speech to voice the question ever with me, the thing that lay as close to my heart as did the welfare of Larry, indeed the whole object of my quest—the fate of Throckmartin and those who had passed with him into the Dweller's lair; yes, and of Olaf's wife, too.

"Lakla," I said, "the friend who drew me here and those he loved who preceded him—can we not save them?"

"I'll volunteer to go into that joint any minute and I'll bet I can get 'em," Larry's face was grim. "Lakla's been buffaloed like all the rest. Give me a hose or just make me one gas cylinder—and I'll get 'em out, don't doubt it."

He had spoken in English and the handmaiden had not understood; she paused, perplexed.

"Tell him what he wants to know—heart's delight," he spoke to her. "If you can," he added.

"The Three say no, Goodwin." There was again in her eyes the pity with which she had looked upon Olaf. "The Shining One—*feeds*—upon the flame of life itself, setting in its place its own fires and its own will. Its slaves are only shells through which it gleams. Death, say the Three, is the best that can come to them; yet will that be a boon great indeed."

"Gassed—let us get 'em away once, Doc, and we'll put up a fight to get 'em back all right," whispered O'Keefe.

"But they have souls, *mavourneen*," he said to her. "And they're alive still—in a way. Anyhow, their souls have not gone from them."

I caught a hope from his words—skeptic though I am—holding that the existence of soul has never been proved by dependable laboratory methods—for they recalled to me that when I had seen Throckmartin, Edith had been close beside him.

"It was weeks before he passed that my friend Throckmartin was taken," I said. "How did he and his wife come together in the Dweller's lair?"

"I do not know," she answered, slowly. "You say they loved—and it is true that love is stronger even than death. By soul, Larry dear, you mean, I think, that which is in us that lives forever. But I do not know—I only know that those whom the Shining One has taken live ever as you see them; fed by its own life, doing as it commands and in a measure partaking of its power. Whether their souls go far—or dwell there, being imperishable, when life fire has been eaten—I do not know."

"Lakla," I said, "this blight the Dweller puts upon what it touches—its power to eat what you call the fire of life—whence comes it?"

"From the time of the first sacrifice," she answered. "Before that its touch was clean. So too of the sounds that accompany it—you heard, like little bells of glass—whence they came I know not; but they were not there before the sacrifices and they, too, grow ever stronger as the Shining One—eats!"

"Can—er—Fireworks go wherever he pleases?" This was Larry. "If he can, why all that ceremony Goodwin and I watched when Olaf tried to do for him? And why the spot-light?"

"Spot-light?" she repeated, wonderingly.

"The path of radiant colors that swept over the Silvery Waters and through which the Shining One came," I interpreted.

"At the first *that* was necessary," she answered, "as the seven lights in the Moon Pool Chamber were, and still are, needed to open its path to the above. The *Taithu* made the light—but as the Child of the Three grew stronger it could pass beyond the Veil unaided, going where it willed about the land beyond the Portal. But the fair haired clung to the forms—and as long as they gave their god all the brides and bridegrooms for whom it lusted—why should it wander?" she asked. "And then I have told you that the Shining One is cunning and has great wisdom. Perhaps it fears to affright too much those who serve it—and feed it," she added.

"One thing I *don't* understand"—this was Larry again—"is why a girl like you keeps coming out of the black-haired crowd; so frequently and one might say, so regularly, Lakla. Aren't there ever any red-headed boys—and if they are what becomes of them?"

"That, Larry, I cannot answer," she said, very frankly. "There was a pact of some kind; how made or by whom I know not. But for long the Murians feared the return of the *Taithu* and greatly they feared the Three. Even the Shining One feared those who had created it—for a time; and not even now is it eager to face them—*that* I know. Nor are Yolara and Lugur so *sure*. It may be that the Three commanded it; but how or why I know not. I only know that it is true—for here am I and from where else would I have come?"

"From Ireland," said Larry O'Keefe, promptly. "And that's where you're going. For 'tis no place for a girl like you to have been brought up—Lakla; what with people like frogs, and a half god three quarters devil, and red oceans, an' the only Irish things yourself and the Silent Ones up there, bless their hearts. It's no place for ye and by the soul of St. Patrick, it's out of it soon ye'll be gettin'!"

Larry! Larry! If it had but been true—and I could see Lakla and you beside me now!

CHAPTER XXXVI

"THE *KETH* HAS POWER"

LONG HAD BEEN her tale in the telling, and too long, perhaps, have I been in the repeating—but not every day are the mists rolled away to reveal undreamed secrets of earth-youth. And I have set it down here, adding nothing, taking nothing from it; translating liberally, it is true, but constantly striving, while putting it into idea-forms and phraseology to be readily understood by my readers, to keep accurately to the spirit. And this, I must repeat, I have done throughout my narrative, wherever it has been necessary to record conversation with the Murians.

Rising, I found I was painfully stiff—as muscle-bound as though I had actually trudged many miles. Larry, imitating me, gave an involuntary groan.

"Faith, *mavourneen*," he said to Lakla, relapsing unconsciously into English, "your roads would never wear out shoe-leather, but they've got their kick, just the same!"

She understood our plight, if not his words; gave a soft little cry of mingled pity and self-reproach; forced us back upon the cushions.

"Oh, but I'm sorry!" mourned Lakla, leaning over us. "I have forgotten—for those new to it the way is a weary one, indeed—"

She ran to the doorway, whistled a clear high note down the passage. Through the hangings came two of the frog-men. She spoke to them rapidly. They crouched toward us, what certainly was meant for an amiable grin wrinkling the grotesque muzzles, baring the glistening rows of needle-teeth. And while I watched them with the fascination that they never lost for me, the monsters calmly swung one arm around our knees, lifted us up like babies—and as calmly started to walk away with us!

"Put me down! Put me down, I say!" The O'Keefe's voice was both outraged and angry; squinting around I saw him struggling violently to get to his feet. The *Akka* only held him tighter, booming comfortingly, peering down into his flushed face inquiringly.

"But, Larry—darlin'!"—Lakla's tones were—well, maternally surprised—"you're stiff and sore, and Kra can carry you quite easily."

"I *won't* be carried!" sputtered the O'Keefe. "Damn it, Goodwin, there are such things as the unities even here, an' for a lieutenant of the Royal Air Force to be picked up an' carted around like a—like a bundle of rags—it's not discipline! Put me down, ye *omadhaun*, or I'll poke ye in the snout!" he shouted to his bearer—who only boomed gently, and stared at the handmaiden, plainly for further instructions.

"But, Larry—dear!"—Lakla was plainly distressed—"it will *hurt* you to walk; and I don't *want* you to be hurt, Larry—darlin'!"

"Holy shade of St. Patrick!" moaned Larry; again he made a mighty effort to tear himself from the frog-man's grip; gave up with a groan. "Listen, *alanna!*" he said plaintively. "When we get to Ireland, you and I, we won't have anybody to pick us up and carry us about every time we get a bit tired. And it's getting me in bad habits you are!"

"Oh, yes, we will, Larry!" cried the handmaiden, "because many, oh, many, of my *Akka* will go with us!"

"Will you tell this—*boob!*—to put me down!" gritted the now thoroughly aroused O'Keefe. I couldn't help laughing; he glared at me.

"Bo-oo-ob?" exclaimed Lakla.

"Yes, bo-oo-ob!" said O'Keefe, "and I have no desire to explain the word in my present position, light of my soul!"

She spoke again to the frog-man. He answered her.

"Kra says he likes to carry you," she said hopefully.

"Lakla, darlin', dear!" Larry was now almost tearful. "Please let me walk! I want to! When anybody carries me it makes me ill, an' I don't get up for days—*va* upon *va,*" he amended hastily. "It's a weakness of mine."

The handmaiden sighed, plainly dejected. But she spoke again to the *Akka,* who gently lowered the O'Keefe to the floor.

"I don't understand," she said hopelessly, "but if you want to walk, why, of course, you shall, Larry." She turned to me. "Do you?" she asked.

"I do not," I said firmly. "I haven't Larry's weakness."

"Well, then," murmured Lakla, "go you, Larry and Goodwin, with Kra and Gulk, and let them minister to you. After, sleep a little—for not soon will Rador and Olaf return. And let me feel your lips before you go, Larry—darlin'!" she added naïvely.

With enthusiasm he responded. She covered his eyes caressingly with her soft little palms; pushed him away.

"Now go," said Lakla, "and rest!"

Unashamedly I lay back against the horny chest of Gulk; and with a smile noticed that Larry, even if he had rebelled at being carried, did not disdain the support of Kra's shining, black-scaled arm which, slipping around his waist, half-lifted him along. The two boomed softly to us as we went, turned their staring, saucer eyes upon each other, talked a bit, addressed us again. And in some odd way as I rocked, cradled in the gentle grip of the monstrous arms, I, all at once, lost any impression that these were—*things*. I realized Lakla's viewpoint perfectly; it came to me that the *Akka* were just very big, very formidable children, with an extremely unfamiliar exterior; gentle, loyal, in fact—*lovable*—child-men. I smiled up at Gulk—and his huge muzzle widened, wrinkled, grinned in the friendliest fashion back at me; the phosphorescence in the eyes softened. Evidently Larry was feeling the same way as I.

"You know, Doc," he called back, "these beggars aren't half bad! Anyway, they're clearly mighty fond of the *colleen*. But what I'm going to do with them when we get back to Ireland beats me—" He groaned again.

They parted a hanging, and Gulk set me softly down beside a small walled pool, sparkling with the clear water that had heretofore been brought us in the wide basins. Then they began to *undress* us. And at this point the O'Keefe gave up.

"Whatever they're going to do we can't stop 'em, Doc!" he moaned. "Anyway, I feel as though I've been pulled through a knot-hole, and I don't care—I don't care—as the song says."

When we were stripped we were lowered gently into the water. But not long did the *Akka* let us splash about the shallow basin. They lifted us out, and from jars began deftly to anoint and rub us with aromatic unguents. Almost immediately every trace of soreness and stiffness vanished. I noted that while the webbed palms of the monster—no never again shall I call them that—of the comradely creature attending me were horny, they possessed a surprising pliability. And, after they had in extremely workmanlike fashion manipulated our muscles, they picked us up and literally *dipped* us back in the pool, stirring us about. Then they rubbed us vigorously with white cloths and began—to dress us again!

I think that in all the medley of grotesque, of tragic, of baffling, strange and perilous experiences in that underground world none was more bizarre, and funnily bizarre, than this—valeting. I began to laugh, Larry joined me, and then Kra and Gulk joined in our merriment with deep batrachian cachinations and gruntings. Then, having finished appareling us and still chuckling, the two touched our arms and led us out, into a room whose circular sides were ringed with soft divans. Still smiling, I sank at once into sleep.

How long I slumbered I do not know. A low and thunderous booming coming through the deep window slit, reverberated through the room and awakened me. Larry yawned; arose briskly; called over:

"I feel simply great!" he announced.

He had described my own sensations accurately, and I told him so.

"Sounds as though the bass drums of every jazz band in New York were serenading us!" he observed. Simultaneously we sprang to the window; raised ourselves; peered through.

I gasped!

We were a little above the level of the bridge, and its full length was plain before us. Thousands upon thousands of the *Akka* were crowding upon it, and far away other hordes filled like a glittering thicket both sides of the cavern ledge's crescent strand. On black scale and orange scale the crimson light fell, picking them off in little flickering points. Yes, and upon scarlet and green and blue scale, too; for now I saw that, like the leopard frogs so familiar to us, the *Akka* possessed an extensive range of coloring. And while all those who guarded the castle of the Three were uniformed in their Princeton armoring, these newcomers flaunted a bewildering variety of hues. At first I thought that Lakla had perhaps yielded to some feminine penchant for livery, but watching those nearest I saw that they were formed in squads and detachments, each under the command of one of the black and yellow batrachians. These latter, then, I presumed, had some special talent for leadership.

Within ordered lines of the *Akka* upon the platform from

which sprang the smaller span over the abyss were Lakla, Olaf, and Rador; the handmaiden clearly acting as interpreter between them and the giant she had called Nak, the Frog King.

"Come on!" shouted Larry. The passages were deserted, and as we raced along the O'Keefe kept up a discomfited monologue.

"Ought to wrap me up in cotton wool! Wonder how much we've missed already? Don't think it's fair of her! Been through a hundred battles, and now she's afraid, if I don't get enough sleep, I'll crack!"

Out of the open portal we ran; over the World Heart Bridge—and straight into the group.

"Oh!" cried Lakla, "I didn't want you to wake up so soon Larry—darlin'!"

"See here, *mavourneen!*" Indignation thrilled in the Irishman's voice. "I'm not going to be done up with baby-ribbons and laid away in a cradle for safe-keeping while a fight is on; don't think it! Why didn't you call me?"

"You needed rest!" There was indomitable determination in the handmaiden's tones, the eternal maternal shining defiant from her eyes. "You were tired and hurt! You shouldn't have got up!"

"Needed the rest!" groaned Larry.

"Yes—and why did you *let* him arise, Goodwin?" she leveled an accusing finger at me.

"Let me! Let me!" gasped the O'Keefe. "Look here, Lakla, what do you think I am?"

"You're all I have," said that maiden firmly, "and I'm going to take care of you, Larry—darlin'! Don't you ever think anything different!"

"Now, Lakla—" he began. Rador was unable to repress a chuckle. Breathing heavily, Larry glared at him. The green dwarf made an heroic effort to control his mirth; failed signally. Then the humor of the situation struck O'Keefe; he grinned, a bit feebly, it is true.

"Well, pulse of my heart, considering my delicate health and general fragility, would it hurt me, do you think, to be told what's going on?" he asked.

"Not at all, Larry!" answered the handmaiden serenely. "Yolara went through the Portal. She was very, *very* angry—"

"She was all the devil's woman that she is!" rumbled Olaf.

"No word did she speak all the journey," said Rador, "until the Portal opened. Then said she to tell you, *Larree,* that both Lakla and you would pray her each to destroy either before she finished with both. If"—he hesitated—"if matters should go wrong, slay the handmaiden and yourself before Yolara can grip you!" he whispered.

O'Keefe nodded.

"Rador met the messenger," went on the Golden Girl calmly. "The *ladala* are ready to rise when Lugur and Yolara lead their hosts against us. They will strike at those left behind. And in the mean time we shall have disposed my *Akka* to meet Yolara's men. And on that disposal we must all take council, you, Larry, and Rador, Olaf and Goodwin and Nak, the ruler of the *Akka.*"

"Did the messenger give any idea when Yolara expects to make her little call?" asked Larry.

"Yes," she answered. "They prepare, and we may expect them in—" She gave the equivalent of about thirty-six hours of our time.

"But, Lakla," I said, the doubt that I had long been holding finding voice, "should the Shining One come—with its slaves—are the Three strong enough to cope with it?"

There was troubled doubt in her own eyes.

"I do not know," she said at last, frankly. "You have heard their story. What they promise is that they will help. I do not know—any more than do you, Goodwin!"

I looked up at the dome beneath which I knew the dread Trinity stared forth; even down upon us. And despite the awe, the assurance, I had felt when I stood before them I, too, doubted. For I had watched the Dweller at its devilish work, and I had looked upon my own friend Throckmartin and Throckmartin's wife—a clean man and woman from my own sane and understandable world—and I had seen what the Dweller had made of them.

Why should I not have doubted?

"Well," said Larry, "you and I, uncle," he turned to Rador, "and Olaf here had better decide just what part of the battle we'll lead—"

"Lead!" the handmaiden was appalled. "*You* lead, Larry? Why you are to stay with Goodwin and with me—up there, there we can watch."

"Lakla," Larry's tone was stern. "The O'Keefes do not stand and watch while there's fighting going on. Take it from me, Lakla—that's just what they don't do."

"But, Larry darlin'," wailed Lakla, "they will have the *Keth*, and that strange new weapon with which you were smitten— and others. Rador and Olaf will stay beside us, too. You must not go ahead, no."

"Heart's beloved," O'Keefe was stern indeed. "A thousand times I've looked Death straight in the face, peered into his eyes. Yes, and with ten thousand feet of space under me an' boche shells tickling the ribs of the boat I was in. An' d'ye think I'll sit now on the grand stand an' watch while a game like this is being pulled? Ye don't know your future husband, soul of delight! No, ye don't. An' a dozen times have they got to me with their iron—an' I bear the marks of it now—an' glad I am that I do—"

He pulled aside his tunic and showed a great scar that ran around the shoulder.

"Who did that Larry?" whispered Lakla—and I saw that whatever else of his talk passed over her head, she at least knew what this meant.

"A Hun Archie," he said.

She shivered; drew herself up.

"Now when we go from here," the golden voice hardened,

"you shall point out him ye call Ho-oo-on Archie—he who marked you so, Larry dear; and this I promise you—my *Akka* will rend him—yea, with all their strength, with claw and fang and spur shall they rend him!"

Her eyes blazed. O'Keefe gave it up; helplessly he shrugged his shoulders.

"Well, Doc," he said to me, "what can *I* do?"

I confess that all that *I* could do was to grin.

"Well," he said at last, "uncle and you, Doc and Olaf, let's get together. If I've got to sit on the bleachers I want to watch something that we've had some hand in anyway."

Lakla nodded; spoke to Nak. We started toward the golden opening, squads of the frog-men following us soldierly and disappearing about the huge structure. Nor did we stop until we came to the handmaiden's boudoir. There we seated ourselves.

"Now," said Larry, "two things I want to know. First—how many can Yolara muster against us; second, how many of these *Akka* have we to meet them? Never mind the *ladala*," he added. "This war's going to be won or lost on the western front—to use a phrase I've heard for the last four years."

Answering, Rador gave as the strength of Yolara's following what would be the equivalent of a hundred thousand with us; of the frog-men, roughly, two hundred and fifty thousand.

"Good enough," answered Larry. "Two to one. And they're some fighters."

"But, *Larree*," this was Rador, "do not forget that the nobles will have the quaking death and other things; also that the soldiers have fought against the *Akka* before and will be shielded as far as possible against their spears and clubs; also that they will smite with their swords—and that their blades can bite through the scales of Nak's warriors."

"What about the *Keth?*" Larry spoke. "Didn't you tell us, uncle, that it had no effect against the cliffs of the Shining One's lair and that there was some other halters on it?"

And then I remembered. I thrust my hand into my breast pocket where I had been carrying a certain devilish little silver cone; drew it out.

"And all the advantage is not on their side," I boasted. "Something surely can be done with this."

"Where did you get that?" cried Rador.

"Yolara left it behind," said I.

Delicately the handmaiden took the cone; turned it about in her hands. Then she whistled, a low golden note. The frog-woman of the rosy wall entered. Lakla spoke to her; leaving, it was not long before she returned, one arm dissolved in vacancy—and by that I knew she was carrying one of the garments of invisibility. The webbed hand vanished; the arm appeared. Lakla stooped down to the floor and felt carefully about; then, rising, thrust a slender foot into an unseen something that eclipsed it. Withdrawing the foot she pointed the cone downward, slipped the catch.

The green ray leaped from the cone—and was as quickly shut off. But at the handmaiden's feet a shower of writhing sparks burst into sight; swam, interlaced, disappeared. Lakla thrust her foot forward again, cautiously. It did not vanish!

"Those, at least, are no protection," she sighed.

She clapped her hands; a half-dozen of the *Akka* parted the curtains, booming softly, looking at her with luminous, round eyes. The deep monosyllables passed between them; they bowed, went out—returning shortly with a great block of stone. They placed it at her feet; withdrew. And again she leveled the cone at it and again the green ray shot forth. It impacted upon the rock, spread; the boulder began to quiver, to vibrate ever more rapidly; to shine forth; coruscate—and was gone!

"Now must we put our faith in the Three indeed," said Lakla, "for that stone ye saw is the stone of all here, even of the bridge—and over it the *Keth* has power, even as ye have seen!"

CHAPTER XXXVII

"YOUR LOVE; YOUR LIVES; YOUR SOULS"

BUT NO MORE of this. No need to tell of all that passed before the five of us and Nak walked from the castle in pursuance of plans that had ripened there. We crossed the bridge. We paced the crushed ruby floor until I gazed out, Tantaluslike, upon the elfin land of moss and flower. Ten miles it was between the cavern lip and the first green growth, Larry was for setting regiments of the *Akka* close behind the Portal to attack when Yolara's hosts came through—but Rador pointed out that the Murians would race over the roadway in their *coria*, and that as there was no place there for hiding, we would only leave a considerable number of our forces behind, useless.

The *coria* path ended with the astounding forests and those who would pass on to the Crimson Sea must proceed on foot or in litter to the crescent ledge. And so we decided to raise barricades along this path and behind them to garrison a certain number of the *Akka*, who, when the hosts of Lugur and Yolara should pass, would arise and smite them with lance and club while still others flanked them.

Across the cavern mouth we planned another barricade. At certain intervals over the span we placed marks and Lakla directed the frog-men to bring stones and set them there as barriers.

"A hundred Hindenburg lines," said Larry, whose strategy this largely was. "What's the use of the Huns if we can't learn from them?"

Bitterly, as we were pursuing these occupations, I wished for the little pocket camera I had carried with me through the moon door and had left, alas, with my medicine-case and other effects when we fled from our pavilion in the gardens. Instead of the sketches I carried away in my memory, I could have shown my colleagues of the International Association actual pictures of the marching files of the amphibians taking their places behind the walls as they built them; a peek at least of elfland; the prodigious bridge—a thousand marvels that my poor words have really no power to picture. But I *had* left it— and therefore words and sketches must do.

Larry, happy as a lark, busied with the plans of defense.

"If there were only time, Doc," he said to me, "I'd build a flock of planes that would make 'em look like thirty cents."

Lakla hovered about him like a worried honey-bee.

Then, suddenly, without warning, dropped the tragedy.

"Larry darlin'," said the handmaiden, "the Silent Ones bid me say the time is come for them to ask us the question. They say, too, Goodwin, that they would have you there—because should you return to your own world there are things within your spirit to which they would set flame," she added.

The command was enigmatic enough.

"When do we go?" I asked; Larry's face grew bright with interest.

"The time is now," she said—and hesitated. "Larry dear, put your arms about me," she faltered, "for there is something cold that catches at my heart—and I am afraid."

"There's nothing to be afraid of, *alanna*," he whispered, pressing her close.

"No?" Her eyes were fear-touched. "No—and yet; well, after all, there is naught for us to do but obey. And the Three—"

She drew his hand tighter about her, clasped it, began to move slowly with him out of the chamber.

"The Three?" Larry's voice was low, tender. "The Three— sweetheart?"

"The Three love me," she murmured. "I know they do—and you, too, Larry. And yet—it is as though I felt a door closing behind us—the door that leads to freedom, Larry; nay, even a door that bars the road of life!"

At his exclamation she gathered herself together; gave a shaky little laugh.

"It's because I love you so that fear has power to plague me," she told him.

WITHOUT ANOTHER word he bent and kissed her; in silence we passed on, his arm still about her girdled waist, golden head and black close together. Soon we stood before the crimson slab that was the door to the sanctuary of the Silent Ones. She poised uncertainly before it; then with a defiant arching of the proud little head that sent all the bronze-flecked curls flying, she pressed. It slipped aside and once more the opalescence gushed out, flooding all about us.

Dazzled as before, I followed through the lambent cascades pouring from the high, carved walls; paused, and my eyes clearing, looked up—straight into the faces of the Three. They gazed down upon us over the rushing, veined and shadowed mists of curdled moon radiance streaming upward from the rim of their dais; from the marble-white faces, the jet triangles of eyes rilled with the tiny, leaping red flames burned.

The angled orbs centered upon the handmaiden; softened as I had seen them do when first we had faced the Three. She smiled up; seemed to listen.

"Come closer," she commanded, "close to the feet of the Silent Ones."

We moved, pausing at the very base of the dais. The sparkling mists thinned; the great heads bent slightly over us; through the veils I caught a glimpse of huge columnar necks, enormous shoulders covered with draperies as of pale-blue fire. It came to me that these beings must be eighteen or twenty feet tall, giants, indeed—and what were the hidden shapes beneath the half-revealed necks and shoulders?

I came back to attention with a start, for Lakla was answering a question only heard by her; and, answering it aloud, I perceived for our benefit; for whatever was the mode of communication between those whose handmaiden she was, and her, it was clearly independent of speech.

"He has been told," she said, "even as you commanded."

Did I see a shadow of pain flit across the flickering eyes? Wondering, I glanced at Lakla's face and there was a dawn of foreboding and bewilderment. For a little she held her listening attitude; then the gaze of the Three left her; focused upon the O'Keefe.

"Thus speak the Silent Ones—through Lakla, their hand-maiden," the golden voice was like low trumpet notes. "At the threshold of doom is that world of yours above. Yea, even the doom, Goodwin, that ye dreamed and the shadow of which, looking into your mind they see, say the Three. Doom, they say, utter doom and the end of all things; cruelty and wickedness unspeakable; slavery most evil and at the last a dead-alive globe menacing the firmament. For not upon earth and never upon earth can man find means to destroy the Shining One, and free there, enthroned, the Shining One will know the strength it has and that now it does not know it has. Nor, say they, does it need that court which Lugur and Yolara plan to follow it; it does not even need Yolara; power it has to make its own court on earth as soon as free—and *none* of these things does the Shining One yet know. But all of them it will know once it spreads its wings beneath sun as well as moon!"

She listened again—and the foreboding deepened to an amazed fear.

"They say, the Silent Ones," she went on, "that they know not whether they have power to destroy that which they made— even now. Energies we know nothing of entered into its shaping and are part of it; and still other energies it has gathered to itself"—she paused; a shadow of puzzlement crept into her voice—"and other energies still, forces that ye *do* know and symbolize by certain names—hatred and pride and lust and many others which are forces real as that hidden in the *Keth*

and among them—fear, which weakens all those others—"
Again she paused.

"But within it is nothing of that greatest of all, that which
can make powerless all the evil others, that which we call—love,"
she ended softly.

"I'd like to be the one to put a little more fear in the beast,"
whispered Larry to me, grimly in our own English. The three
weird heads bent, ever so slightly; a gleam as of approval flitted
through the eyes and I gasped, and Larry grew a little white as
Lakla nodded—

"They say, Larry," she said, "that there you touch one side of
the heart of the matter—for it is through the way of fear the
Silent Ones hope to strike at the very life of the Shining One!"

The visage Larry turned to me was eloquent of wonder; and
mine reflected it—for what *really* were this Three to whom our
minds were but open pages, so easily read? Not long could we
conjecture; Lakla broke the little silence.

"This, they say, is what is to happen. First will come upon us
Lugur and Yolara with all their host. Because of fear the Shining
One will lurk behind within its lair; for despite all, the Dweller
does dread the Three, and only them. With this host the Voice
and the priestess will strive to conquer. And if they do, then
will they be strong enough, too, to destroy us all. Also, if they
take the abode they banish from the Dweller all fear and sound
the end of the Three.

"**THEN WILL** the Shining One be all free indeed; free to
go out into the world, free to do there as it wills!

"But if they do not conquer—and the Shining One comes
not to their aid, abandoning them even as it abandoned its own
Taithu—then will the Three be loosed from a part of their doom,
and they will go through the Portal, seek the Shining One
beyond the veil, and piercing it through fear's opening, destroy
it."

"That's quite clear," murmured the O'Keefe in my ear.
"Weaken the morale—then smash. I've seen it happen a dozen

times in Europe. While they've got their nerve there's not a thing you can do; get their nerve—and not a thing can they do. And yet in both cases they're the same men."

Lakla had been listening again. She turned, thrust out hands to Larry, a wild hope in her eyes—and yet a hope half shamed.

"They say," she cried, "that they give us choice. Remembering that your world doom hangs in the balance, we have choice—choice to stay and help fight Yolara's armies—and they say they look not lightly on that help. Or choice to go—and if so be you choose the latter, then will they show another way that leads into the passage through which you came, and that opens also into the Chamber of the Moon Pool. There, carrying food and drink, shall we stay until the Moon opens the door; and after that bring what means we may to destroy the Pool and seal up that gateway of the Shining One. Yet they bid me say, too, that if they are beaten, the Shining One will surely find other ways to go forth—though perhaps not in our time," she ended.

A flush had crept over the O'Keefe's face as she was speaking. He took her hands and looked long into the golden eyes; glancing up I saw the Trinity were watching them intently—imperturbably.

"What do you say, *mavourneen?*" asked Larry gently. The handmaiden hung her head; trembled.

"Your words shall be mine, O one I love," she whispered. "So going or staying, I am beside you."

"And you, Goodwin?" he turned to me. I shrugged my shoulders—after all I had no one to care.

"It's up to you, Larry," I remarked, deliberately choosing his own phraseology.

The O'Keefe straightened, squared his shoulders, gazed straight into the flame-flickering eyes.

"We stick!" he said briefly.

Shamefacedly I recall now that at the time I thought this colloquialism not only irreverent, but in somewhat bad taste. I am glad to say I was alone in that bit of weakness. The face that

Lakla turned to Larry was radiant with love, and although the shamed hope had vanished from the sweet eyes, they were shining with adoring pride. And the marble visages of the Three softened, and the little flames died down. Then Lakla started, plainly surprised.

"Wait," she said, "there is one other thing they say we must answer before they will hold us to that promise—wait—"

She listened, and then her face grew white—white as those of the Three themselves; the glorious eyes widened, stark terror filling them; the whole lithe body of her shook like a reed in the wind.

"Not that!" she cried out to the Three. "Oh, not that! Not Larry—let me go even as you will—but not him!" She threw up frantic hands to the woman-being of the Trinity. "Let *me* bear it alone," she wailed. "Alone—mother! Mother!"

The Three bent their heads toward her, their faces pitiful, and from the eyes of the woman One rolled—tears! Larry leaped to Lakla's side.

"Mavourneen!" he cried. "Sweetheart, what have they said to you?"

He glared up at the Silent Ones, his hand twitching toward the high-hung pistol holster.

The handmaiden swung to him; threw white arms around his neck; held her head upon his heart until her sobbing ceased.

"This they—say—the—Silent Ones," she gasped; and then all the courage of her came back. "O heart of mine!" she whispered to Larry, gazing deep into his eyes, his anxious face cupped between her white palms. "This they say—that should the Shining One come to succor Yolara and Lugur, should it conquer its fear—and—do this—then is there but one way left to destroy it—and to save your world."

She swayed; he gripped her tightly.

"But one way—you and I must walk—together—into its embrace! Yea, we must pass within it—loving each other, loving the world, realizing to the full all that we sacrifice and sacrificing all, our love, our lives, perhaps even that you call soul, O loved one; must give ourselves *all* to the Shining One—gladly, freely, our love for each other flaming high within us—that this curse that threatens your earth shall pass away! For if we do this, pledge the Three, then shall that power of love we carry into it weaken and baffle for a time all that evil which the Shining One has become—and in that time the Three can strike and slay!"

The blood rushed from my heart; scientist that I am, essentially, my reason rejected any such solution as this of the activities of the Dweller. Was it not, the thought flashed, a propitiation by the Three out of their own weakness—and as it flashed I looked up to see their eyes, full of sorrow, on mine—and knew they read the thought. Then into the whirling vortex of my mind came steadying reflections—of history changed by the power of hate, of passion, of ambition, and most of all, by love. Was there not actual dynamic energy in these things—was there not a Son of Man who hung upon a cross on Calvary?

"Dear love o' mine," said the O'Keefe quietly, "is it in your heart to say *yes* to this?"

"Larry," she spoke low, "what is in your heart is in mine; but I did so want to go with you, to live with you—to—to bear you children, Larry—and to see the sun."

My eyes were wet with tears; dimly through them I saw his gaze on me.

"If the world *is* at stake," he whispered, "why of course there's only one thing to do. God knows I never thought of it when I was fighting up there—and many a better man than me has gone west with shell and bullet for the same idea; but these things aren't shell and bullet—but I hadn't Lakla then—and it's the damned *doubt* I have behind it all."

He turned to the Three—and did I in their poise sense a rigidity, an anxiety that sat upon them as alienly as would divinity upon men?

"Tell me this, Silent Ones," he cried. "If we do this, Lakla and I, is it *sure* you are that you can slay the—Thing, and save my world? Is it *sure* you are?"

For the first and the last time, I heard the voice of the Silent Ones. It was the man-being at the right who spoke.

"We are sure," he said—and the tones rolled out like deepest organ notes, shaking, vibrating, assailing the ears more strangely than their appearance struck the eyes. Another moment the O'Keefe stared at them. Then I saw conviction spread over his face. Once more he squared his shoulders; lifted Lakla's chin and smiled into her eyes.

"We stick!" he said again, nodding to the Three.

Over the visages of the Trinity fell benignity that was— awesome; the tiny flames in the jet orbs vanished, leaving them wells in which brimmed serenity, hope—an extraordinary joy-fulness. The woman sat upright, tender gaze fixed upon the man and girl. I saw her great shoulders raise as though she had lifted her arms and had drawn to her those others. The three faces pressed together for a fleeting moment; raised again. The woman bent forward—and as she did so, Lakla and Larry, as though drawn by some outer force, were swept against the dais.

Out from the sparkling mist stretched two hands, enor-mously long, six-fingered, thumbless, a faint tracery of golden scales upon their white backs, utterly unhuman and still in some strange way beautiful, radiating power and—all womanly!

They stretched forth; they touched the bent heads of Lakla and the O'Keefe; caressed them, drew them together, softly stroked them—lovingly, with more than a touch of benediction. And withdrew!

The sparkling mists rolled up once more, hiding the Silent Ones. As silently as once before we had gone we passed out of the place of light, beyond the crimson stone, back to the hand-maiden's chamber.

Only once on our way did Larry speak.

"Cheer up, darlin'," he said to her, "it's a long way yet before the finish. An' are you thinking that Lugur and Yolara are going to pull this thing off? Are you?"

The handmaiden only looked at him, eyes love and sorrow filled.

"They are!" said Larry. "They are! Like *hell* they are!"

CHAPTER XXXVIII

THE MEETING OF TITANS

IT IS NOT my intention, nor is it possible no matter how interesting to me, to set down *ad seriatim* the happenings of the next twelve hours. But a few will not be denied recital.

O'Keefe regained cheerfulness—

"After all, Doc," he said to me, "it's a beautiful scrap we're going to have. At the worst the worst is no more than the leprechawn warned about. I would have told the Taitha De about the banshee raid he promised me; but I was a bit taken off my feet at the time. The old girl an' all the clan 'll be along, said the little green man, an' I bet the Three will be damned glad of it, take it from me. An' I'm not thinkin' it'll go that far, anyway. If it does, why when I took the king's shilling I let in the chance of going to glory like Elijah on a flamin' plane, or being sent into—strange how you get the slang of this joint—into the nothingness with a shell. An' the only difference between that an' the *Keth* is that Yolara's dope is slower.

"No, it's all right," he mused. "Only it hurts hard about Lakla. Never, never was there a girl like her, Goodwin, not even in the days of the heroes of the old isle. Stand up and fight for you, kill for you, go to hell with you if necessary—and for you! God keep me good to her!" he added.

Lakla, shining eyed, filled with extremely grateful news.

"The Three say again to have no fear of the *Keth*, nor for aught else of the weapons of light of Yolara," she said. "The *Akka* must face them, it is true—and would I could help my people," she sighed. "But against us here, or the bridge or the abode, those things will be helpless. I have other tidings that I

am afraid will please you little, Larry—darlin'." She was half
fearful. "The Silent Ones say that you must not go into battle
yourself. You must stay here with me, and with Goodwin—for
if—if—the Shining One does come, then must we be here to
meet it. And you might not be, you know, Larry, if you fight,"
she said, looking shyly up at him from under the long lashes.

The O'Keefe's jaw dropped.

"That's about the hardest yet," he answered slowly. "Still—I
see their point; the lamb corralled for the altar has no right to
stray out among the lions," he added grimly. "Don't worry,
sweet," he told her. "As long as I've sat in the game I'll stick to
the rules."

Olaf's fierce joy in the coming fray—

"The Norns spin close to the end of this web," he rumbled.
"*Ja!* And the threads of Lugur and the Heks woman are between
their fingers for the breaking! Thor will be with me, and I have
fashioned me a hammer in glory of Thor." In his hand was an
enormous mace of black metal, fully five feet long, crowned
with a massive head. "I fashioned it at a forge of the frog-men
from something I found here," he went on, "and it is good. *Ja!*
It is very good"—he whirled it around his head as though it
had been a faggot. He paused, thinking. "But I go not from
here," he continued at last. "No, the gods tell me I shall not.
And it is well. If you go through free, let Larry and the white
maiden have the *Brunhilda*. There are none to mourn me up
there; and I know that mine Hilda is to be freed from death-
in-life, and we go out together as we sailed together—to meet
the *Yndling! Ja!*"

My own perplexity—

Why, when Larry made that choice for himself and Lakla,
had such relief, such joy—almost as though the decision had
freed the Three themselves from a desolating slavery—broken
through their unhuman aloofness? Was there something more
involved in their decision than Lakla had been told? Did the
Silent Ones need that abnegation, that self-sacrifice to strength-

en their own powers? Or was it after all but a test, a trap, prepared for inexplicable reasons of these beings? And if they were as alone as the handmaiden had said—whence had come the cloud of angled, flame-flecked eyes hovering behind her when she had "taken the way" to our home in Yolara's city?

I asked Lakla about this, telling her what I had seen. There was no mistaking the reality of the surprise in her face or the sincerity with which she answered.

"I took the way alone," she told me. "I saw them not, nor did I feel any near me." She hesitated. "But it is strange that you saw such eyes long before you stood before the Three," she murmured. "There are none others like them—here. Now I wonder—can it be—" But she did not tell me what she was wondering.

I pass to the twelve hours' closing.

At the end of the *coria* road where the giant fernland met the edge of the cavern's ruby floor, hundreds of the *Akka* were stationed in ambush, armed with their spears tipped with the rotting death and their nail-studded, metal-headed clubs. These were to attack when the Murians debouched from the *corials*. We had little hope of doing more here than effect some attrition of Yolara's hosts, for at this place the captains of the Shining One could wield the *Keth* and their other uncanny weapons freely. We had learned, too, that every forge and artisan had been put to work to make an armor Von Hetzdorp had devised to withstand the natural battle equipment of the frog-people— and both Larry and I had a disquieting faith in the German's ingenuity.

At any rate the numbers against us would be lessened.

"It's not such a devilish good omen, though," grinned Larry; "this coming down upon us in their motors. I'm not forgetting that the whole German army was turned back by some regiments of Frenchmen who got out to the front in Paris taxicabs when Paris was right in the grip of the Hun hand."

Next, under the direction of the frog-king, levies commanded by subsidiary-chieftains had completed the rows of rough walls along the probable route of the Murians through the cavern. These afforded the *Akka* a fair protection behind which they could hurl their darts and spears—curiously enough they had never developed the bow as a weapon.

At the opening of the cavern the strong barricade we had planned stretched almost to the two ends of the crescent strand; almost, I say, because there had not been time to build it entirely across the mouth.

AND FROM edge to edge of the Titanic bridge, from where it sprang outward at the shore of the Crimson Sea to a hundred feet away from the golden door of the abode, barrier after barrier was piled.

Behind the wall defending the mouth of the cavern waited other thousands of the *Akka*. At each end of the unfinished barricade they were mustered thickly, and at right and left of the crescent where their forests began, more legions were assembled to make way up to the ledge as opportunity offered.

Rank upon rank they manned the bridge barriers; they swarmed over the pinnacles and in the hollows of the island's ragged outer lip; the domed castle was a hive of them, if I may mix my metaphors—and the rocks and gardens that surrounded the abode glittered with them.

In one particular we were very greatly handicapped. None but Lakla could speak the language of the frog-people, and therefore none of us three men—I leave Larry out because of the prohibition laid upon him—could command them.

"But it does not really matter," consoled Lakla. "My *Akka* know not fear, and they will fight each *man* of them to the end."

Upon their stick-at-itiveness, fearlessness, and the sheer weight of their numbers we had, perforce, to rest our hopes. It was primitive strategy, no doubt, but what else could we do? And at last, when all was finished, the handmaiden came to us, rather guiltily, bearing with her frog-woman armsful of metallic robes like that she had worn when she faced Yolara in the banquet hall.

"They are shields against the *Keth*," she explained.

"But, darlin', the Three have said that we need not fear the *Keth* here," objected Larry.

"I know," she said; "but I'd feel much better if you wore one, Larry," she ended defiantly.

"Far be it from me to give you any more worry than you've got," answered the O'Keefe—Larry had become astonishingly gentle, at least so far as Lakla was concerned, ever since that last meeting with the Three—and complaisantly donned one. Rador and I—then Olaf, after a little hesitation—followed his example.

Upon Nak, the Frog King, she threw another, showing him how to cover his great eyes, and then, because the folds came hardly to his knees, she cut the hem from another, stitching it rapidly on with a long needle of curious iridescent metal. Of the robes left there were enough to cover three of his captains— and queer enough the four looked as they strode away, out upon the bridge to take their places at the head of their forces.

"Now," said the handmaiden, "there's nothing else we can do—save wait."

She led us out through her bower and up the little path that ran to the embrasure I have described in a previous chapter. Looking from there, down upon the bridge, over its span, out upon the swarming cavern ledge, I again regretted most intensely the loss of the camera that might have revealed to you so much better than these printed pages the unimaginable sights that I beheld—but enough of these regrets.

We watched, all of us—even Lakla, to whom the sight was at least partly familiar—a little awed. Intensifying the awe was the silence that brooded over the place. There were no boomings or croakings from the frog-men, thrown like a glinting carpet across the span, gleaming dimly on the crescent.

Then through that silence came a sound, a sighing, a half-mournful whispering that beat about us and fled away.

"They come!" cried Lakla, the light of battle in her eyes. Larry drew her to him, raised her in his arms, kissed her.

"A woman!" acclaimed the O'Keefe. "A real woman—and mine!"

He kissed her again; set her upon her feet.

"An' never tell me Lakla's not Irish," he said to me.

With the cry of the Portal the silence was broken definitely. There was movement among the *Akka,* the glint of moving spears, flash of metal-tipped clubs, rattle of horny spurs, rumblings of battle-cries.

And we waited—waited it seemed interminably, gaze fastened upon the low wall across the cavern mouth. Suddenly I remembered the crystal through which I had peered when the hidden assassins had crept upon us. Mentioning it to Lakla she gave a little cry of vexation, a command to her attendant; and not long that faithful if unusual lady had returned with a tray of the glasses. Raising mine I saw the lines furthest away leap into sudden activity. Spurred warrior after warrior leaped upon the barricade and over it. Flashes of intense green light, mingled with gleams like lightning strokes of concentrated moon rays, sprang from behind the wall—sprang and struck and burned upon the scales of the batrachians.

"They come!" whispered Lakla. "They have won through! And they use the *Keth* upon my *Akka!*" Her hands clenched; her eyes blazed.

At the far ends of the crescent a terrific milling had begun. Here it was plain the *Akka* were holding. Faintly, for the distance was great, I could see fresh force upon force rush up and take the places of those who had fallen.

Over each of these ends, and along the whole line of the barricade a mist of dancing, diamonded atoms began to rise; sparkling, coruscating points of diamond dust that darted and danced.

What had once been Lakla's guardians—dancing now in the nothingness!

"God, but it's hard to stay here like this!" groaned the O'Keefe; Olaf's teeth were bared, the lips drawn back in such a fighting grin as his ancestors berserk on their raven ships must have borne; Rador was livid with rage; the handmaiden's nostrils flaring wide, all her wrathful soul in her eyes.

Suddenly, while we looked, the rocky wall which the *Akka* had built at the cavern mouth—was not! It vanished, as though an unseen, unbelievably gigantic hand had with the lightning's speed swept it away. And with it vanished, too, long lines of the great amphibians close behind it. It was sorcery!

Down upon the ledge, dropping into the Crimson Sea, sending up geysers of ruby spray, dashing on the bridge, crushing the frog-men, fell a shower of stone, mingled with distorted shapes and fragments whose scales still flashed meteoric as they hurled from above.

"That which makes things fall upward," hissed Olaf. "That which I saw in the garden of Lugur!"

The fiendish agency of destruction which Von Hetzdorp had revealed to Larry; the force that cut off gravitation and sent all things within its range racing outward into space! My heart chilled—and now over the debris upon the ledge, striking with long sword and daggers, here and there a captain flashing the green ray, moving on in ordered squares, came the soldiers of the Shining One. Nearer and nearer the verge of the ledge they pushed Nak's warriors. Leaping upon the dwarfs, smiting them with spear and club, with teeth and spur, the *Akka* fought like devils. Quivering under the ray they leaped and dragged down and slew. Now there was but one long line of them at the very edge of the cliff.

And ever the clouds of dancing, diamonded atoms grew thicker over them all!

That last thin line of the *Akka* was going; yet they fought to

the last, and none toppled over the lip without at least one of
the armored Murians in his arms.

There, my gaze dropping to the foot of the cliffs, I grew tense
with fascination of horror. Stretched along their length was a
wide ribbon of beauty—a shimmering multitude of gleaming,
pulsing, prismatic moons; glowing, glowing ever brighter, ever
more wondrous—the gigantic Medusae globes feasting on
dwarf and frog-men alike!

Larry was rigid, his eyes dazed; Lakla, arm around his neck,
stood as though turned to stone. Across the waters, faintly, came
a triumphant shouting from Lugur's and Yolara's men!

Was the ruddy light of the place lessening, growing paler,
changing to a faint rose? I rubbed my eyes, thinking that the
strain of watching had dimmed them. No, it was not that. There
was an exclamation from Larry; something like hope relaxed
the drawn muscles of his face. He pointed to the aureate dome
wherein sat the Three—and then I saw!

Out of it, through the long transverse slit through which the
Silent Ones kept their watch on cavern, bridge, and abyss, a
torrent of the opalescent light was pouring. It cascaded like a
waterfall, and as it flowed it spread, whirling out in columns
and eddies, clouds and wisps of misty, curdled coruscations. It
hung like a veil over all the island, filtering everywhere, driving
back the crimson light as though possessed of impenetrable
substance—and still it cast not the faintest shadowing upon
our vision.

"Good God!" breathed Larry. "Look!"

The radiance was marching—*marching*—down the colossal
bridge. It moved swiftly, in some unthinkable way *intelligently*.
It swathed the *Akka*, and closer, ever closer it swept toward the
approach upon which Yolara's men had now gained foothold.

From their ranks came flash after flash of the green ray—
aimed at the abode! But as the light sped and struck the opalescent it was blotted out! The shimmering mists seemed to

enfold, to dissipate it—as, it came to me, the rays of an automobile headlight are checked by fog.

Lakla drew a deep breath.

"The Silent Ones forgive me for doubting them," she whispered; and again hope blossomed on her face even as it did on Larry's.

The frog-men were gaining. Clothed in the armor of that mist they pressed back from the bridge-head the invaders. There was another prodigious movement at the ends of the crescent, and racing up, pressing against the dwarfs, came other legions of Nak's warriors. And reënforcing those out on the prodigious arch, the frog-men stationed in the gardens below us poured back to the castle and out through the open Portal.

"They're licked!" shouted Larry, "They're—"

So quickly I could not follow the movement his automatic leaped to his hand—spoke, once and again and again. Rador leaped to the head of the little path, sword in hand; Olaf, shouting and whirling his mace, followed. I strove to get my own gun quickly.

For up that path were running twoscore of Lugur's men, while from below Lugur's own voice roared.

"Quick! Slay not the handmaiden or her lover! Carry them down. Quick! But slay the others!"

The handmaiden raced toward Larry, stopped, whistled shrilly—again and again. Larry's pistol was empty, but as the dwarfs rushed upon him I dropped two of them with mine. It jammed—I could not use it; I sprang to his side. Rador was down, struggling in a heap of Lugur's men. Olaf, a Viking of old, was whirling his great hammer, and striking, striking through armor, flesh, and bone.

Larry was down, Lakla flew to him. But the Norseman, now streaming blood from a dozen wounds, caught a glimpse of her coming, turned, thrust out a mighty hand, sent her reeling back, and then with his hammer cracked the skulls of those trying to drag the O'Keefe down the path.

A cry from Lakla—the dwarfs had seized her, had lifted her despite her struggles, were carrying her away. One I dropped with the butt of my useless pistol, and then went down myself under the rush of another.

Through the clamor I heard a booming of the *Akka,* closer, closer; then through it the bellow of Lugur. I made a mighty effort, swung a hand up, and sunk my fingers in the throat of the soldier striving to kill me. Writhing over him, my fingers touched a poniard; I thrust it deep, staggered to my feet.

The O'Keefe, shielding Lakla, was battling with a long sword against a half dozen of the soldiers. I started toward him, was struck, and under the impact hurled to the ground. Dizzily I raised myself—and leaning upon my elbow, stared and moved no more. For the dwarfs lay dead, and Larry, holding Lakla tightly, was staring even as I, and ranged at the head of the path were the *Akka,* whose booming advance in obedience to the handmaiden's call I had heard.

And at what we all stared was Olaf, crimson with his wounds, and Lugur, in blood-red armor, locked in each other's grip, struggling, smiting, tearing, kicking, and swaying about the little space before the embrasure. I crawled over toward the O'Keefe. He raised his pistol, dropped it. "Can't hit him without hitting Olaf," he whispered. Lakla signaled the frog-men; they advanced toward the two—but Olaf saw them, broke the red dwarf's hold, sent Lugur reeling a dozen feet away.

"No!" shouted the Norseman, the ice of his pale-blue eyes glinting like frozen flames, blood streaming down his face and dripping from his hands. "No! Lugur is mine! None but me slays him! Ho, you Lugur—" and cursed him and Yolara and the Dweller madly, hideously—I cannot set those curses down here.

They spurred Lugur. Mad now as the Norseman, the red dwarf sprang. Olaf struck a blow that would have killed an ordinary man, but Lugur only grunted, swept in and seized him about the waist; one mighty arm began to creep up toward Huldricksson's throat

" 'Ware, Olaf!" cried O'Keefe; but Olaf did not answer. He waited until the red dwarf's hand was close to his shoulder; and then, with an incredibly rapid movement—once before had I seen something like it in a wrestling match between Papuans— he had twisted Lugur around; twisted him so that Olaf's right arm lay across the tremendous breast, the left behind the neck, and Olaf's left leg held the Voice's armored thighs viselike against his right knee while over that knee lay the small of the red dwarf's back.

For a second or two the Norseman looked down upon his enemy, motionless in that paralyzing grip. And then—slowly— he began to break him!

Lakla gave a little cry; made a motion toward the two. But Larry drew her head down against his breast, hiding her eyes; then fastened his own upon the pair, white-faced, stern.

Slowly, ever so slowly, proceeded Olaf. Twice Lugur moaned. At the end he screamed—horribly. There was a cracking sound, as of a stout stick snapped.

Huldricksson stooped, silently. He picked up the limp body of the Voice, not yet dead, for the eyes rolled, the lips strove to speak; lifted it, walked to the parapet, swung it twice over his head, and cast it down to the red waters!

CHAPTER XXXIX

AND THEN—

THE NORSEMAN TURNED toward us. There was now no madness in his eyes; only a great weariness. And there was peace on the once tortured face.

"Helma," he whispered, "I go a little before! Soon you will come to me—to me and the *Yndling*—who will await you— Helma, mine *liebe!*"

Blood gushed from his mouth; he swayed, fell. And thus died Olaf Huldricksson, one of those upon whom the Dweller's blight had fallen, helping to save his fellow men from the Dweller's soul-destroying curse; simple-hearted as a child, faithful, fearless, worthy of any of his conquering forefathers, and passing away even as they would have elected to go—and in their ancient faith. Wounds enough to have killed four lesser men he had got in that battle wherein, without him, Lugur's men could not have been held; and even now my marveling how even his strength could have been great enough to do what he did with the red dwarf is not dulled.

We looked down upon him; nor did Lakla, nor Larry, nor I try to hide our tears. And as we stood the *Akka* brought to us that other mighty fighter, Rador; but in him there was life, and we attended to him there as best we could.

Then Lakla spoke.

"We will bear him into the castle where we may give him greater care," she said. "For, lo! the hosts of Yolara have been beaten back; and on the bridge comes Nak with tidings."

We looked over the parapet. It was even as she had said. Neither on ledge nor bridge was there trace of living men of Muria—only heaps of slain that lay everywhere—and thick against the cavern mouth danced the flashing atoms of those the green ray had destroyed. About the dead, casting them down to the Crimson Sea and its elf-moon feasters, thronged the *Akka.*

"Over!" exclaimed Larry incredulously. "We live then—heart of mine!"

"The Silent Ones recall their veils," she said, pointing to the dome. Back through the slitted opening the radiance was streaming; withdrawing from sea and island; marching back over the bridge with that same ordered, intelligent motion. Behind it the red light pressed, like skirmishers on the heels of a retreating army.

"And yet—" faltered Lakla, and was silent. We fell in behind the unconscious Rador, the dead Olaf, both in the arms of the batrachians; and there was nothing of jubilance in any of our three hearts.

"And yet—" repeated the handmaiden as we passed into her chamber, and doubtful were the eyes she turned upon the O'Keefe.

"I don't believe there's a kick left in them," said he. "That was some stunt the Three pulled off, Doc. Wish I knew about one-millionth as much as they do. Now for the expeditionary force into the hellhole we peeped into—and cheer-o for those friends of yours, old boy; never doubt it—"

What was that sound beating into the chamber, faintly, so faintly? My heart gave a great throb and seemed to stop for an eternity. What was it—coming nearer, ever nearer? Now Lakla and O'Keefe heard it, stiffened, life ebbing from lips and cheeks.

Nearer, nearer—a music as of myriads of tiny crystal bells, tinkling, tinkling—a storm of pizzicati upon violins of glass! Nearer, nearer—not sweetly now, nor luring; no—raging, wrathful, sinister beyond words; sweeping on; nearer—

The Dweller! The Shining One!

We leaped to the narrow window; peered out, aghast. The bell notes swept through and about us, a hurricane. The crescent strand was once more a ferment. Back, back were the *Akka* being swept, as though by brooms, tottering on the edge of the ledge, falling into the waters. Swiftly they were finished; and where they had fought was an eddying throng of women and men, clothed in tatters or wholly nude, swaying, drifting, arms tossing—like marionettes of Satan.

The dead-alive! The slaves of the Dweller!

They swayed and tossed, and then, like water racing through an opened dam, they swept upon the bridge-head. On and on they pushed, like the bore of a mighty tide. The frog-men strove against them, clubbing, spearing, tearing them. But even those worst smitten seemed not to fall. On they pushed, driving forward, irresistible—a battering ram of flesh and bone. They clove the masses of the *Akka*, pressing them to the sides of the bridge and over. Nor did the fact that every huge amphibian that fell carried in his horny arms one of them seem to lessen

their numbers. Back and back they forced those of Nak's warriors who still found footing on the span. Through the open
Portal they forced them—for there was no room for the frog-
men to stand against that implacable tide.

Then those of the *Akka* who were left turned their backs and
ran. We heard the clang of the golden wings of the gateway,
and none too soon to keep out the first of the Dweller's dreadful hordes.

Now upon the cavern ledge and over the whole length of
the bridge there were none but the dead-alive, men and women,
black-polled *ladala*, sloe-eyed Malays, slant-eyed Chinese, men
of every race that sailed the seas—milling, turning, swaying,
like leaves caught in a sluggish current.

The bell notes became sharper, more insistent. At the cavern
mouth a radiance began to grow—a gleaming from which the
atoms of diamond dust seemed to try to fly. And now occurred
what to me was the ghastliest incident—save one, which I have
yet to relate—of all this incredible scene. As the radiance grew
and the crystal notes rang nearer, every head of that hideous
multitude turned stiffly, slowly toward the right, looking toward
the far bridge end; their eyes fixed and glaring; every face an
inhuman mask of rapture and of horror!

A movement shook them, as though at some command.
Those in the center began to stream back, faster and ever faster,
leaving motionless deep ranks on each side. Back they flowed
until from golden doors to cavern mouth a wide lane stretched,
walled on each side by the dead-alive.

The far radiance grew brighter still; it gathered itself at the
end of the gruesome lane; it was shot with sparklings and with
pulsings of polychromatic light. The crystal storm grew intolerable, piercing the ears with countless tiny lances; brighter still
the radiance—

From the cavern swirled the Shining One!

The Dweller paused, seemed to scan the island of the Silent
Ones half doubtfully; then slowly, stately, it drifted out upon

the bridge. My hand was gripped in a bitter clasp; I saw Larry was holding it. Closer drew the Shining One; behind it glided Yolara at the head of a company of her dwarfs, and at her side was the hag of the council whose face was the withered, shattered echo of her own.

Slower grew the Dweller's pace as it drew nearer. Did I sense in it a doubt, an uncertainty? The crystal-tongued, unseen choristers that accompanied it subtly seemed to reflect the doubt; their notes were not sure, no longer insistent; rather was there in them an undertone of hesitancy, of warning! Yet on came the Shining One until it stood plain beneath us, searching with those eyes that thrust from and withdrew into unknown spheres, the golden gateway, the cliff face, the castle's rounded bulk—and more intently than any of these, the dome wherein sat the Three.

Behind it each face of the dead-alive turned toward it, and those beside it throbbed and gleamed with its luminescence.

Yolara crept close, just beyond the reach of its spirals. Rosy shone her flesh through her gossamer veils, blue as pale sapphires were her eyes, and in the radiance of the Shining One the coronal of corn-silk tresses sparkled. Once more, even in our deadly peril, I realized how beautiful was the priestess. She raised her face, looking straight toward where we watched, as though her glance had been summoned by our gaze. She murmured—and the head of the Dweller bent toward her, its seven globes steady in their shining mists, as though listening. It listened, drew itself erect once more, resumed its doubtful scrutiny. Yolara's face darkened; she turned abruptly, spoke to a captain of her guards. A dwarf raced back between the palisades of dead-alive.

Now the priestess cried out, her voice ringing like a silver clarion.

"Ye are done, ye Three! The Shining One stands at your door, demanding entrance. Your beasts are slain and your power is gone. Who are ye, says the Shining One, to deny it entrance to the place of its birth?" There was biting mockery in this last.

"Now will ye open your doors and let us pass, or must we open them for ye?" She paused. No answer came from those upon whom she was calling.

"Ye do not answer," she cried again, "yet know we that ye hear! The Shining One offers these terms: Send forth your handmaiden and that lying stranger she stole; send them forth to us—and perhaps ye may live. But if ye send them not forth, then shall ye too die—and soon!"

An odd paralysis had gripped us, but it was not of fear. None of fear did I feel—at least none for myself—and searching the eyes of Lakla and Larry, I saw no trace of it in either. Rather was it an inhibition—something that stilled all desire to speak, as though a hand had been laid over my mouth. We waited, silent, even as did Yolara—and again there was no answer from the Three.

The priestess laughed; the blue eyes flashed.

"It is ended!" she cried. "If you will not open, needs must we open for you!"

Over the bridge was marching a long double file of the dwarfs. They bore a smoothed and handled tree-trunk whose head was knobbed with a huge ball of metal. Past the priestess, past the Shining One, they carried it; fifty of them to each side of the ram; and behind them stepped—Von Hetzdorp!

Larry awoke to life.

"Now, thank God," he rasped, "I can get the Hun, anyway!"

He drew his pistol, took careful aim. Even as he pressed the trigger there rang through the abode a tremendous clanging. The ram was battering at the gates. O'Keefe's bullet went wild. The German must have heard the shot; perhaps the missile was closer than we knew. He made a swift leap behind the guards, was lost to sight.

Once more the thunderous clanging rang through the castle.

Lakla drew herself erect; down upon her dropped the listening aloofness. Gravely she bowed her head.

"It is time, O love of mine." She turned to O'Keefe. "The

Silent Ones say that the way of fear is closed, but the way of love is open. They call upon us to redeem our promise!"

For a hundred heart-beats they clung to each other, breast to breast and lip to lip. Below, the clangor was increasing, the great trunk swinging harder and faster upon the metal gates. Now Lakla gently loosed the arms of the O'Keefe, and for another instant those two looked deep into each other's souls. The handmaiden smiled tremulously.

"I would it might have been otherwise, Larry darlin'," she whispered. "But at least—we pass together, dearest of mine!"

She leaped to the window.

"Yolara!" the golden voice rang out sweetly. The clanging ceased. "Draw back your men. We open the Portal and come forth to you and the Shining One—Larry and I."

The priestess's silver chimes of laughter rang out, cruel, mocking.

"Come, then, and quickly," she jeered. "For surely both the Shining One and I have long yearned for you!" Her malice-laden laughter chimed high once more. "Keep us not lonely long!" the priestess mocked.

Larry drew a deep breath, stretched both hands out to me.

"It's good-by, I guess, Doc." His voice was strained. "Good-by and good luck, old boy. If you get out, and you will, let the old *Dolphin* know I'm gone. And carry on, pal—and always remember the O'Keefe loved you like a brother."

I squeezed his hands desperately. Then out of my balance-shaking wo a strange comfort was born.

"Maybe it's not good-by, Larry!" I cried. "The banshee has not cried!"

A flash of hope passed over his face; the old reckless grin shone forth.

"It's so!" he said. "By the Lord, it's so!"

Then Lakla bent toward me, and for the second time—kissed me.

"Come!" she said to Larry. Hand in hand they moved away, into the corridor that led to the door outside of which waited the Shining One and its priestess.

And unseen by them, wrapped as they were within their love and sacrifice, I crept softly behind. For I had determined that if enter the Dweller's embrace they must, they should not go alone. There was no one to mourn for me—and it had come clearly to my mind that without them I did not care to live. Nothing of this had I spoken—for well I knew that they would have forbidden it.

They paused before the Golden Portals; the handmaiden pressed its opening lever; the massive leaves rolled back.

Heads high, proudly, serenely, they passed through and out upon the hither span. I followed.

On each side of us stood the Dweller's slaves, faces turned rigidly toward their master. A hundred feet away the Shining One pulsed and spiraled in its evilly glorious lambency of sparkling plumes.

Unhesitating, always with that same high serenity, Lakla and the O'Keefe, hands clasped like little children, drew closer to that wondrous shape of nebulous flame. I could not see their faces, but I saw awe fall upon those of the watching dwarfs, and into the burning eyes of Yolara crept a doubt. Closer they drew to the Dweller, and closer, I following them step by step. The Shining One's whirling lessened; its tinklings were faint, almost stilled. It seemed to watch them apprehensively. A silence fell upon us all, a thick silence, brooding, ominous, palpable. Now the pair were face to face with the child of the Three—so near that with one of its misty tentacles it could have enfolded them.

And the Shining One drew back!

Yes, drew back—and back with it stepped Yolara, the doubt in her eyes deepening. Onward paced the handmaiden and the O'Keefe—and step by step, as they advanced, the Dweller withdrew; its bell notes chiming out, puzzled, questioning—half fearful!

And back it drew, and back until it had reached the very center of that platform over the abyss in whose depths pulsed the green fires of earth heart. And there Yolara gripped herself; the hell that laughed within her soul leaped out of her eyes; a cry, a shriek of rage, tore from her lips.

As at a signal, the Shining One flamed high; its spirals and eddying mists swirled madly, the pulsing core of it blazed radiance. A score of coruscating tentacles swept straight upon the pair who stood intrepid, unresisting, awaiting its embrace. And upon me, lurking behind them.

Through me swept a mighty exaltation. It was the end then—and I was to meet it with them.

Something drew us back, back with an incredible swiftness, and yet as gently as a summer breeze sweeps a bit of thistle-down! Drew us back from those darting misty arms even as they were a hair-breadth from us! I heard the Dweller's bell notes burst out ragingly; I heard Yolara scream.

What was that?

Between the three of us and them was a ring of curdled moon flames, swirling about the Shining One and its priestess, pressing in upon them, enfolding them!

And within it I glimpsed the faces of the Three—implacable, sorrowful, filled with a supernal power!

Sparks and flashes of white flame darted from the ring, penetrating the radiant swathings of the Dweller, striking through its pulsing nucleus, piercing its seven crowning orbs.

Now the Shining One's radiance began to lessen, the seven orbs to dull; the tiny sparkling filaments that ran from them down into the Dweller's body snapped, vanished! Through the battling nebulosities Yolara's face swam forth—horror-filled, distorted, inhuman!

The ranks of the dead-alive quivered, moved, writhed, as though each felt the torment of the Thing that had enslaved them. The radiance that the Three wielded grew more intense, thicker, seemed to expand. Within it, suddenly, were scores of flaming triangles—scores of eyes like those of the Silent Ones!

And the Shining One's seven little moons of amber, of silver, of blue and amethyst and green, of rose and white, split, shattered, were gone! Abruptly the tortured crystal chimings ceased.

And dulled, all its soul-shaking beauty dead, blotched, and shadowed squalidly, its gleaming plumes tarnished, its dancing spirals stripped from it, that which had been the Shining One wrapped itself about Yolara—wrapped and drew her into itself; writhed, swayed, and hurled itself over the edge of the bridge— down, down into the green fires of the unfathomable abyss— with its priestess still enfolded in its coils!

From the soldiers who, rigid as stone, had watched that terror came crazed screams of panic fear. They turned and ran, racing frantically over the bridge toward the cavern mouth.

The serried ranks of the dead-alive trembled, shook. Then from their faces fled the horror of wedded ecstasy and anguish. Peace, utter peace, followed eventually in its wake.

And as fields of wheat are bent and fall beneath the wind, they fell. No longer dead-alive, now all of the blessed dead, freed from their dreadful slavery!

We stood, Lakla and I, silent, stunned, half dead ourselves through the tearfulness of it all; souls well-nigh blasted by what we had seen—and saw.

Abruptly from the sparkling mists the cloud of eyes was gone. Faintly revealed in them were only the heads of the Silent Ones. And they drew before us; were before us! No flames now in their ebon eyes—for the flickering fires were quenched in great tears, streaming down the marble white faces. They bent toward us, over us; their radiance enfolded us. My eyes darkened. I could not see. I felt a tender hand upon my head—and panic and frozen dread and nightmare web that held me fled.

I was happy!

Then they, too, were gone.

Far away was a great shouting. Over the body-strewn crescent strand came pouring regiments of the *Akka;* out of the cavern mouth upon the bridge marched companies of the *ladala.*

Upon Larry's breast the handmaiden was sobbing—sobbing out her heart—but this time with the joy of one who is swept up from the very threshold of hell into paradise.

CHAPTER XL

VON HETZDORP STRIKES!

"MY HEART, LARRY—" It was the handmaiden's murmur. "My heart feels like a bird that is flying from a nest of sorrow."

We were pacing down the length of the bridge, guards of the *Akka* beside us, others following with those companies of the *ladala* that had rushed to aid us; in front of us the bandaged Rador swung gently within a litter; beside him, in another, lay Nak, the frog king—much less of him than there had been before the battle began, but living.

Hours had passed since the terror I have just related. My first task had been to search for Throckmartin and his wife among the fallen multitudes strewn thick as autumn leaves along the flying arch of stone, over the cavern ledge, and back, back as far as the eye could reach. Had they been of those who, clutched in the arms of the amphibians, had dropped by the thousand into the red waters where now myriad upon myriad of the giant Medusae feasted and gleamed? Fervently I prayed that their bodies had been spared that at least.

At last, Lakla and Larry helping, we found them. They lay close to the bridge-end, not parted—locked tight in each other's arms, pallid face to face, her hair streaming over his breast! As though when that unearthly life the Dweller had set within them passed away, their own had come back for one fleeting instant—and they had known each other, and clasped before kindly death had taken them.

"Love is stronger than all things." The handmaiden was

weeping softly. "Love never left them. Love was stronger than the Shining One. And when its evil fled, love went with them—wherever souls go."

Of Stanton and Thora there was no trace; nor, after our discovery of those other two, did I care to look more. They were dead—and they were free.

We buried Throckmartin and Edith beside Olaf in Lakla's bower. But before the body of my old friend was placed within the grave I gave it a careful and sorrowful examination. The skin was firm and smooth, but cold; not the cold of death, but with a chill that set my touching fingers tingling unpleasantly. The body was bloodless; the course of veins and arteries marked by faintly indented white furrows, as though their walls had long collapsed. Lips, mouth, even the tongue, was paper-white. Yet there was no sign of dissolution as we know it; no shadow or stain upon the marble surface. Whatever the force that, streaming from the Dweller or impregnating its lair, had energized the dead-alive, it was barrier against putrescence of any kind; that at least was certain.

But it was not barrier against the poison of the Medusa, for, our sad task done, and looking down upon the waters, I saw the pale forms of the Dweller's hordes dissolving, vanishing into the shifting glories of the gigantic moons sailing down upon them from every quarter of the Sea of Crimson.

While the frog-men, those late levies from the farthest forests, were clearing bridge and ledge of cavern of the litter of the dead, we listened to the leader of the *ladala*. They had risen, even as the messenger had promised Rador. Fierce had been the struggle in the gardened city by the silver waters with those Lugur and Yolara had left behind to garrison it. Deadly had been the slaughter of the fair-haired, reaping the harvest of hatred they had been sowing so long. Not without a pang of regret did I think of the beautiful, gaily malicious elfin women destroyed—evil though they may have been.

The ancient city of Lara, where the enigmatic *Taithu* had

dwelt before the Murians came to it, was a charnel. Of all the rulers not twoscore had escaped, and these into regions of peril which to describe as sanctuary would be mockery. Nor had the *ladala* escaped so well. Of all the men and women, for women as well as men had taken their part in the swift war, not more then a tenth remained alive.

And the dancing motes of light in the silver air were thick, thick—they whispered.

They told us of the Shining One rushing through the Veil, cometlike, its hosts streaming behind it, raging with it, in ranks that seemed interminable!

Of the massacre of the priests and priestesses in the Cyclopean temple; of the flashing forth of the summoning lights by some unseen hands—followed by the tearing of the rainbow curtain, by colossal shatterings of the radiant cliffs; the vanishing behind their debris of all trace of entrance to the haunted place wherein the hordes of the Shining One had slaved—the sealing of the lair!

Then, when the tempest of hate had ended in immortal Lara, how, thrilled with victory, armed with the weapons of those they had slain, they had lifted the Shadow, passed through the Portal, met and slaughtered the fleeing remnants of Yolara's men—only to find the tempest stilled here, too.

But of Von Hetzdorp they had seen nothing! Had the German escaped, I wondered, or was he lying out there among the dead? But how could he have escaped? And even should he by some miracle be able to pass the Portal, what chance was there for him beyond? None, it seemed to me; and slender indeed the chance that he had survived the debacle. Still, it was strange that none of these had seen him with those fear-crazed troops racing straight into their arms.

But now the *ladala* were calling upon Lakla to come with them, to govern them.

"I don't want to, Larry darlin'," she told him. "I want to go out with you to Ireland. But for a time—I think the Three would have us remain and set that place in order."

The O'Keefe was bothered about something else than the government of Muria.

"If they've killed off all the priests, who's to marry us, heart of mine?" he worried. "None of those Siya and Siyana rites, no matter what," he added hastily.

"Marry!" cried the handmaiden incredulously. "Marry us? Why, Larry dear, we *are* married!"

The O'Keefe's astonishment was complete; his jaw dropped; collapse seemed imminent.

"We are?" he gasped. "When?" he stammered fatuously.

"Why, when the mother drew us together before her; when she put her hands on our heads after we had made the promise! Didn't you understand that?" asked the handmaiden wonderingly.

He looked at her, into the purity of the clear golden eyes, into the purity of the soul that gazed out of them; all his own great love tranfiguring his keen face.

"An' is that enough for you, *mavourneen?*" he whispered humbly.

"Enough?" The handmaiden's puzzlement was complete, profound. "Enough! Larry darlin', what more could we ask?"

He drew a deep breath, clasped her close.

"Kiss the bride, Doc!" cried the O'Keefe. And for the third and, soul's sorrow! the last time, Lakla dimpling and blushing, I thrilled to the touch of her soft, sweet lips.

"As soon as we get up above, it's straight to a Christian altar we go," murmured Larry to me. "But what she says is so. Nothing holier than what I felt when the woman blessed us do I ever expect to know, even"—he laughed a bit shakily—"if I didn't realize it was a married man she was making me."

Quickly were our preparations for departure made. Rador, conscious, his immense vitality conquering fast his wounds, was to be borne ahead of us. And when all was done Lakla, Larry, and I made our way up to the scarlet stone that was the doorway to the chamber of the Three. We knew, of course, that they had gone, following, no doubt, those whose eyes I had seen in the curdled mists, and who, coming to the aid of the Three at last from whatever mysterious place that was their home, had thrown their strength with them against the Shining One. Nor were we wrong. When the great slab rolled away, no torrents of opalescence came rushing out upon us. The vast dome was dim, tenantless; its curved walls that had cascaded light shone now but faintly; the dais was empty; its wall of moon-flame radiance gone.

A little time we stood, heads bent, reverent, our hearts filled with gratitude and love—yes, and with pity for that strange trinity so alien to us and yet so near; children even as we, though so unlike us, of our same Mother Earth.

And what I wondered had been the secret of that promise they had wrung from their handmaiden and from Larry. And whence, if what the Three had said had been all true—whence had come their power to avert the sacrifice at the very verge of its consummation? Had it been a test of these two—a test as unconscious in its cruelty as any of those exacted by Divinity, the stories of which fill the legends of mankind? The comparison is not irreverent—for in wisdom, as compared to mankind, the Three were divine.

"Love is stronger than all things!" had said Lakla.

Was it that they had needed, must have, the force which dwells within love, within willing sacrifice, to strengthen their own power and to enable them to destroy the evil, glorious Thing so long shielded by their own love? Did the thought of sacrifice, the will toward abnegation, have to be as strong as the eternals, unshaken by faintest thrill of hope, before the Three could make of it their key to unlock the Dweller's guard and strike through at its life?

Here was a mystery—a mystery indeed!

Then Lakla softly closed the crimson stone and we passed down—down the corridors, out of the abode, to where, upon the span, a few score of the handmaiden's own black-and-or-

ange-scaled warriors awaited us. They were those who had been
pressed back into the castle by the onrush of the dead-alive and
those who had remained to garrison the island after Lugur's
surprise attack. The mystery of the red dwarf's appearance was
explained when we discovered a half-dozen of the water *coria*
moored in a small cove not far from where the *Sekta* flashed
their heads of living bloom. The dwarfs had borne the shallops
with them, and from somewhere beyond the cavern ledge had
launched them unperceived; stealing up to the farther side of
the island and risking all in one bold stroke. Well, Lugur, no
matter what he held of wickedness, held also high courage.

"Yes, Larry darlin'," said Lakla, "my heart is like a bird, free
from sorrow and singing."

"And mine's singing so I can hardly get my breath; an' why
not, when the pulse of my heart is you, *acushla*," wooed the
O'Keefe.

"An' I hope it's now you have no more doubt about the
O'Keefe banshee." He turned to me with his old fire.

"Doubt?" I asked mildly.

"Yes, doubt!" he repeated. "The old lady's given you proof
enough for even your incredulous mind, old dear."

"Proof?" I asked again, perplexed. "But I saw no proof of her,
Larry."

"You didn't!" he cried. "Well, she didn't come, did she?"

"No," I acquiesced.

"And I'm alive, ain't I?" triumphantly. "Well, then, do you
want any more proof than that?"

Another picture—a vision of what might have been—flashed
before me.

"I do not, Larry," I answered. "I concede the banshee. I want
no more proof."

The cavern was paved with the dead-alive, the *Akka* carrying
them out by the hundreds, casting them into the waters.
Through the lane down which the Dweller had passed we went
as quickly as we could, coming at last to the space where the

coria waited. Rador and the frog-king we placed in our own, where sat too the little frog-prince and Lakla's woman monster. Speeding toward the Portal, my eyes were busy with the marvels of the fernland. I promised myself speedy return and exploration. We reached the entrance all too soon. No sign did I see of the dragon worm. Asking Lakla, I learned that its wanderings were limited; that along the *coria* road certain plants through which it would not go grew thickly.

"It is the guardian of the other paths," she said. "There are others—not many; it is said that they were brought here by the people of the Three—after that which I have told you happened—and the Portal was closed upon them."

Rather nervously I mentioned that I hoped we could find a way to get rid of the Things, now that all was peace; that in fact I did not believe I could carry on my investigations here with an entirely easy mind with them crawling around.

"They can be slain," she assured me. "I know the means. We shall hunt them ourselves, Goodwin!"

This did not entirely set me at ease. I must admit, having no great desire to meet again the dragon worm at any distance. I managed, however, to suppress my apprehensions and to thank her. And not long after we swung past where the shadow had hung and hovered over the shining depths of the Midnight Pool.

Here the bodies of the green dwarfs lay thick. Guards from the *ladala* manned the ebon fortresses and the bridge. Loud were their shouts of welcome to us, and clamorous the greetings of the throngs that lined the emerald road as we swept out upon it.

Upon Lakla's insistence we passed on to the palace of Lugur, not to Yolara's—I do not know why, but go there then she would not. And within one of its columned rooms maidens of the black-haired folks, the wistfulness, the fear, all gone from their sparkling eyes, served us. It was a silent meal; both Larry and Lakla so busy with handclasp, with little whisperings, and so taken up drinking in each other, that I felt rather sorrowfully malapropos and lonely. Walking to the side, I looked out upon the frowning wall of the temple, not more than a quarter of a mile away.

There came to me a huge desire to see the destruction they had told us of the Dweller's lair; to observe for myself whether it was not possible to make a way of entrance and to study its mysteries.

I spoke of this, and to my surprise both the handmaiden and the O'Keefe showed an almost embarrassed haste to acquiesce in my hesitant suggestion.

"Sure," cried Larry, "there's lots of time before night!"

He caught himself sheepishly; cast a glance at Lakla.

"I keep forgettin' there's no night here," he mumbled.

"What did you say, Larry?" asked she.

"I said I wish we were sitting in our home in Ireland, watching the sun go down," he whispered to her. Vaguely I wondered why she blushed.

But now I must hasten. We went to the temple; and here at least the ghastly litter of the dead had been cleaned away. We passed through the blue-caverned space, crossed the narrow arch that spanned the rushing sea stream, and, ascending, stood again upon the ivoried pave at the foot of the frowning, towering amphitheater of jet.

Across the Silver Waters there was sign of neither Web of Rainbows nor colossal pillars nor the templed lips that I had seen curving out beneath the Veil when the Shining One had swirled out to greet its priestess and its voice and to dance with the condemned. There was but a broken and rent mass of the radiant cliffs against whose base the lake lapped.

Long I looked—and turned away saddened. Knowing even as I did what the irised curtain had hidden, still it was as though some thing of supernal beauty and wonder had been swept away, never to be replaced; a glamour gone forever; a work of the high gods destroyed.

"Let's go back," said Larry abruptly.

"How long, Larry, do you think we'll stay here?" I asked.

"Not a minute longer than we can help, I'll say that," he answered forcibly.

"We can return, I suppose, by the passageway from the Moon Pool?" I said.

He nodded.

"I asked Lakla," he replied; "she says yes."

I dropped a little behind them to examine a bit of carving—and, after all, they did not want me. I watched them pacing slowly ahead, his arm around her, black curls close to bronze-gold ringlets. Then I followed. Half were they over the bridge when through the roar of the imprisoned stream I heard my name called softly.

"Goodwin! Dr. Goodwin!"

Amazed, I turned. From behind the pedestal of a carved group slunk—Von Hetzdorp! My premonition had been right. Some way he had escaped, slipped through to here. He held his hands high, came forward cautiously.

"I am finished," he whispered—*"kaput!* I don't know what *they'll* do to me." He nodded toward the handmaiden and Larry, now at the end of the bridge and passing on, oblivious of all save each other. He drew closer. His eyes were sunken, burning, mad; his face etched with deep lines, as though a graver's tool had cut down through it. I took a step backward.

A grin, like the grimace of a fiend, blasted the German's visage. He threw himself upon me, his hands clenching at my throat!

"Larry!" I yelled—and as I spun around under the shock of his onslaught, saw the two turn, stand paralyzed, then race toward me.

"But *you'll* carry nothing out of here!" shrieked Von Hetzdorp. "No, by God!"

My foot, darting out behind me, touched vacancy. The roaring of the racing sea stream deafened me. I felt its mists about me; threw myself forward.

I was falling—falling—with the German's hands strangling me. I struck water, sank; the hands that gripped my throat relaxed for a moment their clutch. I strove to writhe loose; felt that I was being hurled with dreadful speed on—full realization came—on the breast of that racing torrent dropping from some far ocean cleft and rushing—where? A little time, a few breathless instants, I struggled with the devil who clutched me—inflexibly, indomitably.

Then a shrieking as of all the pent winds of the universe in my ears—blackness!

Consciousness returned slowly, agonizedly.

"Larry!" I groaned. "Lakla!"

A brilliant light was glowing through my closed lids. It hurt. I opened my eyes, closed them with swords and needles of dazzling pain shooting through them. Again I opened them cautiously. It was the sun!

I staggered to my feet. Behind me was a shattered wall of basalt monoliths, hewn and squared. Before me was the Pacific, smooth and blue and smiling.

And not far away, cast up on the strand even as I had been, was—Von Hetzdorp! Von Hetzdorp, following me to the last— but dead! But was he dead? I tottered toward him, my hands flexing and clawing—for if he had not passed, then surely was whatever spark of life might be within him of short tenure. For I had but one thought—to cast myself upon his throat and choke life from him; yes, even though he lay there helpless.

And I would have done it! But there was no need. He lay there, broken and dead indeed. Yet all the waters through which we had passed—not even the waters of death themselves— could wash from his face the hideous grin of triumph. With the last of my strength I dragged the body from the strand and pushed it out into the waves. A little billow ran up, coiled about it, and carried it away, ducking and bending. Another seized it, and another, playing with it. It floated from my sight—that which had been Von Hetzdorp, with all his wicked schemes to turn our fair world into an undreamed-of hell.

My strength began to come back to me. I found a thicket and slept; slept it must have been for many hours, for when I again awakened the dawn was rosing the east. I will not tell my sufferings. Suffice it to say that I found a spring and some fruit, and just before dusk had recovered enough to writhe up to the top of the wall and discover where I was.

The place was one of the farther islets of the Nan-Matal. To the north I caught the shadow of the ruins of Nan-Tauach, where was the Moon door, black against the sky. Where was the Moon door—which, someway, somehow, I must reach, and quickly! But I had no boat, and over all the waters there was no sign of life; and well I knew none would go by this haunted place at night, or if they did, would dare to respond to the call of my fire.

So at dawn of the next day I got together driftwood and bound it together in shape of a rough raft with fallen creepers. Then, with a makeshift paddle, I set forth for Nan-Tauach. Slowly, painfully, I crept up to it. It was late afternoon before I grounded my shaky craft on the little beach between the ruined sea gates and, creeping up the giant steps, made my way to the inner enclosure.

And at its opening I stopped, and the tears ran streaming down my cheeks while I wept aloud with sorrow and with disappointment and with weariness.

For the great wall in which had been set the pale slab whose threshold we had crossed to the land of the Shining One lay shattered and broken. The monoliths were heaped about; the wall had fallen, and about them shone a film of water, half covering them.

There was no Moon door!

Dazed and weeping, I drew closer, climbed upon their out-lying fragments. I looked out upon the sea. There had been a great subsidence, an earth shock perhaps, tilting downward all that side—the echo, little doubt, of that cataclysm which had blasted the Dweller's lair!

The little squared islet called Tau, in which was hidden the seven globes of Moon flame summoning the Dweller, had entirely disappeared. Upon the waters there was no trace of it.

MOON DOOR was gone; the passage to the Moon Pool was closed to me—its chamber covered by the sea!

There was no road to Larry—nor to Lakla!

This, you who have listened to me so long, is the end of my narrative.

There, for me, the world ended. A canoe of native fishermen, two days later, picked me up. At Ponape I found that the *Dolphin* had never called, that there were rumors of her having been lost in a typhoon, rumors that I afterward verified. The *Brunhilda* I left with the Chinaman who had guarded her so faithfully. I returned to find the interest in my first narrative so great that I knew it to be no other than my plain duty to reveal to what the happenings I had related in it led.

And this I have done truthfully, as fully as I might.

And as a labor of love, a monument to those two bright spirits who I do believe saved this world of ours from unthinkable disaster—

Larry O'Keefe and Lakla, the handmaiden!

Shall I ever see them again? Shall the world ever see them to do them that homage which they deserve?

I do not know.

But this I am sure. In that far land of mystery which seems now so irrevocably set apart from us they live—and are happy—gathering the fruit of their love and their high courage.

As for me—my heart is heavy, and I have much to do preparing the data I gathered in that too short time—hardly a month—for the study of my colleagues of the International

Association of Science; the results of which will no doubt from time to time be placed before the public as it seems wise.

Echoing the words of one of America's immortals, Samuel J. Tilden, paraphrasing a little perhaps his thought, I say: "Having borne faithfully my full share of labor and care in the public service, and wearing the marks of its burdens, I seek the repose of private life."

With my heartfelt thanks to you, and to the editor of the *All-Story Weekly* for his exceeding kindness and courtesy to me, to my associates who have assisted me in this narrative, and, not least, to Mr. Merritt for his guidance and always ungrudging aid, I bid you all—

Farewell!

A. MERRITT (1884–1943)

ABRAHAM GRACE MERRITT was a prominent journalist and editor, as well as one of the premier fantasists of the early Twentieth Century. His handful of novels are noted for their lushly descriptive prose, which the author employed to bring to vibrant life his novels of lost civilizations, preternatural beings, heroic protagonists and exotic gods and goddesses. A sense of spiritual wonder mixed with metaphysical horror infuses his primary works, which are among the earliest science-fantasy novels to delve into the realm of disturbing alien contacts.

Debuting modestly with a 1917 short story, "Through the Dragon Glass," Merritt electrified readers with his ethereal novelette of otherwordly entities haunting an ancient ruin, "The Moon Pool," which appeared in *All-Story Weekly*, June 22, 1918. A novel-length sequel, *The Conquest of the Moon Pool*, followed. In 1919, both tales were revised into a unified work. The story's protagonist, Dr. Walter T. Goodwin, returned in *The Metal Monster*, a 1920 epic of utterly alien beings composed of sentient metal dwelling high in the Himalayan Mountains. With their cross-dimensional incursions and cosmic terrors, these works deeply impressed H.P. Lovecraft, who borrowed from them in creating his early Cthulhu Mythos stories. Merritt seemingly returned the favor in his 1932 novel, *Dwellers in the Mirage*, which focused on the other-dimensional Kraken-like creature, Khalk'ru. Forgotten civilizations and their surviving demigods comprise the themes of Merritt's 1930 short story, "The Snake

Mother," and its lengthy sequel, *The Face in the Abyss* (1931), as well as the novel, *The Ship of Ishtar* (1924).

Abraham Merritt

Beginning with *Seven Footprints to Satan* in 1927, Merritt abandoned his heroic supermen, exotic locales and godlike characters for contemporary thrillers set in urban America with ordinary protagonists involved in supernatural horror. *Burn, Witch, Burn* and its sequel, *Creep, Shadow*, explore modern-day witchcraft and allied occult survivals in the Twentieth Century, and as such are clear precursors to the later novels of Stephen King and other modern masters.

Most of Merritt's major fiction debuted in Munsey magazines such as *Argosy* and *All-Story Weekly*, which were combined for a time. A rare exception was his memorable 1926 fantasy short, "The Woman of the Wood," which was the author's sole contribution to *Weird Tales*. Along with H.P. Lovecraft, Robert E. Howard, C.L. Moore, and Frank Belknap Long, A. Merritt contributed a chapter to the 1935 round-robin story, "The Challenge from Beyond."

Merritt died of a heart attack in Indian Rocks, Florida on August 21, 1943. After his passing, fantasy illustrator Hannes Bok completed two unfinished works, "The Fox Woman" and *The Black Wheel*.

ABOUT THE AUTHOR

THE A STANDS for Abraham. It happened this way. The family on both sides were Quakers. Whenever anybody was born the Bible was taken down and the chapter of "Begats" consulted. His mother's mother headed a revolt and named her children Ida, Phoebe, Ella and Philip—she liked the Greeks. She got away with it by sheer force of character, but when Ida's son was born the conservatives on both sides surged in. As a result the helpless infant was named Abraham after his grand-father. He was lucky, because that was a compromise between Job and Hezekiah.

General Wesley Merritt was his grand-uncle and Fenimore Cooper only a little farther back in his family tree. After having saddled him with the name of Abraham, the family thought he ought to be a lawyer. Why not? Some day he might be President. Abraham Lincoln had the same number of letters in his name as Abraham Merritt. What could be more logical?

So after going through Philadelphia High, he matriculated for the University of Pennsylvania law school. Almost imme-diately thereafter his whole family went broke. There was nothing to do about it, so he did it. He went into the newspa-per game at the tender age of eighteen. In those days writing was paid for at the rate of five dollars a column, and twenty dollars a week was affluence. Two star reporters took him in hand and taught him the art of the inter-written story—that is, one the harassed copy reader could not cut. This was not altruism on their part, because the more money he could make the more they could borrow. He served a little over a year of this peonage, but has never regretted the cost of the training.

Newspapers were newspapers in those days, and politics were politics. It happened he saw one day something that made it awkward to have him within reach of the witness stand. The result was that he spent a happy year at no expense to himself wandering around Central America, poking into ruins, getting in and out of tight places and acquiring a taste for archeology. Also a rather unusual cargo of Mayan, Aztec and, later, Incan legends and the kind of history not taught in the schools. During that time he gained a curious knowledge of Indian customs, religious ceremonies that would have made his Quaker ancestors' hair stand on end, and an equally intimate knowledge of the interiors of palaces, wine shops, haciendas, huts, the jungle and once or twice the *cabozo* or jail.

Returning reluctantly north, he resumed his newspaper fetters, and became immersed in a succession of murder mysteries, suicides, coal strikes, minor and major catastrophes and executions. He unfortunately developed a talent for writing up these latter so vividly that he was always assigned to them. He wrote them vividly because he loathed them. His procedure was always the same. He would attend the ceremony strongly fortified. He would return and write the story, resign with dignity and at once finish his fortification with a complete plasterization. He would return in a couple of days with the wound in his soul scarred over, and that would be all of that till the next hanging. Between times he would seek relief from this dark life of crime and catastrophe by jaunts back to the jungle, and in study of science, of color and of music.

After a few years of this he went to New York, becoming the assistant of Morrill Goddard, editor of the *American Weekly*, of the Hearst Sunday newspapers, whom A. Merritt considers the greatest newspaper editor in the world and to whom he believes he owes a debt of gratitude for patient training he can never repay.

As for the rest, he is somewhat of an authority upon folk-lore and mythology, archeology, Central and South American history and customs, a fair astronomer and a good botanist, with a smattering of other sciences. He has made an intensive study of ancient sorcery, medieval magic and witchcraft, both past and modern.

He dislikes all violent exercise, including bridge, and never walks if he can ride. He keeps bees.

He writes slowly, and primarily to please himself—which is largely why he writes so little. And whenever he finishes a book he is profoundly depressed for a time because it is no better.

ABOUT THE ARTIST

VIRGIL FINLAY HAS worked for nearly every magazine in the science fiction and fantasy field for the last 18 years. He has designed book jackets, magazine covers and illustrated books. His paintings and drawings have been hung in the Metropolitan Museum of Art, as well as in the Memorial Art Gallery and in the Art Center, Rochester, New York. Born in Rochester in 1914, he completed high school, and was self-tutored in art. He started to exhibit when he was only fourteen years of age. Submitted drawings to *Weird Tales* from 1934 to 1936, and was on A. Merritt's staff as feature fiction illustrator for the *American Weekly* (Sunday section of the *New York Journal American*). He married Beverly Stiles in 1938. He was in the Army Engineer corps for 3 years, also a veteran of the Okinawa campaign. Freelanced in New York after his return. A daughter Lail, born in 1949. He says, "I am interested in writing poetry, I like to garden, drink beer and Martinis when I can afford them."

TARZAN AND THE JEWELS OF OPAR
BY ARGOSY'S GREATEST AUTHOR
EDGAR RICE BURROUGHS

WAR LORD OF MANY SWORDSMEN
W. WIRT

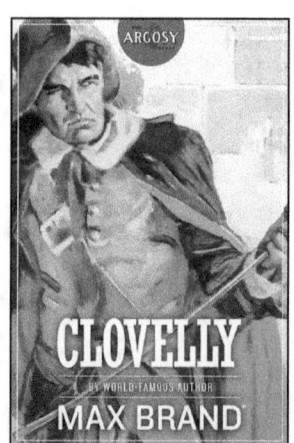

CLOVELLY
BY WORLD-FAMOUS AUTHOR
MAX BRAND

DRINK WE DEEP
THE SCIENCE FICTION CLASSIC
ARTHUR LEO ZAGAT

THE GUN-BRAND
BY NORTHWEST FICTION LEGEND
JAMES B. HENDRYX

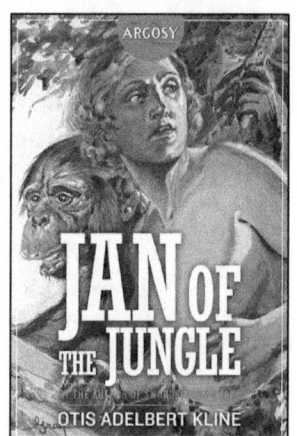

JAN OF THE JUNGLE
OTIS ADELBERT KLINE

THE BLUE FIRE PEARL
GEORGE F. WORTS

THE MOON POOL & THE CONQUEST OF THE MOON POOL
ABRAHAM MERRITT

MINIONS OF THE MOON
THE SCIENCE FICTION CLASSIC
WILLIAM GREY BEYER

ALIAS THE NIGHT WIND
VARICK VANARDY

THE ARGOSY LIBRARY ™

SERIES 3 INCLUDES:

* BURROUGHS * ZAGAT * MERRITT *

* BRAND * KLINE *

* BEYER * HENDRYX *

* WIRT * VANARDY *

* WORTS *

THE BEST FICTION
FROM THE FRANK
A. MUNSEY LINE

www.ingramcontent.com/pod-product-compliance
Lightning Source LLC
Chambersburg PA
CBHW070759030726
47504CB00003B/621